"Good news ~~~~~~~~~~~~~~~~~~~~~~~ ~~~~~ jet, so you
won't have to worry about layovers or security or any
inconvenience. Straight shot to Honolulu Airport."**

"Company jet. Right." She kept forgetting the billionaire
part of this scenario. "And the rooms?"

"We'll stay at Crane Makai, our hotel in Oahu. The
suites there are top-notch."

She swallowed thickly and asked the question she
wanted to ask. "Together?"

"I booked one for each of us."

"I think we could share one, don't you?"

"Dimples." He palmed the back of her neck and leveled his gaze with hers. "Hell yeah, I want to share a room
with you." Then he lost the schoolboy chagrin as the heat
flared in his blue eyes. "Honey, I have imagined you in
a lot of ways and most of them involve you naked in my
bed in Hawaii."

She bit her bottom lip and his eyes went to her mouth.
He lowered his face, hair shrouding them as she tipped
her chin to meet his lips. Then they kissed, gently and
surely, her hands moving to his sweater and gripping two
handfuls. He sucked in a breath and pulled his lips from
hers.

He tasted like heaven.

ACCLAIM FOR
JESSICA LEMMON'S NOVELS

THE BILLIONAIRE BACHELOR

"Lemmon hits the right emotional buttons with this lavish, indulgence-fueled romance."
—*Publishers Weekly*

"Wonderfully entertaining storytelling filled with sharp, sassy banter... Reese and Merina's strong sexual tension and fiery chemistry will have readers hooked."
—*RT Book Reviews*

RETURN OF THE BAD BOY

"Love, friends, family, sweet and steamy romance, and so much more, Jessica Lemmon is an auto-buy for me! Her Bad Boys are just sooo good!"
—**Erin Nicholas, *New York Times* and *USA Today* bestselling author**

"In Lemmon's latest, her signature style of storytelling laced with emotion and grit will engage readers with each turn of the page."
—*RT Book Reviews*

A BAD BOY FOR CHRISTMAS

"Shopping for a hot holiday read? Look no further than *A Bad Boy for Christmas* . . . With charismatic characters, stirring situations, and enough sexy to fill an entire town's worth of stockings, this latest in Lemmon's Second Chance series is 400-plus pages of Christmas magic."

—*USA Today*, "Happy Ever After" blog

"Connor and Faith are strong and complement each other, and their chemistry is explosive. Lemmon is an expert at the modern-day romance."

—*RT Book Reviews*

"Lemmon's sexy and well-constructed third Second Chance romance uses a nice reversal: The man wants marriage and the woman is commitment-shy . . . Likable and realistic characters with believable emotions, and the right balance of fantasy fulfillment, make for some good holiday heat."

—*Publishers Weekly* (starred review)

RESCUING THE BAD BOY

"An amazing read and I can't wait for the next installment."
—TheBookNympho.com

"Nobody does a bad boy like Jessica Lemmon."
—HarlequinJunkie.com

"An amazing read."
—*RT Book Reviews*

BRINGING HOME THE BAD BOY

"Everything I love in a romance."
   —Lori Foster, *New York Times* bestselling author

"Clever, romantic, and utterly unforgettable."
   —Lauren Layne, *USA Today* bestselling author

"4½ stars! A sexy gem of a read that will tug at the heartstrings...A heartfelt plot infused with both emotionally tender and raw moments makes this a story that readers will savor."
   —*RT Book Reviews*

THE MILLIONAIRE AFFAIR

"Fast-paced, well-written, and impossible to put down... Jessica writes with humor infused generously throughout in a realistic, entertaining way that really helps to make her characters realistic people you'll want to know."
   —HarlequinJunkie.com

"Landon and Kimber's banter is infectious as their chemistry sizzles. Smartly written with a narrative infused with humor and snark, this modern-day romance is a keeper."
   —*RT Book Reviews*

"Magnificent writing and characters."
   —NightOwlReviews.com

HARD TO HANDLE

"[Aiden is] a perfect balance of sensitive, heart-on-his-sleeve guy who is as sexy and 'alpha' as they come...A real romance that's not about dominance but equality and mutual need—while not sacrificing hotness factor. A rare treat."
—PolishedBookworm.com

"[Aiden is] a fantastic character. He is a motorcycle-riding, tattooed, rebel kind of guy with a huge heart. What's not to love?...Entertaining and heartfelt."
—RomanceRewind.blogspot.com

"I smiled through a lot of it, but seeing Aiden and Sadie deal with all of their hurdles was also incredibly moving and had me tearing up more than once as well...I can't wait to see what Lemmon will bring to the table next."
—HerdingCats-BurningSoup.com

CAN'T LET GO

"This novella was long enough to get me hooked on Aiden and Sadie and short enough to leave me wanting more...The chemistry between the characters is fan worthy and the banter is a great addition. The writing style draws readers in."
—BSReviewers.blogspot.com

TEMPTING THE BILLIONAIRE

"A smashing debut! Charming, sexy, and brimming with wit—you'll be adding Jessica Lemmon to your bookshelves for years to come!"
    —Heidi Betts, *USA Today* bestselling author

"Lemmon's characters are believable and flawed. Her writing is engaging and witty. If I had been reading this book out in public, everyone would have seen the *huge* grin on my face. I had so much fun reading this and adore it immensely."
    —LiteraryEtc.wordpress.com

"The awesome cover opened to even more awesome things inside. It was realistic! Funny! Charming! Sweet!"
    —AbigailMumford.com

The

BILLIONAIRE
NEXT DOOR

ALSO BY JESSICA LEMMON

The
BILLIONAIRE NEXT DOOR

JESSICA LEMMON

FOREVER

NEW YORK   BOSTON

This book is a work of fiction. Names, characters, places, and incidents are the product of the author's imagination or are used fictitiously. Any resemblance to actual events, locales, or persons, living or dead, is coincidental.

Copyright © 2016 by Jessica Lemmon
Excerpt from *The Bastard Billionaire* copyright © 2016 by Jessica Lemmon

Cover illustration by Tony Mauro
Cover design by Elizabeth Turner
Cover copyright © 2016 by Hachette Book Group, Inc.

Hachette Book Group supports the right to free expression and the value of copyright. The purpose of copyright is to encourage writers and artists to produce the creative works that enrich our culture.

The scanning, uploading, and distribution of this book without permission is a theft of the author's intellectual property. If you would like permission to use material from the book (other than for review purposes), please contact permissions@hbgusa.com. Thank you for your support of the author's rights.

Forever
Hachette Book Group
1290 Avenue of the Americas, New York, NY 10104
forever-romance.com
twitter.com/foreverromance

First Edition: October 2016

Forever is an imprint of Grand Central Publishing. The Forever name and logo are trademarks of Hachette Book Group, Inc.

The publisher is not responsible for websites (or their content) that are not owned by the publisher.

The Hachette Speakers Bureau provides a wide range of authors for speaking events. To find out more, go to www.hachettespeakersbureau.com or call (866) 376-6591.

ISBNs: 978-1-4555-6658-7 (mass market), 978-1-4555-6659-4 (ebook)

Printed in the United States of America

OPM

10 9 8 7 6 5 4 3 2 1

ATTENTION CORPORATIONS AND ORGANIZATIONS:

Most Hachette Book Group books are available at quantity discounts with bulk purchase for educational, business, or sales promotional use. For information, please call or write:

Special Markets Department, Hachette Book Group
1290 Avenue of the Americas, New York, NY 10104
Telephone: 1-800-222-6747 Fax: 1-800-477-5925

For my "cuzin" and lifelong friend, Jenny.

ACKNOWLEDGMENTS

Thank you to Michele Bidelspach for all you do to make my books a success, including this yummy cover. When I requested a long-haired billionaire with facial hair who didn't wear a suit, you didn't balk. Publicity mavens Jodi Rosoff and Michelle Cashman, for making publicity look easy when I know you work your tail feathers off. And Jessie Pierce, for your quiet efficiency.

Thanks as always to my agent, Nicole, for your help and praise. I wouldn't be here without you. Thanks also to my husband, John, who unnecessarily steps out of the spotlight to ensure I have plenty for myself. You're a big part of the reason I shine.

A special shout-out to Tracy Slemker, who talked with me at length about prosthetic limbs. Any mistakes are my own. Lastly, thank you to Brock O'Hurn for sharing your photos (which inspired Tag Crane's physical features) and for your encouragement to chase life's dreams. I wish you continued success with yours.

The
BILLIONAIRE
NEXT DOOR

CHAPTER 1

Eyes closed, Rachel Foster drew in a steeling breath, shut out the din of voices at the surrounding tables in the bar, and said aloud for the first time ever, "Mom, Dad, I resigned from my position at the design firm after Shaun took credit for my work. I moved out of our shared apartment and took a job as a bartender instead."

Other than background chatter, silence greeted her. She held her breath for a few seconds before opening her eyes. The fifty-something guy across from her blinked, fries gone cold on his plate.

"Should I have started with my ex taking credit for my work, then moved to the resignation? Or is it best to open with the bartender bit?" she asked him.

"I think they'll love you no matter what." The man on the guest side of the bar, who'd agreed to play the role of "Mom and Dad," smiled.

Oliver Something. He had kind green eyes, a plain

face, and thick hair dyed a shade too dark for his age and skin tone. He was a regular at the bar where she worked, enjoying the same exact meal (turkey club, no mayo) each and every week. He always ate, but never drank alcohol, only soda. And he had a big, beautiful Great Dane, a dog she would soon be in charge of while living in his gorgeous apartment.

She really needed to learn Oliver's last name.

"You say that because you've never met them." She grabbed the soda gun from behind the bar and refilled his Diet Coke. "Maybe I shouldn't tell them at all."

"Rachel." He brushed his hands on a paper napkin. "I'm old enough to be your father."

"Uncle," she corrected, being generous.

"*Older* uncle. Either way, I have longer perspective than you do given that I'm closer to the grave, and I'm advising you to tell your folks what's going on."

He was right, of course. She hadn't told them anything, and the least they deserved was the truth.

After her and Shaun's relationship had imploded, she'd grieved alone and put on a happy voice for her mother's phone calls. Inside, she'd been aching. Two years was a long time to be with someone. She had begun to accept his faults—like the fact he was grouchy in the evenings and could be abrasive and critical—but when he'd betrayed her and took the promotion she'd earned, she pushed the eject button without a second thought.

"I'll tell them." Eventually. She wasn't ready to call her family in Ohio and drop on their lap that their successful, city-dwelling daughter was *not* watching the gold nameplate go up on her corner office door. Instead, she was stacking dirty dishes in a bus tub and cleaning sticky, disgusting residue out of the rubber mat over which she poured libations for eight hours a night, five to six days a week.

Still better than being stabbed in the back by the man who was supposed to love and protect her.

She took Oliver's plate as he reached for his wallet. He extracted a credit card, which he used to pay for everything to earn miles for his many business trips, and set a gold key next to it.

"Front desk knows to expect you tomorrow. Adonis has been asking about you since you stopped by last week," he said of the Great Dane with whom he shared a life.

She pocketed the key with a smile and settled the bill, swiping the card on the machine a few feet down the bar.

"The front desk was incredibly thorough and scares me a little." Last week when she was there, they required two forms of ID and took a photo of her to put in their database. "I'm surprised they didn't ask for fingerprints." She tore off the receipts and handed them over with a pen. "Adonis is gorgeous, but let's both admit he only loves me because of the liver treats I fed him."

Oliver laughed as he signed the receipt. "His loyalty is easily bought. Like his owner's."

"Truer words." She accepted the pen and the receipt, glancing at the tip line to see that Oliver had once again tipped the amount of his meal, which she used to yell at him for but now accepted that he wasn't going to listen to her no matter what.

"Thank you for doing this, Rachel," he said. "I didn't expect to be in Japan for an entire month."

"You're welcome." She'd confided in Oliver one late

night how her roommate situation wasn't working, and she needed to find a new place to live, never imagining he'd offer to solve her problem. As it turned out, he was due to go away on business and his dog sitter had double-booked herself. He'd asked Rachel if she'd take the gig, sharing that he couldn't stomach the idea of Adonis in a kennel. When he told her his address, Rachel had nearly drooled on the bar top between them.

Crane Tower. *Oh la la.*

Not only would she live in his glorious fifteen-hundred-square-foot apartment, but he was also paying her. *Generously.* She could add the money to her savings and put a deposit down on her own place. It was either that or move back home, but she wasn't willing to concede the battle yet. Chicago may be kicking her around, but she was tougher than she looked.

She hoped.

Once she found a better gig than bartending, a professional and brag-worthy profession devoid of rat-bastard, promotion-stealing boyfriends, she'd be good to go. Not because bragging about her job was important for her, but it was for her parents. They were the ones who were so proud of their daughter, the "city girl."

Oliver bid her adieu and left as Rachel's roommate-slash-coworker, Breanna, stepped through the door he held open for her.

At the bar, Bree slid her coat from her arms and stashed it beneath the register. "Soooo. How's Daddy Warbucks?"

"Bree." Rachel laughed as she washed a beer glass in the double sink. That roommate situation that wasn't working? It had nothing to do with Bree or her significant other, Dean. Rachel adored Bree, and vice versa. They'd become close in the two months since Rachel moved in with her, when both Bree and Rachel swore they'd be roommates for years. Then Dean proposed, Bree said yes, and he moved in and well...Rachel was now a third wheel.

She didn't want to be in the way of what her friends had, which was special. She could tell because she knew what a relationship looked like when it wasn't right. It was strain and silence and frustration and animosity brewing under a surface that no one disturbed.

"I'm going to miss you when you go live in luxury for a month." Bree pouted, pushing her full lips out. Her chin-length brown hair was smooth tonight, her eyes sparkling thanks to glittery eye shadow.

"No, you won't. You and Dean will probably run around naked the moment I leave."

Bree grinned.

Rachel was happy for her friend. She'd met Bree at Dusty's, a bar that was a downscale Andromeda. Bree had been working through the last week of a two-week notice.

They'd bonded almost instantly, which Rachel did with almost no one. By the time she'd made the decision to leave her marketing job, Rachel called Bree to ask if the Andromeda Club was hiring.

It'd occurred to her that when she'd moved to Chicago alone, she intended to be an island. She'd never expected to have a roommate—certainly not one she was dating—and since the whole Shaun debacle, she'd become anxious to reclaim her island status. She'd hate to think she'd lost the ability to be independent after coming to depend on a man who wasn't dependable in the end.

Her recent breakup with her boyfriend of two years, being homeless, and losing the job for which she'd attained her degree was a series of minor setbacks.

Living with a dog was the bridging step from roommate to once again living on her own, and she would take it. Somewhere in her lived a fearless woman who was ready to take on a new adventure.

Rachel was determined to find her.

* * *

Tag's oldest brother and CEO for Crane Hotels, Reese Crane, had no love for the board of directors around the conference table. As of last year, when they'd razzed Tag about lagging profits at the hotel and pool bars nationwide, he had recently put them on his shit list as well.

Today, they'd changed their tune.

"Given that the losses fall within an acceptable range, we are downgrading the bar issues at Guest and Restaurant Services from a code red to a code yellow." Frank smiled at his own joke, but the only thought in Tag's brain was that the older man's teeth matched his *code*. "Thank you for your careful preparation, Tag. Now if you'll excuse us, Bob, Lilith, and I have a meeting to attend downtown. This marks the end of our agenda. Unless either of you have anything to add?"

Tag had plenty to add, but when he opened his mouth, Reese spoke for him.

"Nothing on our end."

Tag felt a muscle in his cheek twitch. Reese cast him a sideways glance as the board shuffled into the hall. The door shut behind them and he faced his brother.

"The term 'acceptable losses' isn't bad news." Reese arched an eyebrow.

"Loss should never be 'acceptable,'" Tag growled. "The board harps on falling profits in the hotel bars last year, but as of thirty seconds ago they no longer care?"

Tag dropped his unused number 2 pencil to push a hand through his hair, then remembered it was pulled back. Long, nearly to his elbows, he preferred wearing his hair down, but for board meetings he wrangled it into a low-hanging ponytail/man bun hybrid. He'd also wedged his wide shoulders into an uncomfortable button-down and wrapped his bulky thighs in restrictive trousers. He felt... not like himself. Agitated about being here, about this whole downgrading thing.

Ever the underestimated brother, he shouldn't be surprised that they'd shrugged him off. Even if Guest and Restaurant Services wasn't his baby—and it was—he'd consider cooperating worth it if the board left him the hell alone and went back to whatever it was they did when they weren't giving the Crane brothers grief.

"I prefer to handle this, not ignore it," Tag said.

"They know you're capable. They're not worried. Take that as a compliment." Reese shrugged easily, taking it in stride. A far cry from where he was a year ago, when he nearly went apoplectic on Frank.

The board had tried to keep Reese from becoming CEO, citing disapproval over Reese's playboy lifestyle. The good news was Reese had ended up with a wife— now ex-wife, soon to be his wife again (long story)—but at the moment, Tag was having a hard time finding his own silver lining.

He didn't consider futility a compliment.

He lifted the report in front of him—the one he'd received months ago. Filled with spreadsheets, numbers, and projected targets, it was seriously structured. And seriously pissing him off.

"Why the fuck did they give me this if they weren't going to follow through?" The cover read "Fiscal Projections for Food and Alcohol." The word *fiscal* was enough to give him hives, but he'd pored over those sheets, those numbers, until his eyes felt like they were going to bleed.

Tag preferred to do things his way, and his way consisted of two main elements: his gut and people. He could rely on himself for decisions and his interactions with the staff to ensure his decisions were carried out. Spreadsheets and charts didn't translate into good business in most cases. He could relate better to an employee over a beer than he could by sending a memo.

"I came in prepared to discuss numbers, and Frank brushed me off," he continued, still grinding his teeth over the wasted time.

"Need I remind you how undesirable it is for them to watch your every move? Care to have the paparazzi chasing you around? Parts of you highlighted on social media with a hashtag?" Reese's wry humor was showcased with a slow blink.

But even the mention of the Twitter debacle and Reese's nefarious *#ReesesRocket* hashtag didn't cheer Tag up.

"Yeah, well, I don't care what they say. I'm going to make the profits sing." Tag stood from the desk. "*Acceptable loss* doesn't factor in to my plans for Crane Hotels."

Reese's lips curved into an almost proud expression

reminiscent of their father. Tag pulled in a breath and stood straighter.

Over the years since Reese had been clamoring for CEO, Tag was content to run GRS. He'd risen in the ranks by paying attention and talking to everyone who worked for him. He'd learned how to invest his inheritance, part of which he'd retained since he hadn't blown it on a college degree.

Tag was self-made, self-confident, and self-aware. He worked for Crane not because he needed to, but because it was his purpose. He had a part to play in preserving their family's legacy and in no way took the task lightly.

"I'm doing things my way," Tag stated. "This"—he held up the report, then dropped it into the wastebasket by the door—"is bullshit."

Reese followed him to the door and flipped off the light. They walked silently through the hall and out into the reception area where Reese's secretary, Bobbie, was typing, her fingers flying over the keyboard.

"Look forward to hearing more." Reese slapped Tag's shoulder. "Don't let 'em get to you."

That gave Tag pause. Reese was almost laid-back since he'd been married to Merina, which wasn't easy to get used to.

"Thanks, bro."

Reese vanished into his office, where he could be found most of the time. The Cranes—their father, Alex; Reese; Tag; and Eli, who was currently overseas serving in the Marines—were in this battle together. Tag liked everything about that. The way he could count on his family to be on his side and the way he'd rise to any challenge they set forth. The Cranes would never bail on each other.

He waved to Bobbie, who acknowledged him with a brief nod; then he collected his coat and scarf from the coat rack next to the elevator.

He rode down to the lobby and strolled through a sea of white leather and past shining windows. Gorgeous as the Chicago home base for Crane Hotels was, Tag preferred his home office, where he could focus on something other than the purring of the receptionist's phone and the pompous chatter of the suits occasionally prowling the floors. When he wasn't there, he was visiting one of the hotels to oversee a grand opening or cut the ribbon on a new restaurant.

The Windy City was living up to her name today, the cold slapping him in the face as he strode out onto the sidewalk. He pulled up his collar and plunged his hands into his black coat's pockets, welcoming the chilly bite of February.

Crane Tower stood exactly three blocks west of the Crane and was Tag's proudest accomplishment. His brother may own a mansion, but Tag had purchased an entire damn building. He'd bought it from his father quietly so as not to draw too much attention to the sale a year ago. His penthouse was at the top floor, forty-nine, and overlooked a sea of buildings. He liked the vantage point. He loved being on top. Ask any of his past girlfriends.

Well, dates. *Girlfriends* was a strong word.

Crane Tower's doorman, a middle-aged guy whose name Tag did not remember, pulled open the door as Tag was angling to walk inside. The respite from wind was brief though, blowing his hair over his face and temporarily blotting out the vision of a woman exiting the luxury apartment building.

He swept his hair behind his ear and stopped dead in his tracks.

She was blond.

Petite, which put her at least a foot shorter than his almost six-and-a-half feet tall, and wearing high-heeled, knee-high boots that met the edge of a long dark coat, belted at the waist. The wind chose that moment to bless him, parting her coat and revealing gray leggings beneath a super short black skirt. She closed the coat over her like Marilyn Monroe trying to push down her dress and then she caught him looking.

And looked back.

Shiny lips. Thick, black lashes. Cute nose.

A pair of black leather gloves rose to tug a few stray hairs from her sticky lip gloss, and Tag felt a definite stir of interest in his pressed-for-work pants.

Then she was gone, hoofing it to a car waiting at the curb. He watched the maroon sedan pull away, a woman in the driver's seat, and blinked as the taillights dwindled in the distance. Then he turned for the door again.

"Mr. Crane," the doorman greeted.

"Hey...uh. Man." He should know this guy's name. "Who was that?"

A brief look of panic colored the other man's features like he might be fired for not knowing. "I don't know, sir. Would you like me to find out?"

Tag looked in the direction where the car had vanished, thinking for a second.

"No," he decided. He liked not knowing. Liked the idea of running into the blonde by chance. Maybe in the gym or the lobby.

Or the elevator.

Yeah, he'd rather stumble across her. Preferably into her.

"Thanks." He nodded to the doorman and strode in, stepping onto the elevator a few minutes later. On the ride up, he realized he was leaning in the corner, smiling like a dope, the bar upgrade issue and the frustration of the board the furthest thing from his mind.

CHAPTER 2

Asharp bark startled Tag, and his arm jerked, dragging the tip of the Sharpie across the Post-it and onto the photograph he had been trying not to ruin. He scowled at the jagged red line, then lifted his face and scowled at his blurry reflection in the window, beyond which was a lit Chicago skyline and pale half-moon.

For most of the evening he'd mentally blocked out the barks that had punctuated the air approximately every ten seconds before narrowing to every two or three seconds. Now they were almost constant.

Woof! Woof! Woo-oof!

He could not freaking work in these conditions.

Judging by the direction of the sound, and the deep, barrel-chested baritone, he guessed the barker none other than Adonis, Oliver Chambers's giant white-with-black-splotches Great Dane. Adonis was generally a quiet dog. Tag only knew him because he often ran into the pair

(Adonis and Oliver on their way to a morning stroll, Tag on his way out) when he rode the elevator down with them.

Tag had been patient—Adonis was a dog, and dogs barked—but the dog had never barked this much, and never this late at night. He'd been determined to ignore it, but he needed every ounce of concentration he could muster.

He was reviewing the setup for the main candidate for a recent bar redesign: the pool bar at the Crane Makai in Hawaii. He'd been there several times, having overseen the grand opening of the hotel and the restaurant run by an acclaimed chef Tag had handpicked. Tag had taken the blow personally when he reviewed the spreadsheets and determined that the Makai boasted the lowest bar sales profits.

He didn't get it. The bar was in *Hawaii*. People went there *to drink*. And the weather was damn near perfect. What the hell? After ruling out theft and pricing, and a staff he had complete confidence in, he'd determined the shortcoming was the design. They'd built onto the Makai over the last decade, and as a result, a secondary pool was an afterthought. What it did have was an ocean view and plenty of seating choices, including cabanas. Theoretically, they should be drowning in profits. Even during the slow season—

Woof!

"All right, that's it." Tag shoved the stack of photos aside and moved through his penthouse, out the door, and punched a button in the elevator. He had nothing against dogs, and he liked this one in particular, but either something was wrong or Oliver had gotten lax with keeping the pooch in line. With so much at stake, there was no way Tag could concentrate with constant—

Woo-woo-woof!

The moment the elevator doors opened, Adonis's barks echoed through the entryway.

The top three floors of Crane Tower were reserved for private apartments. Tag's took up the entire top floor, while the two floors below his were split into two apartments per floor. These were the luxury suites, but given that the other apartment on Oliver's floor was empty, Tag was the only neighbor who was hearing Adonis's yapping.

At the door, Tag knocked. Barking followed scratching, and he winced as he thought of the dog's nails marring the wood. Bending at the waist, he spoke through the door. "Adonis."

Silence, then one more bark.

"Adonis, hey, boy."

The barking stopped.

"Are you a good dog?" A small whine was followed by a more desperate bark.

"There you go. Calm down, okay?" He kept his voice pitched to soothing, feeling like an idiot cooing to a dog through a door, but hey, whatever it took. "I have shit to do," he crooned, "and you're making me insane."

Sniffing at the door preceded silence. Tag stood and waited. No barking. No whining.

Satisfied, he smiled to himself. He had just turned to the elevator when the scratching came again—more desperately this time—followed by a cacophony of pathetic yelps.

Tag ran a hand over his face and climbed back into the elevator.

He wasn't the kind of guy who freaked out over anything. Easygoing, easy to get along with, he was going to let this go for now and talk to Oliver—wherever the hell he was—in the morning. No doubt Tag would run into him in the elevator.

Back in his apartment, he opted to drown out the dog's barks with music, cranking Adele to ear-bleeding decibels. For a guy who viewed his dating life through a lens of common sense, Tag would admit he admired the kind of love she sang about. The kind of love his parents had. The kind of love his oldest brother had found in the most unlikely of places. As much as he admired it, however, he was too practical to be stupid.

He was randomly hit with a memory of the woman outside the building this afternoon. That body. That hair. Women were fun. He adored them... for a while. Letting them down easy was the key to everyone having a good time and keeping the heartache at a minimum.

Sex was fun. Hanging out was fun. When it encroached on relationship territory, there were few couples who could keep the fun alive. Tag preferred to binge on the highs and bail before the lows happened.

It was as good as his personal motto.

He sat down at his desk only to stand up right away. He couldn't look at pictures of bars without wanting to pour a drink. In the fridge, he found a bottle of beer, cracked it open, and enjoyed the first ice-cold swallow.

Outside, wind blew the flags below; the sky was a cavernous gray-black. He shuddered. He'd chosen this apartment with this view because cities made him feel claustrophobic. But neither did he want to live on acres of land like his brother, because something about a *house* was too settled for Tag's taste.

He loved to travel, which was another reason in the con column for settling down. His work took him to other states, where he'd stay away a week or a month, depending on what mood struck him.

Women tended to get pissy when their men didn't come home for long stretches.

Freedom. Flexibility. That's what his lifestyle had afforded him.

He went back to the desk—a large table in the corner of the living room—and frowned down at the plans—and yes, the report he'd chucked into the trash at the board meeting. He'd found an emailed copy (gee, thanks, Bob) and went ahead and printed the damn thing in case there was some insight to be gleaned in the numbers and spreadsheets after all.

Guest and Restaurant Services wasn't all fun and parties, but the board seemed to think so. Frank's obnoxious words a few months back sat like a stone in the center of Tag's stomach.

Just because he drinks at a bar doesn't mean he's qualified to oversee the bar business for this entire company.

Frank, the jackass, was dead wrong. Tag could and *would* handle this. Even though the board had found something else to focus on, Tag wasn't going to allow his bars to bleed money until they deemed it a "code red."

An adrenaline spike flooded his system, and he felt a smile of challenge crest his lips. This was a winnable battle, one he was made for.

He plunked down the beer bottle on the edge of the desk and rubbed his hands together.

"Let's fucking do this."

* * *

Rachel's mother was standing in the Andromeda Club knocking on a table. An annoying *rap-rap-rap*. The rapid-fire series of knuckles to wood was paired with questions like "How could you give up a desk and nice clothes to work *here*?"

Rachel opened her mouth to defend her choices when she jerked out of sleep with a start. She wasn't at the bar, but in bed at Oliver's apartment. And the knocking wasn't her mother, who'd found out the truth and drove to Chicago to interrogate Rachel. The knocking was coming from the front door.

She rubbed the sleep from her eyes and took in Adonis lying next to her, his big, square head on a pillow.

"I hope this isn't disturbing you," she told the dog, her voice craggy. Still foggy from her dream and the late night, she stretched.

The Andromeda had been packed last night, thanks to a nearby company bringing everyone in for happy hour on the boss's dime. She'd already sent Bree home since things were slow, so Rachel had been waiting tables and bartending until well after closing time.

The Andromeda didn't have entertainment aside from a few televisions and a pool table in the side room that was rarely used, but the *clack-clack* of balls rolling on felt hadn't stopped until well after midnight. And only because the remaining twenty or so patrons ringing the bar were doing body shots. Yes, a few employees of Lobby, Inc., would find it hard to make eye contact with one another on Monday morning.

Especially the guy who'd worn his tie on his head.

For those reasons and because one, okay, she'd admit it, *charming* guy who wasn't sauced included her in a round of shots (not body shots—she hadn't done that since college) before she closed, the knock on the door at eight a.m. came way, way too early.

Adonis, in the bed next to her, opened his eyes and met Rachel's, then shut them again as another knock pierced the quiet.

For a dog who'd spent the evening cooped up in the penthouse while she worked her tail feathers off, he was awfully wiped. He'd likely spent the entire afternoon into evening snoring on the couch, so why the major case of the lazies?

The knock sounded again, a deep voice booming, "Oliver? You home? Adonis?"

And now her visitor was talking to the dog.

"Why don't I get that?" Rachel told Adonis as she slid out of bed. Thankfully she'd slept wearing flannel, so there was no need to get dressed or fuss with a robe. Not that she owned one, but she'd bet Oliver had one in his closet. He was the robe type.

"Coming!" She stepped from the bedroom and shuffled across the massive apartment that was more like a house on one floor.

When she reached the door, she pulled her fingers through her blond hair and decided her visitor had earned the penalty of seeing her sloppy hair, leftover makeup, and pale blue flannel pajamas with a polar bear and snowflake design.

She turned the knob and blinked, stunned.

Holy crap, there is a mountain man at my door.

She was faced with wide, round shoulders. A waterfall

of caramel-brown, slightly wavy hair cascaded down his arms. He wore a closely trimmed beard, his mouth flat beneath it. One eyebrow was arched over the bluest eyes she'd ever seen.

"Hello," she managed, before jerking her gaze from his assaulting blues to take in the fitted cream-colored sweater, a pair of gray cargo pants, and laced leather boots.

He was like a sexy city lumberjack.

"Hi."

Oh. That voice. Deep, rich, and low enough that it registered in her belly.

When his eyes dashed away from her face and he smiled, her brain turned to mush. She couldn't think of a thing to say. Not a single thing.

"There he is. Hey, buddy." The giant knelt as Adonis meandered through the living room, pausing to do a downward-dog stretch in front of the man's feet. The dog received a scrub on the head, and she was rewarded with more of her guest's low voice. "You're better today, yeah? Sleep okay?"

Meanwhile, Rachel gawked at the two of them. Her appearance was probably less put-together than the dog's. She ran her fingers through her hair again, making it worse at this point, and straightened her pajama top futilely. There was no escaping that she looked as if she'd crawled out of bed after a late, late night.

The man stood. "Typically, Adonis has had his walk by now, but I didn't see you at the elevator, so..."

She squinted one eye and finally her brain chugged into gear.

Oh. *Oh.*

Oliver had mentioned a dog walker, but Rachel had

sworn he said he'd postponed the walks while she was staying here. But since he was here, he may as well take Adonis. She wasn't anywhere near ready to go for a stroll in the snow.

"I'm sorry. I'm so sorry." She went to where the leash was hanging—on a hook inside the pantry—retrieved it, and chased Adonis for a few irritating seconds while he turned in circles in excitement. "I took him out at three in the morning, so I'm not sure if he'll have to...you know." Dog clipped, she handed the leash to the ridiculously good-looking man at her door. "Do you bring your own poop bags? Or do you..." The man was looking at her like she'd sprouted a third eye, so she swept the topic away with one hand. "You know what? I'll just grab one."

She shot him a tight smile, went back to the pantry, and returned with a bag made for Adonis's business. She offered it to the guy, who was holding tight to Adonis's leash while the pooch lunged for the elevator. The man didn't budge, despite the dog's strength.

"Where's Oliver?" he asked.

She frowned as she crinkled the plastic bag against her body. "You mean he didn't tell you? He's on a business trip. I'm house-sitting."

"You his niece?" he asked after running a long gaze down to her feet, then up to her face again.

She laughed. "No, not at all. He's one of my regulars. Odd, right? But we hit it off and he likes me, so..."

The man's frown deepened, those gorgeous eyes darkening to stormy blue. "I'm not the dog walker." He offered the leash but Adonis stayed in the hallway rather than coming back inside. "I'm an upstairs neighbor."

"Oh. Oh my God! I'm so sorry!" Rachel took the leash

and wrestled with Adonis, who was much, much stronger than she. He knew it. The dog spread his feet wide and stood his ground on the carpeted floor.

"I suggest you find a way to keep him quiet at night while you're out. I work from home and I can't listen to him bark for hours."

Hours?

"If I were anyone else, a noise complaint would be in your future. Oliver follows the rules. He wouldn't like knowing you're breaking a big one." That low voice had dropped lower, the reprimand having the dual result of both pissing her off and making her feel a little tingly.

God. I need more sleep.

"No need to be rude," she snapped. He blinked, surprised. Probably not used to being put in his place.

Look at him. He's a wall. Who would stand up to him?

Then she remembered his kind smile, the way his hands rubbed Adonis's flank with rugged gentleness. A shiver climbed her spine at the same time Adonis jerked hard on the leash.

She expelled a dainty "oh!" and lunged forward at the same time the man in the doorway caught the leash in one hand and her against him. Rachel found every part of her from thighs to breasts plastered to the giant's body. Her palms flattened over two hard pectoral muscles hidden beneath the sweater, her legs bumping his legs, which felt as solid as two marble columns. She tilted her head, met those aqua blue eyes, and...and...remembered she hadn't brushed her teeth yet.

She shoved off his rock-hard stomach, slapping a palm over her mouth. Then she snatched Adonis's leash and gave a hard tug. The dog turned with a sigh and paced back inside. Once he was clear of the door, she sent the hard-bodied hunk at the threshold a glare and slammed the door in his face.

Adonis yipped his disappointment at losing the chance to go outside.

"You'll have to take him out now!" came a shout through the door. "Don't blue-ball the poor guy after taking him halfway."

Adonis wagged his tail so hard, he nearly took out a lamp. The hulk at the door was right. There was no way she could turn down the Dane's pale eyes and smiling pink mouth, perked pointy ears, and lolling tongue.

"Fine," she growled, and stomped for the bedroom. She snatched up her boots and hastily picked out her clothes, feeling both tired and cranky. Yet as she tugged on her coat, she found her mouth curving into a half-smile.

Blue balls.

Who *was* that guy?

* * *

Tag wasn't hiding, per se, but he wasn't making his presence known in the lobby of Crane Tower. Rather than take the elevator up, he took it down, grabbed himself a coffee, and waited.

Surely the blonde would be down with Adonis in tow any second now. As he took the second sip from his cup, he saw her. Well, he saw Adonis first since he was six feet ahead of her, leash a straight, taut line. The blonde's hair was in a sloppy topknot, and she'd changed into jeans and a long red sweater. Her coat was open; her boots came up to her knees. Nothing special about her outfit, but he was hit with a blast of longing so acute, he froze in place.

Damn.

Like the first time he'd spotted her on the sidewalk, she'd once again struck him stupid. Him noticing a woman was not a rare thing, but neither did he stop and stare, dumbstruck. The moment he'd noticed her, and she'd noticed him, had been infused with a palpable buzz of electricity.

"That's stupid," he grumbled against the lip of his coffee cup, sliding behind a divider separating the coffee shop from the lobby.

She strode by in a plume of soft, floral perfume, Adonis in the lead and so focused on getting outside he didn't give away Tag's hiding spot.

Tag shook his head. There was no denying it. Oliver's girl was cute.

"One of her regulars," he mumbled to himself, sauntering over to the front desk after woman and dog vanished into the whitewashed landscape outside.

Regular *whats*?

But he knew. One look at the blonde's smooth skin and blue eyes, even with her body covered from head to toe in flannel polar bears, Tag knew exactly what she and Oliver were *regularly* doing.

It was what any man in his right mind would regularly do with a woman who was as effortlessly sexy as she was.

"Whatever," he said, determined to stop debating how dorky Oliver had landed a super-hot (and way too young for him) girlfriend.

"Talking to yourself again, Tag?" Fiona manned the front desk often, her shifts ranging from day to night to filling in for the afternoon staff. He'd been out with her a few times. She was brunette, savvy, and a great lay. A keeper if he were the keeping type, but then he'd let her go and she'd gone and now she was dating some dude with a law degree. Good for her.

"The blonde," he said, tossing his chin toward the door she just exited. "She's staying with Oliver. I think she works second shift. Can you let me know when she comes in tonight?"

"You mean spy for you?" Fiona's eyes rounded playfully.

"A little intel is not spying, Fi."

She tapped her keyboard, then said, "Rachel Foster. Says here she is a bartender."

Rachel. The bartender.

"One of her *regulars*," he said, his tone shifting into *duh*. He was a restaurant guy—how had he not put that together? They must've met at the bar where she worked. Maybe Rachel and Oliver had some sort of opposites attract thing going on. Who knew, maybe the guy was really charming in that setting.

Tag grimaced. He couldn't picture it.

"I'll let you know of her comings and goings," Fiona promised. "Oh, and, Tag?"

"Yeah, doll." He dragged his attention from the door to focus on Fi's knowing expression.

"This wouldn't happen to be personal would it?" Her voice had a singsong quality.

"She's Oliver's girl. You know better."

"I do." Nostalgia hung on those two words, like maybe she was remembering a time between them. He couldn't call up specifics, only that she'd rated on his scale and she was all wrong for him.

That happened a lot.

"The dog has been barking nonstop. It's not like him."

Fiona nodded. "Ah. I bet he has separation anxiety. Whenever I leave my Pomeranian, Lola, she goes crazy. My dog sitter says she's inconsolable for weeks."

"Separation anxiety."

"Mmm-hmm," Fiona confirmed, folding her arms on the counter in front of her. "There are several things you can do to combat it. Some dogs need more exercise, others special treats. They even have these toys that are like puzzles you hide treats in to keep them busy during the long hours while the owner is away."

"No shit."

Fi's smile widened. "No shit."

Finally. Something tangible. An action step he could check off a list.

"Where's the nearest pet store that would have those things?"

"I love Pup Paradise. They have everything, including services like grooming and dog massages."

Dog. Massages.

"Let's hope it doesn't come to that," he said. "Get me an address, will you?" Movement outside the door showed Rachel Foster and Adonis moving toward the glass entry door. "I'm, uh, I'll be back."

Without explanation he darted off in the direction of the coffee shop, but not before he heard Fi's smart-aleck comment of "Totally spying."

Yeah, yeah. But for good reason. He watched Rachel walk by, that same thread of longing stringing through his entire torso.

He wanted to help the dog. That's it.

At least that's what he'd been telling himself.

CHAPTER 3

"Did you need ketchup?" Rachel asked the man as she put a cheeseburger and waffle fries in front of him.

"Naw, sweetheart. Just another Bud." He winked and her smile turned saccharine. The youngish guy was in jeans and a button-down, had blond hair and eyes that didn't open all the way, and had been hitting on her all evening. And he was laying it on *thick*.

She walked by Bree, who was cashing out another bar patron.

"Bud bottle to seat six for me," she mumbled.

"Sure thing." Bree gave a quick nod.

Neither of them questioned when the other one asked for a favor. Usually the patron took the hint if they double-teamed him.

So to speak.

The rest of the evening flew, and both Bree and Rachel considered themselves lucky they'd escaped without swatting too many guys away. Almost everyone was on their best behavior. No crazy rush (beyond the usual), so Andromeda hit a lull at midnight. Late for a first cut, but Bree could definitely handle the crowd if she left.

"What a night," she said to Bree as she counted and separated the tips.

"I know! This weekend has been nuts. Don't people know it's February? They should stay home where it's warm and binge Netflix."

Rachel spun the bills in her hand so they were facing the same way and put the stack on the counter. She kept her back to the bar while she did, even though she wasn't worried about being robbed. There was muscle at the door in the form of Lex, a college student earning tips while he went to CSU. He was nice, though. Had a girl-friend who lived in Iowa, and from what Rachel had seen, he was completely loyal to her.

Maybe there were a few good guys left on the planet.

"Hey, I didn't tell you," Rachel said as Breanna poured and delivered a draft beer to seat 12. "This guy who lives upstairs from Oliver stopped by at the butt crack of dawn this morning." Ones stacked in her hand, she smiled at her friend. "I thought he was the dog walker and gave him a leash and poop bag."

Bree laughed, a rich sound matching her mahogany hair. "Tell me you didn't call it a 'poop bag.'"

"Okay, I won't tell you." Rachel scrunched her face, realizing how ridiculous her reaction was to the guy.

Yes, sure, he was attractive in a completely unique way. And *yes*, she had looked like a pajama-clad hobo and offered him a poop bag, but really, who cared? She wasn't looking, and he clearly wasn't interested.

"He lives upstairs from Oliver, and Oliver's apartment is *ritzy*," Rachel continued explaining. Oliver's neighbor had been on her mind all day. "This guy didn't look like a guy who lived in a ritzy penthouse."

"Well, what did he look like?"

Rachel decided to leave out the attractive qualities lest Bree take it as an invitation to imaginarily set her up with Mr. Tall, Tan, and Sexy.

"He was uh…" *Built like a brick shithouse, as hard as a brick shithouse.* "He was a big guy, probably a few years older than we are." There. That sounded generic. "And he wasn't friendly. I stumbled into him because Adonis is the size of a horse, and I had a hold of the leash. You should have seen the guy's face when I body-slammed him. He looked severely angry."

And kissable.

"So you went rubbing against Oliver's unfriendly upstairs neighbor?"

"Basically."

"Oh, no. Embarrassing." Bree's face melted into a mask of sympathy. But for Rachel, the moment hadn't been that bad. Aside from worrying about her morning breath. Which, if the guy was as bland as Rachel had made him sound, wouldn't have been embarrassing at all. Okay-looking guys were easy to relax around.

Back in Ohio, Rachel's 140-year-old dentist had retired and a youngish doctor had replaced him. A guy so attractive, she could barely think when she went in for a checkup. Dr. Moore. *Purr.*

"I take it by your frown you're not over it?" Bree asked. "Try to relax. The guy probably thought you were cute and was envious of Oliver's superior taste in women."

Rachel laughed dismissively, split the tips, and put her cash into a pocket. Then she paused, Bree's words wending around her brain until she practically heard them click into place.

"Bree."

"Yeah?" Bree answered, distractedly folding her three hundred dollars in tips and shoving it into her front pocket.

"Do you think the neighbor thought I was with Oliver? Like *with him*?" Because even though Oliver was a super-sweet guy, he was still older and . . . just no. That would be wrong.

Bree shrugged it off and called, "Thanks again!" as a bar customer climbed from his seat. Then to Rachel, she said, "Possibly. It's not uncommon for an older, rich dude to have a hot girlfriend."

"Well, he did ask if I was Oliver's niece."

"Also plausible." Bree leaned against the back counter and crossed her arms over her chest. "What'd you say?"

"I told him the truth. I wasn't, and Oliver was one of my regulars."

Bree offered a shrug; then her eyes went wide and her mouth dropped open. This time when she laughed, she slapped her thigh.

"What?" Rachel watched her reaction, completely perplexed.

"Your 'regular' what?" Bree was still grinning.

"My regular customer," Rachel answered, making the *duh* face.

"Yes, honey, here the term *regular* makes sense." Bree dropped a hand on Rachel's shoulder. "But in the hallway of a ritzy apartment with you looking cute and sexy-frumpy . . ."

THE BILLIONAIRE NEXT DOOR

"Sexy-frumpy? I don't even know what that is."

"He thought you were Oliver's hot mama."

"Eww!"

Bree laughed again. "Stranger things have happened." She walked to the other side of the bar, but Rachel stood frozen.

Was that what he'd thought? That Oliver was one of her...clients?

Don't blue-ball the guy...

A minute later, Rachel said goodbye to Bree, who greeted a group of guys at the bar and waved, then hailed a cab back to her temporary home.

On the ride there, she thought about Oliver's gargantuan neighbor, how warm and hard he'd felt. How obscenely good-looking he was despite the fact he had a mane of hair. Which she did *not* like, by the way. Some girls had a type, and she was one of those girls. She liked guys who dressed smart, not necessarily suit-and-tie, but fashionable. She liked men who had ambition. She liked men who knew how to live the good life. Drank espresso. Cared about thread count.

As she made the mental list of qualities she liked in a man, they added up to Shaun. Which started to make her sad, then morphed to anger. Anger was a better emotion. Better to be pissed at Shaun than go down the rabbit hole of unanswered questions.

Why didn't he put me first? Why wasn't he sorry? Why did I ever introduce him to my parents?

Nope. No good answers lay down that route.

But she could stoke the flames of a current anger. The one where the long-haired upstairs neighbor basically assumed she was a *prostitute*. Just because she was staying in Oliver's apartment and just because she kept late hours was no reason for the guy to assume the worst about her.

Who did that jerk think he was? She felt her lip curl; then an idea hit her.

She rapped on the glass separating her and the cabbie and gave him a different address. "I need to make a quick stop and then back to Crane Tower, please," she instructed. Rachel was sure Bree wouldn't mind if she raided her closet. It was for a good cause.

The mountain man thought she was a lady of the night?

Well, then that's what she'd give him.

* * *

Beer in hand, Tag turned down the music and jogged for his cell phone, plugged in on the other side of his house. He loved the space, loved that he had room to *move*. At six-five bordering six foot six, he was used to ducking for doorways and bumping into walls in an effort to navigate in a smaller man's world.

Here he had all the space he needed.

"Tag," he answered, even though he'd already seen his father's name on the caller ID.

"How's it coming?"

His mouth twisted. Ever since the board mentioned struggling bar profits, Dad had been up his ass. Despite being retired, Alex Crane made it his business to know what was going on.

"My day?" Tag asked, playing dumb. "It's coming along nicely. I cracked open a beer and was about to settle in and watch television."

"Taggart."

He ground his teeth together. Could he hate his full name any more? Not possible.

"I'm talking about the bars," Alex said.

"I know." Tag took a long pull from his beer bottle and glanced over at the plans he'd drawn up. He used the word *plans* loosely, considering he hadn't done much more than scribble with red Sharpie on top of printed photos. Still, he had some good stuff going on. "I've been working on it all day, Dad. You suck at being retired, by the way."

Alex laughed, a comforting raspy sound. "Rhona says the same thing to me all the time."

A warm female voice trilled in the background and Alex laughed again. Tag's neck prickled. Rhona had been his father's personal assistant for years. Hell, decades, now. But lately, he'd been mentioning her more. She'd been around more.

Tag's mom had been gone since he was eleven, but he still felt territorial over his father. He'd have to ask Reese if he'd noticed anything. No, scratch that, he'd ask his brother's fiancée, Merina. Reese was a goose egg on figuring out people, but Mer had more intuition than all the Crane brothers put together.

"I ask because I wanted to give you Howard Schiller's contact info."

"Dad, I know Howard." Howard Schiller was the architect who had designed at least a dozen of Crane's interiors. It wasn't as if Tag lounged at the pool when he did site and build visits. He put on a hard hat and met with developers. "I have his contact info."

"Then why aren't you using him?"

"How do you know I'm not?" Tag snapped, setting the beer bottle down too hard and spilling some of it from the neck onto the photos. "Shit."

"I know because I'm your father and I like to make sure you don't wind up penniless and homeless and..."

"Without a pot to piss in," Tag finished for him as he cleaned the spill with a nearby napkin. "Stop being ridiculous. Go drink your Metamucil or something." Rhona's giggle punctuated the air and Tag added, "And take your Cialis."

"Never, son," Alex said, his tone bow-strong. "Never question your old man's cock."

On that note, a knock came at the door. A light trio of raps. "Someone's at my door. Thanks for the advice and mind your own damn business."

"Later, kid." Alex chuckled and Tag found himself smiling. Cantankerous old man.

He ended the call as he approached the door. Through the peephole, he saw a woman facing away from him in a short black dress, tall black spiky boots, and blond curls trailing down her back.

"Well, well," he muttered, reaching for the knob. He did a quick run-through of his list of curly-headed blondes and came up with a few. Tina. Margo. Oh, maybe Brittani. Although the last night he'd brought her home, she drank way too much Sour Apple Pucker and passed out on the sofa. So maybe not her. He didn't have the energy.

Since he'd started this bar upgrade business he hadn't gone out at all. His evenings were long and late, and peppered with Adonis's barking—which rang out now, shrill and unwelcome.

Hearing that would be fun while trying to twist up the sheets with the blonde standing in the hallway.

He popped open the door, cranking his expression to seduction mode, and then the girl turned and the smile slipped from his face.

Blond curls, red lips, tight, tight black dress pushing her tits out, and the short skirt exposing only a few inches of bare pale legs above the boots. It was Oliver's girlfriend. Adonis's caregiver.

"You," he snarled, having no luck wrangling his lust-filled thoughts into a neutral corner. Here he'd thought he was opening the door to an evening of sex and instead was faced with this one.

"Hey," she purred, strolling toward him, eyes at half-mast, shoulders pulled forward slightly, her cleavage on parade.

He held up one hand and took a step away from her.

"What's the matter?" Doe eyes. Pouty mouth. Another step forward.

"Listen, honey, I'm not sure what you..." She walked toward him, and he maintained his grip on the doorknob, pulling his other arm back before he had a handful of breast. And yeah, he'd thought about what that'd feel like. When she'd stumbled into him outside Oliver's door, he'd noticed every inch of her soft body pressing against him. Braless breasts cushy against his torso, small hands clenching his pecs...

"Not sure of what?" She tipped her head back, hair falling down her back, smile widening, and—*sweet Jesus*. Dimples. Two of them, one on each side of her red apple of a mouth.

He swallowed around a lump of lust. He wasn't sure

what she was doing. Well, he *thought* he knew what she was doing, but right now thinking wasn't easy. The blood wasn't exactly flowing to the head on his shoulders.

Then, the diversion he needed happened. Three quick barks followed by a pathetic, high-pitched howl crept through the floor.

Rachel's smile vanished as her top teeth stabbed her bottom lip. Suddenly she didn't look like a tempting seductress bent on snaring a man in her web; she looked...worried.

"Is that what he does when I'm gone?" she asked, her voice small.

"Yeah."

"The entire time?" Her pale eyebrows bowed.

"Pretty much."

She blew out a breath and with it, sent some of her curls billowing in front of her gorgeous face. He narrowed his eyes and took her in, like he was seeing her for the first time. Something was off. He realized he'd officially met her in the morning so she hadn't been dressed to go out, but he'd also spotted her out front of the apartment building and saw how she dressed normally. Sexy, yes, and in a skirt, but this...this skintight getup wasn't her.

"What going on?" he asked.

Her eyes went to his face. "What do you mean?"

He lifted one of her blond curls, intending to drop it, but wound the silken strands around his finger instead. When he'd met her, her hair was wavy at best, not a tornado of curls. "*This*. What are you doing here dressed like this?" He gave her hair a gentle tug, then dropped it, figuring there was only one of two reasons she'd be at his door dressed like a decadent dessert. Either she knew he was a Crane and was an opportunist, or she was playing it up to teach him a lesson. He narrowed his eyes in thought.

He'd bet it was the latter.

"You thought I was a hooker," she said, her top lip curling.

Tag chuckled. "I did not."

"You did! I said Oliver was a regular, and you thought I meant one of my tricks." She did air quotes and everything.

His chuckle turned into a belly laugh and he had to put a hand on his stomach to catch his breath. "No, sweetheart, I thought you meant you were one of his regular girls. *Girlfriends.* Not that you curled his toes for money."

Busted, she blushed, and that made him happy. Definitely she was not doing Oliver. His day was looking up.

"I hadn't ruled out you slept with him for perks, because he's a wealthy dude and I'm sure he sees a lot of that kind of attention, but I didn't think you were a *working woman.*" He smirked.

"It's not funny." She'd folded her arms, which had the side effect of pushing her tits together, creating enough cleavage that he nearly lost the thread of their conversation.

He pulled himself together by looking at her boots. Patent leather, shiny, pointy-toed.

"What were you trying to prove by gussying yourself up?" He gestured at her body, but he couldn't dismiss her. She rocked that dress, even though he'd bet it was a size smaller than what she was used to wearing. Maybe it belonged to one of her friends. Rachel had amazing curves, and they were testing the limits of her outfit . . . and Tag's ability to stay on point. "What were you planning to do, anyway? Were you coming up here to seduce me?"

A not at all unpleasant idea...

"You wish." She snorted—an honest to God snort. "I'm not the least bit attracted to..." She shrugged, which was cute. "What you have going on."

"No?" He felt his eyebrows lift. "Because this"—he gestured to his body—"has worked for plenty of women."

"What women? Women who want to help you brush your hair? Women who are into the whole you-Tarzan, me-Jane scenario?"

Damn. And she was funny.

"I'm not opposed to role-playing," he teased with a grin. She flinched, and he let the comment hang. He couldn't remember a woman ever brushing his hair, save for his mom when he was a kid, but he'd let Rachel keep poking him. Tag knew women, and this one seemed like she had no idea what she wanted. Maybe she'd known at one point, but now...now she wasn't sure.

"Rachel Foster," she introduced, shooting a hand out for him to shake.

A handshake? Who was this woman? He took her hand and she answered that question, too.

"Oliver is a regular at the bar *where I work*. He found out I was saving money to move out of my roommates' apartment and offered me a gig house-slash-dog sitting for him."

So, completely professional acquaintance. He should have guessed. He'd always suspected Oliver was gay. He'd never seen him with a woman. Then again, he'd never seen him with a man, either, Tag thought with a mouth shrug.

"And you are?" she asked.

Was she playing him, or did she really not know? Her eyebrows were slightly raised in an expression of genuine curiosity.

"Tag," he answered, letting go of her hand.

"Tag? As in *you're it*?"

Tag as in Taggart, but he'd die before she found out he was named after his great-great-grandfather Crane.

"Yeah. As in *you're it*." They shared a not uncomfortable silence, eyes on each other. He could swear the air between them thickened. He opened his mouth to ask if she was going to give chase when Adonis's bark killed the opportunity.

She gestured at the floor, beneath which was her apartment and a very unhappy pup. "What am I going to do about him? I work second shift, so it's not like I can be home with him in the evening. I take him out five times, day and night, snow or sunshine."

"He has separation anxiety," Tag said over another of Adonis's mournful howls. "The internet suggested a few things."

"You...you researched it?" She looked confused and a little grateful, and now that he knew she wasn't Oliver's girlfriend, a whole lot tempting.

"Yeah." After he'd spoken with Fi, he'd pulled up a few websites on his phone. "I didn't want to file a noise complaint."

"Thanks," she muttered quietly, followed by an even quieter, "I need this job."

A bartender who needed a side job. This smacked of a woman who was trying to take a bite out of success in the big city and the city bit back. He wondered what her story was.

"What'd it say?" she asked.

"What did what say?"

She frowned. "The internet."

Right. He really needed to keep his thoughts on track when she was around, or she'd assume he was some idiot with a trust fund who was living in a penthouse because he was spoiled. She wouldn't be the first person who'd underestimated him. When he was younger, being underestimated was his shtick, but then he grew up and opted to tell the truth. He was intelligent, he'd made his own millions, though his portfolio upgraded his title to billionaire by the time he was twenty-six, and he preferred the term *blessed* over *spoiled*. He refused to apologize for living the good life.

He crooked a finger and beckoned Rachel deeper into the house. She came, which gave him an immense sense of satisfaction. She closed the front door behind her and wobbled a little in her high, high boots, and he bit back a smile. He must have burrowed under her skin if she'd gone to the trouble of putting as much of her body on display as possible in clothes that weren't hers. When she'd stumbled into him in Oliver's doorway the other morning, she'd slammed into him about chest high. With the boots, she was almost to his chin. He tried not to think about where else they might line up, but the images came.

Hot, sweaty, panting images.

"Front desk didn't tell me you were on your way up, or I'd have met you at the door with this." He picked up a large brown bag from Pup Paradise, a place on the Magnificent Mile where he'd purchased anything and everything to help with Adonis's issue.

"The front desk was supposed to tell you when I arrived?"

Shit. Now he sounded like a stalker.

"I didn't want to miss you."

"Oh." Her full lips pursed to a tempting degree.

"There are treats, toys, and something called a Kong. You're supposed to fill it with peanut butter."

She took the other handle of the bag and dug through the contents with him. Soft skin brushed the back of his hand and made him wonder if she was that soft everywhere. "Peanut butter?"

"You're supposed to help him look forward to being alone," Tag said, clearing his throat and his mind of his lecherous thoughts. "He probably thinks Oliver left him for good."

"Adonis has had sitters before." She pulled out a squirrel toy and squeaked it. Then traded it for a book on dog behavior and gave him a dubious look. "Really?"

"He doesn't know you. Maybe you two should bond."

"He sleeps in bed with me." She dropped the book into the bag. "We've bonded."

"Sounds cozy." Forcefully, he pulled his gaze from her mouth. A mouth he'd bet tasted like candy.

"Shut up." She snatched the bag, but there was a teasing glint in her eye. She turned for the door and he kept his eyes on her ass, realizing belatedly she'd turned around. He rerouted his gaze to her frowning face. "Thanks, I guess."

"You're welcome, I suppose."

She glared at him.

He grinned.

She opened and shut the door and he jogged to the

peephole and watched as she waited for the elevator. She pulled out an oversized stuffed ball and sent another unsure gaze at the door.

"God, she smelled good," he said to himself. The elevator doors opened and she stepped inside. "And she likes you."

Kind of liked him.

Or else she wouldn't have come up here to put him in his place. Plus that electric zap that hummed in the air hadn't only radiated from him.

He had a feeling she was fighting attraction he knew she'd felt. If she was fighting, he was willing to pull on his gloves and climb in the ring with her.

Suddenly, he was really glad he was having an issue with his downstairs neighbor.

Game on.

CHAPTER 4

"How's Shaun doing?" Rachel's mom asked.

Rachel stopped stirring the canned soup she was heating on the stove while Adonis stared a hole into the side of her head. "I fed you. Go eat," she told him. He looked forlornly at the dish of kibble, then back at the stove.

"Dear, who are you talking to? I hope not Shaun," Keri Foster said with real concern.

Rachel froze mid-stir, phone to her ear, and realized she was going to have to take Oliver's advice and tell her parents what was going on. They didn't know that (a) Rachel no longer was dating Shaun, (b) Rachel was no longer working in the marketing department at Global Coast, and (c) that Rachel was temporarily living with a dog roughly the size of a mule.

"Uh…" She stalled, trying to think of what to say. "I'm dog sitting, actually."

"You are? How fun! Is it Shaun's sister with the

schnauzer puppy? What was her name? The puppy, not the sister."

"Yes. Her name is uh…" What was that dog's damn name? "Adonis." No sense in snaring herself in another lie. The Dane's head tipped in interest and he licked his chops. He chuffed, and Rachel shushed him. Her mother couldn't see him, but if she heard him, she'd know Rachel was not sharing a house with a small dog.

"Adonis. Not very feminine." Clattering came from the background as her mother dug out what sounded like a metal pot. It was rare Rachel had a day off to make calls at dinnertime, but she'd made an effort to keep up the ruse that she worked nine to five. "Did Shaun get the promotion he was angling for?"

Her mom had been asking for a few months. Rachel had put her off by saying things were "on hold for another month." Then another.

"Weren't the two of you going to look for a new apartment soon? Your lease is up next month, isn't it?" Another clang and bang sounded as her mom went for more cooking implements. "I ask"—a chopping sound followed by Keri crunching a bite of whatever she'd chopped—"because I heard in Chicago, the best view is—"

"Mom, stop." She couldn't do this. Not any longer. It'd been crushing her to keep the lies spinning like plates on poles. Rachel was an adult, and it was past time to take her medicine.

"What is it, dear?"

The line fell silent and the words clogged Rachel's throat. Well. Take *part of* her medicine. She wasn't quite ready to tell her mom the whole truth.

"Shaun and I . . . split up."

A gasp.

"It's fine. It was amicable," Rachel was quick to add to keep her mother from worrying unnecessarily. The truth was it wasn't fine, nor was it amicable, but Rachel had the benefit of eight weeks to absorb it and her mother had only had about eight seconds.

"What happened?" Her mother's tone was alarmed. "I thought you two were so happy."

We were until he betrayed me like the punk ass he turned out to be.

"Sometimes . . . things don't work out," she hedged, pulling the soup off the burner to cool.

"Is there someone else?"

For Rachel there wasn't. She hadn't been ready to jump into the dating pool after things went south with Shaun. Not after said pool tested positive for pond scum.

"Two years is such an investment. I can't imagine," her mother was muttering.

It was an investment. A big one for Rachel. She'd loved him and had assumed they'd get married. Until Shaun's familiar nighttime ritual "love you, Rach," stopped and "G'night" replaced it.

She wondered when he'd stopped loving her. Had someone else grabbed his attention, or was it because of the guilt that he'd accepted the boss's praise/promotion combo? A preemptive strike before Rachel found out he'd betrayed her?

After moving in with Bree and seeing firsthand what she and Dean had, Rachel started wondering if Shaun had ever loved her at all.

". . . thought the two of you might even get married."

She tuned in her mom mid-litany about how sad it was to lose a future son-in-law.

"I'm sorry," her mom cut herself off to say. "I did not mean to say that. Honey, I'm so sorry. Where are you living? Is working with him every day weird?"

"I'm dog sitting for a...friend who's letting me stay in hi—uh, her place." Yeah, saying she was living in another man's house would not sound innocent, even though it was. "I'll be here for the month and find my own place after."

Surely she'd make enough money on this gig to put down the first month's rent and deposit elsewhere. From there, she would have to secure a job that paid more than cash tips in exchange for working until three in the morning.

"And work?"

"Work's good, Mom." Finally, the truth. "Busy." Also true. "I have to go. Adonis needs to go out."

He woofed.

"Goodness, she sounds like a large schnauzer."

"*He's* a Great Dane. Like Marmaduke. Except prettier." She scrubbed Adonis's head, admiring his white-with-black splotched coat. He smiled, tongue lolling. "We're bonding."

"Well, sounds like he's a great fill-in while nursing your broken heart."

At her mother's statement a pang speared the center of her chest. Rachel had been brokenhearted and had gone through it alone. Rather than share too much with Bree, Rachel had stayed busy. With work, moving, and getting used to her new bartending gig, it wasn't hard to distract herself. Now, in Oliver's silent apartment with only Adonis for company, she was feeling that uncertainty and pain from the breakup anew.

"You call me every evening, okay? I want to make sure you're safe."

"Mom. No." She was not doing the check-in thing.

"I'll worry."

"Don't worry."

"I will."

"I love you," Rachel said.

"I could worry myself literally sick and then how bad would you feel?" asked Keri Foster, master of manipulation.

"Tell Dad hi."

"Love you too," her mother said, giving up. "Can I downgrade my call to a text?"

"I'm hanging up now."

"Fine." A sigh.

"Good night."

Rachel pocketed her phone with a smile. She loved her parents. They were the reason she was doing what she was doing. Her mom bragged to everyone who would listen about her daughter who was "making it" in the big city. In the small Ohio town where Rachel grew up, Chicago was *big time*. So big, her parents had only ventured out her way twice in the two and a half years since she'd moved here.

She didn't want to disappoint them, and while they may not be disappointed in her job as a bartender, they would definitely be more concerned and possibly offer to send her money, which she would flat-out refuse to take.

If only they knew what her life was really like.

Two days ago she'd put on a ridiculously tight dress

and boots, hell-bent on teaching her upstairs neighbor a lesson. Tag had seen right through her, and after she'd clopped back into Oliver's apartment, she realized she was not surprised.

She'd felt more self-conscious than sexy wearing that getup, and she'd witnessed how confounded Tag had been. He'd backed away as she stepped forward. Not exactly the actions of a man who was interested. Not that *she* was interested, she thought, chewing on the side of her cheek.

Maybe her mother had uncovered the crux of Rachel's bizarre behavior when she mentioned Shaun and heartbreak. Rachel didn't feel like herself and had never, ever done something as bold as slink into a man's apartment wearing six-inch-heeled boots.

It was nice of Tag to buy Adonis all of those toys, though. She took her mug of soup and a sleeve of crackers into the living room and placed them on the coffee table. She reached into the shopping bag, pulled out the stuffed squirrel, and squeaked it. Adonis's head cocked to one side and she threw the toy down the hallway.

Adonis turned his head but refocused his attention on the crackers.

"These taste about the same as what's in your bowl," she said, giving up and handing over a Ritz. Then she ate one. Heaven. Buttery, salty heaven. "Well, maybe not."

She finished her soup, sharing more crackers with Adonis, her mind on Tag and the way he'd looked at her when she suggested that women liked to brush his hair. It made her laugh when she remembered it right afterward, and it made her laugh now as she washed the mug and spoon and put them into the dishwasher.

Tag was ridiculously outside of her playing field, though, right? He was massive, both wide and tall, had a thick but well-groomed beard, and longer hair than she'd ever seen on anyone—male or female. She hadn't been far off with the Tarzan zinger, either. He looked like a trail guide in a jungle, or maybe a wrestler on television, grimacing and flexing until the veins in his neck popped out.

She laughed aloud but it paired with her fanning her face. Because imagining Tag oiled up and shirtless...or sweat-covered in a safari outfit...Those were warming thoughts indeed.

Two months wasn't that long to be without someone, but it was longer if she counted back to the last time she and Shaun had sex. She had done the math once, and the halting of "love you, Rach" and the death of their sex life coincided. They also coincided with the hiring of a cute girl in the design department who had purple streaks in her hair.

That chest-crushing feeling returned. Rachel had trusted him. With her heart, and as a friend. Shaun taking credit for her hard work was reason enough for her to end things. But there was a sting of embarrassment when she thought about how clueless she'd been for so long. How much she'd trusted him—how well she thought she knew him.

Never could she have guessed underneath that neatly buttoned shirt and penchant for double espressos was a man who would step on her head as he climbed the ladder instead of lifting her alongside him.

Adonis chuffed, snapping her out of her reverie.

"What's it matter, right, boy?" she asked his gray eyes. He chuffed again. "Want to go for a walk?"

He danced in a circle and she smiled.

The apartment and dog were more than a step toward independence; they were a step in helping her deal with unresolved feelings over Shaun.

This time, for good.

* * *

Biceps straining, Tag blew out a breath from his mouth and pushed the bar up to his best friend's smiling face. He made it, and then because he knew Lucas was waiting to catch him quitting early, lowered it to do another.

Lucas laughed. "Oh man. He's doing it." He looked to his right, talking to someone Tag couldn't see. "He hates to lose money." Then he bent over Tag's face— Tag's sweaty, red face by the feel of it—and readied his hands. "Just say when, you pussy. I'll take it off your hands."

Smug bastard.

With a grunt of achievement, and a hell of a lot of effort, Tag pushed the bar to the brackets and dropped it with a heavy *clang!* A few of the guys in the gym clapped their hands, and Lucas swore under his breath. By the time Tag sat up and rested his spent arms on his knees, a folded twenty-dollar bill landed on the bench between his legs.

"I have to quit giving you my money." Lucas sat on the leg machine across from Tag. He tipped a water bottle to his mouth and drank. "You probably keep the cash you win from me in a big bin and swim in it like Scrooge McDuck."

Tag laughed and reached for his towel, wiping his

brow. He'd been friends with Luc for going on a dozen years. They'd met in high school when Lucas moved here in his junior year, and learned they'd had the same thing on their minds then and now.

Girls.

Even when Luc went to college, they still met and picked up girls—competing to collect the most phone numbers. Then Lucas won the lottery. He won Gena, sassy black-haired bombshell, now wife and mother of two to Lucas's rug rats. Gena took no shit and was as cool as they came.

The competition for phone numbers stopped for both of them then. Luc because he was gone for Gena, and Tag because there was no game if he was playing alone. Tag settled for the more sophisticated, but no less rewarding, picking up a girl for dinner and sex—one or both. Usually both.

"Been a while." Lucas tugged his earbuds from his ears and looped them around his neck. He was rarely without them. As a music producer, he was often listening to either his musicians' latest albums or potential new clients.

"Since I took your money?" Tag asked, shoving the twenty into the pocket of his shorts.

"Since I saw you. Is it because of work, or because you can't be around my smoking hot wife without dying of envy?" Lucas grinned, an idiot in love. His dark hair was short and spiky, but he used to wear it longer and shaggier. The tattoo of a dragon on his leg hadn't gone anywhere since college. He may be a husband and dad, but Luc was also a badass. It was admirable.

"The last one." Tag stood, his arms feeling like limp noodles, and did a few windmills. While he was teasing his buddy, it hadn't been a line. A part of him was envious of Luc, who'd managed to have a beautiful family and thriving career and keep his fun-guy personality. "Well, that and I'm tired of turning down Gena's advances. She loves me."

Lucas chuckled, taking the ribbing good-naturedly. They both knew Gena too well to believe that lie for a second. She was one of Tag's favorite people, but probably because she gave him more shit than Lucas, and that was saying something.

"Beer?" Luc asked.

"You don't have to be home for bedtime tonight?"

Luc loved to read to his kids. His family was his lifeline. What a great dad he'd turned out to be. Tag thought of his own father and how dedicated he'd been. Even after his mother died in the car wreck, his dad had been there for his boys. Some of the shine had gone, though. The life that only Lunette Crane seemed to bring to his father's eyes. That must be the trick to landing a good woman— getting her to stay—and if she didn't, not losing that light.

"No curfew for me." Luc slapped Tag hard on the shoulder and headed for the showers. "Tonight is boys' night."

"You pick the place," Tag said, following. "But if you score a phone number, I'm ratting."

A little later, Tag was clad in jeans and a sweater and brushing the snow out of his slightly damp hair. "The Andromeda Club," he read off the sign. "Sounds like an old folks' home."

Lucas popped open the door. "It's a cool place. Great food."

Inside, Tag looked around. C-shaped booths in the corners, exposed brick walls, and rich, warm woods throughout. There was an adjoining room with a pool table, and the bar was at the back of the room, a pretty brunette at the helm. A few servers milled around, but the place wasn't formal, as hinted by the "seat yourself" sign.

They headed for the bar and bellied up.

"What can I get you?" The brunette bartender tossed a few coasters in front of them.

"I'm Lucas."

Oh, shit.

"This is my friend, Tag."

"Luc, shut up." This was an old wingman bit, and not one Tag was looking forward to resurrecting. He hadn't needed help picking up women for a long time.

Lucas gripped Tag's shoulder and squeezed, giving him a good shake. "Tag here is in the hotel business. He runs Guest and Restaurant Services."

"Oh really? Sounds exciting." The brunette was smiling and friendly, and then she started playing with the stack of coasters in a really obvious way. Tag noticed the engagement ring. So did Lucas.

"I'm married, father of two. Have you been married long..." He drew out the pause to get her name.

"Breanna, and no. I'm engaged, not married."

"Do it if he's not a prick," Lucas said smoothly.

"He'll be in here later, and he's definitely not a prick." She was still smiling, but not flirting, which Tag respected.

Lucas ordered beers for both of them, sending Tag a shoulder shrug that said, *Welp, I tried.*

"You are rusty on the wingman game," Tag said after Breanna had delivered both beers and went to help another customer. He took a drink from the tall mug. "You, the married guy, should know to check the left hand first."

"I admit, that was a rookie move," Lucas said. "But we'd better get to it since you're probably behind."

Tag swallowed another mouthful of beer. "Behind on what?"

"I figured you and Reese split Chicago singles right down the middle, but with him engaged"—Luc dipped his voice to add the word *again*—"that puts you in charge of sexually pleasing the remainder of Chicago's females."

Tag couldn't help laughing. "You're an ass."

"With great power comes great responsibility, my friend."

Again, the oddest twinge of envy pricked him. He'd never marinated long on settling down, never pictured himself married with kids and the whole picket fence thing. Especially in the midst of boys' night over beers. Tag's sights should be set on the single women in the room. That thought brought forth the vision of one woman, and one woman only.

Guess who that was?

"Menus, guys," Breanna said. "Are you eating?"

"Always. Look at these guns. We need protein," Lucas said. "Breanna, tell me something."

She leaned an elbow on the bar to listen. As was always the way chicks behaved around Lucas. He drew them in with his charm. If Tag didn't like Gena so damn much, he may have had a moment of mourning for Lucas's dormant pickup skills. It was hard to watch one of the greats hang up his gloves.

"Do you think my game is rusty or out of fashion?" Luc asked. "I admit, I'm deliriously happy with my wife and have no desire to return to the singles scene, but it'd be nice to know if I still had it."

"Hmm." Breanna pretended to size him up, which was perfect. Tag would have to tip her extra for egging on his friend, who needed to be checked for his sheer cockiness. "Your approach would work on me if I were single, but I'm not sure you're everyone's cup of tea."

"I will take that as a win." Lucas lifted his beer.

"What about you?" Breanna tipped her chin at Tag. "Do you think your friend still has it?"

"Well, I'd take him home," Tag said with a smile, and Breanna held his eyes a little longer than she'd held Lucas's. Engaged or not, he noted a passing appreciation. Luc picked up on it, too.

"Fuck," he muttered when she walked away. "What is it? The long hair?"

"Chicks dig the hair." Tag shrugged one shoulder.

"Better watch it because her fiancé will be in here later. He might kick your ass."

"I'm not getting into a fight over a taken woman. There are plenty of available ones around." Like his neighbor. Rachel Foster with her blond curls and tight dress, or her tangly locks and polar-bear pajamas. He hadn't figured her out yet. He liked how she was a mystery.

"I haven't told you about my hot new neighbor," Tag started.

Lucas elevated his beer, a look of interest on his face.

"And my brief but memorable foray as a dog walker…"

CHAPTER 5

H_{ot?"} Rachel asked Bree.

"That's what he said." Bree wiped down the bar in front of her. "I only caught bits and pieces of the conversation, but I clearly made out the phrase 'hot neighbor' and by the time he mentioned the black and white Great Dane, I knew he was talking about you."

Rachel had the day off work but popped into the bar to drop off the dress she'd stolen from Bree's closet. The bag was in her hand, and she hadn't yet brought up the fact she'd borrowed her friend's clothes. In a plaid button-down, jeans, and boots minus the heels, by comparison Rachel was downright slumming.

She hadn't slept well last night thanks to Adonis waking her three times to go out, so she'd spent the day cleaning and doing laundry before crashing for a three-hour midday nap.

As a result, her brain was chugging along groggily.

"I'm about to use part of my dog sitting pay to take a certain Great Dane to a kennel," she said around a yawn. "He's exhausting."

"Why didn't Oliver kennel the dog?"

"He said Adonis is used to being at home. Apparently, he's used to being with the usual dog sitter, and I'm not an acceptable replacement." Or maybe it was because the dog sitter Oliver typically employed had one job: dog sitting. Rachel had two, and being here forty-plus hours a week was putting a serious dent in her quality time with Adonis.

"I want to hear more about the long-haired, muscled neighbor you have. You underplayed him." Bree leaned a hip on the bar. The Andromeda was in the middle of a lull, which wasn't surprising given it was nine o'clock. "He's still here, you know."

"Here?" Rachel's eyes went wide as she looked around. "Now?"

No way could she have missed him. He simply took up too much space. Tag was easy to notice. Like the time she'd spotted him briefly outside of Oliver's apartment building.

The sound of low, male laughter echoed off the adjoining room, and she turned around to see Tag and an attractive dark-haired guy standing at the pool table. The other guy held out a hand and she heard him say, "I'll take my twenty back now."

"What's he doing here?" Rachel whispered, trying to remember if she'd mentioned she worked at Andromeda. She didn't think so, but if she had, that would mean Tag had come in here to see her.

Surely not. A ripple of excitement flowed through her at the thought.

"You mean did he ask about you?" Her friend's smile was shit-eating.

"No." Rachel drew out the word, hoping Bree would believe her.

Reaching into the Pup Paradise bag in which her dress and boots were being held, Bree asked, "Where did you go in *this*?"

"Nowhere. I chickened out."

Bree shook her head and took the bag. "Fine. Keep lying to me. Lie to me, lie to your parents..." She stashed the bag beneath the bar.

"Hey, I will have you know I told my mom I broke up with Shaun."

"You did not." Her friend's eyes went wide.

"I did. I told her we broke up. I told her I moved out." Rachel bit down on her lip. "I did *not* tell her I was bartending instead of sitting in my own office."

"Progress. You are making it." Bree moved to the taps and pulled a beer. Then she gave Rachel a real smile as she filled a second glass. "Now go make some more progress, and take these to the two gentlemen playing pool."

"Me? It's my day off." Rachel held up her hands in protest, and Bree put the beers into them.

"Go say hi to the large, pretty man with the beard and the gun show."

"I can't. He's...too much."

"Too much? What, like you can't handle him?"

Rachel thought for a minute. Not that she *couldn't* handle him, but...Yeah, kinda that she couldn't handle him.

"He's over six feet tall, and there's so much hair, and...the sheer width of him." She gestured said width with the beer mugs in her hands. "I don't know. Shaun was reasonably sized. Somebody I could picture myself with until he turned into a jerk."

Bree's eyebrows lifted. "I didn't say settle down with the guy. I said take him a beer. Talk to him. Maybe have a hot, steamy make-out session in the corner by the pool table."

"Breanna!" Rachel hissed.

"What? You're off the clock."

Rachel was saved by a couple who walked up to the bar. Bree shuffled off to wait on them, but not before she turned and said, "Thanks for delivering those beers, Rach."

With a growl low in her throat, Rachel turned on her heel and headed for the pool table.

Tag, in a low-slung man bun, was bent over lining up the cue ball. Rachel took brief inventory of his wide thighs decked in denim but quickly jerked her attention to his face when his dark-haired friend elbowed him. From his hunch over the table, Tag turned his head and pegged her with a look that was borderline animal. Then a bearded smile curved his mouth.

He straightened, put the pool cue stick on the floor, and stood with it at his side like a staff. At that moment she realized her assessment of Tarzan was incorrect. He looked more like a Viking. Or a supersized Aragorn from *Lord of the Rings*.

"Bree was in the weeds, so she asked me to bring you your beers," Rachel lied. Because she had to have a reason for bringing him booze. She couldn't hover in the doorway while Tag pierced her with those fierce blue eyes.

"You work here?" Tag asked as she put the beer glasses on a narrow ledge along the wall behind him.

"You didn't know?" Disappointment sank into the pit of her stomach. Part of her had hoped he'd sought her out.

"No idea."

"It's my day off. I stopped in to..." Well, she couldn't tell him she was dropping off the clothes she'd gone upstairs to his apartment wearing, now could she? "I just stopped in."

"Do you drink beer?" Tag's friend asked.

"Yes." Rachel sent a look from him to Tag. Tag shook his head, but his smile remained. She was missing something.

"Good. I have to go home to the old ball and chain." The friend held up his left hand and wiggled his wedding band with his thumb. "You can have my beer. And Tag can pay for everything since he owes me money for whipping his ass at pool tonight." He snagged his coat off the coat rack—black leather—and slid his arms into it.

"I'm telling Gena you called her a ball and chain," Tag said as his friend moved across the room.

"Tell her whatever you want. She barely believes you anyway." Then he leveled Rachel with a warm amber gaze. "Lucas. It's nice to finally meet you."

He extended a hand and she shook it, noting his extra emphasis on the word *finally*. She apologized for her hand being damp from the glass. Then Lucas was gone and Tag and Rachel were in the billiard room by themselves. She put her hands in her coat pockets and gave the beer a dubious look.

"I should get back to Adonis." She wasn't in any hurry to go home, but faced with the prospect of hanging out with Tag alone, she would rather leave. She thought of how Bree had challenged her a minute ago. Surely, Rachel could handle being in the same public place with him. Though, at the moment the small room felt more intimate than the night she went up to his house dressed in almost nothing.

"Do you play pool?" he asked, interrupting her thoughts.

"Well," she answered. Whenever it was slow here, she practiced. And before then she and Shaun used to play at a dive near work.

Where I used to work.

"In that case"—Tag did a neat little move where he lifted the pool stick and let it slide along his hand until the bottom hit the floor—"we'll drink instead of play. I've lost enough money tonight."

After putting away both pool cues, he came to her and held out a hand. It took her a few seconds to realize he was asking for her coat. She slipped the buttons through her black wool coat and handed it over, then watched as he hung it on the coat rack on the wall. The way he moved exuded strength and confidence. And the way he looked in jeans and a sweater...well, that was heat and sex and temptation personified.

Too much. He's just too much.

On his way back, he palmed both beers, dwarfing the drafts in his big hands. "It's one drink, Dimples."

She blinked, taking in his earnest expression. Her entire life, she'd never been called anything but Rachel or Rach. She tried to decide how she felt about the new nickname. Tried to call up her inner feminist and be properly offended, but she couldn't feel anything short of flattered.

She accepted one of the glasses and Tag lifted his in a silent cheers.

"Do you and Lucas work together?" she asked after taking a drink.

"Nah. Lucas is in the music business. I'm in the hotel business. But we've been friends for a long time." He leaned a hip on the pool table. He was so...big. Dominant.

Delicious.

No, not delicious. He was not the same word she used to describe cheese-covered fries. He was something different. Something she wasn't cut out for. She could sense it.

"Cool. Music. That's awesome."

"Yeah, the girls were always drawn to him. Music is a sexier profession than hotels." Tag's smile was self-deprecating.

"You poor thing." She had zero doubts he'd collected his share of phone numbers, and she knew exactly what it was about him that made her shy away.

The boy was a Player. Capital *P*.

"Did he put a dent in your average?" she asked, lifting her glass for another drink.

He grinned and his expression was so blindingly beautiful, she lost track of what she was going to say. He took one step, then another. The closer he came, the more nervous she grew. Each step was purposeful, capable. Whatever he did in the hotel business, he sure as hell wasn't a maintenance guy. He smacked of power. Of commanding it. Of wielding it. An answering zing in her stomach sent a flutter of butterflies into her chest cavity.

When he was close enough to touch her, he did, gently

resting a palm on her shoulder. Warmth saturated her, sending those butterflies on a hectic migration through her limbs. He redirected his gaze to the dining room, but not until after he'd started speaking. "Hey, guys, table's open."

"Thanks," one of them answered.

Rachel turned to see a pair of guys walk into the room and fish quarters out of their pockets. When she looked back to Tag, he was watching her with a quiet intensity that made her want to turn and run.

"Pick a place to sit," he said. "We're not done yet."

* * *

Flirting with Rachel came easy, but her reactions weren't what he was used to.

The wariness was normal. Women often reacted suspiciously when they first met him, but Rachel's reaction was more than suspicion of what he might want from her. She acted almost afraid of what *she* might want from *him*.

If she was anyone else, he'd make an excuse and bug out, knowing what would follow: her walling up and shutting down each of his advances. She'd given him an inch when he called her Dimples, and damn what he wouldn't give to see her flash those pair of divots again, but then she'd clammed up the second he mentioned Lucas had been popular with the ladies.

Rachel's guard was way, *way* up. She'd been hurt, and if he had to guess, it hadn't been that long ago.

Nearly every table in the place was open. A few business types hanging out in curved booths. A cluster of women dressed for happy hour at a group of tables pushed together. Rachel sat at a table as opposed to a cozy booth—on purpose, he'd bet. She wasn't looking to get cozy with him tonight.

He sat across from her, dwarfing the wooden chair. A candle in a jar threw golden light onto her blond hair, creating a halo around her that looked like it belonged there.

"You're single?" he asked, cutting right to the chase. If she was going to throw up walls, he wanted to know how many questions he could ask before she bricked him out. A risky tactic, but if she stood and stormed off, he knew where she lived.

One eyebrow arched. "Are you?"

"I am tonight." He held her gaze and leaned on the table, crowding the small space.

Rachel sat back in her chair and lifted her beer, creating physical distance. "Do you always come on this strong?"

"No," he answered honestly.

Often, he watched, would take a read on a group of girls across the room. Usually, one would break out of her safety zone and come to him. Ask about his hair. Mention she had a bet going with a friend and ask if she could touch it. He always let them touch. Touching led to them agreeing to come home with him, so it was a smart move.

"Adonis favors the toy beaver over the squirrel. What do you think that means?" Her brows closed in as if she was actually considering the absurd question.

Tag laughed. "You're funny."

"So I've been told."

Okay. Well, the girl didn't lack self-confidence, so her trepidation wasn't because of timidity. She shouldn't be timid. She was gorgeous. And single.

Strange.

"How long have you lived in Chicago?" he asked.

"A few years. You?"

She was good at throwing the conversation back at him.

"Lived here since birth." He reached for his beer, anticipating her next question.

As predicted, she went with, "Where do you work?"

"Crane Hotels," he said after a moment's hesitation. Normally, he'd only mention he worked for a big hotel chain. But Rachel didn't know he was a Crane, and once she did, he was curious how she'd react. "I run Guest and Restaurant Services."

"Ah, then you can write this visit off, I'm assuming." She narrowed her eyes in faux suspicion. "Are you here to steal Andromeda's bar secrets?"

Write-off. Not a term often spouted by a girl who worked in the service industry, unless she owned the place.

"What's the deal, Dimples? How did a businesswoman end up slinging shots in a bar?" It was a guess, but it drew a response. Her mouth softened and dropped open. Then she frowned, probably trying to figure out what she'd said to give herself away.

"I...um. Didn't like to dress professionally." She took a drink of her draft beer. He liked how she drank out of a big-ass frosty mug, filling her cheeks before she swallowed. She hadn't argued about the beer. Didn't balk and order something pink and served in a martini glass, which suited her.

Rachel had more secrets than Victoria...which made him wonder what kind of underwear she'd hidden beneath her casual, relaxed outfit. Their conversation had been laced with his questions and her snappy comebacks. He had no idea who she was, but her evasiveness only made him want to know more.

Dressed down, she was turning him on more than she had in the skintight dress she'd worn to his penthouse. Much as he liked a girl spilling out of her clothes, Rachel looked ready to go on an adventure, awakening the explorer in him.

"I don't believe that for a second." He kept his tone casual instead of accusatory.

"That's all you're getting." She stood from the table, propping a hand on the tempting curve of her hip. "I'm going to go. Thank you for the beer."

"Taking a cab?" He kept his voice at normal volume instead of calling after her as she beelined for the billiard room to collect her coat. She had to stop and turn back to him to respond.

Perfect.

"Yes." A glance to the windows. "I mean, probably. It's snowing."

"It is snowing." Outside, fat flakes fell from sky to ground in a delicate dance. It wasn't windy, wasn't too cold. Luc had driven him here, which left Tag to his own devices. "Nice night for a walk."

He stood and handed a few bills to her before she turned him down, which face it, was likely. "Give this to your friend. I don't need change. I'll grab our coats."

"Tag." She was already shaking her head and holding out the money for him to take back.

"We live in the same building. We're going the same direction."

"I could be going to my boyfriend's house," she said when he started away from her. He paused and leaned close, watching her eyes flicker to his lips. He liked being this close to her. She smelled good.

"I'm flattered, but not really boyfriend material, Dimples." He winked. Which was overkill and earned him a flat-mouthed grimace, but she went to the bar to talk to her friend like he'd asked.

He grabbed their coats and met her as Bree dropped cash into the tip jar. She grinned approvingly at Tag, happier than Rachel about what was transpiring.

"Hey, are you sure I can trust you with my girl?" Bree asked.

"I'm not sure I can trust *her*." He shot a thumb in Rachel's direction, then leaned on the bar and lowered his voice. "Did she tell you she came up to my apartment last night dressed in the tightest black dress I've ever seen? Red lipstick—"

"Tag! He's kidding," Rachel interjected, her cheeks staining a delicate pink. He was content to see her flustered.

"—high-heeled boots. Short, short dress." He pursed his lips and let out a short whistle.

Bree's smile held but a shocked expression joined it. "He's why you borrowed my dress!" She pointed at Rachel. "Do I need to launder it?"

He laughed.

"I did it because he accused me of being a hooker!" Rachel said a little too loud. A table of guys lifted their collective heads in interest. Tag took the opportunity to straighten and wrap an arm around her; then he pulled her close and slid his palm from her waist to her hip. Everywhere his fingers brushed was met with Rachel's body shifting, but she didn't pull away from him. Not even a little.

Bree didn't miss anything, her eyes following the display.

He looked down at Rachel, who was flushed and flustered and trying not to look at him. She liked him way more than she wanted to admit, and he liked that a whole hell of a lot. He gave her a soft squeeze before letting her go, but moved his hand possessively to the small of her back.

"It's just a walk. We're not trading services of any kind." He offered her coat.

Rachel's pinked cheeks went ruddy as she narrowed her eyes at him. Then she snatched the coat and started to the door without him.

He looked to Bree for encouragement, but Bree's loyalty to her friend was rock solid. "Good luck," was all she said.

CHAPTER 6

"This is so much colder than a cab," Rachel said through chattering teeth. The bar was probably fifteen blocks from the apartment. What was she thinking agreeing to walk? She couldn't feel her nose.

"But cleaner," Tag said. She was currently taking two steps for every one of his, given his gait was longer than hers, even at a leisurely pace.

"I do better when it's a nice, even seventy degrees." She buried her chin in her scarf as she watched her boots cut through the gathering snow. "I guess it'll be a few more months until we see milder temps."

God. She was hopeless. Walking down the sidewalk next to a gorgeous guy and talking about the weather. But Tag didn't balk.

"I like extremes," he said, as if this was perfectly acceptable conversation. "If it's hot, I like it really hot. If it's cold, there'd better be snow or it's a waste. I like the ocean because you can't see the end of it. If I'm in a forest, I prefer one filled with massive sequoias."

"Because you can relate to them," she teased. "Giant."

He turned his head and smiled and she admired straight, white teeth surrounded by a golden brown beard. He'd pulled his hair down and the light brown waves fell haphazardly over his black coat. Which was so sexy she couldn't think. Especially since there were snowflakes in the strands. Not that she could blame them. Nestled warmly in those locks wasn't a bad place to imagine being.

Again, she wondered at her attraction to him. Though he did kind of look like Thor, and while she wasn't a die-hard comic book fan, she could appreciate the actor in the movie.

"How tall are you?" she asked, mostly to stop her inane train of thought. The more she was around him, the less she understood her basal reaction to him.

"Just under six-six. You're what? Five-five?"

"Yeah. How'd you do that?"

He shrugged and looked ahead, but she didn't doubt how he'd done it. He'd likely honed his carnival skills and was stellar at guessing weight and height. It wasn't hard to imagine him using his intuition to figure out a woman's weak points so he could attack where she was most sensitive. He'd probably had a ton of practice.

Was that where her concern was coming from? That he'd find her weak spots and use them against her? That's what Shaun had done, she thought with a token amount of bitterness.

"How'd I do what?" A puff of air came from Tag's lips, buried in his beard. She'd never liked facial hair. Until now, apparently.

"How'd you guess my height?" she shot back, feeling peeved more with herself than him. Lack of sleep, or maybe too much, she wasn't really sure what to blame her reaction on now. "How'd you know I was a businesswoman before? I'm a great bartender, by the way. I was a bartender for longer than I worked in marketing." She pushed her hands deeper into her pockets, lamenting not bringing her gloves with her. Her hands were freezing.

"Just observant. I'm good with people," he said.

She absorbed that for a few seconds.

"What exactly do you do in Guest and Restaurant Services?" She air-quoted those words, which brought her bare hands from her pockets. He noticed.

"Where are your gloves? Do you realize it's February in Chicago?"

"I forgot them."

Tag stopped walking, a deep sigh working its way from his wide chest as he tugged off his gloves.

"I'm fine." But he wasn't listening. Once he'd had his baseball-mitt-sized gloves off, he lifted her smaller, freezing hands to his mouth, cupping them in his palms, and blew on them to warm her fingers. He did this the way he did everything else.

Slowly.

Intentionally.

And looking right at her.

He brushed his lips over her knuckles as a drove of chills shot down her spine and legs. She became fascinated by how soft his beard felt against her freezing skin, and then those chills were replaced with heat. Pooling in her belly, between her thighs, and infusing her face with color.

"Thanks," she muttered when he let her go. She stuffed her hands into his gloves—they were warm, and after his personal attention, so was she. They finished their walk to Crane Tower, and once they were in the lobby, she put that together with Crane Hotels. "You're pretty brand loyal aren't you?"

"Honey, you have no idea." His voice was low and raspy and the pit of her stomach did that pinging thing. Or was it a zing? Whatever it was, it was unnerving.

She couldn't shake the idea that she hadn't wanted to walk home, yet he'd talked her into it. She didn't want to get played by the player. *To get taken advantage of like Shaun took advantage of you.*

Since she lived on the floor below Tag, she had no choice but to walk to the elevator with him. Just when she worried about being in an enclosed space with him alone and having nothing to say, another couple stepped into the elevator with them.

Phew.

They pressed the button for the floor three floors below Rachel's, so they were going to be in here a while. Which meant she and Tag would have chaperones. Before she could let out a breath of relief that she wouldn't have to force conversation, she noticed the girl's eyes were kind of glassy and the guy's smile was a little wonky. *Drunk.* The second the elevator doors swished shut, the guy lunged and the girl caught him tongue first.

Gawd. Clearly the inebriated couple had no problem with PDA.

Rachel wiggled her hands out of the gloves, leaving them in her pockets, and glued her eyes to her iPhone screen. Which helped, but didn't shut out the suctioning sounds. She gave up, dropped the phone in her coat pocket, and scooted closer to Tag to avoid the flying arms and legs. Tag was leaning against the back of the elevator, one boot on the wall. She risked a glance up at him when the girl made a mewling sound and Tag looked back down at her, one eyebrow arched into a sexy tilt. When his mouth joined, Rachel looked away.

Looking at him while a couple in front of them sucked face was...awkward. Because it made her wonder what his beard might feel like against her lips.

There were too many rampant hormones in this tiny enclosed space. Too many pheromones per square foot or something. Maybe she'd been infected like some sort of airborne virus.

The elevator stopped and the doors opened, but the two lovers weren't finished yet. As the doors started to shut, Tag stepped forward and stopped them with a hand. "Hey, buddy, this you?"

The other guy slid his lips away from his girlfriend's— or whoever she was—and blinked, dazed. "Thanks, man."

Then they stumbled out, adhering to each other the second they cleared the lift.

Tag looked at the floor, a secret smile gracing his face. He shook his head, which made Rachel wonder what he was thinking, but she didn't dare ask. Namely because he might blurt out that he was thinking of kissing her and then she'd be powerless to say anything but *"Yes!"*

In the end, neither of them spoke as they rode the few floors up to her temporary penthouse. When the doors opened this time, she practically ran from the elevator, but Tag followed behind her.

"Care if I say hi to Adonis?" he asked.

"Is that really why you're following me to the door?" She was suddenly nervous as she pulled her house key from her jeans pocket. "Or did those two turn you on because you're some kind of pervy voyeur?"

Her comment was supposed to lighten the tension between them, but as Tag's heat blanketed her side, it intensified instead.

"It's neither," he said into her ear, his voice a low rumble that made her close her eyes. "I want to make sure you get inside safely. Then I'll go." With that, he stepped away and left a yawning gap of cool air between their bodies. "It was just a walk, Dimples."

Sure it was. She licked her lips and unlocked the door. Adonis ran directly to Tag.

"He really likes men," she grumbled, miffed at having been bypassed. The Dane offered sloppy kisses to Tag, which he expertly dodged.

"He's used to Oliver." He scratched Adonis's flank.

"You and Oliver are hardly the same." Oliver with his gentle mannerisms and quiet midrange voice versus Tag's calm confidence and low, baritone reverberating off her ribs. Oliver was like an uncle. Tag was like...a bad idea. In the flesh.

So why are you disappointed he's not trying to kiss you?

"Adonis. In," she commanded. The typically well-behaved dog tromped back into the apartment and stood inside the door, tail wagging.

"Thank you," she turned to tell Tag. "For walking me home."

"You bet." He was already at the elevator and had pushed the Up button. The doors opened instantly.

Another wave of disappointment she couldn't explain covered her. She didn't want him to pursue or kiss her. She didn't want to be at the receiving end of a man who would use her and toss her aside. Yet the disappointment stayed when she realized there was no chance of lingering in the private entryway with her neighbor.

"'Night," he said.

It was so final, she let out a sigh.

"Good night."

He stepped in, hit a button, and the doors closed on his handsome face. She walked into her borrowed apartment with her furry companion, determined to shake off every last confusing thing Tag had made her feel tonight.

* * *

Rachel had tried to return Tag's gloves the very next morning, the day after, then yesterday, at different times of the day and night. After earning motion sickness from the elevator, she'd finally determined he must be out of town. And the way she'd determined was by asking the front desk and lying by saying she'd found his gloves in the elevator.

The woman had smiled like she didn't believe Rachel's story, but at least she'd confirmed: Tag was out of town and expected back today.

So.

Rachel waited until after her shift, a really busy one where she could avoid Bree's scrutiny. Her bestie had been consumed with prying out the details of Rachel's and Tag's walk home when Rachel had already told her several times nothing had happened.

Well. Nothing *much* had happened. She was fairly certain Tag warming her hands and forgetting his stupid gloves was a scam. The man knew women and Rachel refused to be another bee in the hive. He wasn't getting her honey.

Enough with the metaphor.

Right. She was here on serious business. Return the gloves. Go to bed.

Her own bed. Because imagining Tag in bed was... gosh. Distracting.

Delicious.

She shook her head to dislodge the thought. Where he was concerned she was beginning to think she couldn't trust any of her female anatomy. Her brain had its guard up, and as long as she wasn't around him for extended periods of time, she could fend him off.

Yes, it'd been two months since she'd broken things off with Shaun, much longer since she and her ex were romantic, but in no way was she looking for a man to occupy her time. She had a very simple list of goals: find a job, get her own place.

There was no item number three involving sliding lips with her sexy neighbor.

Properly fortified, she knocked on his door three times and waited, gloves at the ready so she could thrust them in his face and go directly downstairs. Do not pass go. Do not attempt to converse with the guy who scrambled her brain.

Then the door opened and her brain was promptly scrambled. And scattered, covered, smothered...

Tag was wearing...next to nothing. No shirt, so his beautiful chest and shoulders were exposed, leading down to a pair of enormous biceps. He had a pair of large, white headphones over a ball cap, under which his wavy brown hair hung over his shoulders, half out of its ponytail.

There were no words. None to describe the expanse of his chest dotted with a faint bit of golden hair, expanding more with the deep breaths he was taking. Or the rippling six-pack leading to the perfect indent of a belly button, then to the delineated lines that cut a sharp *V* shape along his hips above a very, very, *very* low-slung pair of sweats.

By the time her eyes reached his waistband, she jerked them north to meet his face instead. His skin was covered with a sheen of sweat and he was breathing heavily, chest glistening with perspiration.

He took off the headphones and hat, smoothed his hair, and then put the hat back on. She watched every choreographed move like he was putting on a show for her and her alone.

Say something.

"Hi."

Nice going.

Half of Tag's mouth lifted into a smile. "Hey, Dimples. Come in."

"No, I..." But it was too late. He'd already turned and was walking into his penthouse, his stride casual. Like women knocking on his door and him answering barechested was an everyday occurrence.

She followed behind him, and try as she might couldn't keep her eyes from feasting on the way his tight butt swaggered across his living room and into the kitchen.

He nabbed a water bottle from the counter and

chugged down several greedy gulps. She watched his throat move, his Adam's apple bob. Even drinking water, he was a glorious sight to behold.

"I tried to return them sooner," she said needlessly, waving the gloves before tossing them on a glass dining room table. Beyond, half a wall of windows revealed the dark city skyline. Tag had a great view. Given his penthouse was twice the size of Oliver's, he also had a great amount of space.

"Something to drink?" His voice echoed off the sparsely furnished kitchen and dining area.

"No, thanks."

"I have wine."

He stood at the counter, palms flat on the surface, biceps straining, chest temptingly bare.

"No," she said more forcefully, then covered with, "Rain check."

"Hold you to it," he said with a nod.

She turned away and tried to think of something to say, when her saving grace came into focus. On the kitchen table next to the discarded gloves was a collection of photos of bars. Pool bars, she noted. She lifted the eight-by-tens and flipped through the pictures.

"Is this for work?" she asked, admiring the ocean view for this one. Tropical. Hawaii, maybe?

"Yeah." His deep voice grew closer. "Redesigning the bars in a bunch of Crane hotels. He dug under another stack and pulled out a blueprint-style drawing. "Just had these drawn up."

She took the prints, a bird's-eye view of the pool bar with seats and blenders, liquors, and beer taps. "Where's your server's well?"

"The what?"

"Come on." She slanted him a disbelieving glance.

He grinned. Yeah, she thought he was giving her shit. He couldn't be in charge of Guest and Restaurant Services and not know there was an area where servers picked up their customers' drinks.

"Here." He pointed.

"It's tiny." She held the drawing closer to examine the itty-bitty square of space. "Bad idea."

"What do you mean?" This time he wasn't teasing her; he sounded interested in her opinion. He crossed those massive arms over his massive chest and waited.

"Well . . ." *Don't think about how good he smells, even sweaty.*

She didn't like sweaty guys. She liked suited guys. Clean-cut guys. No facial hair. A respectably short haircut. What was happening to her?

"You don't have enough space for the servers to wait for their drinks," she said, grateful she'd found her former thread of thought. If Tag had an inkling of how he affected her clothed—let alone shirtless—he'd never leave her alone.

Which suddenly didn't sound so bad. Which was why she needed to keep talking. Outside the door, she'd determined why he was a bad idea and why she wasn't ready for someone of his caliber in her life. In here, she was having a harder time reminding herself why she couldn't roll onto her toes and sample his mouth.

"Sure they do." He took the papers, scooting closer to point out the map. "One here, and one here, on the opposite side."

"You have servers on two sides of the bar? So your

bartenders have to run from one end to the other." She shook her head and repeated, "Bad idea."

He took the plans, studied them for a long, silent minute, then handed them back to her. "What else sucks?"

She let out a small laugh. "It doesn't suck."

But his brow was creased, his expression concerned. She took another look and then pointed out the flaws that jumped out at her immediately.

"Here. The liquors are out of reach. If you have a bartender who doesn't have particularly long arms"—she gestured to herself—"you run the risk of breakage and spillage, which is costly." She laid the plans on the table next to a spread of photos. "You're right to carry through on a redesign. The way it's designed currently isn't *good*, but the plans aren't much better."

When he was silent for a few seconds, she lifted her chin to take him in. His eyes were shadowed by the bill of his cap, his mouth pulled flat. He nodded subtly.

"Interesting," he murmured.

"I'm no expert but—"

"But you kind of are." Those electric eyes arrowed to her soul. She could sense his brain churning. Tag cared about this stuff. In a flash she saw past the player who had talked her into a beer followed by a walk home. He cared enough to bring his work home and spread it out on the table. Cared about his job as much as he cared about his body. And he must. To work it out to such perfection. Her eyes slipped from his face to acres of tempting flesh.

"Do you mind if I pick your brain some more?" His eyes narrowed. "I could use another opinion. I was trying to figure out the kinks, but I gave up and worked out instead, which didn't get me anywhere." He offered a cocky smile. "I mean, it got me these." He spread his fingers over his glistening abs. She imagined running a finger over those bumps. One, two, three...

Good Lord, he had an eight-pack.

"You like what you see, Dimples? Because you keep looking down there."

She moved her eyes to his and instantly regretted it. Their gazes locked and when he stepped forward, she was again in the position of stepping away or standing her ground. She should step away. Excuse herself. Her brain tried to call up details of the lecture she'd given herself at the door, but she came up blank.

"What do you want from me?" she asked, her tone light so he didn't think she was panicky.

He stopped advancing and leaned with one hand on the back of a chair. "I want you to admit you like what you see."

"Ha!" She couldn't help it. The audacity of this guy was incomparable. Who talked like he did? "You want me to stroke your ego? No, I don't think so."

"Dimples, whatever you're offering to stroke, I'm in."

The quip should have earned him a slap, or at least a heel-pivot and a march straight for the door. She should be hoisting her middle finger in the air and leaving. But instead she laughed. Again.

"Don't look offended," he said around an impermeable grin. "I was talking about my hair."

"Yeah, right." She crossed her arms protectively. She'd die before she admitted it, but the thought had crossed her mind. "Because *alllll* I want is to run my fingers through your luxurious manly mane of hair."

Arguing with him was her only defense at this point. He emitted testosterone like a mind-altering drug.

He didn't look the least bit insulted as he prowled— yes, prowled—to her. She cleared her throat. Backed up one step, then another.

"I'm not into players. An-and I know that's what you are." Another step back and her ass collided with the back of the sofa. She reached behind her to grasp the edge.

Tag stood no farther than a foot away, his expression animal, his body making her forget her own name. All that bared skin...

He kept coming, dipping his head to take some of the inches off his height.

"You're into me," he stated.

"Am not," she choked out. Barely.

"Touch me," he said. A simple request.

"What?" Her heart hammered against her ribs, reminding her how she wasn't ready for this moment. Maybe in the future with some harmless, neutral guy who made her feel attraction instead of chest-exploding anxiety.

"I want you to touch me. You've been eating me alive with your eyes since I opened my door. You look at me like you're shopping for something you can't afford."

"I can't afford you." Her confession was a whisper. She hadn't meant to say that out loud. It was too honest. Too revealing. Wasn't she supposed to be protecting herself after she'd been thoroughly let down? She hadn't meant to stand frozen while he made demands. *Inappropriate* demands. Then she remembered Bree's advice from yesterday.

Why not let yourself have some fun, Rach? He looks fun.

Her eyes danced over his rounded shoulders and pecs, rock-hard abs and narrow hips. He did look fun. He looked like a damn carnival ride.

"You're doing it again," he accused, and this time she didn't argue, because she was busted. "Touch me."

She should say no but heard herself whisper, "Where?"

He shrugged one round shoulder. "Anywhere you want."

She licked her lips, swallowing thickly and watching as if an observing outsider as her fingers breached the gap between their bodies. Then she did what she'd imagined a few seconds ago and touched his ab muscles with the tips of her first three fingers where his smooth, slick flesh was stretched over hard muscle. Slowly, she brushed along the second bump, then the third. Ran her index finger around his belly button and the wiry hair surrounding it, then dragged her blunt nails the opposite direction up his right side.

When she'd reached the end of her exploration, she hesitantly lifted her face to his chest and saw it expand with one huge breath. Despite the fact she was terrified to look, she met his eyes next and was nearly floored by the responding heat she found there.

Snow fell rapidly outside Tag's windows, but between them it was Florida in July. An active volcano. The buzz in the air between them shook her bones. Jetting from her spine to her breasts and lingering in the space between her legs.

She wondered about the space between Tag's legs, and with a great amount of effort avoided checking the front of his sweatpants for signs she wasn't alone in her attraction.

But she wasn't alone.

She could see it in his expression. Sense it in his barely controlled posture.

"Have your fill?" he asked, his voice a thick, lust-filled growl.

Not even close.

"Yes. Sorry. I'm sorry. I have to go." She slipped away, half surprised Tag didn't grab her arm, pull her back, and kiss her. Or maybe press her against the door and kiss her. Or throw her on the couch and kiss her.

Wow. She'd take all three.

"Dimples," he called as she jerked the door open.

"Yes?" she asked without turning, her eyes on the patterned carpet leading to the elevator. *To freedom.*

"I was serious about needing your help."

She didn't answer. She didn't turn. She simply nodded, then shut the door behind her, slamming a palm into the elevator button and praying to God Tag didn't come out to wait with her. At this point, she didn't trust herself not to lunge at him and have some of the fun she'd been imagining.

When the elevator took its time, she opted for the stairwell. She jogged down to the next floor, working off some of the unfulfilled desire hammering her bloodstream and arriving at her safe haven to a Great Dane with pale gray eyes.

That was a close one.

Too close.

CHAPTER 7

It was an early night for Rachel, and she was relieved to be home before two in the morning. She hadn't been home before ten in a while.

In the swanky lobby of Crane Tower, she inhaled the fresh, floral smell that likely came from the vases of real flowers dotting the room. She hadn't spent much time down here but had noticed as she passed through how residents often loitered in the swanky space. Especially in the evenings.

It wasn't hard to see why. Gold carpeting and wide chandeliers, cozy leather furniture in nooks, and a sprawling area in the middle made for an inviting third space. There were plenty of small tables interspersed with seating where one could rest a drink and coaster from the in-house bar.

She'd never been in a place this ritzy before and wondered how she'd acclimate to non-luxury living when she was done with her dog-sitting gig.

"Dimples."

She stopped in her tracks on the way to the elevators. The deep, sexy voice had come from her right. Tag was sitting on an armchair, papers spread over a low table in front of him, in a nook with another matching armchair and a couch. He was the only one in the tiny area and took up most of it.

But then he took up space wherever he was—even when he was in his massive top floor penthouse threatening her personal space.

Touch me.

"Hi." She sidled over to him, hands in her coat pockets so he couldn't see the slight shake that worked through her as she remembered touching him. "What are you doing down here?" Then her smile fell as she put two and two together. "Oh, no. Not Adonis. Is he . . . ?"

"He's fine." Tag was quick to shake his head. "I needed a change of scenery. I'm not really an office kind of guy."

"Do you have an actual office?" she asked, unable to picture him behind a desk.

"A big one." He gestured to the chair next to him. "Join me. I'll buy you a drink."

"I should . . ." She pointed upstairs. "The dog."

"Fair enough." He turned back to his spread of papers and a little ping of regret zapped her when he didn't argue. Where he was concerned, she couldn't decide what she wanted. Did she want him to leave her alone or pursue her? Ignore her completely, or continue offering her drinks and flirting?

The ride up to Oliver's apartment didn't deliver an answer.

She made quick work of changing, tugging her hair from a for-work bun. She slipped into a pair of black yoga pants and a thick fleece, and pulled her coat on. By then, Adonis was dancing by the door, ready for his after-hours jaunt around the block.

Because she was a lost cause, she brushed her teeth and touched up her lip gloss before heading downstairs. When she strolled by, Adonis ahead of her, she casually turned to smile at Tag only to find he was no longer sitting there. But then had she expected him to wait when she'd turned him down?

The next day, she recounted the story to Bree in between flinging drinks to eager customers. Bree's fiancé, Dean, was at the bar to visit, nursing his beer as he listened with half an ear.

"So you like him," Bree said.

"I don't know." Rachel was exasperated by him. Conflicted by the idea that he should be the last person on earth to draw her interest, yet he snagged it without trying. But did she like him? Not like Bree meant.

Again the thought, *Too much*, flitted through her brain. Even in the lobby, casually leaning over a wide coffee table, he was too much for her to handle. She'd grown nervous thinking about walking past him with the dog.

Oh, no. Maybe she *did* like him.

Another hour passed, Dean now lounged back on his barstool, yelling at a basketball game on the television overhead. Rachel, her back to the room, counted the tips so Bree could get out of here. She was first cut tonight, but Rachel was in it for the long haul, which was fine, because she had plenty of bar-back and a burning desire to make a lot of money. Apartment deposits didn't pay themselves.

"Rach," Bree said.

"Thirteen, fourteen, fifteen, sixteen." Rachel finished counting the ones aloud, then added them to the stack of two hundred dollars and handed it to Bree. "There you go. Pleasure doing business with you."

Bree's wide-eyed, barely contained excitement stopped her cold.

"What?"

"You have company." Bree stuffed the cash into her pocket and waggled her eyebrows.

Rachel turned to find Tag leaning between a few empty seats on the bar, his eyes serious. She took in his expression and her heart hit her stomach. "What is it? What's wrong?"

"Adonis has been barking for going on an hour. Thought I'd borrow your key and take him out. You close tonight, right?" His eyes flitted to Bree. "I'm assuming since you split your tips." A friendly smile for her co-worker, then his eyes were back on her.

"Yeah, I'm here until close," Rachel answered.

"Key." He held out a hand.

"Tag, you don't have to—"

"Adonis is one unhappy pup, Dimples. I'll take him out, walk him around. The exercise will be good for both of us."

"Miss?" a guy at the far end called to her.

"Be right there," she called back. With little time to debate and no other option, she pulled her keys out of her pocket, twisted Oliver's house key off the ring, and pressed it into Tag's hand. "Thank you."

"No worries." With a wink, he turned and was gone.

Rachel tended to the man at the edge of the bar, cashed out a couple next to him, and served refills to seats two and three. By the time she was heading to the other end, she was surprised to see Dean and Bree staring at her.

"I thought you two had plans. Were you hanging out?" Rachel asked. "Need something to drink?"

"Do you know who that was?" Dean's face was ashen.

Rachel's eyes went to the man at the end of the bar who she'd just served a Bud Light. She shrugged. "No."

"Not *him*," Dean said. "The guy you handed your key to."

"I had no idea," Bree said, awed, her smile a little dreamy.

"Tag?" Rachel was more confused than ever. "He's my neighbor."

"Tag *Crane*," Dean amended.

"Okay..." Rachel gestured for him to tell her his meaning; then a very big puzzle piece clicked into place. "*What?*"

"As in Crane Hotels," Bree said.

"As in the *billionaire* Cranes. Reese Crane. Tag Crane. Alexander 'Big' Crane." Dean blinked at her in exasperation. "We designed their billboards last year. We're up for bid on another advertising project for them this year."

"I know Crane Hotels." Rachel's lips felt numb. Tag had said he was in the hotel business. "I've heard of Reese Crane..." The billionaire CEO had become a celebrity of sorts after a Twitter scandal last year. She wasn't into the social scene enough to know more about him.

"Tag is Reese's brother," Dean said. "Tag runs the restaurant side of Crane Hotels nationwide."

"Guest and Restaurant Services," Rachel murmured, remembering how he'd told her everything, and didn't at the same time.

Dean nodded. "He owns Crane Tower, too. Where Bree told me you're temporarily living."

"He *owns* it?" Now Rachel's face was numb.

"Excuse me," came a request from behind her.

"He owns the building I'm staying in." Her mind tried to process that information, but a tumbleweed blew across the barren landscape. "My long-haired, bearded neighbor, who closely resembles Tarzan, is a billionaire hotel magnate?"

"Yep," Dean said, lifting his beer.

"Excuse me, miss?" the customer called again.

"Yes, I'm sorry, be right there." She snapped out of it, then shook her head at Dean and Bree. "I can't process this right now."

Bree started to pull off her coat. "Let me help you back there."

"No, I'm good." Rachel forced a smile. "Just...the news surprised me." To say the least. The man who was intimidating physically had just become intimidating monetarily.

She compartmentalized the newly learned info and responded to customers waving money and holding up fingers to signal they were ready to drink some more. Over the next few hours, the conversation with Dean and Bree receded to the back of her mind.

Until the cab ride home.

Tonight, the sky was spitting and wet and freezing and she refused to walk, no matter how much she needed the exercise. During the short ride, she hadn't fully wrapped her mind around Tag being Tag Crane: Billionaire.

She chewed on her lip, considering what this changed. Nothing and everything. Why didn't he tell her? Why wouldn't he mention he owned the damn building? At her floor, she reached for her keys only to find one missing. The one for the door. Great.

Although maybe...

She twisted the handle and the door opened, which gave her a brief moment of alarm. She didn't like the idea of leaving Oliver's house unlocked and open to whomever...

A gasp stole her breath as she spotted a large figure spread from end to end of Oliver's couch. Somehow—and it had taken some strategy—Tag and Adonis were both sprawled on the sofa, Tag's arm wrapped around the dog, whose paws were hanging over the edge of the cushions.

Adonis lifted his head, spotted her, and emitted a startled, "Woof!"

When the dog lunged off the couch, Tag opened his eyes, blinking as if he was disoriented, or maybe surprised to find himself still there.

Rachel patted Adonis's head as he whined happily and nudged her hard enough that she nearly lost her balance.

"I was worried you'd left the door unlocked on accident," she told Tag.

"No." He sat up, pulled his hands over his face. One lamp was lit in the corner, creating a soft, yellow glow on the disheveled man in the living room. He pulled his hands over his hair and expertly twisted it into a low man bun like he'd done it a million times.

Or a billion times, she mentally corrected, remembering what she'd learned about him tonight.

"You're a Crane," she said, deciding to take a page from his book and blurt out what she was thinking. He didn't filter much. She could learn a thing or two from him.

Elbows on his knees, he blinked tiredly at her and nodded. "Yeah. I'm a Crane." He stood and walked to where she stood. "Adonis went out about"—he squinted past her to read the clock in the kitchen—"thirty minutes ago. So that'll save you having to take him out in this mess." He surveyed her damp coat. "Hope you took a car."

"I did."

"Good."

"We're not going to talk about it?" How he could gloss over the fact that he technically owned every square foot of space she now stood on?

He took her purse from her shoulder, pulled off her coat, and tossed both onto a nearby chair. Then he looked at her, as calm and patient as he ever was.

"Never mind, I'm too tired," she said. Suddenly, Oliver's not-small-at-all penthouse felt like a cramped closet.

A big warm hand enclosed hers and Tag tugged her to the couch. He sat, then winced, stood, and pulled a rawhide bone out from behind his back. He threw the bone, which Adonis happily chased and then flopped down in the hallway to chew.

Tag still had a hold of her hand and tilted his head to the cushion next to him. Rachel sat. Stiff as a cadaver, but she sat. This close in the intimate, softly lit confines of Oliver's living room, her hand wrapped in Tag's larger, warmer palm, she couldn't think of a thing to say.

"What do you want to know?" Tag let go of her hand

and put his arm behind her on the couch, which didn't do much to calm her. If she sat back, she'd be nestled into him, a welcome idea since she was chilled from the cold and thoroughly exhausted.

"Now's not the time, really." She knotted her hands together and glanced at Adonis.

"You brought it up." His words were low and quiet. The way the timbre of his voice danced over her was like sliding into a hot tub. Being engulfed in warmth. Her entire body relaxed on contact.

"I did. I was...surprised."

"How'd you find out?" he asked.

"Bree's fiancé recognized you."

Tag let loose a tired little smile. "Ah."

"Is it a secret?"

"Not a secret, Dimples. Just like you don't want to tell me personal things about you, there are some things I don't share if I can help it." He propped an arm on his knee and faced her, crowding her but not crowding her. She guessed it wasn't his fault her nipples tingled when his heat blanketed her side.

She licked her lips, nervous. "Makes sense."

And it did make sense. She hadn't shared anything with Tag. Whenever he'd asked questions, she'd glossed over them like she was in the witness protection program.

"Does that change things between us?" Given the curious tilt of his head, he was being sincere.

"Why would it?" she asked.

"Because you don't want to deal with a megalomaniac?"

"Are you a megalomaniac?" she asked with a smile. Because yes, he was cocky, but drunk on his own power? She didn't get that vibe.

He pulled his arm out from behind her and sank a fingertip into one of her cheeks. Thick lashes dipped then raised when he met her gaze. "No, Dimples. I'm not."

The eye contact lasted a few extra seconds, and then a few more. He leaned the slightest bit closer, heat blooming between them again. The tingle in her breasts moved south, and the moment she was sure Tag was going to kiss her was the moment she opted to get the hell away from him.

"Sorry. I'm...I probably smell like beer." Rachel bolted off the couch, letting out a laugh that sounded slightly unhinged. "I'm going to..."

She pointed toward the back bedroom where she was staying, pictured Tag's mouth on hers, his capable hands removing her clothes. His big body settling between her thighs...

"Thank you for taking care of Adonis," she chirped as she shuffled to the room. She shut the door and through a tight throat called, "You can leave the key on the table!"

Heart jackhammering, she held her breath to listen, palms flat on the door. She heard the door opening, a soft click as it closed. She counted to twenty—not hard to do since her heart pounded out the count—then opened the bedroom door. Adonis stood halfway between the bedroom and the front door staring at her, the rawhide bone in his mouth.

Rachel tiptoed to the living room, leaned in to check the peephole, and saw the hallway empty, the elevator doors shutting on a tall, crazy-handsome man who happened to be Chicago royalty.

Her shoulders dropped as a breath left her lungs.

"Ready for bed?" she asked Adonis, who cocked his head.

He chuffed and padded into the bedroom. Rachel followed, along the way trying to convince herself that she was relieved she hadn't crossed a line with Tag.

After the death of her relationship with Shaun, she wasn't ready to be burned again. And the man she'd found sleeping on Oliver's couch was capable of a nuclear explosion. With his means, his *history*, she'd bet Tag could love and leave with the best of them. Rachel had recently been loved *and* left, and she wasn't anxious to get another punch on her membership card.

Keeping her distance from Tag was the only way to ensure she wouldn't repeat past mistakes or make spectacularly bad new ones. She put toothpaste on her toothbrush and regarded her reflection, proud of her reaction even though Tag probably thought she was loony.

"You did the right thing," she said aloud.

Because once his lips touched hers, there'd be no going back.

CHAPTER 8

Once the quarterly reports were in, we could see...
Tag?" Reese slid into view when he leaned on the conference table and pressed his palms into the glass. "What's up with you?"

Tag blinked at his brother, then his brother's fiancée, Merina, who was sitting next to Reese, hand wrapped around a mug of coffee.

"Sorry. Didn't sleep." He slept fine on Oliver's couch, until Rachel returned home. He'd tried to kiss her, but then she'd leapt away from him like he was emitting deadly fumes. Afterward, he rode the elevator up, turning the moment over and over in his head. Then in his penthouse, he'd turned over another moment in his memory—the one where she touched him. The moment her delicate fingers had stroked his bare skin. The way her pink lips parted and her eyes widened with lust-filled curiosity...

He'd been so sure she liked him. Now he wasn't so

sure. What was up with her? Maybe there was something wrong with *him*. He'd never been off-kilter when it came to women. Hell, women occupied his mind only up to a certain extent. He wasn't one to fantasize and space out and lose sleep over a woman. But Rachel ... He couldn't shake her. He couldn't quit thinking about her. What her touch did to him. No other touch had ever been as welcome as her tentative fingers brushing his abdomen. Damned if he could figure out why.

"Seriously, what's going on? You look ... weird." His oldest brother was frowning now.

"No, he doesn't." Merina touched Reese's hand and rolled her eyes. "You don't look weird, Tag. You look"— she assessed him, and he squirmed in his chair, worried she could read his thoughts—"consumed."

He was consumed. With the woman he even now couldn't shove out of his psyche.

"Is it the bar project? It's a massive overhaul you've taken on."

"I can handle it," he grumbled. He ground his back molars together. Did Merina assume the project was too much for him?

"I wasn't implying you couldn't." Her eyebrows tilted. Then her eyes narrowed and he could practically feel her reaching for the real reason for his lacking attention span.

"Yes," he blurted, taking the out Merina had offered and running for the goal line. "The bars are all I think about."

"I approach problems the same way. Completely buried until I work my way out." She sipped from her mug. "Have you considered taking a mental break? Shift your attention to something else for a while?"

Like Rachel?

"He has no time to take a break," Reese said, formal tone set to lock, but his eyes glimmered with challenge.

"I'm not taking a break."

Reese straightened and fiddled with a cuff link. "You could, you know. The board isn't concerned with GRS."

He was doing that on purpose. He knew damn well Tag wouldn't take a break while his department lost money no matter how the board rated it.

"The board isn't concerned with your shitty racquet-ball skills either, but it doesn't stop you from trying to beat me."

"Okay, boys," Merina said with a chuckle. "If you want to get them out and measure them, I'll turn away." She gestured at Reese's pants.

The quip earned a hearty laugh from Reese, who put his arm around his soon-to-be wife and kissed her square on the lips. "You'd like that, wouldn't you?"

Again, Tag was hit with the strangest desire to have what his brother had. A woman at his side, good-naturedly jabbing him. A woman who made an effort to be involved and informed about his work. The desire was disconcerting and threw him so far off, he might not find *on* again.

What Tag needed was to get laid. Preferably by the cute blonde with the dimples currently mangling his brains. "I'm done if we're done."

Reese, not taking his eyes from Merina, said, "We're done. Close the door on your way out."

Tag did as asked, leaving the Crane with no real destination in mind.

First, he stopped in to Andromeda, said hi to Bree, and

ordered a beer. After pretending he wasn't looking for her blond cohort, he casually slipped into the conversation the question of whether Rachel was working today. Bree had narrowed her eyes and offered a knowing smirk when she'd said, "Rach has the day off."

At the lobby of Crane Tower, he considered another beer, figuring he could loiter until she walked by with Adonis. Which sounded pathetic. Sternly, he reminded his balls he wasn't a fifteen-year-old any longer.

"Come on, man," he scolded himself, standing halfway between the bar and the hallway leading to the elevators. Indecision wasn't typically his MO.

She'd turned him inside out, and he had no idea why. Although it could be argued he'd never had a woman behave almost scared of him the way Rachel was. He didn't get the impression she feared him or his actions, though. More like she didn't trust herself with him.

Which intrigued him.

What was she afraid might happen?

He had a big personality. No problem pushing. But in her case, he hadn't wanted to push her away. Which was a new approach for him. He'd never had to be careful. Either a woman wanted him or she didn't. And if she didn't, there were always more. Hell, there were *plenty* more. He'd clocked a leggy, black-haired, mocha-skinned beauty at the bar watching him the second he'd set foot inside the lobby.

But he didn't want the leggy woman currently staring at him over her wineglass. He wanted a cute, dimpled blonde.

Worse, the situation with Rachel had created a niggling in the back of his skull that felt a lot like doubt. His gut wasn't telling him anything, and his people instincts were failing him miserably.

There was only one of two foreseeable paths to take in this case. Either seal the deal with his neighbor or forget about her. Those two choices left him with no choice at all.

"Fuck." He used the word to propel him to the elevators and to Rachel's apartment. He wasn't going to give up or back away from what he wanted. And what he wanted was Rachel.

He had come up with a plan earlier today to involve her in his bar-rehab project. She'd had a lot of opinions the evening she'd stopped by his place unannounced, and he was a man in need of another opinion. Hers, preferably.

She wasn't in Crane Tower forever. Her job as Adonis's caregiver would end, and then she'd be gone. Tag wasn't letting her go without at least getting her phone number.

He knocked, rolling his shoulders and licking his lips in preparation to see her. The front door opened to her wearing tight black stretchy pants and a long pink sweater. Her blond hair flowed over her shoulders, and her blue eyes went wide and innocent. Every inch of him wanted to sweep her into his arms and kiss her senseless.

So he did.

He looped an arm around her waist and pulled her against his body. Small hands met his shoulders, and he lowered his lips to hers to taste that pout. It was the briefest touch of their lips but tightened every muscle in his body.

She was warm. She was soft. She tasted better than he could've imagined.

He lowered her to her heels, pulled his lips away, and slid his hands from her back.

"Been thinking about kissing you for roughly fifteen hours," he said, looking down at her.

Her fingers had gone to her lips, but she remained speechless. Which made him uncharacteristically nervous since he couldn't tell if she'd liked it.

Surely she'd liked it.

"Um..." She let out a little breath that sounded like a laugh. "Did you... want to come in?"

Okay. Definitely, he was off script here. By now, they should be ravishing each other, hands and limbs everywhere. He wasn't a total pig, he didn't expect to get laid after kiss number one, but he expected her reaction to be at least... favorable?

"Yeah. Okay." He took an awkward step forward as she stepped back. He'd come to get answers, but so far was only left with questions.

"I have beer and wine."

The offer of a drink was a good sign. "Beer."

"I was hoping you'd stop by," she said from behind the refrigerator door.

"Oh, yeah?" Another good sign. He relaxed some, leaning a hip on the kitchen counter.

"I wrote down the things I love and the things I don't like about the bars where I've worked. I thought it would help with your plans."

Right. The bar plans. That kiss had erased his short-term memory.

He accepted the beer bottle with a tight smile. *Refocus,* he told his other head, the one currently stuck on *Seduce the Girl.* Evidently, Rachel didn't want to be seduced. Not tonight anyway. Her blasé reaction had seriously messed with his head.

The one on his shoulders.

She came to him next, unfolding the papers and flattening them on the counter. A soft scent wafted from her hair and mingled with his senses. Her arm brushed his and his legs went rigid.

"I borrowed paper from the printer at work." She looked up at him with a sheepish and completely adorable smile.

Damn. He wanted to kiss her again. His gaze went to her lips, but she averted her eyes quickly. He'd pick his timing more carefully the next time.

"You worked at the Winshop in Miami?" he asked, his eyes landing on her neat, curly penmanship. Winshop Luxury Hotels was one of Crane Hotels' major competitors.

"Very briefly, I was the bar manager." She waved a hand. "It was my first attempt to escape Ohio. I thought Florida might be for me, so I followed a friend down there and moved in with her. Six months later, I was home and decided a college degree was a better idea."

Impressive.

"You're one up on me, Dimples. I never did the college thing."

"No?" Her brow dented. "I assumed that's how you knew Lucas."

"Oh, we trolled the college bars, but I never cracked the books."

Her eyes slipped to one side and he realized bringing up his days of picking up girls in bars was not to his favor.

"So the Winshop," he said, choppily steering the conversation back to where he'd untethered it.

"Yes. The Winshop. I learned a lot there. Granted, it was six or seven years ago, but I bet I could share some trade secrets." She winked conspiratorially, pale lashes closing over one blue eye, and he shook his head to reset his brain.

"Yeah, I bet you could," he said, his voice low, his mind back on scooping her up again and seeing how many tricks he could teach her with his tongue. The attraction wasn't solely physical, but the desire to take care of her, to make her feel incredible, encompassed every moment he was with her. The urge had surpassed him getting laid or having a night of fun. He wanted to crack her open, know why she liked the things she liked.

Which definitely put him in *where the hell am I?* territory. He wiped his brow, unsurprised to find a few beads of sweat there.

She frowned, so he refocused on the papers.

He couldn't remember a time he'd struck out this badly. And Rachel wasn't a chick in a bar. She was in her house, or, well, her temporary house. He should have more game than this.

"This is great, Rachel, thanks."

"No problem. I figure if you want to pick my brain, this will give you a starting point." She offered him a bottle opener and he realized he hadn't thought to take a drink of the beer she'd given him. "What are your plans tonight?"

Meeting her curious gaze, he considered his plans were whatever she was willing to do with him. A distant warning siren blared in his head. He wasn't calling the shots when it came to her. Was that why he was so thrown?

"I could take a look at your photos again," she said when he didn't respond. "I mean, if you don't mind working after hours."

"You want to come up?" He smiled, tipping his head toward the door. His turf. His place. Maybe that's what he needed to get on even ground. He waited for the flush to steal her cheeks. Instead, her eyes shuttered.

"Um, why don't you come down here? Adonis." The dog lifted his head from the couch where he was lazing. "He's been clingy today."

Tag could relate.

"Fair enough. Be right back." He left the beer bottle on the counter, turned, and walked out the door. He'd either lost his touch or had seriously miscalculated the attraction between him and his neighbor.

Unless it was one-sided.

Which was alarming in every way possible.

* * *

Bree's eyes were the size of dinner plates. "Then what happened?"

The bar was deader than the proverbial doornail as Rachel crossed her arms and leaned against the bar. She'd been cut fifteen minutes ago, but stayed to share what had happened last night. And Lord have mercy, did she need some advice.

"Then he came back downstairs and for the next two hours, we discussed how he could improve the bars at Crane Hotels across the US." Rachel heard the abject disappointment in her own voice, and evidently so did Bree.

"He kissed you," she said, clearly not understanding why more didn't happen. "Didn't he kiss you again? Like, when he left?"

"No, but I..." Rachel shrugged helplessly, which summarized how she was feeling about the entire situation with Tag. Like she was stuck in suspended animation. On Pause instead of Play. "I wanted him to, but I didn't act like it," she admitted.

Bree's face scrunched in blatant misunderstanding, and was it any wonder? Her friend with her sparkly eye shadow, her provocative yet tasteful style in clothes, and her sassy confidence would never understand not taking what she wanted.

"I'm going to his apartment tomorrow," Rachel said in a lame attempt to save face.

"A date?" Bree looked hopeful.

"We didn't define it." What he'd said was he liked her ideas and needed her input. He also offered to pay her, which she'd quickly declined. When he insisted on dinner as compensation for her time, she'd agreed on Chinese food. Takeout seemed to be a fair middle ground.

With tomorrow looming, Rachel was getting more and more scared. Well, not *scared*. But definitely intimidated. Of Tag, of sex. She wasn't sure. No one was within earshot here at the bar, and Rachel needed advice. Lowering her voice and taking a quick survey to make doubly sure they weren't being overheard, she told Bree her worries.

To her relief, her friend didn't laugh. "Totally understandable. Shaun did a number on you."

Rachel's head jerked on her neck in surprise. Since she'd moved in with Bree after the demolition of the relationship, Bree had only met Shaun once, when Shaun brought over a box of books Rachel had mistakenly left behind.

"From everything you've told me," Bree continued, "he was overly critical. Making you think your idea at work was subpar and then taking credit for it behind your back. What a dick."

Rachel chewed on that ugly thought. Shaun was overly critical. During the last year or so they were together, she'd felt as if she couldn't do anything right.

There at the end when things started unraveling, and he'd stopped saying "love you, Rach" before bed, Shaun had been downright bossy. Unsatisfied. With work, with their home life.

With sex.

She hadn't told Bree about their sex life, only hinting how it had tapered off, but turning it over in her head now, she wondered if the secret to why they'd stopped sleeping together was not because of an outside force, but because Shaun was dissatisfied with her...performance.

Rachel cringed at how true that felt. No wonder the idea of Tag intimidated the hell out of her. She wasn't sexy. Not overtly. Shaun had mentioned on more than one occasion that he wanted a writhing, confident woman in bed. How could she deliver when he'd been so hard to please?

Or hard for *her* to please.

"Oh, God." Rachel sank onto a stool on their side of the bar, her knees turning to jelly as she arrived at a very unattractive conclusion. "I'm afraid of sex."

"No. No, no, no." Bree waved her palms in front of her and shook her head, sending her silky hair sliding against her cheeks. "No, you're not. You're nervous about getting back on the horse." Her eyes went to the side in thought. "Tag Crane is a Clydesdale."

"He's too much," Rachel murmured, nodding to herself. "That's why I didn't kiss him back. Why I keep pushing back. I can't handle a Clydesdale right now. If ever."

"He's not too much. He's just right. You deserve to overindulge after being under Shaun's thumb. You can't indulge much more than a Viking billionaire."

Despite her worries, Rachel laughed. "Seriously, Bree."

"Yeah, seriously." Bree wasn't laughing. "He can handle you if you walk away afterward, which is what you need. Nothing tying you down. Nothing putting you back in Shaun Territory."

Bree meant relationship territory, which admittedly had Rachel skittish in a myriad of ways. Once she'd trusted him implicitly and he'd tossed her aside. With Tag, there was a safety net built in because he struck her as a guy who often tossed women aside. Maybe going in with eyes wide open was the key to getting some of her power back.

"And look at Tag," Bree continued, hovering over Rachel like her own personal life coach. "You *know* he's good in bed. The kiss...tell me about it." Her features softened. "Tell me what it was like."

"I already told you."

"No you didn't. You said you didn't kiss him back; you wanted him to kiss you again, but you didn't tell me what the kiss was *like*." Bree crossed her arms. "This is the part where you prove you're not afraid of sex. Describe it to me."

"It was..." Rachel's tongue refused to push the words from her mouth.

It was sexy as hell. The feel of his broad palms on her body. The way his beard was soft on her skin. Firm lips. Hot tongue.

"Really nice," she finished lamely, feeling her face heat.

"Uh-huh." Bree grinned. "You're not a dirty talker, are you?"

"No." Shaun had requested she talk dirty in bed once, but she'd clammed up. Shut down. She'd felt ridiculous doing the things he asked, knowing he was her worst critic. "Do I need to be?"

"You don't have to do anything you don't want to, Rach. But I hear you saying you want to push your own boundaries, and there was a perfect candidate literally at your front door. It's my job as your friend to tell you to go for it. You're already spending time with him."

Rachel found herself nodding in agreement, as Bree made a very good point. Rachel did want Tag. She wanted to kiss him. She wanted to do more than kiss him. But fear was holding her back. Fear he'd be disappointed. Once he uncovered her *unsexiness*, he'd stop pursuing her altogether.

Rejection.

Maybe that was her big fear.

And maybe it was time to overcome it.

* * *

Tag and Lucas bypassed the weight room and hit the indoor courts. Basketball wasn't something either of them was great at, but it gave them something to do while they shot the shit.

Luc wasn't available for beers tonight since he was taking care of putting the kids down so Gena could go out with her friends. For that reason, they were here before six, and Luc was on the clock.

"Game," Tag announced, sinking his next throw.

"Shit. What are we up to, forty bucks?"

"Naw." Tag dribbled the ball as they walked across the court. "I owed you for pool."

"Right. I left without my money so you could hit on the honey." Lucas darted forward, stole the ball, and dribbled it over to the rack, where he rested it next to a line of orange balls. He followed Tag to the bench and sat next to their stuff. Water, towel, and, for Tag, a gym bag with a change of clothes. He'd planned on lifting tonight anyway, Lucas or no.

"How'd that go?" Luc asked.

They hadn't talked about Rachel yet. Tag hadn't brought her up for a very good reason, but Luc had asked, so the question running in his brain like a tireless hamster in a wheel tumbled out of his mouth.

"Have you ever kissed a girl and she didn't kiss you back?"

"What?" Lucas's face screwed into a horrified look.

Frustrated, Tag stood and crammed a towel into his bag. "Nothing."

"You kissed her and she dodged?" he asked, using their old lingo. *Dodged* was a term for when a girl didn't go for whatever attempt was made. And whenever either of them were dodged, Tag and Lucas had moved on. Moving on was key. There were plenty of women who wanted to be pursued, so why waste time on the ones who didn't?

At least, that used to be the rule. Tag had been out of his element lately.

"She didn't dodge. I think I surprised her." Tag frowned. Because that sounded like bullshit.

"Then what did you do?" Lucas was amused. He was still sitting on the bench, leaning his head against the wall, water bottle in his hands. "Come on. Don't run away from your feelings." He grinned bigger. The asshole.

"I hate that you're married," Tag grumbled, dropping the bag and settling on the bench again. Looking straight ahead, he answered his friend. "She invited me in, we had a beer, and talked about the plans for the Crane Makai pool bar."

"Sexy."

He glared over at Lucas, who sat up and quickly lost his smile.

"Okay, I'm done. But honestly, she didn't react at all?"

"She didn't slap me. But she sure as hell didn't react like I thought she would." He thought she'd climb him like a tree. Though *hoped* might be a better word. He'd imagined Rachel's legs wrapped around his hips a few times.

"But you're not done with her." Lucas's tone was cautious.

"Not yet," Tag answered honestly.

"Huh."

"It's not a big deal." He felt like ants were skittering over his skull. He pushed a hand into his hair.

"What's keeping you from rolling out?"

The ultimate question. What *was* keeping Tag from rolling out? After a few seconds of fruitless deliberation, he answered, "I have no idea."

"Is it to prove to yourself you haven't lost your touch, or is this a situation like when I met Gena?" Luc's eyebrow rose knowingly. Watching him go gaga over a girl was a sight to be seen. He'd been as confused as Tag was right now.

"Gimme a break. You married people get extra points for recruiting singles into your secret society or something?"

"Uh-huh." It was a blow-off, and Lucas knew it. He pressed his lips into a smirk and stood from the bench. Lucas started out of the gym, but not before leaving Tag with a parting jab. "Heading home to the rug rats. Keep me posted on whatever is happening with you and the dodger."

"She's not dodging!" Tag called after him.

"Whatever you say!" was his buddy's response as the doors to the gym shut with a bang behind him.

Tag leaned back on the bench and conked his head on the wall. He wasn't done with Rachel yet, for better or worse. As he grabbed the bag and headed for the weight room, he had a premonition his friend wasn't as far off the mark as Tag would like him to be.

CHAPTER 9

T ag sat, elbow on his kitchen table, chin in hand. He watched Rachel's tongue flick out to touch the side of her mouth as she drew a line on the paper in front of her and thought again how he'd like to take her mouth captive.

She'd been mapping out bar designs with him for a few hours, and he was impressed with her ideas as well as her ability to concentrate on the project in front of her without once wavering.

His concentration had been shot since she arrived. She wasn't wearing a sexy, sleek dress, but the stretch pants and long sweater paired with a knee-high pair of boots made her look cozy and cute. Her lips were free of gloss, her hair down in soft blond waves. She looked warm and touchable, and, as he knew after cradling her against him, achingly soft.

He'd been reeling from Lucas's suggestion that she was dodging. Not the best confidence booster, but then

Tag had never needed his confidence boosted before, had he? New territory all around. If the woman across from him was unmapped territory, he wanted nothing more than to explore her from head to toe.

Problem was, he didn't know whether to hack past her boundaries with a machete or lie in wait like a photographer waiting for the perfect shot of a timid deer.

"You should come to Hawaii with me," he blurted. *Okay, machete it is.*

Her pencil stilled on the paper and her lips softened, her mouth parting.

"Crane Hotel on Oahu," he elaborated. "That's the pool bar you're drawing. It'd help if you were on site advising. Talking to the staff. I'm better hands-on."

Her top teeth came down over her lip. He kept going. Kept hacking.

"Snow's killing me," he said. "I could use some sand and ocean and sunsets. Couldn't you?"

Moreover, he could use some alone time with her where she didn't run to work or back to Oliver's apartment. He didn't think she knew why she was running, and he was still perplexed why he was chasing. What he did know was that she'd burrowed under his skin, and no matter what he did, he couldn't stop wondering what they'd be like together.

Together together.

He would concede that part of the allure of Rachel was the challenge, but mostly it was her. Her quick comebacks and hesitation. The way she stared at him with her eyes but feigned disinterest with her mouth. She was a mystery he wanted to solve, and the key to uncovering her was getting out of their my-penthouse-or-yours routine.

She flipped the pencil to the eraser end and tapped the pink nub on the paper. "I have a job."

"Take a vacation."

"I don't have vacation. I've only worked there a few months."

"Take an unpaid vacation." No wasn't an option. He needed to get out of here. She needed to get out of here. Them getting out of here together was an even better idea.

"I—"

"I need your help," he said sincerely. He tapped the drawing with the tip of his finger. "A fresh pair of eyes on the bar would be a huge service. Consider yourself a consultant for Crane Hotels. Any food, drinks, and accommodations are on me."

When he expected another no, she surprised him with "I have my own money."

He blinked, surprised. And relieved. That was definitely not a no. He refused to let her pay for anything. If he were to hire another consultant, he'd book a room, provide a per diem for food and drinks. No way would Rachel shell out her own money for those things.

"It's settled, then." He sensed if he pushed her on the money thing, she'd balk.

She licked her lips and shook her head, her blond waves moving like silk over her shoulders. "I don't know what to do with you."

Boy, did he have a few suggestions. Every last one involving her and nothing between them but a thin layer of sweat.

"Meaning?" he asked instead of saying what he was thinking. Machete, yes, but no need to use a bulldozer.

"Meaning..." She abandoned the pencil and turned toward him, leg folded beneath her on the kitchen chair. She let out an exasperated sound and put her hands over her face, then raked her fingers through her hair.

"You're nervous. Around me." Every inch of her body language said so.

She nodded hesitantly, like she was ashamed to admit it.

"But you don't want to be," he fished.

She shook her head in confirmation. Oh, damn. He wanted to rub his hands together at how excited he was to take on *this* challenge.

"Why are you nervous? Are you a virgin?"

"No." Her eyes popped wide.

"Take it easy." He lifted a hand. "I didn't mean to offend you."

"Do I act like a virgin?" she asked, a cute little worry line bisecting her brow.

Kind of. He knew better than to share that thought.

"You act like you don't like me," he said instead.

"Oh." She didn't refute that, which he didn't like. How did she continually knock him off balance?

"Do you?" he asked. "Like me?" Fantastic. Now he sounded *and* felt like an eighth grader. Maybe he should jot the question on the paper in front of him with *Yes* or *No* checkboxes.

If Lucas could see him now, he'd laugh himself into an early grave.

"Yes. I like you." Her cheeks tinged pink, making him think the tame statement was a bold one for her. Then she got bolder. "I wished I would have kissed you back the other night, but you surprised me."

He pulled a deep breath into his lungs. Now *that* was some good fucking news.

"You mean it?" He had to know.

"I mean it. I've been kicking myself for screwing things up every minute since."

Really.

"Then why didn't you kiss me the second I opened my door?" His mouth twitched with the urge to smile, but he didn't want her to think he was laughing at her. Far from it. She'd absolutely floored him.

"Because...you're..." Her smile widened. "Too tall?"

"Too tall to kiss?"

She wrinkled her nose. "I'm blowing this, aren't I?"

Not even a little.

"Come on." He offered a palm.

She looked at it for a few seconds before slipping her smaller hand in his.

Trust. He liked that. He stood and tugged her until she was on her feet; then he led her into the living room. She followed. Slowly, but she followed.

He sat on the couch and she sat next to him. Sort of. There was a lot of space between them.

"Closer, Dimples. I'm not going to do anything you don't want me to do." He gave her fingers a gentle squeeze and she lifted off the cushion and scooted closer, until her hip was touching his.

"I'm not afraid of you, you know."

"Prove it." He let go of her hand and wrapped his arm around her shoulders. "Now's your chance to make up for the kiss you didn't return."

"But I had garlic chicken tonight." She put her fingers to her lips.

"We both had garlic chicken," he said with a laugh. "Do you always worry about everything?"

"Pretty much." She looked nervous again. Unsure.

The woman was a puzzle with a secret, which made her an unsafe pastime. And a fun one. If she'd let her guard down enough to have some fun with him.

"Been a long week." He pushed her hair off her shoulder, brushing his fingers along the delicate line of her neck when he did.

Her eyes closed and a subtle shiver shook her.

"It's only half done. Put me out of my misery," he murmured. "Let me taste your mouth again."

Blue eyes sought his, and again he waited to be turned down. Then she obliged, leaning in and touching her mouth to his. Tag gripped her shoulder, all of him going up in flames. Like the electricity snapping the air between them had made contact with a metal rod. He kept his other hand fisted at his side. He'd only tasted her once before and since had damn near gone out of his mind with need. This timid, adorably cute, confusing creature...

Her tongue tentatively swept his lip, leaving a warm, wet trail. He opened for her, allowing her to lead. She stroked his tongue with hers and he responded by kissing her back, all of him leaning closer. Her hand came up and touched his chest, but not to push him away, to *feel* him. She glided her fingers over his thin sweater, sending a trail of gooseflesh climbing his arms, then down, lower, *lower*, until she lifted the edge of the material and found the T-shirt he wore underneath. Tentative fingers raked worn cotton as a whimper came from their joined mouths—from her.

She finished off the kiss and his lips chased her, not quite ready to let her go. She put her fingers to her mouth. "Sorry."

"Why?" His brain was shaken, his pulse through the roof, his pants uncomfortably tight. What the hell was she sorry about?

"I didn't mean to"—a small puff of air that might be a laugh—"go right for your body again."

Again. Like the night she explored his naked abs. The same night he'd showered and taken himself in hand, her touch on his mind while he stroked out his sexual frustration.

"You don't need to go slow with me, sweetheart." His voice was gravel-laden, his body aflame. "I'm matching your pace, not the other way around."

"What's your pace?" She lifted her sweet face, and in her expression he saw she wanted the truth. So he gave it to her.

"My pace? Honey, you'd be in my bed naked, screaming my name because you couldn't take another second of pleasure."

"Oh." She looked worried, then looked away. Which he didn't comprehend. He lifted his hand to her cheek and stroked baby soft skin with his thumb.

"What's yours?" He wanted to know everything about her—why she forced herself to stop when she was clearly enjoying what was happening. What was holding her back?

"My pace?" Her delicate throat moved when she swallowed. "I'm a few...encounters away from there."

"Okay." He dipped his chin. He was fine with a few more encounters.

"But I want to...do what you said. I want to..." She laughed full out. "I can't say it." She started to stand, ready to run again. He caught her wrist and pulled her back down. This time she sat even closer to him. He could see the pulse fluttering against her neck.

"You want to do what I said." He threaded her hair through his fingers. "You want to enjoy this."

She nodded, barely, and he mentally punched the air in triumph. That nod was like finding a hidden trail on the map that was Rachel Foster.

"You're not sure if you can," he guessed.

She closed her eyes. He didn't like the way she couldn't admit it. Had someone done a number on her, or was she woefully inexperienced? No, no way was she that inexperienced. She'd kissed him, and the woman could *kiss*. His heart was just now ticking down to a normal rate.

"I'm not sure of anything," she whispered.

Well. He tightened his grip on her neck, massaging his fingertips against her scalp. If this wasn't a challenge he was made for, he didn't know what was.

"You're in good hands, Dimples." He brushed his nose against hers. "You'll enjoy yourself. I'll see to it. Only satisfied women leave my bed."

"I'm not worried about my satisfaction." She pulled back some to focus her eyes on his, and in them reflected real concern. "I'm worried about yours."

He nearly laughed because the idea was fucking ridiculous, but her worry was so tangible, he swallowed his reaction. The root of her fear was whether or not *he* would enjoy himself? There was a crass but simple way to alleviate her concern.

He grasped her hand, put it over his aching cock, and asked against her lips, "Do I feel dissatisfied to you?"

When he thought she might leap away from him, she

surprised him, gripping him harder. He grunted, a sharp exhale leaving his lungs.

"No," she said on a harsh whisper, then kissed him. Kissed the life right out of him. He groaned into her mouth, accepting her tongue again and again, his hips shifting toward her insistent, stroking hand. He was going to come in his pants if she didn't stop touching him.

Their kisses grew deeper, his tongue sparring with hers at a feverish, desperate pace. Her hands wandered away from his fly to his T-shirt. She lifted it, palming his hot, naked skin. He was all for it. He lay back on the arm of the couch when she pushed him, allowing her to drape half on top of him while her chilly hands rubbed up and down his torso.

When she pulled her lips from his, he was panting, his hard-on pressing against her giving body. He hooked his thumbs on her jaw before she scrambled away from him again.

"What's this pace?" She was out of breath, lips swollen pink from his beard raking her softer skin. Gorgeous. Ridiculously gorgeous and plastered to him with way too many clothes on.

"You're still setting it," he answered, sweeping his thumb over her bottom lip. "You don't have to take me to bed tonight."

She nodded and his cock gave an argumentative twitch. Tag gritted his teeth. No, it wasn't what he'd wanted to say, but it was what she needed to hear.

"Maybe we could make out some more?" Her request came out like a question. Even though it would be the most torturous make-out session ever, he answered instantly.

"Yes."

She crawled off his lap, sat next to him, and arranged her hair. He watched the thick waves tumble, remembering what they felt like between his fingers a moment ago.

She reached for the band holding his hair back. "May I?"

"Always." He was so amused by this woman. She wasn't timid, more afraid of his reaction. A spark of an epiphany pushed forward but fizzled the second she started pulling at the band. She let his hair down slowly, then put her hands in it and pulled the long strands over his shoulders.

"Tarzan." She smiled. "You're more like Thor. Those shoulders." She raised her eyebrows. "Bree called you a Viking billionaire."

"That's a new one." A low laugh echoed in his chest, releasing some of the tension between them. She was easy to be around when she was being her fun, flirty self. When she let down her guard and stopped trying to keep him at arm's length. More proof they were good together. That she wanted this.

If she needed to be made comfortable enough to enjoy herself, he was *in* like fucking *Flynn*.

He leaned forward and she closed her eyes, lips waiting. He bypassed her mouth and put his mouth to her ear, nipping her lobe with his teeth, then swirling his tongue. She moaned. Oh, yeah. She liked this just fine.

One hand holding her head to the side, he tilted her neck and explored there, dotting her jawline and her throat with hot kisses before dragging his tongue back to her ear.

He was rewarded with drooping eyelids and blown-out pupils. He officially did not get it. This girl was a sexual firecracker waiting for a flame, yet afraid of igniting.

"What are you thinking right now?" he asked.

"You make me want to take my clothes off," she whispered.

His turn to be shocked right down to his gutter-dwelling thoughts.

"Dangerous." Her eyes glanced off his mouth.

"Fun," he corrected when he could find his voice.

"Fun." She smiled, and he was rewarded with the dimples he'd nicknamed her after. She leaned in for a kiss that felt really final. Turned out it was. In a flash, she climbed off the couch, leaving him wanting and hard as steel. "I'm going to go, but thank you for dinner."

Maneuvering the erection pressed against his fly into a manageable location, he stood and limped forward as she gathered her purse. Because he couldn't resist her scent, he leaned in for a cheek kiss. Then because he couldn't resist watching her squirm, he nipped her ear and kissed behind it.

"Can I see you again?" she asked, her voice a satisfied sigh.

"You'd better." He'd been asked a similar question by women in the past. His answer was always the same: a varying version of a gentle blow-off. Of course, he'd usually sealed the deal by now, but instead of being disappointed at not getting Rachel naked and underneath him, he was irrationally excited about having another shot at pushing her boundaries. Or watching her take something she wanted from him.

Was that what she needed? A chance to assert herself?

"Good night." She gave him a tight-lipped smile, one that pushed those shallow divots into her cheeks, then left. He stood at the threshold as she popped the door open on the stairwell and headed down to Oliver's apartment.

Half of him wanted to follow, drop her off with another longer, wetter, deeper good night kiss, and the other half of him (the half above his waist) decided to let her simmer. Because if he followed her downstairs, he would have her in bed in five minutes flat.

Tempting, but he was looking forward to next time.

He shut his door and locked it, his thoughts torrential and his frustration at a peak. He couldn't remember the last time he'd wanted a woman more than she'd wanted him. Wait. Yes, he could. Jennifer Byron. He'd been sixteen when he asked her to a movie and was terrified she'd say no. She did, and then dated a shorter, less interesting guy named Tom.

Since those dark days of high school, Tag hadn't felt this particular type of lightning rod attraction. For Rachel, there was no substitute. Every encounter drew him in, made him want to know more.

No matter how he felt, he decided he wasn't going to jerk off and lose the fire for her. He adjusted himself through his jeans, wincing at the discomfort. No matter how much it killed him, he vowed not to come until she was at the controls.

This was a thirst only she could slake.

* * *

Against Oliver's front door, Rachel blew out a breath of pure torment. Every part of her wanted to strip Tag's clothes off and savor every last naked inch of him. From the feel of his hardness in her palm tonight, there were a lot of inches to savor.

He'd wooed her and coaxed her and she'd given herself

silent permission to take what she wanted. He let her control the pace, and though she'd voiced that she wanted to slow down, a switch had flipped the moment he kissed her earlobe.

She'd practically attacked him.

She shivered, pinching her eyes closed and trying not to relive the moment. Impossible. She lifted her head off the door and bonked the back of her skull lightly on the wood. "Pull it together, Foster," she told herself, earning a curious whine from her canine companion.

Instead she'd sleep next to a big, slobbery dog. What a consolation prize. She turned and looked at the doorknob for a good five seconds, then backed away as if it had caught fire.

Tag made her bold, which in turn made her almost… afraid? Her heart rate ratcheted up at the thought of him. She was sexually excited, yes, without a doubt, but also… nervous. When she'd first moved to Chicago, she'd been fearless. Bold. When she dated Shaun, she'd been the same way. She went after what she wanted unapologetically.

Somewhere between moving in with him and losing what they had together, that boldness had fizzled. Shaun had rattled her, and as a result she'd lost the ability to trust her own sexual prowess.

Now she was out of practice, but then she'd been at her prime. Yet according to Shaun, she'd done everything wrong. A fact she could hide from a normal guy, but Tag?

She winced. There was no way to fake it with that sex god. Tag knew what he was doing. She tugged on her earlobe, remembering his warm, wet kisses.

Really knew what he was doing. And she was simply too overwhelmed to try.

She'd stripped out of her sweater and yoga pants and was pulling a pair of flannel pajamas from the dresser drawer when another idea struck. The idea of soaking in a long, hot bath and relieving some of the sexual tension ricocheting in her bloodstream.

Without having to involve Tag further.

It'd been a long while since she'd touched herself, since she'd needed to. With Shaun, sex was on the back burner, and then off the stove, and at the end, not even in the kitchen. She'd focused on work and, after she quit, focused on finding a new job and moving out.

She hadn't indulged in anything more fun than wine nights with Bree, and even those had been rare considering one or both of them were usually clocked on and slinging drinks at Andromeda.

Maybe tonight she'd give herself the gift of imagining Tag. She may not be brave enough to strip herself bare and be with him, but alone in the quiet of the giant spa tub in her borrowed penthouse, Rachel could have her cake and eat it too.

Genius.

Bubbles brimming at the edge of the tub, she put one foot in and then the other. She'd shut the door to keep the dog out, lit a vanilla candle she'd found in the back of a cabinet in the kitchen, and turned the lights off. The only glow was the warm, yellow flame matching the one burning inside her.

Closing her eyes, she sank deep in the water, slid her fingers over her body and down between her legs. She started a slow caress designed to take her where she needed, and...

Completely lost her concentration.

Her eyes snapped open and she listened for the sound of Adonis padding outside the door, but no sound came. Only the crack of the windowsills when the wind blew outside.

She closed her eyes and tried again, a hand on her breast, fingers stroking between her legs, but once again gave up after a few futile and wholly unsatisfying seconds.

She pushed herself up and braced the sides of the tub, feeling like a failure. Her body didn't want her hands. Her body wanted Tag.

There was no substitute for him. No matter how achy and needy she felt. She grabbed a bar of soap and finished bathing in a utilitarian manner.

After toweling off, she dressed head to toe in flannel pajamas—white with tiny pink hearts—and buried herself under a mountain of blankets.

Outside the snow fell, and eventually Rachel's eyes slid closed. She thought of Tag and the things they could have done together if she wasn't completely intimidated by him. Her insecurities were far deeper than just her performance in bed; this had to do with a dormant part of her—the fearless, take-charge part of her.

Even as she pinpointed the issue, she couldn't escape the clinging uncertainty that the real thing might end up as unsatisfying as both attempts to find her release in the bathtub. The idea of the sexiest man she'd ever kissed looking at her the way Shaun used to—like he was disappointed and left disappointed—made her want to crawl in a hole and die.

CHAPTER 10

In a moment of bravado, she'd asked Tag if she could see him again, but now Rachel was having second thoughts. After work, she trudged into Crane Tower, ready to sneak into her living room for a movie marathon—she could watch at least two before her eyes grew heavy—but didn't make it to the elevators before she spotted Tag lounging at the bar to the left of the lobby.

His hair was down, his long-sleeved navy Henley hugging impressive biceps. A draft beer stood virtually untouched at his right elbow and his eyes were glued to a paperback novel.

He was quite possibly the sexiest vision she'd ever seen. An answering tingle started at her lips and radiated to her breasts before fluttering in her tummy. She could have him whenever she said the word. He'd made that abundantly clear.

Her penetrating fear was strong…but she was beginning to think her desire for him was even stronger.

"Thor," she tossed out his nickname.

He lifted his head and a smile pulled his beard; then he turned to her and raised an eyebrow. A second later, the book was shut, and he swiveled to face her. She floated to him like he had a gravitational pull.

"What are you up to?" she asked. "I don't see many readers at my bar."

"Waiting on my date." He pulled out the barstool next to him. "She just got here."

Rachel rolled her eyes. "I take it you've had practice learning to be irresistible." She dropped her purse over the back of the chair, then took off her coat, which Tag helped her with.

"You find me irresistible?" He folded his elbows on the bar, leaning close when she sat. His blue eyes, wavy hair, the tempting curve of his mouth she now knew tasted both spicy and inviting…He knew he was irresistible.

"I'm not answering that question." She mimicked his body language and folded her arms on the bar top. The bartender, an older woman with short gray hair, took Rachel's order and delivered a glass of white wine.

"What are you reading?" Rachel lifted her glass and sipped.

"Murder mystery." He showed her the cover. The book wasn't new, with a few well-worn creases in the spine and dog-eared pages. She cringed.

"You need a bookmark."

"Use is a sign of love," he said simply, dropping the book back onto the bar.

She couldn't tear her eyes off him. Once, he'd accused

her of just that. She couldn't help it. He was crazy beautiful. Being this close to him was like being granted access to the tigers at the zoo. Something about him was dangerous, but she knew he wouldn't harm her. She was more concerned she'd swim in way over her head and drown.

Drown happily, the vixen currently residing inside her suggested. There was no other way to regain her fearlessness other than to be fearless. Being bold took practice. Boldness was something the man before her wasn't short on.

"Were you..." She started to ask him if he was really waiting for her, but that sounded needy in her head, so she paused and rerouted. "Did you have a good day at work?"

He laughed, a low rumble she liked far too much. "Is that what you really want to ask me, Dimples?"

Busted, she answered honestly. "No."

He leaned close, keeping his arms in front of him, and challenged her with his eyes and his words. "Then why don't you tell me what you want."

So tempting. So, *so* tempting.

"Okay." She reached for her wineglass and downed half the golden liquid before turning back to him, swiping her lips with her tongue and saying, "You."

Tag was off his stool in a flash, tossing money on the bar.

"We're done here," he told the woman behind the bar, then snatched his book and Rachel's coat and purse, before offering a hand.

Rachel laughed in shock. She'd never dreamed he'd react instantly. She was trying to flirt, to tease him, and thought he'd flirt back.

"Not *now*," she whispered.

"Oh, yeah," he argued. "Right now."

She didn't move, frozen in place, hand still on her wineglass. This was it. Really it. Oh God. She wasn't ready.

Tag dropped his hand, took a deep, and possibly impatient, breath, and leaned so his lips grazed her ear. "Dimples, hop off that stool and take your gorgeous, round ass upstairs and into my bed."

Her nipples grew hard, the heat in her belly trickling lower until parts of her were pulsing mercilessly. He pulled back and some of her hair stuck to his beard.

His mouth. She wanted his mouth all over her. She wanted her mouth all over him.

Oh boy.

"*Now*," he said, and his tone brooked no argument.

She slid from the stool and followed obediently, loving the command in his voice, the cocksure strength and confidence in the way he spoke to her. Shaun had been bossy, but also whiny. She thought as she walked with Tag to the elevators how this was different. Tag wasn't being bossy; he was demanding she obey. There was a subtle yet fulfilling shift. One she was willing to embrace.

In the elevator, he waited until the doors shut, then crowded her to one corner. Her coat, purse, and his book were in one of his hands and he pressed the other against the wall over her head.

"Are you ready?" he asked.

"For you?" Her voice was paper-thin. "I don't think so."

He grinned. It was predatory and wicked and downright yummy. Her pulse skyrocketed. At the top floor, he reached for his key.

"Adonis." She'd totally forgotten about the poor dog. "Shit." She turned to punch the elevator button, but a big hand wrapped around her wrist.

"How mad would you be if I told you I made a copy of Oliver's key when you gave it to me the other day and I've already spent the evening with Adonis?" Tag's eyebrows rose as he waited for her answer.

"Not even a little." Relief flooded her. Going downstairs to tend to the dog would have definitely given her time to think. In this case, thinking was not advised. *Fortune favors the bold, right?*

Her eyes roamed over Tag's broad, tall build as he swaggered into his penthouse and dumped their belongings on a chair.

Yeah. She was so *not* mad.

Inside, she shut the door, and he faced her, rubbing his large hands together and smiling as his eyes roamed over her body. "Man. I don't know where to start."

Her face lit. She felt the heat hit her cheeks and spread down her neck.

"This is your fantasy, Dimples. Why don't you tell me what you want?"

There was an invitation if she'd ever heard one. Her fantasy. And how accurate was that? Tag Crane at her disposal. But her fantasy wasn't to tell him what to do; her fantasy was to let him lead.

As sex lives went, hers had been terribly lacking. Even when she'd done the horizontal mambo, Shaun had made some uncomfortable suggestions. He'd asked her to talk dirty. He'd commanded she arch or stretch in a certain way so that he could get off properly. In short, Shaun hadn't found her very sexy, and her memories of

being with him were more about the humiliation of trying what he wanted and failing miserably at satisfying
him.

Was it any wonder they'd stopped having sex if neither
of them were enjoying it?

At the thought, her shoulders curled in, her hands
clasped in front of her nervously. Tag noticed and walked
to her.

"Where'd you go just now?" he asked, taking her
hands in his. "Fun and flirty Rachel swapped places with
tentative, frightened Rachel."

"I'm not frightened," she said, shaking out of his grip.

"You're something. Want to tell me about it?" He
looked serious, his eyebrows centered over his nose, and
now she was seriously humiliated.

"I'd rather die." She crossed her arms over her stomach
protectively, realizing she was once again chickening out
like she did last night. Her evening would end with a
movie marathon she wasn't the least bit excited about any
longer.

"How about instead you level with me." Tag unfolded
her arms.

"Why does it matter?"

"Because I want to know you." There was so much
sincerity on his face right then, she didn't know how to
react. Had anyone ever said those words to her? The request was simple yet radiated in the center of her heart.
She wanted to be known.

"I'll make you a deal." Tag's cocksure smirk was back
in place, sincerity switching places with his typical
bravado. "For each embarrassing secret you tell me, I'll
take off an article of clothing."

She laughed. "You're going to strip for me?"

"Why not?" One eyebrow arched. So dead sexy. This was insane. "Whatever part I expose, you can touch. How's that?"

She swallowed past her very dry throat, taking in all of him. So much of him. So much to touch...

"That is a yes if I've ever seen one. My God, woman." His nostrils flared as he took her head in the palm of his hand. "One kiss and then we'll start."

Without waiting for her response, he lowered his lips to hers for the briefest, gentlest kiss. A kiss that still managed to turn her inside out. Then he walked to the kitchen, hooked a chair with one hand, and put it in the center of his living room. He sat her on the couch and straddled the chair.

"You don't have to do this," she said. He looked like a dream come to life with his thick arms folded over the back of the chair, his hair rolling over his wide shoulders.

"I do have to, or we'll keep doing this dance where you only want me for a few minutes and then you bolt. To be honest, I don't think my balls can take the abuse."

She laughed again, this time embarrassed. But he wasn't going to back down. And hell, they were here anyway. May as well tackle her fears. Then him. In that order.

"Last time you had sex," he said, reaching down to untie his boots. He paused to look up at her, hand on the heel of one shoe.

"A...while."

"Be more specific." He tossed one boot to the side and stripped his sock off.

She did a quick calculation. "Last year, Valentine's Day."

He blinked but doled out no judgment.

"Is that when you and the ex-boyfriend broke up?" He moved to his other shoe.

"No. We broke up later. Around Thanksgiving."

Shoe and sock off, he rested his arms on the back of the chair. "Assuming you don't want to touch my feet."

"They're very nice, but no," she said with a grin. He grinned back and for a moment they did nothing but stare at each other. They might make it through this inquisition after all.

"Fair enough." He narrowed his eyes in thought, then reached for the neck of his shirt. Her breath caught in anticipation of seeing his naked chest. "Why didn't you like it?"

"Like what?"

"Sex. With your boyfriend. What did he do wrong?" He tugged the Henley, revealing a slice of his firm belly, then stopped. He was holding her hostage for the answer.

"Who said he did anything wrong?" she hedged.

"Beautiful girlfriend he doesn't fuck for nine months, he was doing something wrong. Either he cheated, or he admitted he was gay, or he was suffering from early onset ED."

That last barb made her smile slightly but when she remembered the real reason why, her discomfort crept back in. "None of those."

"Then why?" Tag stood from the chair, came to her, and pulled his shirt off. Her eyes feasted on golden skin and rippling muscles. "Tell me, honey."

He took her hand and put it on his body. His flesh was hot and hard and made her want to sin. She squeezed her eyes closed and told him the truth.

"I'm...I'm...rigid."

Rigid and boring. That was what Shaun had always told her.

"You're going to have to be more specific. Explain while you take my belt off."

She was staring at his belly button because she couldn't bear to look any lower. But then she did. And she saw the outline of his manhood pressing against the canvas of his pants.

Wow.

"Do it, Rachel. Let's get through this."

Hands shaking, she slid the thick leather from the metal buckle. As she tugged the belt from his pants loops, she told him some more truth.

"Shaun found me boring in bed. Sometimes he couldn't even finish. He said it was because I'm..."

"Don't say 'rigid,'" came Tag's already familiar, low, and commanding voice. She screwed her eyes up to meet his penetrating gaze from overhead and saw he looked as serious as he sounded.

"I'm not good in bed, Tag." Belt free, she dropped it into her lap. "I don't even know what I'm doing here."

"Open my pants."

She frowned up at him.

"Now. And while you do, tell me what you're thinking about."

Heat stole her face as she reached for his fly. She undid the button and drew the zipper down, her heart pounding so hard she swore they could both hear it. What she thought about was him naked. Him in control. Him taking her in a way she'd never experienced before.

"I'm not hearing any talking, Dimples." He pulled his

pants off and stood before her in naught but a pair of tight, black boxer briefs. "What do you want?"

"I want to..." She shook her head, rubbing one eyebrow as she shielded her face. She couldn't do it. Which proved Shaun right about her, but she still couldn't freaking do it.

Tag bent, took her wrist in his hand, and said, "Look at me."

She did.

"Want me to tell you what I'm thinking about?"

Probably a blow job. Wasn't that what most men were thinking about? She'd never cared to dole those out, but Tag standing in front of her made her think she might actually enjoy it.

She nodded, anticipation squirming in her tummy.

"I want to strip you bare and lay you flat on your back on this couch."

He reached for her sweater and the shirt she wore beneath it and whipped both over her head. She gasped when the cool air in the room hit her feverish skin.

"I'll start by kissing your breasts," he said, tugging off her boots and dropping them to the floor.

Meanwhile, her brain was racing to comprehend how good his mouth on her breasts would feel.

He made short work of her jeans before tearing them down her legs. "Then I'll move down to your belly"— her socks went next—"and tease the inside of your thighs with the tip of my tongue."

And now she couldn't breathe.

He smiled at her reaction—unadulterated *want* she had no doubt was reflecting in her eyes. He wrapped his hands around her and unhooked her bra. Her gasp this time had nothing to do with the cold and everything to do with her nerves. This was it. Really, really it. No running from her desires this time unless she wanted to stand stark naked in the hallway.

"Breathe." He took off her bra and she breathed, feeling his eyes dance along her bare breasts though he still hadn't touched them.

"But the real fun will come"—he worked her panties down her thighs, keeping his eyes on hers as he slipped them from her legs—"when you open your legs and let me kiss you *there*." His gaze snaked down her body and she pressed her thighs together.

"I'm really bad at that, too," she said quickly. Because her ex hadn't enjoyed going down on her, and she couldn't blame him. It had never seemed very sexy to her. She'd only ever panted and moaned to make him think she was done.

"Then that's where we'll start." Tag's mouth parted into a grin that was positively drugging. He kissed her and she caught his head, feeding her fingers into his hair as he lifted and laid her flat on the couch. Her heart thudded out an SOS.

This was a bad idea.

"No," she said between kisses. He backed off immediately with his mouth, but his fingers pinched and pulled each of her nipples. A ripple of satisfaction tore through her, and before she'd meant to, her back was arching and she was crying out in pleasure.

"Funny, *that* didn't sound like a no." He gave her an affected, confused expression and moved his fingers between her legs.

"Tag…" But no words followed.

"Yes or no, Rachel." He hesitated and left her dangling from the ledge where desire met danger. "I'll do whatever you say."

His insistent touch was too much for her to deny. He wanted to know her, and she wanted to know him. Like, biblically.

"Yes," she breathed.

"Have you imagined me here?" He stroked her center, finding her clit and moving over the tender bud. His touch was rough, firm—absolutely perfect. "It'll feel like this." Her eyes shut, her head falling back as she enjoyed his words as much as his touch. "Except hot. *Wet.*"

She loved the way he talked. The way he guided her, never making her feel forced, only pampered.

"Tag." Her voice was a whimper and she let her legs fall open as he continued to finger her. He felt so much better than her own hands that she thought if he only did this, it might be enough.

"I know, sweetheart. You need it, don't you? I'm going to give it to you. And you're going to let go. Put your ankle on my shoulder."

Her eyes flew open. "What? I can't!"

She'd be open and exposed and—

But then he did it for her, giving her no choice. He placed a few torturous kisses on first one inner thigh and then the other as he'd promised.

"Breathe, Dimples." His warm breath rolled over her flesh as he lowered his mouth and though she breathed, her arms were strung tight, fists gripping the fabric of his sofa cushions.

Then his tongue slicked along her swollen center and she let out a moan that relaxed her muscles on contact.

Yes, yes, yes.

He continued the torturous assault, reaching up to gently pinch her nipples in tandem with his flicking tongue. She forgot about faking. The pleasured sounds coming from her mouth were the real deal. Real and raw and desperate. She'd never felt this free, this *good*, not ever.

A sharp, thin breath came from her mouth followed by, "Tag, please."

He took her plea to heart, increasing the speed of his tongue, pinching her nipples again. With one powerful arm, he held her thighs open, gently pinning her so she was unable to do anything but lie there and writhe, and...

Oh, God.

Spots dotted her eyelids, sparking into miniature fireworks that blotted out her mind; then she was coming, her orgasm cresting into a wave before crashing her to earth and leaving every bone in her body liquid.

She was vaguely aware of Tag moving, resting her legs on the couch, and reaching for his shirt. When she opened her eyes, she saw him swipe his face with his discarded Henley.

His smile was as satisfied as if he'd also had a flooring orgasm.

"Wow. I—you're good at that." Surprisingly she didn't feel heat flush her cheeks. She was too pleased to do anything but smile.

"So are you." He winked. "You taste good, Dimples."

CHAPTER 11

Rigid, my ass.

Tag pulled his hands down Rachel's supple thighs and smiled back at her, aware his smile was sort of dopey, but he couldn't help it. Her face reflected exactly how she was feeling. Relaxed, satisfied, and definitely *not* rigid.

Her ex had done a number on her.

"Come here." He lifted her into his arms, stood, and then sat in the chair. Sure, it was a little *Magic Mike* to strip for her, but he'd had an inkling she hadn't been able to let loose with the dickbag she used to date, and Tag wanted to give her a chance. His assessment had been right. If her ex had known what he was doing and this had been his result—Tag stroked her cheek with his knuckles and watched as her smile broadened—there was no way the jackass would've let her go.

He paused when her blues met his, considering the

out-of-place thought. He didn't make empty promises to the women he was with, but neither had he ever pictured holding on to one for good. Rachel letting him in, letting him dig the truth out of her, made him want to get to know even more of her.

He shut the train of thought out before it ran off with him. He didn't know if he could trust that voice suggesting anything more than sex or a good time. It'd never confided in him before now.

He wasn't worrying about the future. Only tonight.

"The rest is up to you, gorgeous." He moved his fingers down her neck and over the crest of one breast. They were the perfect handful, with dusty rose nipples sitting up and begging for his tongue. He'd promised to kiss her there, then skipped right over them. Pity.

Lazily, she draped her arms around his neck and for a second he got lost in her eyes, deeper blue than his own, surrounded by long lashes, not too much makeup.

"The rest?" she asked, her voice bringing him back to earth. He'd been adrift for a few seconds, his mind hazy at the idea of this woman trusting him so implicitly.

He cleared his throat and adjusted his hold on her, bringing her closer.

"How much more did you want to do tonight? I have a big shower, a bigger bed, and I can come up with a list of a hundred things to do to you involving more bone-crushing orgasms on your part."

She bit down on her plush bottom lip, which made him want to do the same. He brushed her wild blond hair away from her face and put a soft kiss on the center of her mouth. He wasn't lying. He could spend the rest of the evening exploring every inch of her with his mouth.

With his other body parts. Especially the steel in his boxers currently nudging her hip.

Rather than answer, she slipped her hands from his neck and moved gingerly from his lap. She covered her breasts with her arms, which made her look demure and enticing, especially with the rest of her gloriously exposed. She took a step away from him and he felt his heart sink.

Damn. He'd wanted to continue with her.

Then she surprised him.

"Take off your boxers."

He felt one eyebrow climb his forehead. No way did he ask if he misheard her. He stood up and pushed his boxer briefs to his ankles, stepping out of them and showing her how much turning her on had turned him on. When she licked her lips, her eyes fastened between his legs, his cock gave a happy bob.

"I was thinking," she said, her voice husky, like her throat had filled with lust, "that we could do it on the chair?" Only then did her façade slip, did she demonstrate she wasn't sure of herself. Thanks to the last guy who did her way too wrong, Rachel wasn't sure she was good at sex.

He sat, spreading his legs slightly to allow for his erection; then he held out a palm, inviting her.

She stepped forward and then so tenderly his chest crushed, slipped her fingers over his hand. He took hold of her just as delicately, wrapping his other hand around one of her hips. She lifted her leg and he muttered an expletive, and not because of how inviting she looked opened up to him.

"Condom. Give me two seconds." He stood carefully, watching to make sure she wouldn't run. She didn't. Only gave him a jerky nod. He walked to the nearest bathroom, pulled a condom out of the medicine cabinet, and raced back.

"Thank God," he said as he tore the wrapper. "I was afraid you'd leave."

She shook her head and her smile grew a little sinister. He liked the look on her way too much. He'd like to assist her in embracing this side of herself more often.

"Sorry, buddy." She tilted her chin. "I'm not giving you up."

Quickly, he rolled on the condom, watching what he was doing and stealing a glance at her to see if she was watching too. She was. With a mixture of anticipation and wonder and maybe a dab of uncertainty.

"Dimples, you know you don't have to—"

He didn't say any more before she rushed him, rolled onto her tiptoes, and kissed him solidly. She cupped his face, slanting her mouth, her tongue sparring with his. She'd gone from hesitant to greedy and demanding, and damn, he liked her like this. He'd known in his gut she was a sexual firecracker. She just needed the right guy to explode with.

You found him, honey.

His hands went to her hips as he sat. She threw one leg over his lap, straddling him. He supported her weight, lifting her some before placing her on his thighs, below where he wanted her. By the time her fingers were buried in his hair and she'd pulled her mouth from his, he was panting, his lungs and heart working double time to keep him conscious.

He put one hand on her lower back and the other on her arm, alarmed to feel he was shaking. Anticipation had coiled him as tightly as possible without snapping him in two.

"Tag," she whispered. "I'm ready."

God. So was he.

He palmed her ass as she tipped her hips over his erection, and then started to slide down. There was no need to readjust, to have her assist. His cock slipped past her warm, wet folds and nudged her opening like she was outfitted with a damn homing device.

Between hectic exhalations and ragged inhalations, he worked his length inside her. Until she closed her eyes, dropped her head back on her neck, and held on to his shoulders for purchase.

He sank all the way in, losing the ability to keep his own eyes open after being wrapped in her heat. Short fingernails dug into his flesh with a slightly painful bite.

"Oh, wow. Tag. Wow."

He pried his eyes open to find Rachel's mouth dropped, her irises blown out, and her cheeks a welcoming, rosy hue.

"I can't reach the floor," she said.

He couldn't keep his smile away as he verified. Sure enough, her toes barely touched the carpet.

"I have no leverage to help." A tiny pout.

He gripped her hips firmly, lifted her off his lap, and plunged her slowly back down, watching her face contort into pleats of pleasure.

"You don't have to help." He lifted her again, grunting at the loss of her tightness before bringing her down again. "You just have to—ah, Jesus." He lost his train of thought when she clamped tightly around him and as quickly let up.

"I'm sorry."

"Do it again."

"What did I—"

His hands gripped her body almost too tight as he endured another mind-melting squeeze. "*That*. God Almighty, Rachel. That right there."

"You like that?"

He let out a raspy chuckle and moved her again, feeling sweat bead at his temple. "You hugging my cock with your warm, wet pussy? Yeah, honey. I like that a lot."

"Your mouth..." When he thought she'd take him to task for talking dirty, she smothered him with another kiss designed to take him straight to heaven in way too short of a time.

He continued rocking her and she continued squeezing him and they continued panting between kisses. She pulled his hair and quickly apologized. He just as quickly told her to shut up and hang on, no apologies necessary. By the time he was slamming her down onto his lap for the hundredth time, they were both sweaty and his eardrums were filled with her screaming out another long orgasm.

This time when she pulsed around him, Tag followed. His release robbed him of his voice and the strength in his legs. He didn't remember ever coming so hard, so thoroughly. He held on to her, arms wrapped around her back as his face rested against her breast.

When he snapped out of it, she was lovingly stroking his hair and he was regaining feeling in his tingling toes. When she spoke, the smile was evident in her voice.

"Thanks, Tarzan."

It was a smile he returned.

* * *

"I'm a slut! I'm a dirty, filthy slut!" Rachel said as she and Bree lifted the chairs off the tables in the dining room and put them on all fours.

Bree stopped their opening routine and crossed the dining room to where Rachel was standing. Presently, there were two kitchen guys in the back doing prep, and Rachel had been sure she'd made her confession quietly enough so they didn't overhear.

"Sit." Bree pointed at a group of chairs. Rachel sat, Bree taking the one closest to her. "Talk. Leave no details out. I have to hear everything."

"Tag and I...we...well." Rachel lifted one shoulder and dropped it.

Bree gasped, slapping her hands to her mouth, a smile in her eyes. She dropped her hands. "Is he hung? Is he any good? Did you have a...you know."

"You're—you're taking this really well."

"I'm thrilled for you! After Shaun, I wasn't sure you'd be brave enough to take on another man for a long time."

"You're making my point! I'm a slut! I have no relationship with Tag."

"You're friends."

"He's a billionaire playboy."

"Which means he knows what he's doing." Bree narrowed her eyes and put a hand on Rachel's shoulder. "Did you use protection?"

"*Yes*. He insisted."

A quick lift of Bree's eyebrows showed she was impressed. "Go on."

"I don't know how to do this."

"Babe, sounds like you do. Did it end badly or something? Was it awkward after?"

"No. It was...nice." A lame descriptor to describe what came after. Once she and Tag had spent themselves on the chair, he'd walked her to the shower and they soaped each other up and down. Rachel leaned closer to Bree and whispered, "He washed my hair."

One hand over her heart, her friend's expression melted. "So romantic."

"He knows how to do it, too. Since he has a head full of very nice hair."

"Great sex, no awkwardness after, and he washed your hair." Bree grinned, clearly pleased. "Did you stay?"

"I didn't," Rachel answered with a headshake. "I had to get back to Adonis."

"Oh right. The dog. Shame. So, what... You feel guilty because you had incredible sex with a guy you aren't technically dating?"

"That's the thing." Rachel stayed close as she spoke. "I *don't* feel guilty. At all. But shouldn't I?" Her mother would be appalled. Her father—oh, Lord, her father would have an aneurism if he knew.

"I get it." Bree nodded.

What a relief—someone understood her crazy brain.

"Just because you have never slept with a man who you weren't committed to doesn't mean you did anything wrong," Bree continued. "Sounds to me like you're both on the same page." Her gaze flitted to the side. "Kind of."

When Bree stood, Rachel stood with her. "What does 'kind of' mean?"

Bree started taking down the rest of the chairs and
Rachel helped. Mainly so she could pry out the answer to
her question.

"He's pursued you pretty hard, Rach."

"He has?"

"Hello? He came in here and walked you home. He
stopped by one day to pick up the key so he could take
care of Adonis. He washed your hair."

True.

"He likes you."

"Well, I hope so considering what we did last night,"
Rachel said with a haughty laugh, but the outburst made
her stomach flip. So did Bree's next question.

"How did you leave things?"

"He wants to take me to Hawaii." Tag had brought up
Hawaii and Oliver. He asked when she was done dog sitting and reinvited her to Oahu.

"Chair sex. A trip to Hawaii with the local billionaire."
Bree put the last chair on the floor. "I am officially jealous
of your life."

Rachel had to smile. When she thought of what had
been happening to her lately, it was pretty damn enviable.

"What'd you say?" Bree asked.

"I said I couldn't possibly leave you in a lurch here at
Andromeda."

"Fuck you, Blondie!" Bree exclaimed so loudly that
the guys in the back fell silent. Javier came to the window, eyebrows raised in alarm. She waved him off with a
"We're joking around." Then she turned back to Rachel.
"Seriously, ladybug. You are going to say yes. You are
going to take some time away from here, and if I'm three
deep around this entire bar, I'll not only leave with all

your tips, but I'll also feel good for giving you the gift of sex on the beach with Tag Crane."

Sex on the beach. That would be a first, and Hawaii was the ideal destination for it.

"When you put it that way..." Rachel allowed herself to grin.

"Grab life by the balls, girlfriend." Bree pointed at the CLOSED sign on the front door. "And open up for us. Let's hurry through this week so you can get to next week."

CHAPTER 12

T ag was whistling when he went to work the morning after the best chair sex of his life. Helping was the fact Rachel was petite and he could lift and pull her down onto him. It helped more that she was willing and excited, matching his attraction to her.

At least he hoped it matched. When she insisted on leaving to sleep in her own bed, turning him down when he offered to take the dog outside for her, he had to wonder.

He also wondered if she'd eventually accept his offer to go to Hawaii. It surprised him how much he wanted her there. For one, he could use her advice, and for another, the girl was an untapped sexual powder keg. He wanted to be the one to make her blow.

Sex on Oahu would be a great addition to her repertoire. He'd had sex in Hawaii before, but he suspected with Rachel it would be different. With her, everything was different. Which made him worry slightly about the location of his balls. He'd like to think he still had them on his person and hadn't handed them over to the tiny blonde currently turning his brains into paste.

Tag arrived at his brother's office and spared a shit-eating grin for Bobbie. Reese's secretary didn't like him much, but he was determined to draw a smile from her. He'd achieved the feat once, about four years ago. He was convinced there was another one in there.

"Bobbie. Dumpling."

"Mr. Crane," she said flatly.

"Reese in there?"

"Yes."

He sat on the corner of her desk, hearing the wood creak beneath his weight. She gave the surface a worried assessment.

"Do you have a favorite flower, Bobbie?"

"What on earth are you talking about?" Black eyes darted to his.

"Roses? Daffodils?" He snapped his fingers. "Wait. I've got it. Tulips."

"None of the above. Mr. Crane, would you kindly remove your derriere from my desk?"

He did as she asked, walking to his brother's door. "Okay, but I'm going to keep guessing."

"Please don't."

"You'll cave eventually," he said as he turned the doorknob.

She spared him a glare and then picked up the phone and started punching numbers furiously. Probably an excuse to get him to go away. No smile yet, but he'd keep trying.

"Bro!" he said as he walked in to Reese's office and found him tapping at his keyboard.

Reese looked up from his computer screen. "To what do I owe the honor?"

"Always so formal." Tag sat in the guest chair in front of his brother's desk. "I'm going to Hawaii in a few days, so I'll miss the next board brouhaha." He tossed the folder in his hand on Reese's desk. "Details about what I'm doing there, if they care."

Reese chuckled, warmth lighting his eyes. Maybe it was the infusion of sunlight bouncing off the buildings and the white, reflective snow, but his brother looked lighter lately. Less worried.

"How are things?" Tag asked.

"Things?" Reese closed the folder and set it aside. "Meaning?"

"With Merina. You seem...weird," he said, using Reese's words from the other day.

"Ha-ha."

"Good, though?" Tag asked. "I mean, you seem good. It's nice to see you happy."

In a rare moment of sharing, Reese said, "Merina makes me happy." Then his smile wiped away when he tacked on, "Had no idea what a miserable bastard I was before she came into my life."

"I did." Tag smiled, and in a snap, his brother and he were back on familiar ground. Either of them would go to battle for the other one, but they always gave each other hell.

"How long will you be on Oahu?" Reese asked.

"Week. Maybe two." Tag averted his eyes. "Depends on how long my advisor wants to stay."

"Calling in help, eh? Who is she?" His brother's eyes twinkled.

"It's not what you think."

"You're not looking to have some fringe benefits while on the island?" One side of Reese's mouth lifted.

"She's in the business." Tag's defenses rose, more because he didn't want to admit that her pleasure was mostly why he wanted her to go.

Reese blew out a breath from his nose. "Well don't take advantage of the poor girl so you can get laid."

Offended, Tag bit out, "I already got laid." The word sounded crude, so he rerouted. "Made love—whatever." He felt his face warm when he mumbled, "Have some respect."

Reese wasn't often flustered, but his succession of quick blinks when Tag glanced back at him did showcase his surprise.

"This is new," Reese drawled.

Tag shifted uncomfortably.

"Don't you usually wiggle out of further commitment at this point? Disentangle yourself with a wink and one of those here's-looking-at-you-kid taps to her jaw?"

"Not...always." But most of the time. He wasn't a one-and-done freak like Reese used to be before Merina, but Tag had never made it a habit to stick around. Where Rachel was concerned, he wasn't in a hurry to see her go. Different, true. But it was what it was.

"What does she do besides what she does with you?" Reese leaned back in his chair, amused. Tag wished he'd have handled this with an email instead of stopping by.

"Rachel is a bartender with a background in marketing. She is very skilled at what she does." *In and out of the bedroom,* he thought, and then quickly buried a budding

Jessica Lemmon

smile. He'd never been so invested in a woman's pleasure before Rachel. He hadn't been lying when he'd told her only satisfied women left his bed, but when it came to Rachel, "satisfied" didn't cover it. He wanted her thoroughly sated, boneless. Deliriously exhausted.

He put a finger to his lips to suppress a grin.

"A bartender," Reese repeated, and Tag realized he'd spaced out there for a second.

"She's smart. And she used to work at the Miami Winshop. She gave me some insight."

At the mention of Winshop, Reese perked up. "Nicely done. We could use insight on our competitors." He scooped up the folder and stood, stopping a few inches in front of Tag. "You know, if you like this woman, it's okay to admit it."

Tag shook his head. "You know the deal. Cranes play fast and loose."

"You're the one who used the term *made love*," Reese said, slapping Tag on the arm with the folder. "Have a great trip, baby brother."

Reese exited the side door, sending a know-it-all big-brother smile over his shoulder before he left. Then Tag was alone in the office, staring out the windows and feeling like "fast and loose" may have described him before he met Rachel, but now not so much.

He stood and walked out, muttering, "Made love" with a low chuckle.

Bobbie sent him a displeased frown.

"Later, sugar," he said with a wink. No smile, but he'd swear a blush highlighted her slackened cheeks.

* * *

"It's impossible to pack for this trip!" Rachel shouted from her room in Bree's apartment.

Bree appeared around the corner, pulling her hair into a ponytail for her shift this evening. "What do you need? Raid my closet."

"I . . . I don't know." Rachel gestured at the uninspiring wardrobe hanging in front of her. "T-shirts, long-sleeved T-shirts, leggings, a random dress I wore to a wedding a year ago. Wait, no . . . *two* years ago. And an array of black pants and blouses that are definitely boring with a capital *B*." Aghast, she regarded her friend. "This is not the closet of a woman heading to Hawaii with a billionaire!"

"He wants you naked, Rach." This helpful hint came from Dean, who walked by the doorway brushing his teeth. He spared her a foamy-mouthed smile.

"He's right," Bree said. "Plus, you're going to advise on bar stuff. Dress like you would for work or vacation."

"I can't," Rachel sighed. "I don't have any vacation clothes." Beach vacations weren't exactly on her schedule when she'd lived in Ohio. Once she moved here, met Shaun, and entered the corporate world, where ladder-climbing was an Olympic event, she hadn't had time for a vacation. And she certainly hadn't bothered stocking her wardrobe with vacation wear.

"Then go shopping. Isn't Oliver giving you your dog sitting check this week?"

"Yeah . . . but I'm saving for a deposit on an apartment so I can get out of your hair." She gave her friend a sheepish smile.

Bree walked into Rachel's bedroom and put a palm on her shoulder. "Rach. I know it'll take time. You're not going to be here forever."

"Thanks." But Rachel didn't want to prolong moving out. She wanted to be on her own. Be her own woman and reclaim her independence. Living in Oliver's pad and now staying in Hawaii with Tag was going to put a massive gap between the kind of apartment she could afford and the kind of treatment to which she'd become accustomed.

"Plus you never know what might happen with you and Tag," Bree said as she turned to leave the room. "For the long-term."

"We're not going any further than where it is," Rachel called after her. Bree hummed in the back of her throat and disappeared down the hallway, leaving Rachel with her dilemmas, *plural.*

Wardrobe, Hawaii, and Tag included.

It was okay for this to be what it was: an enjoyable pastime and a once-in-a-lifetime experience of consulting for a massive hotel chain. She'd talked herself into going because (a) she could put it on a resume, and (b) she refused to allow Tag to pay her.

Whatever happened with him while she was there would be fun, but long-term? No, she wasn't ready for anything longer than a week or so. Overcoming her sexy fears with Tag was fun, but she didn't doubt for a moment he'd be over her and back to the game soon enough.

Anyway, she thought as she rolled a summer dress and stuffed it into her suitcase, she knew he wasn't interested in her for more than a brief foray. It was a good deal for both of them, so maybe she should take Bree's advice. Have fun, enjoy herself.

"And don't think about the future." Rachel capped the statement by tossing in a few pairs of slinky underwear with the tags still on them.

She'd vowed to recapture her boldness.

This was a step in the right direction.

* * *

Oliver handed over the check, and Rachel could swear it felt heavy. It was a lot of money and, after living in the lap of luxury on Oliver's dime, seemed almost unreasonable to accept. But she did.

He was clear on what he hired her to do, and she'd done the job he asked. Hawaii wasn't going to be cheap, and while she should be investing the check toward her future apartment, she refused to let Tag take care of her while she was there. She didn't mind him buying a dinner or two, but she was completely capable of paying her own way.

"Thank you for taking care of Adonis," Oliver said. "He's going to miss you. I can see it in his eyes."

His stormy gray eyes. So pretty. She knelt and gave Adonis a nuzzle, though doing so put her below where his giant head stood.

She straightened and shook Oliver's hand. "Thank you again."

"What's next for you?"

"Oh, um..." She debated telling him the truth. Would he think she was a woman for hire? Bouncing from job to job after money? "Well..."

The elevator behind her dinged, and she turned her head to see the doors part and reveal a long-haired, sexy Adonis in his own right.

"Tag Crane," Oliver greeted him. Rachel turned to see Oliver's brow furrow in confusion. She could see the questions on his face. *What is he doing on my private floor? Is there a problem with the building?*

"Hey, Oliver. Adonis." Tag reached forward and scrubbed the dog's head. Then he did something that made Rachel want to hide. He lifted the largest of her bags and slung it over his shoulder. "Ready?"

Oliver slid a glance from Tag to Rachel.

"Uh..."

"Rachel is joining me in Hawaii as an advisor on my latest project."

Rachel sent Oliver a sickly smile. Even though she didn't owe him an explanation, she couldn't help but feel as if he were the father figure in this scenario and she was a teen in need of discipline. Oliver grinned, which totally threw her.

"Congratulations, Rachel. Crane Hotels is a fine company. Does this mean you're out of the bar? Don't misunderstand me, I prefer you to wait on me and I'll miss you, but this is the professional job you wanted, right? A second chance outside of the corporate shadow of your—"

"No!" she interrupted before he kept going and mentioned Shaun. She hadn't had that conversation with Tag and didn't want to—especially not in Oliver's entryway. "I mean, yes, this is a great opportunity, but I haven't left the Andromeda. Working with Tag is a temporary gig."

The trip to Hawaii *and* being with him.

She sent a glance to Tag, who watched her for a few beats before smiling at Oliver. "No one is more qualified to give me an unbiased opinion. I'm lucky she jumped on it, even though it's temporary."

She'd also jumped on *him*, which made her feel flushed and warm all over.

So not the place to do this, Rach.

"Have fun," Oliver said, and she could see he meant it. "You are going to love the island. Make sure to take a surfing lesson while you're there."

"Oh, I don't—" she started, but Tag interrupted her.

"We will. Thanks, Oliver. Oh, and Rachel had an emergency at work so I made a copy of your key. If you'd like it back, I'm happy to return it. If not and you ever need me to check on Adonis, here, I'm glad to."

"Hey, you own the building," Oliver said with a teasing wink. "Frankly, I thought you already had keys to the residences. Keep it. Adonis was in good hands while I was gone. Thank you both."

They finished up their goodbyes, and Rachel lifted her other bag and followed Tag into the elevator. When the doors closed, she turned to him. "How'd you know I was here?"

"Adonis has a happy bark." Tag sent her a lopsided smile, one that curved his beard and made her want to kiss him. If only to feel the warmth of his lips. "He does it whenever you come home."

Aww. That made her smile. She shook her head in thought. "I can't believe how quickly the weeks went."

"On Oahu, time will go slower. We'll make sure of it." He paired that statement with a big palm on her back, sliding down, down until he rested it above her butt. Tingles shivered down her arms. "We fly out at midnight. I figured the later the flight the more likely you are to sleep through the whole thing," he said as the elevator opened on his floor. He held the doors open for her. "It's unlocked."

She opened his front door and walked into utopia. Seriously, his penthouse was massive.

"Do you want to take a nap before we go? Shower?" he asked, his voice rumbling through her.

"Um. No, thanks. I'm good." And nervous all of a sudden. Which was ridiculous. She couldn't be bold while battling nerves.

He carried her bag and her suitcase to the master bedroom. "I'm going to stash your stuff in here. Make yourself at home."

She stood in the center of the living room, unsure what she was supposed to do with herself for the next five hours until they were airborne. Or what she'd do when she was in Hawaii with Tag. It occurred to her she hadn't asked about sleeping arrangements, and she probably should before things went further.

"Tag?"

"Yeah?" He appeared in the doorway of his bedroom—a room she hadn't set foot in yet—and then walked toward her. No, stalked. *Stalked* toward her like a lion. Or a panther. Or some big, muscled cat.

Definitely a lion. Because he has a mane.

"You okay?" he asked. "You look...not okay."

She pulled in a deep breath and he lifted one of those "paws" of his and placed it on her face so gently, she snuggled into it.

"Overwhelmed, I guess. I've never...flown that far." Flying was a legit fear. More legit than being nervous to go on a trip to an exotic tropical island with an exotic man.

"Good news. We're taking the company jet, so you won't have to worry about layovers or security or any inconvenience. Straight shot to Honolulu airport."

"Company jet. Right." She kept forgetting the billionaire part of this scenario. "And the rooms?"

"We'll stay at Crane Makai, our hotel on Oahu. The suites there are top-notch."

She swallowed thickly and asked the question she wanted to ask. "Together?"

"I booked one for each of us. And no, you're not paying for it; I don't care how much you bitch at me about it. This is what I do, Dimples. I am entitled to provide a room for you and not take your money."

She had to laugh, which did wonders for calming her down. Her insistence on paying for the room seemed silly when he put it that way, but it was sillier to stay in separate rooms when she damned well knew they wouldn't use both.

She took his hand in hers and swallowed down her fears. Once she was a woman who asked for and received what she wanted. She still was. She was just out of practice.

"I think we could share one, don't you?"

He smiled gently and something else occurred to her.

"Unless..." Her eyes widened. "I mean if you don't want to, that's fine, too."

He might need his space. She hadn't even considered that.

"Dimples." He palmed the back of her neck and leveled his gaze with hers. "Hell yeah, I want to share a room with you. I had a great time the other night, and I was hoping on this trip we'd see what else happened." Then he lost the schoolboy chagrin as the heat flared in his blue eyes. "Honey, I have imagined you in a lot of ways, and most of them involve you naked in my bed in Hawaii."

She bit her bottom lip and his eyes went to her mouth. He lowered his face, hair shrouding them as she tipped her chin to meet his lips. Then they kissed, gently and surely, her hands moving to his sweater and gripping two handfuls. He sucked in a breath and pulled his lips from hers.

There. There it was. That surge of bravery that infused her every cell when he kissed her. She didn't know if it was because his touch disabled the worrying section of her brain or what, but Tag was becoming an essential part to her finding her old self.

Plus, he tasted like heaven.

She tightened her grip on his sweater and kissed him again. Tag wanted her, in his *bed*, in his room. She wanted it, too.

And she was going to take it.

CHAPTER 13

Rachel Foster had never been so pampered.

When she'd lived in Ohio, she hadn't wanted for anything—her basic needs were always met. Christmases brought lots of presents, and her mother was fond of surprising her with gifts or dinners out. So yeah, she had been brought up in a small town but by no means had been destitute.

Moving to Chicago on her own had been an upgrade, and when she moved in with Shaun, she'd been able to afford a few of the finer things. Expensive handbags and shoes, and a few nice dresses. No, her closet wasn't bursting with designer clothing, but she had enough to make her look good at work and make her look good for Shaun.

But she'd never experienced luxury like this...She took in the cabin of the private airliner from where she sat at the breakfast table. This was really something.

She wasn't yet over the opulence of the buttercream leather sofa and chairs, cushy armrests, and reclining seats.

They'd boarded the plane at midnight, and after they were in the air, she'd gone straight to the cabin and slept like the dead. She awoke to turbulence around seven in the morning Chicago time, took a quick shower—an experience like none other—and dressed before she came out to the main cabin.

Though this room wasn't like being on an airplane either. The cushy seats and leather couch and a dining area were all formal enough.

She'd forgone breakfast, but took her coffee with lots of cream while watching Tag peck at his laptop at a comically slow speed. Each tick of his fingers was like watching a giant try and operate a delicate device.

She knew personally what those fingers were capable of. How sure and strong they were. They were being wasted on whatever email or document he was typing at the moment.

She let out a longing sigh.

Tag didn't look up from the keyboard when he said, "For being nervous about flying, you don't act very nervous."

Finally, he raised an eyebrow and met her eyes.

She wiggled in her seat, heat coating her. This morning his hair was in a low ponytail/bun, and he wore a casual pair of jeans and a V-neck tee showing a hint of chest hair. All she'd been able to think about was making love with him again, and how they likely didn't have time to do it this morning since the plane landed in an hour or so.

"Why is it you look like you're thinking something

sinister?" he asked, that eyebrow arcing higher. "And don't lie to me, Dimples. I have a sixth sense." She watched his slow smile, white teeth appearing as his trimmed beard parted. Her nether regions buzzed like she'd sat on a vibrating phone.

"I'm surprised..." she started, feeling daring. Must be the Kona coffee.

"Because?"

"Because I expected you to induct me into the Mile High Club by now. This is my first private flight." She looked at him through her lashes, her coy smile in place.

Tag wore an all-out grin, which made her inordinately pleased. Where she was concerned, he wasn't immune. And she liked that. *A lot.*

"Excuse me." Smoothly, he shut his laptop, stood, and walked from cabin to cockpit.

Okay. That was interesting. She hadn't expected him to leave. Maybe she didn't have the same power over him as he had over her.

She turned to look out the window, but the nighttime landscape was nothing but blackness. She imagined a sea of clouds and blue skies once the sun rose, anticipating being someplace where the high was above freezing. She wondered what the temperature was on—

"Let's go." Her hand was snatched a moment later as Tag pulled her out of her seat and led her to the bedroom.

"Wait," she said through her laughter as she hustled after him. "What are you doing?"

In the bedroom, he released her, closed the door, and whipped off his shirt. She gasped, her eyes eating up his tanned muscles and bulky arms.

"Making you a member." He caught the back of her head in his hand and kissed her. She melted beneath his touch. She was hopelessly attracted to him. Just an absolute goner.

When she caught a breath of air, she said, "Where did you go?"

"Told the pilot to take the long way."

"There's a longer way to Hawaii?"

"There is now." He continued tickling her neck with kisses, making his way down her collarbone and over one shoulder as he slid the strap of her dress aside. Then the zipper was down, and he was lifting the material over her head.

"I like this season on you." He tossed the garment aside. "More skin. Less clothes," he mumbled in between kisses.

"Hey! Don't wrinkle it. I wanted to get lei'd in that dress." She smiled.

"Oh, now you're cute?"

"I don't know. Am I?"

Something serious overtook the moment, thickening the air in the bedroom as Tag brushed his knuckles along her cheek. His eyes flickered with warmth, his touch enough to tantalize and savor at the same time.

"Yeah, Dimples. You are." His next kiss was slower, more purposeful, when he bent his head and covered her lips with his. Rachel lost herself in the feel of his mouth, noting the shift in the moment. He'd dragged her to his apartment for a sexy game of cat and mouse before, but this was different. He hadn't come in here to prove himself. He'd come in here to grant her request.

That same surge of power joined a surge of passion

when he laid her down on the bed. He kissed the space between her breasts, then circled her belly button with his tongue. Her hands went to his hair, guiding his lips as he sneaked his tongue beneath the edge of her panties.

By the time he'd put his lips on her most private and sensitive part, gone were the pesky questions buzzing in her head. He hummed against her sex, sending vibrations into her belly and her brain into orbit. Her lungs seized when he set the pace, flicking and laving her until her orgasm crested.

When she came, she did so as quietly as possible, which until Tag Crane had never, *ever* been a problem. No man—and there had been embarrassingly few—between her legs had ever been this good. She'd never had to worry about smothering her cries with her ex because he'd never taken her there. But with Tag she was in tune to his particular brand of attention. To the way he was able to turn her inside out in record time.

He kissed a path up her body, and she unthreaded her fingers from his hair, widened her legs to accommodate him, and then tucked him in as close as she could.

"So good at that," she whispered, repeating her praise from the first time he went down on her.

"You didn't need as much coaxing this time." He put a kiss on her chin, pride radiating his entire being. "Minx."

"Tell me you have a condom."

His eyebrows went up.

"I want the gold membership, Tag. Don't short me."

He pushed off the bed and went to the adjoined bathroom, calling, "Trust me, Dimples, there's nothing short about me."

As evidenced when he stepped from the bathroom, naked, cock encased in a condom and pointing due north. She made a "come here" motion with her hands, and he did, sinking between her legs and nudging her entrance the moment his weight hit the bed.

"You continue surprising me; did you know that?" he asked.

"I'm surprising myself." Already, she'd begun to recapture who she once was before receiving a felling blow. Yes, in part it was the sex, but she sensed it was also the man over her, his blue eyes trained carefully on her face, the edge of his smile making her want to know what he was hiding under it. He was big and he was bold, but he was also tender. He cared about her, was careful with her, and that was something else she'd never experienced before.

"Am I crushing you?" he breathed, an exhalation sawing out of his lungs as his arms tucked in next to hers.

"No. I like you here." The comfort of his weight, of his attention.

"I like me here, too." Eyes on hers, he tilted his pelvis and slid, slowly, slowly until he was buried to the hilt. With a gasp, she dug her heels against his ass. Then he began to move, rocking into her at the same time the plane hit turbulence.

There was nothing like being thousands of feet above the earth while they came together and apart, her cries piercing the piped air of the cabin.

He rested his hand on her jaw as every thrust hit its mark deep in her core. She'd been wrong about him. He wasn't too much for her. He fit. Tightly, but each stroke found her most hidden place and sparked like flame to kindle.

"Tag." Her voice was breathy.

"Close," he grunted as he worked.

"I want you to come." She pushed hair off his face with her palms and his pupils darkened in response. He wanted that, too.

"You first."

"One's enough." She shook her head. He'd given her so much. She wanted that same satisfaction etched into his face.

"Not on my watch, Dimples." He wedged one big hand beneath her butt and tilted her hips. His biceps strained as he shifted and drove into her solidly, proving he was a man of his word.

She called out in surprise but mostly from the decadent pleasure of having him seated so deep. Deep in her body...but she couldn't let him embed himself in her heart. Once, she thought she'd get married to a man who threw her aside for a petty promotion, and despite the closeness between her and Tag, she couldn't dismiss that he'd be done with her soon. He may not cheat her out of a future at a company, but he would go when things between them were too much.

She was okay with that. She had to be.

"Working hard over here," he said on a growl. "You with me?"

She pushed his hair from his face and absorbed his grin. "I'm with you."

"Good."

Then there was no more talking. Only the sounds of Tag working her into a frenzy and her trying not to yell too loudly lest the onboard concierge come running.

Tag, oh Tag was perfect. Complimentary and strong. Thick and long. Smooth yet rough. There, on the way to an island she'd never been to before, she clutched, squeezed him tight, and took him with her when she came.

His face was pleated, the sounds in his throat almost animal as he worked through his release, and she couldn't help smiling.

She'd never seen anything as beautiful as Tag's face during an orgasm.

Especially one she'd caused.

* * *

The Crane Makai hotel on Oahu matched the island. The decor was soothing turquoise blues, jade greens, and soft golds. The front desk employees were smiley and professional, the guests milling about dressed in festive Hawaiian shirts and flip-flops. Everyone was laid-back, including Rachel, but she would bet her bank account her relaxation had come thanks to the airplane sex.

She pressed her lips together to hide her smile as she unpacked her clothes from her bags to the dresser in hers and Tag's shared room. It wasn't small by any stretch of the imagination. There was an en suite bathroom and another off the main space, which boasted a living room and kitchenette. A sliding door opened to a balcony, but no one was above them, seeing how Tag had requested the top floor. He'd mentioned he liked to be on top, giving her a saucy wink at the front desk.

Rachel could attest to that, so she hadn't argued, simply tried not to look like a satisfied recipient of his attention.

He appeared in the doorway now, hands bracing either side of the jamb as he leaned the top half of his body into her room. Her eyes went to his biceps, bunching beneath his short T-shirt sleeves. When she redirected her gaze to his face, he was shaking his head.

"I'm sorry. I was uh..." She trailed off, at a loss for an excuse.

"Objectifying me?" His smile split into a grin, and she felt her cheeks go warm. He gave up staying away and came to her, capturing her mouth in a soft kiss. "I'm yours to use up, Rachel." He ran both palms along her arms and goose bumps sprang to the surface of her skin. "Ready to see the bar?"

She had to blink out of the sex fantasy that had just formed. She was here for something other than pleasure.

"Oh. Okay. Sure."

He kept hold of her hand and they headed out of the room, to the elevator, and then outside to the pools. She liked her hand in his, the way their palms fit together comfortably. Again she was struck with the memory she'd thought he was too much for her. How ridiculous was that? All of him seemed to fit her just fine.

There were two pools, one a standard square with chairs lined up like soldiers around the edges and another lagoon-shaped pool with rocks, a slide, and covered cabanas. A bar stood between the two pools, teeming with women in bikinis and men in trunks or Speedos.

"Wow. Busy."

"What the hell..." His face pinched as he studied the area. "It's never this disorganized."

He kept hold of her, and she noticed that one of the women working the bar stopped what she was doing to examine their linked hands. Rachel felt her heart palpitate. For all she knew, the dark-haired beauty shaking up a fruity cocktail used to date Tag. Rachel's stomach flopped, and she purposefully shook off the thought. Now was what mattered. The past didn't matter, and the future would take care of itself, as it often did.

Disorganized was a good word for the bar area. The long bar in the center of both pools was on a limited amount of concrete, forcing drinkers to smash together in a crooked line while waiting their turn to order. There was nowhere for the people ordering drinks to stand while they waited, and those who had received theirs hadn't immediately returned to their designated areas, hanging out and further clogging the bar.

"Hey, Tag. Aloha!"

Rachel turned her attention to a wide-framed, wide-bodied Hawaiian man with a kind smile. He wore the loudest royal blue shirt she'd ever seen, matching the bright blue sunglasses resting on his wavy, short hair.

"Greg." He shook the other man's hand and then introduced her. "This is Rachel. She's advising on the bar project." Tag turned to her. "Greg's our on-site maintenance manager."

"Nice to meet you."

"Bar project?" Greg's eyebrows went up in interest.

"Yeah. Speaking of, what's going on with this mess?" Tag gestured to the crowd.

"Swim-up bar's shut." Greg pointed to an area on the far side of the pool with the waterfall. She hadn't noticed it at first, but sure enough, palm-frond decor was covering the bar and there was a small CLOSED sign hanging from one of the bamboo poles supporting the roof.

"No one cleared that with me." Tag took a step closer to Greg. "What's wrong with it?"

"Sinks were acting up or something."

"How about you find out what the 'or something' is and get back with me on how fast you can have it repaired?" Tag's voice dipped low with authority, sending a shiver through her. She'd never heard him speak like that. Who knew he could be sexier? "How long has it been closed?"

Greg, despite his size, looked chagrined when he answered, "Few weeks."

"I want an answer in an hour."

"You got it, boss."

Tag held Greg's gaze and extended a hand for a farewell handshake. "Thanks for taking care of this."

Greg's next smile was one of relief. When Tag released him, Greg looked to Rachel. "Enjoy the island."

When he hustled off—and yes, even at his size, it was a full hustle—she smiled up at Tag, who'd reclaimed her hand.

"What?" His eyelids slipped, his entire demeanor snapping back into relax mode.

"You pack a lot of authority for a guy so laid-back." She wasn't able to resist him either way.

"I know how to get what I want." He lowered his face to hers and stole a quick kiss. Against her mouth, he muttered, "You personally know how authoritative I can be, Dimples. You want to transfer that control, you let me know."

He angled through the crowd as Rachel turned over that enticing idea.

They sidled behind the bar, not an easy task with the bar area packed and three bartenders slinging booze left and right. The two men and the woman behind the bar wore smiles on their faces and they kept the banter going as they worked.

Rachel had personally witnessed worse behavior in a

rush of this size. She doubted the staff was an issue. Tag was nothing if not a people person, and watching the way he'd engaged with Greg told her he was both respected and admired.

Tag greeted each of the bartenders by name, informed them that Greg was taking a look at the swim-up bar today, and then ordered two drinks.

"Want me to bring them out?" the woman he'd called Karina asked. She was the one who had eyed their joined hands with interest. Her almond-shaped eyes darted to Rachel briefly before zooming back to Tag.

"No. You're too busy," he said. "We'll wait."

"I'll get it," another bartender offered.

Karina appeared taken aback but let it go.

Rachel was getting some vibes from the other woman where Tag was concerned. Once the male bartender handed over the drinks, Tag accepted them and they navigated through the crowd again. He didn't explain to guests why he'd cut the line and helped himself to drinks, and didn't seem to care.

"People are looking at us." She flinched when a few dirty looks skated her way.

"It's because you look hot in your dress," he said, his long legs taking them to an unoccupied cabana off to the side of the pool. On it rested a gold-plated RESERVED sign. "You can toss that underneath," he instructed with a smile. "It's for us."

"Membership has its privileges." She dropped the sign in the sand. Her eyes went to the closed swim-up bar. "Don't you want to handle that first?"

With genuine confusion, he tilted his head. "I did. You saw me talk to Greg."

"You don't want to question any other bartenders? Maybe talk to the hotel staff?"

"You have to give people a chance to prove themselves, Dimples. Greg's a big boy. If he screwed up, he can fix it. If he doesn't fix it, I'll take the next step."

She wasn't able to argue his simple yet impressive logic.

Simple yet impressive. *Just like him.*

Hands full, he nodded. "Climb in."

She did, kicking off her shoes and propping her legs on what was basically an outdoor bed. White privacy panels were draped on all four sides but tied back to give them a view of the ocean and the mountains beyond.

"It's incredible here." She pulled in her first deep breath of warm air and accepted her cocktail: pink with a chunk of pineapple, a cherry, and a slice of mango floating in it. "This is pretty."

"If I said 'so are you,' would you think it was a line?" Tag's drink was a mojito, mint leaves and lime floating on the surface. He sat next to her, propping himself on the wide pillows arranged at the head of the cabana.

"Probably."

"Well, far be it from me not to live up to your expectations." His eyes dashed to her lips before he took a gulp of his drink. She watched as his bottom lip swiped a few droplets from his upper lip. He had the best mouth she'd ever felt.

"Wait. What'd that mean?" She frowned.

"You think this is my game?" He gestured with the cup. "Get you here, get you out of your clothes."

She let out a slightly uncomfortable laugh, then challenged him with "What if that's *my* game? Come here and get *you* out of your clothes?"

"Is it?" He smiled full-on, white teeth and arched eyebrows, the whole huge, hunky package glistening in the tropical sunshine.

She muttered a noncommittal "I'm not answering that" and they enjoyed their drinks in silence. Comfortable, companionable silence, the likes she'd never experienced with a guy she was dating. If what they were doing could be called dating.

"These drinks are huge," she said, shifting the subject to the other reason she was here. She fully intended on working, not only flirting with Crane Makai's head honcho.

"Cranes don't skimp." He bottomed out his drink, having no problem finishing it in record time.

"Maybe you should consider sizing them down. It would help for repeat business, and in this heat, keep everyone with a cold beverage." Her iced drink had already warmed in her palm.

He canted his head to take her in. "You don't waste any time."

"This is why I'm here." She turned to look at the ocean before she accidentally added that she was also here for him.

"What else did you notice?" He rested a cool hand on her knee. When she looked at his palm, he slipped it higher up her thigh, stopping short of inappropriate-in-public.

"Um." Words. She spoke English. Where were her words? "The layout of the bar isn't conducive to this many guests. Even with the swim-up bar open, patrons will probably choose not to drink or they'll sneak in their own liquor rather than wait in the line." She told him her earlier observations, building on them as she described the way the crowd was hot and sweaty and smashed together. How there was no room to maneuver and no way any of the bartenders were making good tips since they would be blamed for the delays. "Clearly, you don't have a staff problem. They're efficient, friendly."

"They are. Karina's been here from the start. Hired her myself." He smirked, proud.

"She watches you." Rachel sneaked a peek over her shoulder and spotted the back of Karina's sleek hair. "Did you two...? Never mind."

When she looked back at Tag, he was wearing an absolutely unreadable expression. A mix of confusion and bemusement, his eyes slitted and mouth pursed like he was thinking of what to say. In the end he said nothing, which was an answer in itself.

"I'm going to work a few shifts," she said after a minute of silence.

"I beg your pardon?" he asked flatly, the same eyebrow raised in protest.

"Oh, I won't take tips."

"Rachel..."

"Absolutely not. You're letting me stay in your room. I didn't pay for this drink. The least you can let me do is what I promised to do, which is help you improve the bar."

"I didn't bring you here to put you behind the bar, Dimples. I want you to advise, not work your ass off." Tenderly, he stroked his hand back down her leg to her knee. "I want you with me."

Nothing made thinking more difficult than when he touched her. Unless it was the bald admission that he wanted her with him. Sweet, and damn hard to resist. But she genuinely wanted to help, and there was simply no way for her to get a feel of the bar without working it personally.

"I appreciate that," she said, finally finding the words. "But to know how things work from the other side, I literally need to be on the other side."

"Fine. I'll pair you with Karina for training. She's the best, and you're a fast learner." He held up a finger. "One night."

"Two," she insisted. Though she wasn't excited about the prospect of working with Karina, it'd take more than one night to figure out the best approach to the redesign. Rachel couldn't be sure what kind of sordid past Tag had with the other woman. She hoped she didn't have to find out. Compartmentalization was the only way to be with him. "One night and one day. It'd help to see how things go during a weekend afternoon."

He sighed, resigned. "Fair enough."

She turned her head to take him in. He fit here on Oahu better than he fit in Chicago. With the heat and his tan and the way his blue eyes sparkled like the surface of the ocean. He turned to face her, admiration awash on his expression.

"But not tonight," he said, proving himself less amicable to her bargain after all. His next words made her shiver. "Tonight you're mine."

CHAPTER 14

Rachel, flower tucked into her blond waves, walked beside Tag through the resort. Her legs shot out of a pair of short white shorts, a frothy top covering a white tank. Gorgeous. Every inch of her.

They'd come from a beachside restaurant, one with the best pulled pork he'd ever tasted.

"Dinner with a luau included," she said with a sweet smile. "That's a first."

"I like when you have firsts with me." He liked treating her. She didn't get enough special treatment; he could tell. Especially when she'd argued about helping pay for dinner. Absolutely *not*.

"Now what do we do?" Dimples dented her cheeks when she flashed him another quick smile. Still cautious. He liked that about her. Liked being the guy who pushed her boundaries and watched her boldly step over them. Mile High Club indeed.

She surprised him at every turn, and he'd ended up surprising himself. He'd never been one for baby-stepping through dates. She was refreshingly different and made him want to discover more and more about her.

"I arranged surfing lessons for tomorrow before your evening shift." He intended to have a few more firsts with her while they were here.

"Is that what you were doing while I was dressing for dinner?" She made a face like she'd tasted something bad.

"What's wrong?" He steered them toward the beach. The sun had set, the moon reflecting white on black water. "Too much of a city girl for surfing?"

"I'm from a farm, thank you very much. I mean, sort of. We didn't have cows or anything." She pulled a few strands of hair away from her mouth and studied the dark ocean waves. "I'm not sure if working after a surfing lesson is smart. I'll probably need a massage after I bust my ass."

"That can be arranged." He leaned close when he said it.

Her laughter filled his chest in a not uncomfortable way. Come to think of it, he was having a few firsts himself. She squeezed his hand and tugged him closer to the water, and he followed without hesitation. He opted *not* to read into that.

"Tag Crane, you brought me here to do a job, not play. Don't you want me to do it?"

At the edge of the surf, he told her the truth. "Not really."

Her forehead crinkled like she didn't know whether to embrace the idea that he may have brought her here mostly to spend time with him. It didn't sit all that well with him, either, but dammit, it was the truth.

"Now that I have you here, I don't want to let you out of my sight." He pulled her closer, pressing her soft curves against his body. Her eyes closed and her chin tipped in unspoken permission, so he gave them what they both wanted and met her lips with his. She tasted spicy from the barbeque and sweet from the piña colada. The scent of coconut suntan lotion scrambled his brain.

The only sounds around them were the distant drumbeat of a band camped by the glow of a beach fire, the warm lapping of the water at their feet, and the gentle suction of Rachel's soft kisses.

"You have to let me work while I'm here, Tag," she said when she pulled away. She put her hands in his hair and tingles shot down his arms. He loved the feel of her fingers in his hair. "I already feel guilty that you won't let me pay for anything."

"Shit, Rachel." He huffed.

"What?" she argued, her tone suggesting she was ready for a fight.

"Hasn't a guy ever treated you well? Bought you things just because he wanted to?" When the questions were out of his mouth, he stopped, sort of stunned he'd asked. Money had always been available to him, had always come easily. Not many people argued when he paid. Then the person he wanted to treat most comes along and she fought him every step of the way.

"I have my own money," she said instead of answering him, crossing her arms over her breasts. A breeze caught her hair and lifted the white ruffles on her top.

He gripped her upper arms. "Stop being so stubborn."

"I'm not being stubborn!"

So fucking cute.

"She says, stubbornly." He let his smile break free.

Rachel shook out of his grip and turned, walking along the shoreline away from him, butt wiggling in those damn shorts. He followed. That was becoming a habit.

"You'd give me your ideas for free, wouldn't you?" he called after her.

She stopped and turned to face him, arms still crossed. "I'd tell you what I thought without compensation, yes."

"Your opinions have worth. You have worth."

She frowned but said nothing, like she was having trouble accepting that. His heart lurched. Had someone convinced her she wasn't worthy?

"You don't have to earn the right to be here." Tag watched her carefully. She straightened the bright pink flower behind her ear and bit her lip in thought.

Voice small, she said, "I'm still going to work behind the bar."

"Figures." He snagged her hand and unfolded her arms, then tucked her against him again, his palm going to her jaw. "I've been waiting to take you back to bed all day." His voice was a low rumble, his cock stirring at the mere suggestion. She made him crazy in the best way, and remembering the ecstasy on her face paired with her high-pitched cries of pleasure made him impatient for more. "How much longer are you going to make me wait?"

"You promised me a beachside stroll." She smiled wickedly, enjoying her power. He enjoyed her taking it.

"A little longer, then," he said.

"You're the one who wants to know me."

"I do. You actually going to tell me about yourself?" *Or dodge some more?*

She held up her hands. "I'll talk. I'll talk."

Seriously. Cute.

"Fine. But after this 'stroll' of ours, it's straight to heaven via my mattress."

Her mouth dropped open, eyes widening. "I accept."

"Let's get to know each other, Rachel Foster." He offered a hand and she interlaced her fingers with his. He set the pace for their walk, careful to not out-stride her since her gait was much shorter than his. Brought him to a shuffle, but he could live with that.

"Parents?" he asked. Warm breeze covered them, the smell of salt mingling with sweet plumeria.

"Two." He didn't have to look at her to hear the smile in her voice. "Still married. Still in love. They live in a small town in Ohio outside of Columbus. They consider Chicago the big time."

"Why did you come to Chicago?"

"I wanted to escape Derby, Ohio." Her voice flattened.

"Derby."

"*Derby*. I came here with a marketing degree. I worked with my now ex-boyfriend."

"Ah, finally pried that nugget out of you." But he didn't get more because it was her turn to pepper him.

"What about your parents?"

"Dad retired last year, when my oldest brother Reese took over as CEO. Mom died in a car wreck when I was eleven."

Her steps faltered. "Tag, I'm so sorry."

"Me too. She was the best." He was being sincere. His mother, Luna, had been loving and open, honest and strong. Most of his memories from his childhood were of the laughter and love surrounding him and his brothers.

A memory crawled out of the back of his mind. One

he hadn't thought of in years. His mother, the kitchen, a PB&J sandwich. Tag had mentioned a girl on the bus he wanted to be his girlfriend.

"You know, someday, Tag, you'll meet the girl you want to marry." Her blue eyes sparkled when she shared this horrible news.

He took a bite of his sandwich and gave a heartfelt "Yuck."

"Just remember, the girl for you will challenge everything you think you know about yourself. That's how you know she's a keeper."

The fringes of the memory faded and he blinked at the moon, feeling unhinged. Where had that memory come from?

"I can't imagine how hard losing her must have been for you and your brothers." Rachel's voice sliced into his consciousness, and he realized they'd walked a few more yards while he'd spaced out.

"Yeah. Reese dealt with losing her by achieving. Eli brooded."

"And you?"

He looked down at her and raised his arms in "ta-da" fashion, one hand still linked with hers. "Entertainment."

"I bet."

A few more moments of silence passed and Rachel stopped walking altogether.

"Tell me why you asked me here, really," she said. "Do you actually need my help? Or do you only want to sleep with me?"

"I'm assuming you want the truth."

"It's not like you to mince words."

It wasn't. So he didn't.

"I want you here because I value your opinion and trust your instincts. And because I haven't been able to stop thinking about you since the second you opened Oliver's door wearing polar bear pajamas."

Surprise colored her features. "How do you know they weren't penguins?"

"Polar bears. Wearing little red scarves."

She beamed and pride coated him.

"Truth is, Dimples, I want both. I want your advice. I also want you naked and on top of me. I want to watch your eyes go dark and hear the way you say my name in a breathy, heated voice while you're coming."

"Tag . . ."

"Just like that." He dropped her hand, opting to put her to the test as well. "Now tell me why you're here." Had she come for the free vacay, or did she come to be with him? His heart pounded as he pressed his lips together and waited for her answer.

"Helping with the bar design will look good on a resume . . ."

He swallowed, his throat dry and his mind racing. If her resume was the only reason she was here, he wasn't sure he would take that news well. But a few seconds later, she put him out of his misery.

"Truth?"

"Preferably," he croaked.

"I came here to be with you."

* * *

Unwrapping Tag Crane was like opening a present.

Being with him unleashed her confidence, and after the

evening they'd had, she couldn't resist him another second. He'd told her she was worthy. He'd made her feel desired. The player, as it turned out, wasn't playing her.

This wasn't Tag on his A game. This was Tag, the layers peeled back. His subtle charm feathering into the very real truth he shared about his childhood. It was him telling her exactly what he wanted, and what he wanted was to treat her well.

Rachel was on board with that. She deserved to treat herself.

She didn't falter when she tugged his shirt up to reveal his bare, flat belly. She didn't hesitate when she unbuttoned his shorts or when she wedged her thumbs beneath the band of his boxer briefs to explore his hot, golden skin.

He captured her face in his hands and kissed her while she touched him, his low male groans reverberating in her belly and bringing her desire to a peak. Everything about him made her want to lick him from head to toe. Which gave her an idea...

Did she dare?

His hands vanished under her tank top, her ruffled shirt already on the floor at her feet. He walked her backward until her back was pressed against the wall outside his bedroom door. Her chin tilted up, she took in the man surrounding her, hair, massive arms, and bare chest.

Hell yeah, she dared.

"Tag." She tilted her head to one side, giving him room to explore her neck with rasping kisses.

"Yeah, Dimples?" he murmured against her skin as both thumbs brushed over her nipples through her bra. Her back arched, her tight breaths making her next words a high squeak.

"I want to..." She gasped when he did it again. "Do something."

He stopped kissing her.

"What something?" he growled, muscles taut and eyes unerringly locked on hers.

Licking her lips, she reached for his manhood and cupped him. "Something...I'm not confident I do well."

His eyes turned into twin erupting volcanoes. His hands tightened around her waist as he hovered over her. "If you're offering what I think you are..."

"Going down on you?" She was barely able to push the words out of her constricting throat.

His nostrils flared and he froze in place.

"I'm offering."

"I've got a fantasy involving you and just that, Dimples."

She couldn't help it, she grinned. Never in her life had she been this brazen, but hearing this incredible man had a fantasy about her made her want to hear every last dirty word of it.

"Will you tell me what it is? In detail?"

His throat bobbed with deep laughter.

"Are you fucking kidding me?" His teeth stabbed his lip briefly, which was the sexiest thing she'd ever seen. "You like when I talk dirty, Rachel?"

She nodded. "It makes me feel wanted." And not like she was rigid or lousy in bed. As he'd proven to her twice, wait...three times, she did *fine* in his bed. Well, on the couch. The chair, the airplane bed...They hadn't been to-gether in a bed on land yet.

"I want you, sweetheart." He offered his hand. "Let me show you how much."

Pants open but still hanging on his hips, he led her to the en suite. Tag pulled open the sliding glass door on the shower.

"It involves us in here," he rumbled. "And you sitting on that bench."

The seat at the back of the shower was the perfect height for…oh. *Oh, my.* Putting a hand to her cheek, she felt the heat there. Could she actually do it?

"I expect you to instruct me," she whispered, unfamiliar words tumbling from her mouth. "I want this to be good for you."

"As you wish." His smile twitched like he was trying to keep from grinning from ear to ear. More evidence he wanted her. Who knew how empowering that could feel?

They stripped, taking their time pulling off remaining articles of clothing. She felt Tag's heated gaze on her body like a touch when he turned on the water and tested it with one hand. Steam billowed out, drenching the room in moisture and heat.

"Ready?"

As she'd ever be. She wanted to do this. She *needed* to do this. She was tired of believing what Shaun had told her. This was another way to prove to herself she was great in bed. *Great in the shower*, she thought with a self-satisfied twist of her lips.

"Get wet," Tag instructed, the command enthralling on its own. She climbed in and stuck her head beneath the spray, hot water loosening her muscles and easing her nerves.

He followed her in and stood behind her, dominating the small space, parts of him brushing parts of her. He unwrapped a bar of soap, lathered it between his palms, and began smoothing rhythmic circles over her back with his hands. Every inch of her being tended to with smooth but firm pressure. He moved to each butt cheek, cupping them as he dropped kisses on her shoulder. Next, he coasted around to her stomach and over her breasts.

"Tag," came her whisper of delight when those fingers soaped her nipples.

"Turn around." He moved his hands to her hips and assisted her. She slid under his soapy palms. "Do me."

She started at his chest, moving in sensual circles over each rounded pectoral muscle and up over his collarbone. Then down to his stomach and over the hard-on jutting impressively between his legs. His breaths had escalated the closer her hand came, expanding his chest, but he didn't tell her to touch him. He did continue soaping her breasts, then moving one hand between her legs and gently swiping his fingers there.

She jerked in pleasure as he touched her, taking the lead and wrapping her hand around his shaft to give him a sudsy stroke. Then another. He was thick and long, and she wanted him so badly, she could hardly think.

"Now what?" The water temperature was perfect—hot but not too hot. "Tell me, Tag."

Rather than answer, he took his time rubbing his hands under the spray to clean the soap from his body, then did the same with her. He slid big, firm palms over her skin, and by the time he'd finished, every inch of her was turned on and ready to go.

Once they were suds-free, he gripped his cock and instructed with a chin lift, "Sit."

She lowered to the bench and, oh what a sight he was. One powerful hand wrapped around several inches of burgeoning manhood, stroking once more as he came to stand in front of her.

"Lick your lips," he said.

She darted her tongue out, seductively swiping it over her top lip as she moved her eyes from his cock to his face. With great effort, he swallowed.

"Do you want to suck me off?"

"Yes." Liquid heat pooled between her thighs as her nipples peaked.

He put his hand under her chin and lifted her face gently. Big as a mountain, he looked down at her, water dotting his body, his wet hair tangled and resting on his shoulders. He was a fantasy in the flesh.

"I want to watch you take me into your mouth, Rachel. After, I'll tell you what comes next."

She nodded and the first hint of his good humor broke through when he smiled. She was safe with him. What they were about to do was going to be as fun as everything else they'd tried. She knew it in her gut.

He thumbed her chin in silent request and she placed a soft kiss on the plump head of his penis before opening her mouth and taking the tip onto her tongue.

A sharp exhalation came from Tag, who immediately dropped his hand onto her head. His fingers flexed in her wet hair, but he didn't force her. He stood so still that his thigh where her hand rested felt as rigid as rebar. A lot like the part of him in her mouth.

His cock was velvety smooth when she tested the underside of his length with her tongue. He let out a guttural sound of pleasure. A zing of excitement went through her as she gripped his other leg. She was *so good* at this. More importantly, she was enjoying herself.

His hand gripped her hair firmly and he drew out of her mouth. She sat back to look up at him and saw he was barely harnessed. His chest lifted and dropped with each ragged breath he drew, his mouth dropped open, water dripping from his hair and beard.

Between clenched teeth he asked, "How was that for you?"

Her confidence abruptly ebbed. Was it not good for him? Maybe the lust-blown look she thought she saw was disappointment. Or...anger? For her, the experience had been phenomenal, but she didn't know how he felt. She'd only been guessing.

"Tell me the truth," he demanded.

Earnestly, she shook her head and then looked right at his penis, which bobbed in front of her, slick and inviting. She moved her eyes back to his face. "I don't want to stop until you come."

His eyes closed. "Do you have any idea how hard it's going to be for me to last longer than twenty seconds?"

She frowned. Was that...bad?

"Your mouth is...God, Rachel. You make me feel like some inept idiot when I'm with you." He slammed a fist into the shower knob, shutting off the water, and helped her stand.

"Mind if we take this to the bedroom?" He stroked her cheek as he brought her against his body. Between them a steamy buzz of electricity shocked the air.

"Only if I can finish you off in there," she purred.

"I insist." A muscle in his jaw ticked as he bit down.

She grinned, pleased. Mostly with herself.

* * *

He was having an out-of-body experience, his head thoroughly disconnected from his neck. Rachel's warm, luscious body was draped over him, one hand around his dick and the other locked around his leg. Her mouth was doing the most unimaginably sinful things.

And this was far from his first blow job.

But what she was doing—the swirl thing…

"Ah! Jesus." She did it again and he knifed up, hand wrapping firmly around one of her ass cheeks and squeezing the plump flesh.

She let him go, licking her damp lips, and he nearly came right then and there. "What'd I do wrong?"

Sweat beading his temple, he managed a stuttering laugh. "*Wrong* is not the word, honey. You're doing things so right I'm pretty sure I'm experiencing life in a way I never have before."

"What do you like the best?"

Heat shot to his face as she held his gaze. Tag was about as far from shy as London to Tokyo, but she'd unraveled him with her mouth, giving him everything he needed and wanted—the very thing he'd dreamed of—with no thought about her own pleasure.

"The swirling thing."

"You mean this?" She darted her tongue out and drew a torturous circle around the moist head. His hips bucked.

"Yeah." His voice was a puny wheeze.

"Let me taste how much you like it, Tag." She smiled, triumphant, then closed her mouth over him and began again.

Damn, he liked her like this.

He didn't lie back down, holding on to her rump with one hand while his other fisted the comforter. He had to find a way to ground himself while his brain cells incinerated to ash. Rachel's head bobbed, taking him deeper, then shallow, swirling her tongue and suctioning him with her exquisite mouth.

He lost his last shred of control on a shout. Her name on his lips, he pumped his hips helplessly. She swallowed every last drop as he spilled into her mouth, her hand gentle around his shaft, her soft blond hair tickling his thighs. His mind exploded like the cosmos as his eyes shut of their own volition. Finally he collapsed, his fist still tight around the bedding, his hand clamping her bare butt.

Cool air hit him as she released him from her mouth. She crawled up his chest, her breasts brushing his torso and he groaned in abject ecstasy. She mumbled to him, but her words were lost behind the pounding of his heartbeat and the rush of blood roaring against his eardrums.

"Hmm?" he managed, and she was lucky he'd said that much.

She peeled her body off his to lie next to him on the bed. "I asked if I was as good as the me in your fantasy."

"No." He opened his eyes to see a flash of hurt in hers. Then he grinned—a lopsided, half-assed grin all he could manage. "You are a million times better."

She looked down, almost shyly, the most endearing expression he'd seen her wear. How this girl could be laying him open one second and shy the next was a hell of a feat.

"I need to know if you'll forgive me," he murmured, losing the battle with his eyelids as they shut again.

"For?" came her voice, almost at a distance.

"For resting here a minute before I return the favor."

Silky laughter poured over him and she kissed the corner of his mouth.

"Now *that's* a compliment," she whispered.

CHAPTER 15

Tag had more than made up for his brief catnap after she'd rendered him temporarily out of service. She'd never rendered a man helpless before, especially not with her sexual prowess, so watching the big guy melt into sleep after she'd had her mouth on him was the most rewarding experience of her sexual history.

Boo-freaking-yah.

She'd crawled out of bed and slipped into one of the room's thick white robes before getting a bottle of Perrier out of the fridge and taking it to their room's balcony. Halfway through drinking it, Tag came outside behind her, took the bottle from her hand, and lifted her into his arms. He was still naked, long hair damp and wavy, and since he was carrying her, really had reminded her of Tarzan. Which was not a bad thing. Not at all.

He'd laid her on the bed and kissed her breasts, languid strokes of his tongue over her sensitized nipples while she'd dug her fingers into his blond-brown strands. Then he'd worked his fingers between her legs and found the spot that made her squirm before replacing his fingers with his tongue. She'd never known before him how good it could feel to have a man's mouth between her legs.

After, he'd pulled her close and tucked her back to his front while she caught her breath, suffering from tiny aftershocks of pleasure shaking her to the core.

"Hope you'll forgive me," she'd managed, her eyes heavy from her last powerful orgasm.

"For?" he'd asked.

"Disappointing you. I just want to fall asleep and make love to you in the morning."

"Make love. I like that." His deep chuckle had made her smile. "Dimples. I don't think you could possibly disappoint me."

She'd liked it too. As much as she'd been tempted to slot Tag into the fun-for-now column, she couldn't help noticing that every time he interacted with her, he hinted that he wasn't going anywhere.

She was still grinning like an idiot the next day when she walked with him to the pool bar at the Crane Makai. He'd taken her to a surfing lesson that morning as promised. Mostly, she'd practiced paddling on the sand and then paddling in the water. Popping up on the board was difficult for her. Tag had done it with relatively little effort.

He was irritatingly good at everything he did. It was unfair.

Of all things, her toes hurt, having used the muscles in her feet the most to keep her balanced. She'd managed to push upright, but into more of a hunch than a stand. She'd tumbled into the waves several times. Tag pulled her to the surface and praised her on her attempts and then delivered wet, salty kisses to her lips.

Yeah. She liked surfing.

She was beginning to wonder how she'd return to life after Hawaii, as this was the most pleasant daydream of her life. Since she'd met him, she was living in a fantasyland in every imaginable way.

Queen bartender Karina greeted Rachel pleasantly enough when Tag introduced them. He pointed out where he'd be hanging out with his laptop and notebook—a chair on the far side of the pool.

"You need me, Dimples, you just yell," he told her, and then right in front of Karina, planted a kiss on Rachel's lips before walking to his seat.

"How long have you been dating?" Karina asked after a brief instruction on the cash register. As luck would have it, it was the same brand they had at Andromeda, so there wasn't much of a learning curve.

"Oh. Um. I don't know. We're friends. Neighbors, sort of," she said. "Or, that's how we started. Things develop sometimes."

Karina harrumphed, her dark eyes rolling as she wiped down the surface of the bar. Rachel watched her for a moment before deciding she wasn't going to avoid the question bouncing around like a pink, winged elephant.

"You look at him like either you've dated him before or you want to. Which one is it?"

The bar towel stopped mid-swipe, and Karina's eyes bulged. Rachel had shocked her. Tag's ability to make bold statements had rubbed off on her. She stood waiting for an answer, not the least bit apologetic for asking.

"It's okay," Rachel told the other woman. "I'm not

jealous. I noticed the way you look at him. I can tell it's one of the two."

Cheeks ruddy, Karina managed a smile of reproach. "I—we've never dated. I'm attracted to him. I mean how could you not be?" she mumbled.

Rachel gave a nod of agreement, remembering how she'd been confounded at her attraction to him. He was the exact opposite of what she thought was her type.

"He never saw me the same way," Karina continued. "Not the way he looks at you. He's got a puppy love thing going."

Puppy love. Things between Tag and Rachel were nowhere near that innocent, but Rachel wasn't about to expound.

They got to work, her and Karina for the first hour; then the same male bartender she'd met previously—Craig—stepped behind the bar to help. He was even more excited to hear Rachel wasn't accepting tips since it meant he and Karina would split the cash fifty-fifty.

A few hours in, Rachel had hit her rhythm and there was no need to ask where anything was or how the flow of the bar worked.

But that didn't mean it was easy.

She had plenty of suggestions on how to improve things after being back here for one evening. The crowd thinned around ten o'clock, and Rachel did her share of the closing duties. She found Tag right where he said he'd be, and somehow he'd looked up as if he felt her watching him.

His smile was small, but one reserved for her. She held up both hands to show she'd be done in ten minutes.

He gave her the thumbs-up and a wink that made her stomach clench.

* * *

Watching Rachel in action—and not only when he was getting some action—Tag was becoming increasingly aware this thing between them wasn't going to end when they arrived home to Chi-town.

There was no way he was done with her, and given her reactions, he had a good idea she wasn't done with him either.

She was fun to shower with. Fun to have sex with. Fun to talk with over dinner, to watch as she fell in the water and tried, tried, and *tried* again to surf. He didn't care if she was ever good at it; he cared that she was willing to try.

She didn't give up easily, she was a fast learner, and as he'd observed tonight watching her run the bar, she was damn good at her job.

Marketing required different skills than bartending, and yet she was adept at both. Behind the bar she was friendly and fast, and he could tell every time he'd glanced up at her that she was assessing the most efficient way things should be done.

Yet she didn't run roughshod over Karina, even though during his observations, he'd noticed Rachel debating whether or not to move a bottle of liquor to a lower shelf. Instead, she'd stood on her toes and put it back on the high shelf where it'd gone.

He'd been counting down the hours until she was off work, unsure when the crowd would die down and give her an excuse to make a break for it, and not for reasons anyone would have guessed. Not to take her into bed.

Well, not right away.

He watched her drying a stemmed glass and reaching to hang it overhead, her tiny T-shirt lifting to bare a slice of skin at the waistband of her shorts. She pushed the back of her hand to move hair that'd fallen over her eye and caught him looking. He only smiled.

She cared about his bar issues like they were her own, and he couldn't get over the idea of a woman sleeping with him and working with him seamlessly.

Tag's phone vibrated on the seat of the lounger where he sat, laptop open on his legs.

His brother Reese. It was the middle of the night in Chicago.

"Hey, bro," Tag answered. "You're up late."

"Sleeping is overrated. How's Oahu?"

"Tropical."

Reese blew out a brief laugh. Since he'd attained his life goal of CEO and met Merina, he was in the process of becoming the man Tag had always known he could be.

It felt odd to say he was proud of his older brother, since Reese had always been the one to push him, but that's what Tag felt: proud.

"When are you coming home?" Reese asked.

"Few days."

"Thanks for pinpointing that for me."

"Hey, you know me." Tag was distracted by Rachel again, this time because she'd started viciously scrubbing the bar top. Her ponytail was coming down, her arms damp, her breasts swaying as she worked a particularly stubborn spot...

"...over dinner when you get back." There was an unnaturally long pause in the conversation before Reese said, "Hello?"

"Here." Tag blinked and looked away from Rachel, rubbing his eyes with his fingers. "Sorry, I'm here."

"How's your advisor?" Reese let his tone dip to show he knew exactly what had Tag so distracted.

"She's a terrible surfer," he offered.

Reese let out a hearty laugh.

"I have a question for you, actually." Tag had thought of calling sooner, but he'd been so mired in work and Rachel, he hadn't taken the time.

"What's that?"

"Did Mom ever give you advice? Like on women?"

"Women."

"You were older than me. I wondered if she ever brought up girls."

There was silence as Reese thought it through, and in that silence, Tag could feel the heaviness. Since Reese was the oldest, he had the most memories of her. "She told me to be respectful. Honest."

Sounded like Mom.

"Why, did she ever say anything to you?" His brother's voice had softened. They all missed her so damn much. It didn't matter how many years had passed. She was gone and it hurt whenever they remembered her smiling face.

"She said the right one would challenge me."

"No shit," Reese said in agreement.

Tag had to grin. "Merina a challenge, is she?"

"If there is a button for it, she pushes it." Reese didn't sound upset about it, though. "Buttons no other woman bothered to locate."

Tag was beginning to understand what that was like. Someone taking time to get to know him, to figure him out. To have new and different experiences with him.

"So being out of your element…" Tag fished even though he was giving his oldest brother a lifetime of ammo to use against him. "Not knowing what comes next…"

"Completely normal."

When silence stretched again, Tag opted not to say more. He didn't know what he was dealing with when it came to Rachel, not really. No sense in trying to work it out on the phone with his brother, who was thousands of miles away. Tag didn't have the words for what was between him and the blonde currently tightening her ponytail.

"I'll let you go. Enjoy the tropics," Reese said.

"Will do. Thanks."

"Oh, and, Tag?"

"Yeah." Tag smiled at Rachel, who was heading his way, ponytail swishing behind her, short shorts showcasing legs he'd had wrapped around him on more than one occasion. Damn. He was lucky.

"We're due for a drink. The four of us," Reese said.

"Four?" His eyebrows closed in.

"Yeah. Bring your girl."

"Bring…Rachel?"

"The challenger." Reese's laugh was low. "This I gotta see."

Tag hung up on his brother. He really shouldn't have brought up Mom or girls or feelings. Reese would never let it go. Of course, Tag didn't let up when Reese went doughy around Merina, so turnabout was fair play.

"Did I hear my name?" Rachel cocked her head as she stood in front of him.

"Hey, how'd it go?" He placed the laptop on the table

next to him and set his phone on top of it, hoping his question would distract her from the other question.

"Where are you 'bringing' me?" She sat on the lounger next to his, facing him, her elbows on her knees.

Challenging, indeed.

"Oh, uh. My brother invited us to cocktails when we get home."

"Cocktails." She pressed her splayed fingers to her collarbone. "With the CEO of Crane Hotels."

"What, the guy who runs Guest and Restaurant Services doesn't impress you any longer?"

She squinted one eye and seesawed her hand back and forth.

He reached out and took that hand. He couldn't be this close to her and not touch her. "He's like me."

"No." She shook her head and assessed him. "You're different."

Threading his fingers with hers, he admitted, "So are you."

She smiled at him. "What'd you have in mind for tonight?"

"Full report on the bar over dinner. Then we'll go back to the room and we'll see what other tricks you have up your sleeve."

"Tag!" She swatted him playfully. Then she peeked over her shoulder at Karina, who was bustling in circles around Craig behind the bar. "Did you know Karina likes you?"

"She...what now?" He caught Karina watching him, and her eyes widened before she looked away.

"*Likes* you, likes you," Rachel continued. "I'm probably lucky I escaped with all my hair."

Karina was pretty—dark hair, full mouth—but her demeanor was more military than soft. She was curt and abrupt, which made her a great manager, but dating potential? Even if there was a notable amount of attraction between them—and there wasn't—her personality and Tag's didn't mesh.

"She's not for me. I like women who—"

"Aren't entangled with your work?" Rachel cut him off.

He yanked her over to his lap and caught her when she would've lost her balance. He tucked her close, one arm around her back, the other palming her jaw.

"You are entangled in my work, honey."

"I'm guessing this isn't something you normally do."

That was true, too. He preferred the subtle blow-off. Sleeping with the people he worked with wasn't only frowned upon, but it could also make future encounters awkward. He didn't want to do his dates any damage, but neither did he want to continue leading them on when he knew things wouldn't amount to anything long-term.

Looking at Rachel now made him realize he hadn't had a single thought like that about her. Hadn't worried she was getting the wrong idea or that he should start laying the groundwork for disentangling himself from what was rapidly becoming an "us."

"This isn't normal for me, Dimples," was all he said. He palmed the back of her neck and pulled her lips to his, tasting her gently before letting her go. His eyes on hers, he watched as she studied his mouth.

"Me neither," she whispered.

"Because you dated a guy in marketing who never treated you like he should've?" It was information she'd given him during their beach walk.

"Right," she agreed, putting another soft kiss on his mouth. She reached up and stroked his beard with one finger. "He was clean-shaven with short hair and only a few inches taller than I am."

"Sounds like a sissy," Tag teased.

Her grin faded. "He didn't appreciate me. I should have left sooner."

She should have, but pointing that out wouldn't do her any good.

"You're out now." He swallowed the urge to promise her she wouldn't have to deal with any other guy like that again. Wanting to explore what was between them was one thing, making promises was another.

"Still want to work a day shift while you're here?" he asked.

"You know, I would. I think it would give me a better idea of what you need to do to make this place a success."

"You care, don't you?" His heart swelled. "About this place."

"Isn't that why you invited me?"

Yeah, but she cared for more than that reason.

"I'm paying for dinner tonight, too."

"I'm capable of—"

He put a finger over her plush lips.

"Shut up and enjoy it, Dimples." *Enjoy me*, he wanted to say, but didn't. He wasn't sure what was going through her head. He wasn't one for holding back, but this was new territory. The first time he'd suspected he liked a girl more than she liked him.

Rachel held back constantly, until she didn't. He'd like more of her moving toward him instead of away. Even after Hawaii. A wave of certainty and nausea swept through

him. Maybe it was being here that had made him senti-
mental, but he was sure something new was happening.

With her being the first woman in a long, long, *long-*
ass time he was interested in moving toward, not away
from, he wasn't about to let her go.

CHAPTER 16

Their flight out of Hawaii was scheduled to leave early. Rachel was awake at dark packing her bags when Tag appeared in her doorway, cup of steaming coffee in hand.

"Oh, you're an angel." She reached for the mug, but he stepped away.

"You're drinking this on the beach. Sun's up soon. Let's go." He tipped his head and vanished around the corner.

Groggily, she slipped into her flip-flops and shuffled ahead of him as he grabbed a coffee mug for himself. She opened the door for him and pushed the button on the elevator. In a few short minutes, her feet were sinking into the sand at the shoreline, where there was a reserved pair of beach chairs waiting at the ideal spot.

"Really going to miss this kind of treatment," she told him as he handed over her coffee.

"You'll have to come back then."

With him? She couldn't reconcile who she thought he was with his behavior. He'd seduced her as hard as he'd wooed her. Her lips pursed in thought. Had she ever been wooed before? Shaun half-assed everything with her. *"No need to go out for Valentine's Day, right, Rach? We don't need to go out to dinner to know we love each other."*

But she sort of did. Not because she was a princess who needed to be pampered, but because if he'd have made any effort at all, or appreciated hers, she would have felt loved by his actions.

She started to sit, and Tag stopped her with one hand. He plopped into the sand and gestured between his legs. "Sit here, Dimples. We're doing this right."

"You don't act like a billionaire." She arranged herself and rested against his solid chest.

"I take it you weren't impressed with the whisking-you-away-to-Oahu-by-private-plane bit? Because I have to tell you, that's my go-to move."

"You know what I mean." She clucked her tongue.

"Having money means getting to do fun things." He rested his hand with the coffee mug on one knee and leaned in to kiss her neck. "Thanks for coming here with me."

She reached her free hand behind her to cup his face, his soft facial hair brushing her cheek. "Thank you for asking me."

In silence, they sat, sipped their coffees, and watched the sun lift over the ocean. Her fantasy was rapidly coming to an end, during a sunrise rather than a sunset. Soon they'd be back to cold, windy Chicago and…and then she didn't know what came next.

Well, yes, she did. Work at the Andromeda, pound the

pavement for a new marketing job, then apartment hunting. She let out a sigh, feeling the heaviness of what was to come.

Part of her never wanted to leave the crook of Tag's legs, or Hawaii.

He reached forward and threaded their fingers together. "We can talk strategy for the bars on the flight home. Unless you had something else in mind?"

She knew the wicked lilt of his voice when he was thinking of her naked, and she had to admit since she'd met him, she often thought of him the same way.

"You know . . ." She gave him her weight as she relaxed against his chest. "I think we can fit in both."

"I like the sound of that." He kissed her neck and again, the thought of returning to Chicago made her melancholy. "Do we have time to stop by a store to pick up a few souvenirs?"

"Sure. For Bree?"

"Yes, and my cousin. Her wedding is coming up, and I'd like to buy her something unique. She's getting married at my parents' house the month after next."

"Weddings. Yikes." The statement was throwaway, but for her it dug in like a burr.

"Not one for matrimony?" she asked, frowning.

"No." His answer was swift and brief. "I avoid any get-together that involves the Chicken Dance."

"It does get old," she murmured. It had been on the tip of her tongue to ask if he would be her date, but clearly, weddings weren't his scene.

"I get invited to a lot of weddings"—a pause while he sipped his coffee—"and I make it a point to avoid them."

"Didn't you go to your brother's wedding?"

He shifted...uncomfortably? "Well, yeah, but I didn't take a date."

He'd said that like it was the most obvious statement and Rachel bristled.

"Why not? Surely Reese could afford a plus one." She was trying not to snap, but her tone had come out clipped.

"It was...you know. The girl I was seeing wasn't..." He paused as if realizing what he was saying. "Shit, now *I* sound like a douche." He took a breath that lifted his chest and pushed her forward a few inches. "Truth is"— he flexed his fingers around hers—"I don't want to give wrong impressions, and weddings give wrong impressions."

She turned that over, counting the next three beats of his heart against her back before speaking.

"Makes sense," she finally said.

"Good. I was burying myself there." He laughed, back to his at-ease self.

He was a man who didn't want things to get serious. Not ever. It was a sobering realization, when it should have been a relief for her to hear. With Tag, she'd be in no danger of being asked to stay.

Which is a good thing. So why did it hurt a little?

The truth was, she was damn busy, or would be when she arrived back home. And, she continued justifying, she was in no way ready to settle in with a boyfriend after Shaun—especially one that she'd have to drag along in a relationship.

Living in the lap of luxury would transform back into a pumpkin, and her billionaire prince would find another princess to occupy his time.

Staying had never been on her agenda. She'd come

here to enjoy being with Tag and to push her own boundaries. Find her boldness before she launched Rachel 2.0.

But during the quiet times like this one, when Tag's warmth enveloped her and his lips easily found that spot behind her ear, imagining distance between them became harder and harder.

* * *

After a long but smooth flight Tag unloaded their bags into a waiting SUV in the swirling Chicago snow. The driver, a young guy about half the size of Tag, had tried to help, but after struggling with Rachel's largest suitcase, Tag had sent her a wink and stepped in.

They climbed into the backseat and Rachel shuddered violently. "It's freezing here." Her voice faded into a whine as she laid her head back on the seat.

"You're zonked," he observed.

Without opening her eyes, she grunted.

"Kevin, forget that first address. Go to my place."

"Yes, Mr. Crane. Ms. Foster, there is a vent by your legs if you'd like to adjust the heat."

The seat shifted next to her as Tag leaned forward. A second later, warm air was blowing on her frozen limbs. She let out a long hum.

She opened her eyes. Wait...did he say...?

"No, I need to go home," she told Tag. "If I go to your house this late, I'll fall asleep and won't be able to leave."

"Deal." His slow spread of a smile made her stomach flip.

She should have argued, but she was too exhausted. And he was too...something. Too *everything*.

"It's no big deal. I have a big bed. You have luggage."

She guessed it wasn't. Maybe she'd been the one hyper-focused on everything between them. Maybe she should chill out. Not hard to do here in the tundra.

"Thanks."

"Welcome," he answered. She rested her head on the seat again and closed her eyes, enjoying the feel of his broad palm on her thigh.

* * *

Tag woke his houseguest the next morning by diving beneath the thick comforter. He applied kisses to every inch of Rachel's body as he stripped her bare, damn near suffocating under the blanket because she complained she was cold.

Soon enough, though, her complaints were muzzled. She'd tossed those blankets off and came—multiple times—under his ministrations.

After Kona coffee at his breakfast bar, she was already working, and on a *roll*.

"If you push back the bar rather than have it in the center of the two pools, you could create a place for the guests to hang out," she was saying. "Milling around would be easier if they weren't in danger of slipping into the swimming pools by taking a step to the left or right."

She pointed at the drawing with her pen. He could see what she meant. The bar being moved would allow more room for guests who were ordering and, as she'd suggested, offer more seating for guests who already had drinks.

"Even with the swim-up open again, you'll increase

your ability for more traffic if the bar is elsewhere." She then pointed the pen at him. "*And* I was right about the setup. Your server's wells are too far apart. You need one designated area, and preferably one bartender who prioritizes the servers and helps the other two bartenders during downtime." She put the pen down, fire in her eyes as well as her voice. "Once you have it redesigned, I'm betting you can use this as a template for some of your other hotels. I know Hawaii is a different setup given there are multiple pools, but I think..." She trailed off and broke into a smile. "What?"

He shook his head, dropping his arm from where he'd been resting his chin in his hand. "Nothing. I'm listening."

"You're staring." She tucked her hair behind her ear, fidgeting. Adorably. "Sorry, I'm passionate."

Didn't he know it. He hadn't realized she'd caught him zoning out, eyes on her. Hell, didn't know he'd been doing it until she pointed it out. He'd been listening to her ideas and watching her draw for the last half an hour, his mind on how perfect their trip had been.

"Reese is going to love your ideas." He lifted the paper she'd been sketching on and studied it further. "Why'd you leave marketing for the glam life of bartending?"

Her eyes darted to the side. "Just...It was time to go."

"Why?"

A one-shouldered shrug, then, "Truth?"

"You have to ask?" He raised one eyebrow in challenge. She should know by now he preferred things laid out.

"My ex-boyfriend," she said after blowing out a sigh of defeat.

"Damn." He slapped one palm on the counter. "I knew it was his fault."

"We were partners on a project, and he took full credit for what amounted to seventy-five percent my ideas. Management gave him the promotion I was angling for."

Tag scowled.

"I know, right? Dick move to pull on your girlfriend. We had a big fight at work. My boss suggested I resign before I was written up and possibly fired."

Now Tag was pissed.

"Your boss sounds like as big of a dick as your ex."

"Can't argue with that." Her lips twisted.

"So what do you want to do?"

She shook her head, but he could see the wheels turning. She knew; she just wasn't telling him. What made her keep pulling away? And what made him continue asking?

That was the more concerning issue. Not that it was unreasonable to care about her or what she was into, but the chasing was new.

"Do you see yourself in marketing again?" he pushed, evidently content to ignore his own concerns.

"Not really. I like bartending." She smiled and looked down at her drawing. "I liked sharing this project with you. It's been fun."

In more ways than one.

He held her gaze. She looked away first.

"But joining another corporate circus? I don't know. Employees can be vindictive. Each out to stomp on other people in their race to the top." She fiddled with the pen next. "Bartending is one for all, all for one. You band to-gether and do the job. Survive the rush. Make tips. Split the bar so you make sure each bartender is waiting on the person they'll extract the most money from."

"Smart," Tag said with a smile. "Who knew you were such a good player?"

"Am I?" She wrinkled her nose again and he felt all of him lean closer. She drew him to her in every way. "Guess I kind of am."

"Yeah, I guess you kind of are." He grabbed hold of her and pulled her closer. Her eyes slid shut and she pursed her lips, accepting his kiss easily.

Tag wasn't exaggerating about Reese loving her ideas. He was in love with them himself.

CHAPTER 17

The rest of the morning was domestic in a way she hadn't expected. Rachel couldn't very well go home in her travel clothes after spending all day on a plane in them, so when Tag offered to toss them in with the laundry, she took him up on it.

She sighed happily as she pulled on her warm jeans and sweater fresh out of the dryer.

"Much as I hate to watch you put clothes *on*, I have to say, you're damn cute when you do it."

She lowered the cowl neck of her sweater from her nose and smiled. She liked this. Liked being here with him. Hell, liked being anywhere with him.

His cell phone rang and he dug it from his pocket. As he stepped into the other room, Rachel pulled a few shirts and pairs of his (giant) jeans from the dryer. When he stepped back into the laundry room, she was about to make a joke about how folding them was like folding a tent...

Until she looked at him.

His face had gone ashen, phone in hand, his eyes unseeing. "I have to go."

His monotone voice and vacant stare had concern flooding her bloodstream. She rushed over to him.

"What is it? What happened?"

He swallowed thickly before his mouth opened. The only word that came out was, "Eli."

Two cracked syllables paired with wetness in his eyes.

Her heart hit her stomach.

The brother who was stationed overseas.

The brother who was supposed to come home in a few months.

Was he...oh, God, she couldn't think it.

"I'm coming with you," she said, having no idea where they were headed. But she wasn't going to send him out on the snowy roads of Chicago by himself when he'd received bad news.

He moved through the apartment, grabbed his keys and wallet, and reached for the door. Rachel snagged his coat off a chair, put hers on, and grabbed her purse. Once they'd pulled out of the parking garage in a black Mercedes, she asked the question she'd wanted to ask right away.

"Where are we going?"

He blinked like she'd interrupted very deep thoughts. "Hospital. He was injured last week." Bitterness eked into the worry in his tone. "They flew him home to Chicago Memorial. Dad knew—received the call when it happened—but Eli demanded he keep that to himself."

"So that was your dad on the phone?"

"Yeah." Tag cleared his throat. "He said Eli was out of surgery and Reese and Merina were already there."

She heard the grit in those words and felt her ire rise in his defense. Why was Tag the last to know?

"I don't even know what he had surgery *for*."

"I'm sorry." If this were her family, she'd know every bit of information and speculation before anyone knew anything. Like a live news report, they'd guess and wonder, and each unfolding minute would play out via text and phone calls.

The rest of the drive was silent, the only sound the wipers as they gathered snow from the windshield. At the hospital, they sat in the dark of the parking garage for a long moment, Tag with one hand on the steering wheel.

She wanted to ask if he was okay, but he wasn't. She could see it in every taut muscle of his body. The way he wore worry like a second skin.

"My family hasn't seen me with a woman in a decade," he said, fingers flexing on the wheel. "Expect some shocked expressions."

Her heart thudded, stopped, then restarted.

"Not something I make a habit of." Without a glance in her direction, he climbed out of the car and came to her door to help her out.

Inside, he made short work of navigating the hallways to the room number his father had given him. She hurried beside him to keep up, worry and fear eating a hole in her chest. She didn't have a lot of practice with emergencies. One close call with her mother in the hospital for what ended up being anxiety and a grandmother who'd had a heart condition and died when Rachel was six were the totality of her family crises. She was woefully ill-prepared to be here, but neither would she have let Tag come alone. She'd never remembered seeing anyone as devastated as he looked right now. She cared about him, and whether he knew it or not, she could tell he needed her here.

In the waiting room, he beelined for a cluster of chairs. A tall, handsome, dark-haired guy wearing a dark suit stood to greet them. Reese Crane. His build, his facial features, and even the scruff on his jaw told her this was Tag's oldest brother.

Before Reese could speak, Tag said, "Nice of you to let me know."

His brother narrowed his eyes, anger seeping into his expression, and a woman with dark blond hair shot out of her seat to stand next to him. Reese's wife-turned-ex-wife-turned-fiancée, no doubt.

"We only just found out ourselves, Tag." She extended a hand to Rachel. "I'm Merina Van Heusen."

"Crane," Reese corrected.

"Not yet," Merina said with a pointed look. Rachel shook her hand.

"You must be Rachel." Reese shook her hand next.

"Yes."

"Thank you for coming."

"Cut the formality, Clip." Tag's anger was on a short leash. Rachel wrapped her hand around his forearm gently so he knew she was on his side. "What the hell is going on?"

"I'll explain," came an authoritative voice.

Every head swiveled to the older, white-haired man with a matching white goatee. Thick, muscular build, flooring blue eyes.

This had to be Alex "Big" Crane.
Tag's father.

*   *   *

The next few minutes were a blur.

Tag grilled his father for information, of which Alex gave as little as possible. Evidently Eli's request that he keep quiet took precedence. That also included not sharing details of the surgery.

"You know I love you all equally, so stop trying to guilt me. Anyway, you can ask him yourselves." Alex's forehead was crinkled, his eyebrows meeting over a strong, straight nose as he snapped his eyes from Tag to Reese. "I don't want a lecture from either one of you."

"We should know what's happened before we go in there," Reese grumbled. Tag was glad his brother was as pissed as he was. Keeping secrets was bullshit, and not a habit the Crane men had when dealing with each other.

"We're ready," Alex said, beckoning a nurse. "Reese. You're the oldest. You first. I'll go in with you and Merina."

"Tag..." Merina looked to him, but he shook his head and put his arm around Rachel. He understood the importance of Reese taking her with him. She shouldn't go in there with anyone else.

"Not the way I envisioned first meeting your brother," Merina said to Reese, her smile pale. Reese tucked her against his side and kissed her forehead. Tag's gut twisted. Being here, everyone behaving somberly, was a premonition of something bad, and he hated that he didn't know what it was.

His father's assistant, Rhona, had come as well. Again Tag considered her presence, as well as the way her eyes were rimmed red, her hands laced in her lap, knuckles white. Definitely she and his dad were more than co-workers. She had taken the news as personally as any of them.

Which made him consider him and Rachel and what it meant that she'd insisted on coming with him. He couldn't think of a single other woman from his past who would have offered. Face it, this wasn't the most comfortable way to meet his family.

"Let's sit," Tag said to her, his voice gentle. He'd been growling like a caged lion since he arrived. Not only did it not help him pry information from his dad, but it also hadn't put the scared woman at his side at ease.

Rachel sat next to him, fingers linked with his while her other hand rubbed his arm, consoling him. She was so damn sweet.

"He's okay," he told her, covering her hand with his. "If he's making demands that none of us know what's wrong until he tells us, then he's okay." Tag had to believe that or he'd go insane. When their mother died, Eli had handled losing Mom in much the same way he was handling this scenario—he'd locked up, shut down, and processed internally.

"I'm sorry we can't tell you," Rhona interrupted, her voice fragile. Worry was etched across her face, her blond-with-gray-streak ponytail sloppy like she'd hurriedly pulled it back. She was dressed casually, and so was Alex, which made Tag again consider how much time they spent together. "Eli was adamant."

That she knew made Tag feel an ache of betrayal.

"I'll know in a few minutes," he said anyway, aware

that taking out his anger on Rhona wouldn't help the situation. Definitely she and his father were more serious than he'd thought.

Tag had a brief slap of insight at that thought. He hadn't told his family about Rachel, until Reese had pressed. And here he was with her. They appeared together in every way. He couldn't exactly fault his dad for not laying things out. Maybe, like Tag, Alex didn't know what he and Rhona had either.

"Tag," came Reese's voice, pulling him out of his thoughts. "Rachel. You two can go in now."

Reese's pallor was sickly, his expression grim. Merina didn't look much better.

Tag's stomach sank. He stood, then glanced at Rachel, who rose from her seat cautiously. His girl, blond hair down and beautiful, eyes wide with worry. She was scared. She was concerned. And she was in a hospital with his entire family. She'd stayed by his side.

His sister-in-law-to-be swiped tears from her cheeks, a look of devastation covering her features. When Reese enclosed Merina in a comforting hug and met Tag's eyes over her head, Tag's knees nearly went out from under him.

What the fuck had happened to Eli?

"Rachel, I'm not sure this is the best time for you to meet Eli," Alex stated. The look he sent Tag next made him feel like puking.

"She's going," Tag stated. He needed her. More than he'd imagined.

"Tag." Rachel gave his hand a squeeze. "Maybe it's best not to bombard him." Sincerely, she continued. "It's okay if I don't go in. I came here for you."

I came here for you.

She'd said it in Hawaii, and at the time the meaning had been so very different.

"I'll go in with you," Reese said. Merina was wiping her eyes with a tissue and visibly trying to pull herself together. He addressed Rachel next, sincerity in his eyes. "Merina can take you home if you need to leave."

"She's fine," Tag bit out. But he turned and saw Rachel wasn't fine. He wasn't fine. None of this was fucking *fine*.

He bent and kissed Rachel softly. The way her arms wrapped around his waist told him all he needed to know. She was barely hanging on, and she'd done this for him.

"Dimples," he said against her hair, keeping his voice low. "If you need to go, I get it."

She nodded against his chest, squeezing him a little tighter. He let her go, sent her a tight smile, and left it at that. Her wide blue eyes confirmed she was better out here with Merina than in Eli's hospital room.

Tag followed Reese down the hall.

Eli's room was private, dim, the only light coming from the white swirling snow outside the window. Reese walked to the far side of the bed, leaving the chair closest to Eli available.

Eli's face was dotted with cuts, some deeper than others, but mostly shallow, surface. His right arm was bandaged from elbow to fingers—all five of them sticking out of the cast, his left arm lying on his left leg over the blankets. But it was his right leg that weakened Tag's knees and sent him straight to his ass on the chair by the bed.

Beneath his brother's knee, the sheet was flat.

Tag covered his mouth as he mumbled, "Jesus, Eli," into his hand.

Eli turned his head to take him in, dark blue eyes cold and distant, brown hair grown out some from the buzz cut he'd worn for years, his beard scraggly.

"Just Eli is fine. No need for formality," he said, his voice a dry chafe. The humor didn't hit its mark.

Eli licked his lips and reached for the plastic cup at his bedside, shifting his weight and moving his leg—what remained of it—beneath the sheet.

Tag's eyes went to Eli again, his only thought how it was the same knee Eli had injured during a game of backyard touch football that had turned into tackle. Eli had limped for a month and bitched at Tag for causing his injury.

Hand stroking his own beard, Tag sent Reese a nod of thanks for accompanying him. Reese nodded back. No way did Tag want Rachel in here. Merina was right to suggest she not come in.

"It was a bomb," Reese said, arms over his chest.

"Grenade," Eli corrected, eyes going to the muted television overhead. "Benji and Christopher." His mouth compressed as he shook his head. "Didn't make it."

Eli may have been in a hospital bed looking at a TV, but he wasn't here. Tag could see by his vacant stare that his mind was back on a moment of tragedy he likely felt responsible for.

Tag reached out and took his brother's arm above the cast, squeezing as hard as he dared to bring him back to the present. "But you did," he managed, voice shaking, eyes filling with dampness.

Only then did Eli lock gazes with him. His own chin trembled when he said, "Not all of me."

"Enough of you." Tag's voice was a raw whisper.

They had a brief staredown.

Wordlessly, Eli reached out with his unbandaged arm, grabbed a fistful of Tag's sweater, and hauled him against his chest.

Then Tag held on to his older brother and cried like a baby.

CHAPTER 18

Rachel let Merina drive her home from the hospital. A huge part of her had wanted to stay for Tag, but one look around the room at his family confirmed he had plenty of support.

During the drive, Merina explained how Eli had lost his lower right leg, lucky considering two other soldiers hadn't survived the blast. Merina and Rachel shared an awkward moment of silence before Merina admitted, "I didn't mean to hurt your feelings by suggesting you not go in. It was a hard way to meet him for the first time, that's all. And I've been with Reese for a while."

Rachel understood, and told Merina as much. She hadn't wanted to make Eli feel any additional discomfort, either. Per Rachel's request, Merina dropped her at the Andromeda instead of her apartment. All Rachel wanted to do was talk to her friend, have a drink, and, now that

she realized she'd gone two hours past dinnertime without food, have something to eat as well.

"Hey, toots!" Bree said as she filled a shot glass and
delivered it to a customer. By the time she put the tequila
bottle back on the shelf, she was frowning. She knew
Rachel had been at Tag's place, and now she was alone.
"What's going on?"

"Change of plans." Rachel hoisted herself onto a
barstool and plunked her purse in front of her.

"Oh, no." Bree already had a wine bottle in hand—
if that wasn't friendship, Rachel didn't know what was.
"Did something go south?"

"Yes, but not like you think."

"Miss?" called one of the patrons at the bar, and Bree
gave Rachel the "give me a minute" look.

The rush died down gradually. Rachel wolfed down a
salad with grilled chicken, and Bree refilled Rachel's red
wine glass with a generous amount.

"I'm all yours," she said, placing the bottle on the bar
between them. "Where is Tag? Why are you alone?"

"Tag is at the hospital. Or, was, anyway ... I'm not sure
where he is now." Rachel briefed her bestie as succinctly
as possible, watching as Bree's face melted into a mask
of concern.

"Awkward," she whispered when Rachel was done filling her in.

"I feel awful. Like I should have stayed. But I was rocking the third-wheel gig pretty hard." Everyone had been
paired off. Reese and Merina, Alex and Rhona, Tag and ...
she didn't know in what capacity she was there. Rachel
lifted her wineglass and took a hearty sip, taking a full, relaxing breath. Yep, she definitely needed this tonight.

"You did the right thing. Tag told you to leave if you wanted to."

"Yes, but what if he was only being nice and really wanted me to stay?"

"He's a guy," came a low, oddly familiar, voice to her right. She and Bree turned to find a mildly attractive man leaning on the bar, cold rolling off his leather coat.

"Shaun." Rachel had barely spoken her ex-boyfriend's name before he continued.

"Guys always say what they mean. Which makes it harder when they majorly fuck up and have to apologize later." He pressed his lips together in a brief show of chagrin and sat on the stool next to her. "Hey, Rach."

Bree's eyebrows climbed her forehead. "Been a while. I forgot how weak your chin was."

Shaun frowned.

"You remember my roommate," Rachel said. "Bree, we're fine. Bring him a draft Bud Light."

"Make it a bottle," Shaun said. "No offense, but I don't trust you not to spit in it."

"You might not be as big of a dumbass as I thought." Bree gave him a tolerant smile, bent to retrieve his beer, and delivered it without saying more.

"Well?" Rachel asked when Shaun took a drink and Bree walked away.

"What have you been up to?" he asked. Absurdly. "I thought you worked here."

"I do work here." She felt her face pinch. "It's my night off. Why are *you* here?"

"Wasn't my idea." He shrugged and averted his eyes, looking over his shoulder at the entrance.

"Are you meeting someone here? Do you have a date?"

"Met her on Tinder. Half of me thought maybe it was you playing with me. Like the *Must Love Dogs* movie, you know? Where she went on a date with her own dad." His mouth lifted into a half smile. She used to find that attractive like she had the rest of him, but now his clean-shaven face and weak chin—Bree had nailed that descriptor—did nothing for her.

"That's not exactly the same scenario," she said. "What time is your date?"

"If she shows. I keep getting stood up at these things. Dating is hard, know what I mean?"

"She doesn't know what you mean," Bree interjected. "She's had no problem getting—"

"Bree," Rachel interrupted her well-intentioned friend.

Bree held up both hands in surrender and moved back down the bar.

"Have you met someone?" Shaun asked, his face showing the first hint of concern. Rachel liked that look on him so much, she simply sat in silence for a few seconds and enjoyed it. After all she was in the process of overcoming, much of it could be blamed partially, if not mostly, on the man sitting here talking with her like they were buddies.

"I met someone," she said, liking the way that sounded.

Her life was different now that Tag was in it instead of Shaun. Tag's gruff, gravel-laden demands and sincere compliments had come a long way to boosting her confidence—and not only in the bedroom. Tag valued her opinion—valued her as a person. When she'd come with him to the hospital, Tag had held her hand, grateful that she was there.

He valued her.

Valued. Once her brain hooked on to the word, it didn't let go...

"You never valued me." She murmured the epiphany so low her comment was lost in the bustling crowd around them.

"What did you say?" Shaun leaned closer, his receding brow crinkling. But she didn't answer. There was another issue that'd been on her mind and until now, she hadn't had the chance to ask...or was it that she'd never wanted to know the answer?

Well. She did now.

"You and the girl with the purple streaks in her hair..."

Shaun blanched, giving her the answer she'd assumed. She asked anyway, enjoying having him on the spot.

"Did you sleep with her while we were together?"

"You mean..." He shifted in his seat, uncomfortable with this line of discussion. "Did I cheat?"

"Just tell me. It's not like we're together anymore." She couldn't call up jealousy or the feelings of inadequacy that had plagued her as recently as a few weeks ago.

"I didn't...not when...we were together," he managed. "I mean I let her uh..." He grew fidgety, his gaze lingering on the beer bottle's label. "You know...*do* things to me."

Rachel squinted one eye in confusion before his meaning hit her. When it did, she blurted, "Oh my God, she blew you?"

"Rach!" came a harsh whisper. Shaun never liked when she spoke her mind, as proved when his upper lip curled in disgust. "Not like you'd ever do it, and when you did, you weren't exactly good at it."

The insult glanced off her. Eyebrow cocked, she considered her recent experience with Tag. Wouldn't he beg to differ?

Do you have any idea how hard it's going to be for me to last longer than twenty seconds?

She wasn't going to share her intimate moments with Shaun. It was enough to know the truth in her gut.

"Good thing I was tested after we split." She lifted her wineglass, a wry smile pulling her lips. "Who knows what kind of weird STDs you picked up. An almost-year-long hiatus was proof enough I was okay." Come to think of it, that was a really long time for Shaun to be sexless. "Oh man! You were seeing her the entire time."

Ugh. Gross, gross, gross. She was going to have to take a hundred more showers.

"You really are a dick." She shook her head, feeling sorry for her former self.

"Fine, you got me. I was wrong." His jaw moved like he was grinding his teeth before he grumbled. Leave it to him to apologize and make her try and feel bad about it. "You know what they say about hindsight."

"That it's the only sight you have when your head's up your ass?" she asked sweetly.

Bree giggled, overhearing; then her laugh faded. "Oh, look who's here."

Rachel pushed her hair behind her ear as the front door opened. Tag swaggered in, hair down, long overcoat covering his clothes. The moment he scanned the room and found her, warmth poured through her from the roots of her hair to the tips of her toes.

Eyes locked on hers, he moved through the crowd on his way to the bar, maneuvering toward her like she was the only woman in the room—no, the *city*. He had a way of doing that, of making her feel important and special. Until she was sitting directly next to her ex did she realize she had been unaccustomed to that kind of treatment.

"Save a seat for me, Dimples?" Tag asked when he reached her. He slipped a proprietary hand onto the back of her neck and chills wandered down her spine when his fingertips began massaging. He slanted a glance at her ex, roughly the size of a field mouse next to Tag. "Who's this?"

"This is Shaun Sanders. Shaun, this is my um...Tag. Crane," she tacked on after a short pause.

"Tag Crane," Shaun repeated, recognition on his face.

Yeah, buddy, Tag Crane. Damn. She was proud of knowing someone of such high caliber—of course, Shaun would be impressed with Tag's money, but Rachel knew who Tag was underneath it. A good man with a big heart and a penchant for doing her right.

Tag turned his attention to her, moving her hair from her neck and over her shoulder seductively. It was a subtle touch, but it still sent tingles through her limbs. He didn't sit, sort of hovering over her and Shaun at the same time. He dropped his voice, but Shaun had to have heard, given he was sitting at the corner seat directly adjacent to her.

"Is Shaun Sanders bothering you?" Tag rumbled, his voice accidentally sensual.

"We're old friends and co-workers," Shaun interjected.

Tag straightened to his full height and studied Shaun until he wiggled in his seat and shot another look at the front door. Still looking for his date, or his escape? Rachel plunked her chin on her fist and enjoyed watching him squirm.

"Shaun." Tag pointed at him but addressed Rachel. "The douchebag ex-boyfriend who stole your marketing promotion."

"Listen, man, I didn't come in here to fight."

"Then why'd you sit next to her?"

With jerky movements, Shaun slid off the barstool and pulled his wallet out of his pocket. He threw a few bills onto the bar top. "I don't have to take this."

"It's fine, Tag," Rachel said, resting her hand on his chest. "He helped with a few unanswered questions I had."

"Get the answers you needed?" Tag asked.

She tipped her chin to look up at him. He was insanely gorgeous. Between him and wine, she was feeling warm and happy. And in the midst of Shaun Sanders. Who'd have thought?

"I did."

"Good." Tag reserved a small smile for her, and she puckered. He lowered to give her a kiss and that, too, felt like a win.

"You can't leave yet, Shaun Sanders." Tag sounded like he looked—hard, but calm.

What happened next happened fast. He grabbed Shaun by the front of his coat, twisting the collar. A few low gasps came from the bar patrons surrounding them. "You're going to apologize before you go." He tugged Shaun closer.

"This isn't your business," Shaun managed, swiping at his shirt.

"Sorry, but it is. You come in here, sit next to a girl who isn't yours, and expect no retribution." Tag tsked. "My business, bro."

Rachel felt a blush steal across her cheeks and glanced over at Bree to find her friend wearing a matching satisfied smile. Tag released him and Shaun nearly fell back. He straightened his coat and squared his shoulders.

"I'm waiting," Tag prompted, arms folded. "Make it good. One strike, you're out."

Shaun licked his lips like he was debating. In the end, he must have reconsidered challenging Tag, who stood like a mountain daring to be climbed. Shaun's jerky gaze snapped to her. "Sorry, Rach. If it makes you feel better, Larry said he wouldn't have promoted you anyway since—"

"And you're out." Fist wrapped around Shaun's coat again, Tag physically moved Shaun through the bar and around tables, shouting, "Clear a path!"

Bree dropped to her elbows next to Rachel, and they watched as both men staggered out into the cold. When the door swung shut behind them, Tag gave Shaun a shove. Shaun practically sprinted down the sidewalk.

"What will we tell his Tinder date when she shows up?" Rachel murmured as Bree laughed.

Tag walked back into the bar and cheers rose from the crowd.

Bree joined the applause and arched one dark eyebrow at Rachel. "Marry that man."

* * *

"I thought it was nice for Bree to offer you a job as a bouncer." Rachel faced Tag on his bed, resting on a pillow opposite his.

"I'll keep the Andromeda Club in mind if this whole

Crane Hotels thing doesn't pan out." Tag's smile was tired. He pulled a hand over his face. He'd stayed for a few beers while Rachel finished her glass of wine. Then they shot some pool and she realized Tag *couldn't* do everything. He was a horrible pool player. She'd smoked him.

He hadn't brought up the hospital, his family, or Eli. Rachel let him have the reprieve, figuring he'd open up when he was ready.

They were fully dressed, relaxing on top of the blankets of Tag's bed. When he'd stepped into his apartment tonight, he'd gone straight to the bedroom and flopped onto the bed. Rachel followed.

She'd planned on returning to her apartment, but after the day they'd had, she couldn't get motivated to leave him. Even though her bags were packed and standing at the front door.

"I shouldn't have escorted your ex-douchebag out of Andromeda," Tag said around a yawn.

"No?" It wasn't like him to have regrets.

"No." He gave her a lazy-cat blink. "I should've thrown him in the street after I put a dent in his face."

"That would have been great to witness," she said with a small smile. She liked Tag defending her honor. Making Shaun apologize. Mostly, she'd liked that she hadn't allowed Shaun to steamroll her the way he used to. She'd stood up for herself.

"He made you think you weren't sexy, Rachel." Tag brushed her cheek with his fingers, his touch gentle and at odds with his harsh tone. "Do you know how sexy you are?"

He ran those same fingers down her neck, over her gray sweater and cupped one breast.

"How often I think of you naked?" He tilted one eyebrow and pegged her with those ocean blues. A blush stole across her cheeks. Her entire body. She'd never been in the position of being complimented the way Tag complimented her.

Often. And like he meant it.

"Is it as often as I picture you that way?" she asked, leaning closer.

Slowly, he shook his head. "Doubt it."

When he blinked, his eyes nearly stayed shut. She reached forward to cradle his cheek. "I'm sorry I didn't go in with you to meet Eli."

"Don't be. Merina was right. It's better you didn't." Pain lanced through his features at the memory. "Seeing him there...his leg..." He blinked a few times in thought. "I...he could have died. Life without my brother..." He shook his head, unable to continue for a long, silent moment. "Losing Mom was too much. I couldn't take it if Eli followed. I knew there was always risk, him being overseas, but to me he's always been bulletproof. *Grenade* proof."

Tag was such a light, fun, happy guy that it was easy to forget he hid deep, dark hurts behind his resilient confidence. He had so much love for his family, he was bursting with it. Even when he and Reese were squaring off, she could tell how much they cared for each other. People fought the hardest with those they loved the most.

She sat up, rested on her elbow, and stroked a hand into Tag's hair.

"Eli looked out for me when Mom died. He may have been broody and quiet, but he looked out for me."

"I can't imagine how difficult losing her must have

been for you and your brothers. And, oh, your poor dad."

"He was devastated." Tag shook his head, his gaze soft on the window. No snow fell, but the night was frigid all the same. "Even as a sixth grader I knew something was off. I went to the nurse every day with stomachaches. Came home from school more than I was there that year. Damn near didn't make it into junior high."

"Stress," she whispered. She'd been stressed and anxious before, but never to that severity. Losing a parent at such a young age would be like losing half your world.

"I was lucky. Magda, our housekeeper—now Reese's—stayed late every night to help me catch up on my homework."

"That's sweet." She stroked his hair again.

"She's a great person."

"You're a great person," Rachel told him, meaning it. When she'd first laid eyes on him, she'd had no idea about his depth, or how he would turn her world on its head by simply being in her life. "Thank you. For everything."

"You got it, Dimples."

"Come here." She motioned for him.

He did, laying his head on her breast and wrapping an arm around her waist. A deep breath accompanied a guttural male hum that made her smile.

"Rest as long as you need to, and I'll be here." She waited for the quip, the joke to call up their usual playful antics. None came.

"Thanks, Rachel." His fist clutched her sweater.

The response made her chest feel full and her body seize with the realization that Tag was more than playful antics and great sex. He had become part of her world, part of who she was. Her focus narrowed on her suitcases by the front door. They looked out of place there. She wasn't in any hurry to take them to the apartment and unpack. The idea scared her. No longer because she was shying from commitment, but because she wasn't sure how he felt. Yes, they were close, but the truth was Tag might not be any closer to commitment than he was the first night he'd kissed her.

She decided it didn't matter. The point was she was here, and he was here, and his arms felt more right than any she'd ever been nestled in. She turned her head to admire the city lights beyond his bedroom, her fingers in his hair, her mind on this moment and this moment only.

"Anytime, Tarzan."

She was answered by a soft snore.

CHAPTER 19

The next two weeks flew. Rachel and Tag went out for dinner or lunch, depending on her schedule with Andromeda and his visits with Eli, either at the hospital or while readying Eli's downtown warehouse for his return home.

Since Tag escorted Shaun out of the bar, Bree had taken to referring to him as "the billionaire bodyguard," and tonight she didn't mince words when she tied her apron for her shift.

"Are you moving in with him?"

"Bree." Rachel paused drying a wineglass, lunch shift having ended and only a few occupied tables remaining. The dining room wouldn't pick up for another hour or so. "Why...would you ask that?" She pretended to be fascinated with a spot on the glass.

After the night spent holding Tag in her arms, she'd gone back to Bree's the next day. She'd only stayed at

Tag's one time since, and that was fine. If not eye-opening. Whatever was happening between her and him still included everything it had before—she just had to travel across town to go to bed rather than down a flight of stairs.

"I have a not-at-all altruistic reason for asking." Bree grimaced.

Rachel put the spotless glass next to a row of others and faced her.

"Dean and I found a house to rent. It's the perfect location, and available now, and we can break the lease on the apartment for a small fee if we leave the place the way we found it." She took a breath, which was probably needed since she'd blown out the announcement on one exhalation. "Unless you changed your mind about renting it alone?"

Rachel couldn't rent their place alone. It was a luxury three-bedroom, three-bath with a garden balcony. It was located in Edgewater. For the last few weeks, she'd been pounding the pavement with resumes and had received only one callback: an offer for a receptionist position that she'd turned down graciously. She wasn't too good for answering phones, but at the Andromeda she'd make twice as much money as the position offered.

"Um..."

"I'm sorry," Bree said quickly. "I didn't mean to pressure you. It's—"

"Stop. You're too nice. The truth is, I can't afford the apartment on my own. And moving in with Tag would be..." A long pause settled between them before she finished with, "Insane."

At that, Bree cocked an eyebrow. "Dean and I fell in love fast. It could happen."

"No. It couldn't."

"Why not?"

Oh, sweet Bree.

"What you and Dean have is rare, and most of the time isn't what the rest of us find." It was as likely to spot a unicorn as it was to find a couple as in sync as those two. They were on the same page in every way—like the other day when they'd accidently matched in jeans and the same shade of royal blue shirt.

"But if it's real and you're denying it based on your past with some idiot like Shaun, that's not fair to you or Tag."

"Shaun has nothing to do with it. I mean, sure, I was intimidated about sex"—she whispered the word—"but I'm over that. I think it had more to do with me finding my confidence again." And she had. She felt like her old self. In no small way, thanks to Tag.

"I never believed you were scared of sex." Bree's eyes widened. "Oh man."

"What?" Rachel felt her brow crease.

"You're scared of falling in love! That makes so much sense. After Shaun, why would you want to commit only to be left behind again?"

Rachel let out a disgruntled huff rather than reply. It was like Bree had been reading her mind these past few months. Inconvenient when there were certain topics she didn't feel like hashing out.

The front door opened and four men and women marched in, briefcases in hand. Bree grabbed a pen and pad of paper as she headed out to greet the foursome that sat in one of the booths by the window. Before she walked off, she turned to say, "We're not done talking about this."

Rachel went back to cleaning the bar, turning the conversation over and over in her mind, her stomach tossing like a boat in a storm.

Her independence was important. Making it on her own, imperative. Shaun had definitely put doubt in her mind after they'd split. He'd betrayed her when he was supposed to love her.

Even now, the idea of moving in with a man again made her palms sweat. She'd feel so...trapped.

Wouldn't she?

Tag hadn't made her feel trapped or dependent. He'd made her feel...

Amazing.

She gave her head an intentional shake to dislodge the thought. Falling in love with Tag had its own pratfalls. He was a consummate bachelor whose middle name was *Fun*. What would he want with a girlfriend or...or...a wife.

The word hit her like a bucket of ice water.

Either of those roles required a lot of trust. She thought she trusted Tag, but what if she was wrong? She'd been wrong before. And the fallout hadn't been pretty.

She had to protect herself—her heart.

No matter what.

* * *

Tag slid the heavy metal door of the freight elevator aside and made way for his brothers. Eli stepped into his upcycled warehouse, leaning heavily on a pair of crutches, his jeans flat below his right knee.

The doctors had insisted on getting him on his feet as

soon as possible after surgery to increase circulation, and Eli, though wobbly, was doing well. Physically, anyway. He slid a displeased look around his home, specifically to the second floor, where his loft bedroom used to be. His hair was longer, his beard thicker, his frown more prominent.

"Welcome home," Reese said, stepping out of the elevator behind Eli. Unlike Reese, who bought a mansion, and Tag, who opted for a penthouse, Eli went for the more industrial and less homey option. He'd improved the warehouse little by little every time he was on leave. He owned the building and chose to keep the lower floor empty. His upstairs offered plenty of open space to move around, ironically perfect for his mobility now.

Reese dragged Eli's suitcase behind him. "I'll throw this in the bedroom. It's back here, by the way."

Eli's gaze flitted again to the loft and the metal stairs leading to his second floor. Then he walked to the living room area, his arms straining through his Henley as he maneuvered on the crutches. The therapist told them Eli would be fitted with a prosthetic in the next few weeks once his stump had healed. Eli had shared with Tag that he was anxious to get moving like "normal" again, to not be restricted. It'd take time, but Tag knew he'd get there. His brother could do anything he set his mind to.

"We moved everything from the second floor to the main floor," Tag said.

Eli faced Tag, his navy blue eyes hard. "Yeah, I imagine those stairs will come in real fucking handy."

Reese entered the room and blew out a sigh.

"What the hell is all that?" Eli angled to the gym area they set up along the wall below the loft. Tag and Reese had had the area outfitted with a bench and weights and a machine for everyone's all-time favorite: leg day.

"Your physical therapist will come daily, and you'll have a nurse check in on you twice a week," Reese told him. "This is part of the deal, Eli. You have to do your rehab."

"We're close by if you need anything," Tag interjected.

Despite his surly attitude, they knew this was what Eli wanted. He wanted to be at home rather than stay with Reese and Merina any longer. And Eli made it clear he had no interest in staying with Tag. "Penthouses suck," he'd said. He wanted his freedom, and this was the only way to give it to him.

"The nurse is temporary, just until your leg heals. Her visits will taper off after you learn your way around," Reese said.

"Relearn, you mean." Eli scowled at the floor.

Tag's heart ached like it had split in two. What would it feel like to be missing a part of your own body?

"Hey, better than living with him," Tag said, trying to lighten the mood as he pointed at Reese. Eli had stayed with Merina and Reese for the last few days and had been shuttled back and forth to the hospital as needed while Tag readied his warehouse.

"I've had enough of that love nest," Eli muttered.

"It's sickening, right?" Tag joked.

"I'd talk," Reese said. "You're still seeing your blond bartender. Last I checked, it's about time for you to run for the hills isn't it?"

Eli gave them the first hint of a smile—the barest lift of one side of his mouth. "Tell me it's not true. Tag, the ultimate player, benched."

Tag stifled his own smile. He'd wanted to shift the topic from Eli's leg. It worked.

"Merina said you had a girl out in the waiting room. She said you took her to Hawaii on vacation." Eli adjusted his weight on the crutches and rolled one shoulder.

"For work. She was advising on the bar setup." Tag palmed the back of his neck. Okay. The conversation switch had worked *too well*.

Eli and Reese exchanged glances. "He knows I didn't suffer brain damage when I lost my leg, right?"

Reese let out a deep laugh.

When Tag looked up to tell them both to cram it, he noticed Eli suddenly didn't look so good. Then Eli winced, knuckles going white on the crutches, his face pinching. A sound of raw pain followed.

Tag and Reese rushed to him, but before they could each grab an arm, Eli unclenched a hand and held it open, signaling them to stop. He growled one word. "Don't."

Tag froze. Reese locked his fists at his sides. The doctor warned them about this—phantom pains. Intense, spearing, sometimes hot, electric shots of pain in the limb that was missing.

Watching Eli's expression shatter in agony was the hardest thing Tag ever had to witness.

"Stubborn ass," Tag muttered when Eli wobbled like he might pass out.

Tag grabbed one crutch and wrapped an arm around his brother's back, physically moving Eli to a chair and forcing him to sit. Tag laid the crutches within reaching distance, but otherwise let him be. A sheen of sweat covered Eli's forehead as his chest heaved. At least he was breathing through the pain now.

"Fuck me," he panted, lifting one shaky hand to wipe his brow. "I need a beer."

"You can't drink beer with your medication," Reese said. Eli glared at him.

"I can get you a pain pill," Tag said, feeling utterly helpless. Useless.

"No, I'm good." Eli didn't look good, though. He was pale and looked like he'd taken a beating.

"I forgot to eat," Reese said. Out of the blue.

Tag turned to face him and Reese held his gaze. "Takeout? Chow Main's not far from here."

"Chow Main sounds great," Tag said, understanding this was Reese's excuse to stay. "Eli?"

"You two need to go home so I can sleep."

But they wouldn't. Not right away. Certainly not on the heels of Eli's attack.

"After dinner," Reese said, pulling his phone from his suit pocket. "I'll call Merina and see if she wants to stop by. She's probably starving."

"I'll order." Tag pulled his own phone out and hit the button for the Chinese restaurant that had a permanent place in his address book. "Eli, beef or chicken?"

"I don't eat meat."

"Hold on a second, Merina," Reese said into the phone. "What did you just say?" he asked Eli.

"Fish. But not meat."

The man who'd once considered steak the end-all-be-all didn't eat meat now? Tag ingested this information but didn't argue. "Shrimp okay?"

"Or tofu. Either one." Eli rested his head on the chair and closed his eyes. Tag exchanged looks with Reese, who shook his head, shell-shocked.

Tofu? Who was this guy?

"Hey, yes, I have a takeout order," Tag said into the phone. Reese resumed his call, moving to the far side of the room to talk to Merina. Tag completed the order, hung up, and told Eli, "Twenty minutes. I'll get it."

"Aren't you going to call your *girlfriend*?" Eli asked, eyes still closed, his mouth curving into a smile.

"You're lucky we like you," Tag said, pulling his keys from his coat and moving for the freight elevator. The next sound that echoed the room floored him and made him smile in spite of himself.

Because Eli *laughed.*

* * *

Rachel wrung her hands in her lap as Tag pulled up in front of a tidy Tudor home in a cute neighborhood outside Chicago. This was where his best friend, Lucas, lived? The super-attractive, smart-mouthed music producer had a charming little house with flowerboxes? She'd expected a sleek high-rise apartment building. This home was a monument proving players could be tamed.

"Come up with me. I want you to meet the kids," Tag said.

The kids.

"Okay."

She climbed out of the car, careful of her little black dress with the super-short skirt. She'd felt ambitious on her shopping trip earlier this week, and given the temperature, hadn't chosen wisely. The skin exposed between her knee-high boots and hemline was freezing. She definitely wasn't in Hawaii anymore.

"Same rules apply as with my family. Don't mind the bug-eyed looks of shock," Tag said as they scaled the concrete steps leading to a covered front porch.

"Your friends haven't met a girl you're seeing in a while either?" Her nerves were doing the cha-cha.

"Only when you met Luc at the Andromeda that night. But no, not in a long while. Lucas was my wingman for a lot of years, and Gena is the one who spun him."

"Who *what* him?"

A sly smirk, then, "Nothing."

Tag pressed a button and a bell rang. The door popped open and the man Rachel remembered stood at the threshold, a toddler on his hip. Oddly enough, the sight of him with a little girl attached to his side suited him.

Tamed player, indeed.

"Hey, guys, come on in." As she stepped inside, she heard Lucas say to Tag, "Doorbell, man, really?"

"I'm trying to make a good impression," Tag murmured.

Rachel smiled to herself, liking how Tag was still trying to impress her.

"Oh my God, I can't believe it." A petite, tattooed, black-haired woman swung around the corner. She stopped in front of Rachel and propped her hands on her hips. "She's gorgeous, which is not a surprise."

"Meet my wife, Gena," Lucas said as the smaller woman walked a circle around Rachel like she was checking out a prize pony.

"Nice to...meet you." Rachel had to swivel her head to find her. She moved like a mini tornado. Gena's glossy hair was smoothed back into a ponytail, her low-cut, red silk shirt not the least bit understated and her black jeans as tight as possible.

"You've been around our boy for a while." Gena narrowed hazel-colored eyes.

"Claws in," Tag instructed, palming Rachel's back. The second he touched her, she relaxed some.

"You like her." Gena grinned up at him.

"We don't get out much," Lucas said to Rachel in explanation. He placed the little girl in his arms on the floor—or tried to, anyway.

"Tad!" The girl held out both arms and reached for Tag. He obliged, taking her into his arms. "Airplane!" she cried, which sounded like "*awwpwane*" but it wasn't hard to guess this little one had used Tag as her amusement park on more than one occasion.

As have I, Rachel thought with a smirk. Then her smirk died as she eyed Tag with a toddler on his hip. The sight of Lucas had been sweet and unexpected. But Tag? Who smiled as the girl tugged on his beard . . .

Ovary. Explosion.

"No time, Arianna," Gena said, extracting her daughter from Tag's hold.

Tag winked at Rachel, whose knees went the consistency of jelly.

"You can play airplane with Aunt Missy," Gena was saying to Arianna. "Melissa! We're going!"

A dark-haired woman appeared in the doorway of the living room and took hold of Arianna. Melissa was obviously Gena's sister. She looked exactly like Gena but with no visible tattoos and shorter hair.

"The crying is our cue to leave," Lucas said smoothly, handing his wife her coat and pulling on his black leather jacket.

Thirty minutes later, they were at La Prie, a top-notch

steak house with swanky decor and the snootiest waiters Rachel had ever encountered. She normally didn't understand the fuss of a place like this, but tonight, she decided to enjoy being doted on. A bottle of wine stood on the table between Rachel and Gena, who were both working on their second glasses.

Tag and Lucas, beers in hand, were laughing about who-knew-what. Rachel was having a hard time listening in on their conversation since Gena had been dominating theirs. Jury was still out on whether or not Rachel liked the woman. She was...audacious.

"So." Gena elevated her balloon-shaped wineglass in one hand. "I know how you two met—a dog in the same apartment building. But what is it about you that has our boy, Tag, so unwilling to back down?"

"Babe." This from Lucas, who sent an apologetic smile to Rachel. "Think you could hold off the KGB-style questioning until after we eat?"

"Don't you want to know why Tag has invited us out to dinner to meet her?" Gena asked, gesturing to Rachel. "The last woman he was dating that I met was..." Gena froze, mouth open, then clapped her lips shut and regarded Tag. "My gosh. I think it was the night I picked up Lucas."

"You didn't pick me up," Lucas corrected.

Tag leaned close to Rachel and said, "You're in for a treat."

"I did so," Gena argued, putting her glass down. "I saw you and *Flex Luthor* over here working your wiles on a horde of skanks—"

Rachel sputtered into her glass, equally amused by Tag's nickname and hearing Gena refer to a "horde" of skanks. She dabbed her lips with a napkin as Tag patted her back and laughed. Seriously, the man took everything in stride.

"—and I walked right up in between you and said—"

"I know what you said." Lucas smiled genuinely.

"Then tell me." Gena batted black lashes.

"You said, 'I bet by night's end you won't remember a single one of these girls' names, but you won't ever forget mine.'" Lucas's smile went wonky and his eyes turned the color of melted caramel. "Then she introduced herself."

"Is that how a girl lands a player?" Rachel quipped, lifting her own wineglass.

"How'd you snag this one?" Gena asked, tipping her chin at Tag.

Rachel wasn't sure she'd "snagged" Tag permanently, but she had him for now.

"I didn't. Tag made me go to Hawaii."

Gena's brows rose.

"You weren't exactly fighting me," Tag said, a twinkle in his eye. "At all."

Rachel froze, worried about how much more Tag might say. Turned out he didn't say more, only sent her a knowing glance.

"Well, you had her thirty thousand feet in the air. I imagine it was because she had nowhere to go." Gena turned her attention from Tag and leveled Rachel with a look. "You know he's one of the good ones, right? Have you figured out that much yet?"

A rose-red blush stole Rachel's cheeks. She had figured that out.

"Rach, let's go powder our noses." Without waiting for

her answer, Gena stood and took Rachel's hand, dragging her toward the back of the restaurant, around the tidy square tables and diners and waitstaff dressed in black. The restroom was sepia toned, with a gilded gold mirror on the wall. Gena didn't move for a stall but stopped in front of the mirror and faced Rachel's reflection. "Tag has a lot of girl friends."

Rachel blinked at Gena, trying to decide if she was being rude or factual. "A lot of ... girlfriends?"

"No." Gena shook her head as she dug through her purse and came out with a tube of red lipstick. "Girl *space* friends. Two words."

"Oh ... kay."

"Do you know why Tag has a lot of girl friends?"

"Because he's insanely attractive?" Rachel guessed, mentally tacking on *and really good in bed.*

"Yes, and because he's well versed at letting them down. They never hate him." She finished with the lipstick and offered it to Rachel, who turned her down with a shake of her head. "He's charming and sincere and kind and never a prick about it. So they end up liking him. He gets invited to weddings by exes often."

"Weddings he doesn't go to," Rachel said, recalling his reaction in Hawaii.

Gena turned from her reflection to face Rachel. "You know plenty."

"We've been hanging out a while."

"Hmm." Gena's hawk-like eyes grazed Rachel from head to feet and back up again. "But he's given you no such speech."

"Not yet."

"And you're here." Gena smiled and took a step closer

to Rachel. It was the first moment Rachel felt any kind of warmth from the other woman. "We're his best friends. And he brought you to meet us."

She enunciated the words *to meet us* meticulously.

"Do you know why?" Rachel couldn't help asking.

Gena let out a loud *ha-ha!* then grabbed one of Rachel's hands and squeezed. "Rachel, gorgeous. He likes you. A lot. I foresee us spending more time together."

The rest of dinner was less of an inquisition, which was awesome. It was also weirdly normal. Conversation flowed easily between the four of them, sometimes between the couples, but there was also a moment where Lucas and Rachel were talking about music in a cross conversation while Tag and Gena discussed the kids. Rachel found it easy to sink into her seat, wineglass aloft, and laugh at Lucas's jokes or listen intently as Tag spoke about his adventures traveling for work.

When the plates were cleared, Tag reached for the check but Gena slammed her palm onto the black book. "Over my dead body."

"Gena." Tag already had his wallet out.

"No. You're not the only one around here capable of doling out free dinners. This is on us."

Tag opened his mouth but Lucas held up a finger. "Listen to her, Taggart."

Gena burst out laughing. Tag grumbled something that sounded like "thanks, buddy" as he shoved his wallet into his jeans.

"Taggart?" Rachel couldn't help herself. She had to know.

"It's a family name."

"It's a pussy name," Lucas added helpfully as he tucked

his credit card into the book and handed it to the server. "But we love him anyway."

"You weren't going to tell me?" Rachel asked through her own bout of laughter.

"No." Tag polished off his wine, his gaze locked on Rachel's eyes for a very long time. Then he leaned closer, closer, until those beard-surrounded lips touched hers in the softest, most delicious kiss…

"God, they're adorable."

That was Gena. And the moment she spoke, Tag's smile overtook his face.

"I was going to say after-party, but you two look as if you have plans not involving us," Lucas said.

"After-party is just our style," Tag said. "What'd you have in mind?"

Lucas waggled his eyebrows. "You'll see."

* * *

"Paris Layne, I can't believe it!" Rachel shouted over the cheers erupting around them.

Lucas put his fingers in his mouth and whistled. Tag had to hand it to his buddy—Lucas knew how to impress. Front row tickets to a Paris Layne show in the United Center was impressive on its own, but for a concert of this size and a music sensation this popular, well—

Hands cupping her mouth, Rachel howled as Paris came to the edge of the stage where they were standing and sang the beginning of one of her biggest hits. Tag's eyes left the starlet to take in the blonde of his own.

Rachel Foster. Watching her shake her *thang* made him want to lift her up and kiss the life out of her. Made him want to see how many more concerts he could swindle out of Luc. Made him want to hang on to her and not let go.

He let the thought sink in slowly, throughout the concert, and then after as they filed out in a massive crowd of people and into the limo Tag had arranged. Hey, he might not be permitted to pay for dinner or the concert, but the second he learned where they were going, he called to arrange a limo and have his car dropped off at Crane Tower.

"Such a show-off," Gena commented as they clambered into the back of the long, shiny black car.

"Kill an hour, will you, Bill?" Tag passed a hundred through the window and then slid it closed for privacy.

"Kill Bill," Gena said with a snort.

Lucas was already pouring the champagne. Tag had asked for three bottles, chilled, and they were waiting in ice. Luc didn't have to be asked twice.

"I want a pizza," Rachel said, slumping. "I danced off all my dinner."

Her grin was contagious. Tag grinned back.

"Don't say that," Gena warned. "He'll—"

"Bill." Tag slid open the divider again. "Call Uno's and order us two everythings and a cheese and whatever you'd like."

"Yes, sir," Bill said before once again disappearing behind the opaque glass.

"He'll do that," Gena finished. She raised her glass. "To Taggart Crane."

"Taggart!" Rachel and Lucas said in unison.

"Fuck all of you."

"Or just the blond one." Gena sent Rachel a saucy wink, and Rachel burst out laughing. It was hard to believe she'd ever been nervous around him. Nervous to touch him, nervous to be near him. Now she sat, pressed to his side like she belonged there. What he couldn't get over is that he felt like she did.

More firsts.

"Champagne." Gena thrust glasses into Rachel's and Tag's hands.

"You can kiss me if you want to," Rachel said, keeping her voice low when Gena and Lucas started chatting to each other.

"Not afraid of me any longer, Dimples?"

She shook her head, those adorable dents making their appearance on each side of her face. He pushed his fingers into her hair, leaned in, and kissed her, not caring if his friends were wolf-whistling from the back of the limo.

"Like we're kids again," Luc grumbled.

"Aw, I think they're cute," Gena argued.

When the kiss heard 'round the limo was through, Rachel sipped her champagne and gave him a look through veiled lashes communicating one thing and one thing only: she wanted him.

Best news Tag received all evening.

* * *

"Catch you at the gym. Wednesday?" Lucas stepped out of the limo, taking his slightly inebriated wife by the hand. Gena talked like a sailor when she was drunk, and Tag always laughed at the random swear words she made up whenever drunk.

"Come on, shit-weasel!" she hollered, walking backward toward the house.

"Excuse me, I have to remind my wife we have children."

"Okay, shit-weasel, have a good night." Tag waved as Luc shut the door.

Rachel sobered from her giggles and relinquished her flute. "I had way too much champagne."

"Depends. Are you willing to go home with me?"

"Yes." A smile.

"Then you've had just enough." He smiled back.

"I think we should have sex back here." Her eyes went wide.

"You sure?" He couldn't help chuckling. "That was probably the champagne talking. I'm all for taking you to bed, but—what are you doing?"

She was undoing his shirt buttons. That's what she was doing. He was no stranger to being stripped or for a woman to ask to see him naked from the waist up, but this was Rachel, and they were sort of in public. And now she was working on his belt buckle.

Her mouth hit his for a long kiss; then she pulled away and whispered, "Tell Bill up there to take the long way home."

"Honey, I'll tell him to take all night." He cupped her face with his palm. He'd had plenty to drink, too, and sex in the back of this car right now with her sounded like heaven.

She whispered two words: "Do it."

Then he was kissing her, with no further convincing necessary on her part.

CHAPTER 20

She rises."

Rachel groaned as she stepped out of his bedroom wearing his button-down shirt from last night and dragging the blanket from the bed along with her. Her hair was a tangled blond mess, her legs bare and beautiful, and every last thing he did with her in the limo flickered through his head like a movie.

Pushing her skirt up her thighs.

Peeling her panties down her legs.

Going down on her on the seat while she writhed, and when she was wet and ready sliding all the way home.

Okay, enough of that or he'd develop a limp from the hard-on already trying to make an appearance this morning. He couldn't get enough of this woman. She'd saturated his life, and he'd soaked her in, allowing her to take up most of his space. For a guy who liked free rein of said space, he found he didn't mind as much as he'd have thought.

"My queen," he greeted, pouring her a cup of coffee. "How ya feeling?"

"Champagne gives me a headache." She plopped on his couch, and he walked into the living room, her coffee in hand.

"Especially when you drink a vat of it. Here. This'll help."

"Thank you."

"You're sexy in the morning, Dimples."

"Shut. Up."

Next to her, he pushed her hair off her face and leaned in to lay a kiss on her mouth. "I let you sleep, so you have to take a shower with me. Wash my back."

"I do not," she said against the rim of her mug, but she was smiling. "What's on the agenda today?"

"Make an appearance at the Crane for an invigorating conference meeting with the board." He planned on presenting the plans for the Oahu bar.

"Are you giving a presentation?"

"Not officially. But I do have handouts." He barely managed a saccharine smile. There was no love lost between the board that had stuck their noses in his business then out again, then asked for details at the last minute. But he understood it was part of the Crane gig. Plus, he was damn proud of those plans.

"Don't forget to tell them about the redesign and the server's wells." Eyes bright, she turned to face him. "And how you're going to move the bar back and provide extra seating. Oh, and..."

As she talked, he listened, admiring her pluck and her

ability and the fact she was wearing a blanket in his penthouse. She looked at home here. She looked like his.

The thought sent him down another path, one laced with women who had been in this very penthouse, on this very couch, looking sleepy and satisfied like the girl there now. Thoughts about morning sex and breakfast and shared showers were nothing new, but this was the first time he'd ever thought the woman on his couch looked like she belonged with him. *To* him.

Maybe this was how it happened. The beginning of what Luc and Gena had. He remembered his best friend after he'd met Gena. Luc was a changed man. Walked around constantly with a goofy smile on his face. He was exclusive from the start with her. Tag was always exclusive with the women he saw, right up until the point he let them go.

Right about now, he would plan his escape, work out the details of how to send the girl on his couch packing.

"...the map for the liquor placement is important because there will be less spillage. Less spillage equals more profit," she finished with zest.

"Got it."

"Knock 'em dead." She sipped her coffee and hummed in the back of her throat.

"Your turn. What's on your agenda today?" he asked.

"Oh...just some...things."

"Some things."

"Yeah." She bit down on her lip and elevated her coffee cup. He put a hand on her knee and watched her, waiting. Seconds ticked by before she rolled her eyes. "Fine! I'll tell you."

"Only if you want to," he said easily.

"I'm looking for an apartment today."

"Oh yeah?" His chest hammered at the surprise those words caused, and more surprise coated him as he realized he was surprised. She had roommates, but she'd stayed here some, too. He guessed he'd gotten a little used to that arrangement. His forehead creased.

"Which is a little backwards, because I haven't found a job yet," she continued. "I did get one callback, but it paid less than bartending for a receptionist position. I thought it'd be simpler to land a marketing gig since I can list Crane Hotels on my resume." Her face scrunched. "That's okay, right?"

"Of course it's okay. I didn't realize you were looking." He stole her coffee mug and took a sip.

"Didn't I mention it?" She looked genuinely perplexed.

"No." He handed back the mug, once again in the position of being the last to know.

"Oh. Well. Now you know. I've scheduled a few showings at apartments today. I figure if I can find one within a reasonable price range, I can wiggle by until I land the elusive professional job I seek."

"Why the rush?"

"Bree and Dean found a house. They're ready to move out on their own, like yesterday. I don't want to hold them up. Ideally I'd have secured a better-paying job by now, but as luck would have it, I'm doing things ass-backwards."

"Can I help?" he asked, unsure what he was offering.

"No. I've got everything under control. And you have a meeting." She touched her finger to his chin and rubbed his beard.

He frowned, irked, though he wasn't sure why. He wanted do something—help somehow. Maybe he was irked that she hadn't asked for his help. He owned a damn apartment building. He knew about rentals and the area. It would only make sense to ask him his opinion, but she hadn't.

"You know if you needed money, I technically owe you for helping me in Hawaii."

"Absolutely not." Her eyes were fierce, her tone angry.

"Dimples."

"No, Tag. I can't and won't take your money." She pressed her lips into a line, giving him a flat smile. "Thank you for the offer, but I don't need to be bailed out."

He blew out a breath of defeat. That stubborn streak of hers was a mile wide.

"At least let me call you a car so you don't have to take cabs all over the city." She wouldn't let him help her with the place to live, fine, but he could at least get her transportation for the day.

She shook her head.

"You can ride home and decide then. I'd drive you myself if I didn't have work."

Her turn to sigh.

"It's not a big deal."

"Okay. Yes, thank you."

"Yeah?" Her giving him that inch made him feel as triumphant as if he'd won a mile.

"A car would be great. *You've* been great."

"An hour work for you?" he asked as he dialed on his cell phone.

"Better make it two. I did promise you a shower," she replied with a wink. "You have a big back."

* * *

By afternoon, Tag had finished his pitch to the board, ending it with, "Construction starts tomorrow. Oahu is the test."

From the board came nothing but a penetrating silence. He and Reese exchanged glances.

"This is some nice work, Tag," Frank said.

Well, knock me over with a motherfucking feather.

Reese's eyebrows lifted, mirroring Tag's shock.

"This is definitely one way to go about it," added Lilith, the only female board member. She was less impressed, and Tag had expected that. She probably didn't want to agree with Frank publicly either. Those two.

Frank tucked the proposal under his legal pad. "Now. Who's going to Dylan's for Cobb salad?"

The board stood collectively, commenting on dinner and drinks and in general filing out of the boardroom like a pack of lemmings. Or a herd of lemmings. As the last person vanished past the window of the conference room, Tag faced his brother.

"What do you call a group of lemmings? A herd or a pack?"

"No idea." Reese smiled, understanding Tag's reference. "I guess Frank's comment is as close to a compliment as you can expect."

"Whatever." Tag stood and gathered his pencil and blank pad of paper. "I don't need to be coddled."

"Tag," Reese said from behind him. "Great work."

Now that praise he could feel proud about. "Thanks, bro."

"Too bad you're dating her," Reese said as they walked the corridor to his office.

"Why?" Tag stopped short of turning right toward Bobbie's receptionist desk.

"Rachel's smart. Knows more about business than your average bartender." Reese wrapped a hand around the doorknob. "She'd fit in around here, but I'm guessing when you break up with her, you don't want to bump into her at the office."

Tag tracked back to his brother and stopped, crossing his arms over his chest. "Something on your mind?"

Reese folded his arms, mirroring Tag. "You're not in a hurry to blow this one off, are you?"

"Since when do you care about my love life?"

"Since you referred to it as a 'love' life." His lips hitched into a smirk.

Had him there.

"She doesn't want to be entangled with Crane money and me at the same time."

"I respect that." Reese nodded.

"Yeah?" Tag paused to listen, interested in what his brother thought. Because Tag would like to solve her problems, and Rachel wanted to do everything herself.

"You may have found the first girl you can't appease with money. That's probably why she's still around." At that parting observation, Reese opened his office door.

"Hang on. I don't buy my dates, if that's what you're saying." Tag's defenses rose. "I have money. I spend it. End of story."

"And if you weren't footing the bill, how many of those dates do you think you'd have had over the last decade?" When Tag didn't answer, Reese cocked his head. "Rachel being independent isn't a bad thing. It works for Merina and me."

"You two were married before you liked each other." Tag shook his head and smiled. "I think it's safe to say your playbook is unique to the two of you."

"Isn't that the truth," Reese said dryly. "I'm stopping by to see Eli tonight. Coming?"

"He still in a cheery mood?"

"Oh, the cheeriest," Reese deadpanned. "The therapist ramped up his rehabilitation today."

"I bet his swearing can be heard from here if we listen closely."

They fell silent, their smiles slipping away, the seriousness of what had happened to their brother settling in the air between them.

"I hate this for him," Reese said, his voice steel. "I can fix anything. But I can't fix this."

Tag had felt a similar helplessness since the moment he saw the flattened bit of sheet in the hospital room. "I know."

"He doesn't want to admit it, but he's hurting. And not just physically."

"I know." Tag had seen it too. Behind the bitterness and anger, Eli was in pain. The loss he'd suffered, the atrocities he'd witnessed.

"I'd rather have him without a leg than not at all," Reese said, and it might have been the first time any of them had admitted as much aloud.

They shared another penetrating length of silence.

"Tonight then?" Reese asked.

"Yeah." Tag would do anything for his brothers. They'd drag Eli through this kicking and screaming if they had to, but Eli was going to be whole again. That was a vow Tag wouldn't break.

CHAPTER 21

"I used to hate leg day." Tag blew out a breath and pushed his feet against the machine one final time before dropping the weights with a *clang*. He leaned forward and snatched his towel, mopping his neck. "Now I'm grateful to have legs to bitch about."

"Eli," Lucas grunted, finishing a sit-up before lying flat on his back on the mat. The gym was empty today. Typical for spring. Most of the people who'd made New Year's resolutions to get into shape had given up, leaving the diehards to their workouts.

"Yeah."

"How's he doing?" Lucas did one final sit-up and wrapped his arms around his knees.

"He's Eli." Tag lifted an eyebrow. "He's 'fine.'"

Last night Reese and Tag had showed up at Eli's warehouse apartment to find Eli at the end of a session with his physical therapist. They'd hired a male therapist, knowing that Eli's particularly abrasive attitude might be tempered by a guy he could relate to. The therapist they'd found was former military, tough, and didn't take any shit. Eli seemed to be conforming and had done his leg exercises with minimal swearing.

"I'm not used to seeing him without a leg yet."

Tag might never get used to it, and he had no idea how the hell Eli felt about it either. His brother hadn't exactly opened up.

"He has these bouts of pain. Last night they were so close together..." Eli had a big one during dinner—delivered submarine sandwiches. Eli had cried out and slumped over in his chair. Tag had vacillated between unhinged anger that this had happened to one of the best people he knew and the now familiar feeling of helplessness that he couldn't do a damn thing to help Eli through it. After Eli had caught his breath, he'd left his veggie sub uneaten and retreated to his bedroom.

"He's tough as nails, Tag. Always has been," Lucas said gently, pulling Tag from his thoughts. "He's going to make it through this and come out better for it."

God, he hoped so.

"Keep getting in his face. He needs you, even if he doesn't show it."

"I know." Tag reached for his water bottle. No way was he going to bail on his brother. Eli was stuck with him. "What are you grinning like a jackass about?"

"Rachel," Lucas said, pushing himself to standing and snagging his own water bottle in the process.

Tag stood, too, and Lucas kept smiling, even when he took a drink of his water.

"Oh, how the mighty have fallen." Seriously. Lucas looked like the freaking Joker.

"What are you talking about?" Tag tossed his towel over his shoulder and angled for the exit. He knew exactly what Lucas was talking about, and frankly, he didn't want to talk about it.

"You and Rachel." Lucas followed him out of Crane Tower's gym and into the elevator. Tag punched the button for his penthouse.

"You joining me in the shower or something?" he grumbled as they rode up.

"I'm going to use *one* of your showers, and then I will require a beer and an explanation."

"For?" Tag stepped out on his floor and opened his front door.

"Come on. You're not going to admit it?"

"Lucas. What?" Tag elevated his arms, half pissed, half terrified at what his best friend was about to say. Because he knew. God help him, Tag knew exactly what Lucas was about to say. Then with an even bigger shit-eating grin, Lucas stabbed the air and told him.

"You're spun."

"Am not." Tag tossed a hand and walked to his bedroom. "Towels in the hall." But Lucas wasn't shaken.

"Like a Tilt-A-Whirl, Taggart Crane. You are fucking spun."

Tag stopped in the doorway and regarded the ceiling, looking for what, he wasn't sure. Strength? Answers? A clue Lucas was wrong?

Spun was a term they'd used when one by one their friends began falling victims to women, losing their single status and voluntarily handing over their man cards.

Lucas was among the last, save for Tag, who'd kept the dream alive.

"Shit, I thought I was going to be sick the night when we all went to the concert," Luc said. "And not because you and Rachel were kissy-facing all night."

"Give me a break." Tag so did not want to have this convo with his best bud. Not now. Not ever.

"I live vicariously through you." Luc put a palm to his chest. "Through your conquests and exploits. I love my wife, but watching a player that good at the game turn in his balls..." He gave his head a reverent shake. "You are a master. Or used to be, anyway."

"Lucas, for Christ's sake."

"You know when to get out, how to keep the honeys happy. I swear the only thing you've ever been scared of in your life is one of them sticking around."

Tag took a deep breath and wondered if he marched over and punched Lucas in the face if he'd shut up or hit him back.

"You act different with her. And it's because you're spun," Lucas continued. "I think you know it, and I think you want Rachel to know it. Have you told her yet? Have you tested out the three-word bomb in the bathroom mirror?"

"I'm not spun. I'm not scared," Tag bellowed. "And if you'd like to find your own balls and have a manly discussion when I'm out of the shower, I'll offer you a beer. You keep going with this chick shit, you can leave."

Without waiting for Lucas's response, Tag shut his bedroom door, but through the wood, he heard his so-called friend comment, "Never thought I'd see the day."

Tag kicked off his sneakers and went to the bathroom

sink, bracing his hands on the edges. He regarded his reflection, a slightly sweaty guy who needed a shower and a slap in the face.

Wake up, man.

He hadn't practiced the three-word bomb in the mirror like Lucas had suggested, and he wouldn't do it now. But Tag was beginning to think he'd lied to his best friend—that he'd been lying to himself.

Because right now the Tag in the mirror looked both scared *and* spun.

* * *

Since Rachel had the day off work, her plan was to start packing up her room at the apartment before her date with Tag that night.

Today's apartment hunt hadn't fared much better than her recent job hunt. She'd spent the afternoon looking at rinky-dink living spaces that, after deposit and first month's rent, she could only afford for two more months...*maybe*.

She'd have thought the Hawaii gig she'd helped Tag with would shine on her resume, but so far none of the companies where she'd applied had been impressed by her advising on a major redesign. Though, there was one place that would be impressed.

Crane Hotels.

She'd had the thought before—briefly. During her online apartment hunt, she'd even looked up Crane Hotels headquarters. Turned out the building, separate from the Crane where the CEO's offices were located, was hiring.

In marketing.

She'd shut the computer window, determined to find work outside of the Crane realm. Now that she thought about it, though, why couldn't she apply? It wasn't as if Tag had carved out a position for her. If she applied blind, and a manager hired her for HQ, Tag wouldn't find out unless said manager called him as a reference. Unlikely. Tag was in charge of Guest and Restaurant Services, not human resources.

Plus, she was getting desperate.

Her cell buzzed, and Rachel stared at the name on the screen for the length of three rings before pressing the Accept button.

"Hi, Mom."

"Hey, sweetheart! I hadn't heard from you in a while so I assumed you've been busy with work and watching the big dog for your friend."

"You're right about busy, but I'm not dog sitting any longer." Rachel piled books into a box while she talked, unsure why she'd kept so many. Half were college texts and the other half paperback novels she could easily replace if she ever wanted to reread them. She thought of Tag and his well-worn paperback.

Use is a sign of love.

With a smile, she stacked the paperbacks into the box.

"...And your cousin Sheryl is pregnant. So the wedding should be interesting."

"Really."

"I know. Scandal, right?" Her mother sipped, drinking her evening tea no doubt. "But she's only ten weeks, so it's not like she's walking down the aisle with a baby bump."

Through a laugh, Rachel said, "I'm happy for her."

"Yes, so am I. Rich is a nice man," she said of Sheryl's groom. "How's work going?"

"Well. It's going well." Her heart rattled out an unsteady series of beats. She hadn't shared the whole truth with her mom. She supposed now was as good a time as any. "I don't actually have the job you're referring to," she finally admitted. "I didn't want to tell you because then I'd have to tell you how Shaun betrayed me."

"Rachel. What do you mean?" Her mom's concern was palpable. "It's his fault you don't have a job?"

"It's *my* fault I don't have my marketing job." She was the one who'd allowed herself to be bullied out of the company, after all. "But I do have a job. Just not one where high heels are standard." From there, she told her mother everything, from the presentation to Shaun taking all the credit, to the moment when she took the dog sitting job from a male regular at the bar. She debated for a few seconds before sharing the part about Tag knocking on her door.

"Are you and Tag . . . ?"

"We're seeing each other." Which was a parent-friendly way to say they were sleeping together. But her mother didn't need to know the details or that Tag was a billionaire, for God's sake. Baby steps.

"I helped him out with a bar project recently. In Hawaii."

"Hawaii!"

"I didn't want you to worry. Or get the wrong idea," Rachel was quick to say. Even though the idea her mom had was probably pretty close to the right one. "Anyway, he wanted to pay me for going, but I didn't let him."

"Smart girl."

At that, Rachel's shoulders pulled back. Her mother had always respected Rachel's independence. It felt nice to have that acknowledged. "It's been a few weeks and I haven't had any luck finding a corporate job, but there is an opening at...uh, the place Tag works."

"Would he put in a good word for you?"

Rachel nearly laughed, swallowing down the words *You mean with his brother the CEO?*

"That's just it. I don't want him to." She wanted to do this on her own. Prove she could do it on her own. "Do you think it'd be wrong to apply and not tell him?"

"I think you should apply, and I think you should tell him," her mother stated without hesitation.

"I don't want him pulling any strings."

"Then tell him so."

Rachel sighed.

"Don't start off your relationship with a lie, Rach. It won't end well."

She appreciated her mom's advice, but Keri Foster wasn't all the way in the know. Rachel and Tag had a non-traditional relationship. When it ended, she didn't want her employer thinking the only way she'd landed the job was on the merits of the man she had been sleeping with. It had been all too easy for her last employer to believe Shaun had done the heavy lifting. Her hard work had been completely overlooked. She refused to let it happen again.

"Thanks, Mom," she said anyway. "That's good advice."

"That's what I'm here for."

They chatted a while longer before exchanging "I love

yous" and hanging up. Rachel dropped her phone on the bed next to her, thought for a second, then pushed out of bed.

She dug her laptop out from under her work clothes and pecked in the Web address for Crane Hotels HQ. Sure enough, the listing for marketing manager was still available.

Biting down on her lip, she decided to go for it. Maybe they'd never call and she wouldn't have to worry about it. But maybe they would, and she could finally put down a deposit on her own place and rest in the knowledge that she'd taken care of her own problems without the help of her billionaire boyfriend.

* * *

Tag's fingers danced over her bare shoulder as they faced each other in his bed. They'd gone to dinner at a no-muss, no-fuss pub. She'd chatted about her day spent packing boxes and conveniently avoided the topic of putting in an online application at Crane Hotels. Tag talked about work some, but mostly listened to her.

Afterward, they'd come back to his place and immediately stumbled into the bedroom and out of their clothes. Neither of them was interested in remaining dressed when they were together.

"What are you best at?" His voice was a silken murmur as he ran the pads of his fingers down her shoulder to the bend of her elbow.

"What's that supposed to mean?" Her mind on the fantastic way they spent the last forty minutes, she had no idea where his question was leading.

"I've created a monster. Told you that you were good in bed." His throat bobbed when he laughed.

She couldn't keep her smile from emerging. He had created a monster. She'd never had this much sex with Shaun, and she had been with him for almost two years. Tag was like a drug. A long-haired, bearded, wide-bodied, addictive drug.

"I'm asking about your skills outside of my mattress, Dimples. What skills did you highlight on your resume? There has to be a reason you're not turning up any leads."

Oh, right. Her resume.

She hadn't intended on bringing up her job hunt tonight at all. The less she talked about it, the less bad she felt about circumventing him for the position at Crane HQ.

"Are you sure marketing is your bag?" Tag asked, continuing to chase chills down her arm as he ran his fingers down and up again. "Do you like sales? Would you like to work in the service industry?"

"I do work in the service industry," she said with a smile.

"You know what I mean. Would you like to do something like I do?"

"What is it that you do?" She scrunched her brow and feigned confusion. "Travel, party, write your own dress code..."

A laugh burst from her when he rolled over the top of her, careful to keep from crushing her. Elbows tucked at her sides, she was thoroughly trapped beneath him, which was the best place to be. His weight, his warmth, the veil of hair shrouding them...He was so sexy it hurt.

"Is this conversation too responsible for you?" He ran

his lips along the edge of her ear, sending droves of tingles down the length of her body.

"Yes. I'd like to be irresponsible." She raked her fingers into his hair and he faced her, his head tilted, his eyes twinkling. Something about that twinkle made her heart *ka-thud*. The way his eyes held hers for the span of several hectic beats, and the way Tag lowered his lips in the softest, sweetest kiss.

"Are you staying with me tonight? I'll make you breakfast."

"How can I turn down breakfast?" she asked with a small smile. "You make better coffee than my roommates."

"My view is better."

She shook her head and smoothed one hand along Tag's beard, her eyes flitting down to his tempting mouth. "Right now, mine's pretty good, too."

Thunder crashed outside and rain pelted the wide windows.

He rolled over but kept her tucked against him, his arm locked around her waist. "Smart of you to stay."

She sighed, taking in the heavy dark clouds dominating the black sky, the feel of Tag blanketing her back. Being in his arms made her feel safe and cherished.

A big part of her wanted to lean into that feeling and let herself fall. But after recovering from a brutal tumble that had left her nearly homeless, practically jobless, and had taken a bite out of her confidence, she wasn't able to let go all the way.

Maybe a little, though, she thought as she closed her eyes and breathed in Tag's spicy scent.

Just until morning.

CHAPTER 22

Tag had spent the last week and a half consulting contractors and having plans drawn up for Oahu. As soon as they tested the design and had a fair amount of data, then he'd be on to creating a set of plans for each Crane hotel and delegating to the hotel managers. After that, he'd check on progress, visit several of them randomly, and watch the profits outweigh the expenditures.

With everything he'd had to do for work, the whole "spun" thing had retreated to the back of Tag's mind. He and Rachel went to dinners, had sex, and had shared an overnight, and no part of him had retreated into freak-out mode.

He saw no reason to put a label on what they were doing. It was what it was. She was cool; he was cool. *C'est la vie*.

Meeting over, workday hoopla handled, he invited Reese to racquetball. Twenty minutes later, he and his brother were sweating from pounding a blue ball into the wall at the Crane's gym downstairs from Reese's office. Tag swiped at nothing but air, giving Reese the winning point on the tie-breaking game.

"Shit!" Tag said, his voice echoing off the empty room.

"Them's the breaks." Reese, breathing heavily, rested his hands on his hips.

"Smugness suits you," Tag panted, putting away the racquets and the ball. Water bottles in hand, they walked to the locker room.

"By the way, I was surprised you reconsidered," Reese said.

"Reconsidered what? Challenging you to racquetball?"

"Not what I meant, but that would be a wise move." Reese shot a stream of water into his mouth from his bottle.

"What is up with the sudden insurgence of mad skills?" Tag asked, snagging a towel. "Have you been practicing?"

"I'll never tell."

Cheating bastard. He'd been practicing.

"I meant I was surprised you reconsidered the hiring Rachel thing."

Tag freed the band tying back his hair. "What are you talking about?"

"Headquarters. The marketing position?" His brother's brows lifted, then lowered over his nose. "I thought you pushed that through. She applied a week ago, and today I received a call to conduct a second interview."

"You only do that for upper management."

"And for my brother's girlfriends."

"She's not my girlfriend."

Reese laughed, a hearty, real, and rare belly laugh. "I remember you saying something similar when you were thirteen and a neighbor girl was following you everywhere. You haven't changed much."

Tag scowled, the accusation not sitting well with him at all.

"It's Mom's fault," Reese said quietly. So quietly, Tag wasn't sure he'd heard correctly.

"What is?"

Reese pulled in a deep breath before he continued, and Tag swore the air pressure in the room increased. "She died. She left us. No warning, no premonition. One day she was there, and then we never saw her again."

Tag's chest felt like an elephant was using him as a recliner. His ribs crushed as his breathing went shallow. The casket had been closed at Mom's funeral, so when Reese said they had never seen her again, he wasn't exaggerating.

"I can't remember the last thing we did together," Tag said, heavy from sadness. "I have memories, but that day in particular. Nothing. Vaguely, I remember my teacher pulling me out of class. That's it."

"Tag, you were eleven." Reese's hand hit Tag's shoulder and squeezed. "You didn't know what the hell to do with that news. None of us did."

A pair of guys squeaked by on their way to the court and Tag and Reese stepped aside to let them pass. It was the interruption they both needed to get out of the mire of memories of Luna Crane. Losing her was one of those life experiences that would forever be unresolved.

"My point is," Reese said after the locker room was

empty again, "Mom left behind three boys who grew into men allergic to commitment. We learned at a young age that loss happened"—he snapped his fingers, the sharp sound making Tag flinch—"like that."

"Does Merina have you in therapy or something?" Tag asked.

"She should." Reese raised an eyebrow self-deprecatingly and the air lightened. Tag felt like he could breathe again.

"Your nervousness over having Rachel close is not that unusual."

"I'm not nervous," Tag bit out. He was tired of everyone examining his feelings for him. "I didn't know she applied at Crane HQ, that's it. The news surprised me."

Reese nodded, his mouth flat. Then he said, "I can cancel the interview if you like. Or turn her down."

"Is she right for the position?"

"Lonnie loves her. He couldn't say enough about how well she'd interviewed and how well he thought she'd fit in to the department."

"Then don't cancel the interview."

"Okay." Reese gave him a curt nod and headed for the showers.

Tag sat on a nearby bench and dropped his head back on a locker. He didn't mind if Rachel worked for Crane. What he minded was that she didn't tell him. Hell, he'd brought up the topic of her job hunt while they were lying in bed the other night, bare-assed naked and looking right into each other's eyes.

Why hadn't she told him?

He was beginning to think he wasn't the only commitment-phobe around.

* * *

Rachel was grinning to herself at work. So she thought. Bree caught her.

"You look happy."

"I'm pretty thrilled about the apartment."

She'd found the perfect apartment this morning. After a few days of fruitless searches online and in person, she was about to beg Bree and Dean to take her with them to their new house. Then she'd found the place. With her first Crane interview having gone so well, she only had to get through the second one, and she was home free.

"There is something I didn't tell you about yet," Rachel said, sidling over to Bree behind the bar. There were a few beer drinkers sitting there, but the Andromeda was otherwise slow. "I interviewed at Crane Hotels for a marketing position."

"That's great!" Bree shook her head, but she was smiling. "Tag Crane is your lucky rabbit's foot."

"Oh, well, he doesn't know. I wanted to see if I could get the job without his help. I even asked the manager who interviewed me yesterday not to say anything to him. He said he wouldn't. He asked me back for a second interview tomorrow."

"So you're telling Tag soon?" Bree's question sounded more like a suggestion.

"I'm going to do the second interview first, but right after, I'll tell him. I promise. Do you think I should take him to dinner or drinks for the announcement, or maybe strip naked in his penthouse?"

"The last part will definitely soften the blow," her friend said with a giggle.

* * *

"Tomorrow" came quick. Rachel was nervous and excited, but overall feeling confident. Hopefully, she'd be popping a cork from a bottle of champagne with Tag after work today.

Things were coming together. Or at least she'd thought so until her phone rang, the display reading THE CRANE. She gulped down her trepidation before answering with a chipper "Hello?"

"Ms. Foster, this is Bobbie from Reese Crane's office. He'll be conducting your second interview at the Crane. Do you know the address?"

Her interview was with Reese? Rachel's shoulders slumped.

"I do."

"Wonderful," the other woman said, not sounding like she meant it. "See you at one."

"Thanks." At one o'clock she would meet with Reese. If Reese knew she was coming for an interview, he'd likely mentioned it to Tag. She debated a second, then dialed Tag's number. When he didn't answer, she further debated a text before deciding against it.

No need for her to feel guilty. Nothing had changed, not really. If he found out, she would explain why she'd circumvented him. Because she'd wanted to earn the job on her own. That sounded lame now that she imagined their conversation, but she mentally brushed it aside.

Everything would be fine.

That was her mantra until she stepped into the white-washed lobby of the Crane Hotel and spotted Tag.

He was leaning on a wall near the counter, dressed casually in a waffle Henley, sleeves pushed to his elbows, long necklace with a pendant hanging to the middle of his chest. She trickled her gaze down his jean-encased legs, crossed at the ankles and ending in a pair of laced boots.

Worried about his reaction, her heart sank to her feet.

He smiled—not at her, but at the girl behind the counter. Then his maned head swiveled to Rachel and his smile flattened. She tightened the belt on her turquoise coat, nerves eating her.

He pushed off the wall and stalked over as she approached him, her advancing steps growing less and less confident.

"I tried calling," she blurted when he was near.

He stared at her, silent.

"I didn't actually think I'd get a callback. I was desperate. See, I found this apartment, and—"

"Ready to do this?"

"Uh..." That threw her. She thought he'd demand an explanation. "Why? Are you coming in with me?"

"Sorry, Dimples. You're going to have to do the interview on your own." His features softened and he held out a hand for her to take. "I'll walk you up, though."

She slipped her hand into his, and gently, he grasped her fingers.

They strode to the elevator, Tag's steps casual. "You look amazing."

"Thank you." Guilt swathed her and she knew it was legit, because Tag hadn't said anything to make her feel guilty. She felt that way because she should have told him. Her mother was right. Her not telling him felt more like lying. She couldn't escape the idea that she'd hurt his feelings.

"Watch this," he said when the elevator doors opened. "She's utterly immune to me." He stepped out and in a big, boisterous voice, greeted Reese's secretary with a "Bobbie, darling."

"Mr. Crane," the woman replied tartly.

"You are ravishing in black," he told her.

"Here is the file you requested." The woman shot out her arm, at the end of it a manila folder.

"Thanks, doll. This is Rachel Foster. She has a one o'clock with Reese." He took the folder, turned, and winked at Rachel. When he passed her, he leaned down and said, "Dinner on me tonight. Literally if you like."

"Tag..."

"Knock 'em dead, Dimples." He nodded, his blue eyes warm; then he vanished into the elevator, leaving Rachel with the pucker-faced receptionist.

She'd make it up to him tonight. She'd explain why she didn't ask for his help and he'd understand. Though... it seemed like he understood already, and that didn't sit well with her, either.

Bobbie announced Rachel's arrival into her desk phone, jerking her out of her thoughts. She didn't have time to figure out what would happen with Tag after. Right now, she needed to land this job. Nail this interview. The double wood doors leading to Reese's office whooshed open and her throat tightened.

She took one step forward, and then another.

Tag's suited brother stood from his desk to greet her.

"Ms. Foster," he said. "Nice to see you again."

Here went nothing...

* * *

After the interview, Rachel treated herself to a Starbucks coffee with about a thousand calories, went window-shopping for clothes she hoped to someday afford, and finally headed to Crane Tower on foot.

She only hoped Tag was serious about dinner tonight. He hadn't called or texted, and neither did she. She'd rather show up unannounced. Maybe because part of her worried he might cancel, and all of her knew if he did, she'd deserve it.

Inside the apartment building, it so happened a friendly older guy walking a very big black-and-white splotched dog was headed her way.

Adonis let out a happy-sounding *woof!* They approached, Oliver wrapping his free arm around her in a quick hug.

"I've missed you," she said, meaning it. "You used to come in every week, and I haven't seen you lately."

Oliver sighed. "Lots of work, and I'm dieting." He patted his slightly round stomach.

"Well, take a cheat day. I'd like to buy you dinner before I leave the Andromeda."

"Leaving?" His eyebrows went up.

"Eventually. I'm job hunting. I suspect something will come along sooner than later." Tentatively she added, "I interviewed for a job at Crane headquarters today."

In her gut she felt the interview with Reese had gone well, but the man had an intimidating air about him that didn't give her many warm fuzzies. Tag was intimidating in his own way—but more because charm oozed out around him like an oil spill. Reese wasn't like that. He was severe, serious, and incredibly sharp.

Rachel hadn't gone in on her best foot after Tag had

surprised her, but she'd compartmentalized her feelings and called forth her professionalism. She'd half wondered if Reese would bring up Tag, and he did. First he'd mentioned that Lonnie, the manager who'd interviewed her prior, had highly recommended her for the position. Then he'd said, "He felt it'd be best if I interview you since you and Tag are involved."

Reese had said it without inflection and, she hoped, without judgment.

"I didn't want special treatment," she'd told Reese, "so I didn't tell him I applied. The truth is I consider working for Crane Hotels a great opportunity. A company I can stand behind."

Reese had nodded, his expression giving nothing away.

"How'd the interview go?" Oliver asked now.

"Well. I think. Maybe."

"The Cranes are royalty in Chicago. Good luck to you," Oliver said as she bent to pet Adonis. The dog's entire backside was wiggling, his tail slashing the air. "He misses you."

Adonis chimed the affirmative with a whine. Rachel told the giant dog she'd missed him too.

"So nice to run into you." She patted Adonis again. "I owe you dinner. Come see me."

They said their goodbyes and she chewed her lip on the ride up to Tag's penthouse. At his door she rapped lightly, hearing Tag's muffled voice on the other side. "I'll tell her. Gotta go."

He opened the door, dressed the same as he'd been earlier today, wearing that same unreadable expression. "Hey, Dimples."

"Tag. Hi." She walked inside, her nerves rattling from the caffeine, or maybe because she'd really stepped in it today. "Listen—"

"Guess who I was talking to?" he interrupted.

"Tag."

"Rachel." He gave her a headshake as if to say *Let it go.* "Guess."

She lifted a hand and dropped it. "I don't know, Mick Jagger?"

The smile that crept onto his face was so genuine, her heart did a flip.

"The CEO of Crane Hotels," he said. "Also known as my big bad brother."

"Did he...tell you anything?"

"Yep." Tag folded his arms and backed up a few feet so he could rest a hip on the surface of his clutter-free desk.

She hovered at the threshold of his door, fingers wound together around her purse strap. "Are you going to tell me what he said?"

"Maybe. But you have to come in first."

"I suppose I earned this torture," she said, stepping inside and shutting the door.

"Hey, I meant to ask, how'd the interview go?"

She gave up and let her purse slide off her shoulder before dropping it at her feet. "Are you really going to let me off the hook this easily?"

"I thought I was torturing you."

"You should."

Tag fisted her coat in both hands, yanked her firmly against his body, and lowered his head. There between his legs, her hands resting on his thick thighs, she was turned inside out by one of his signature tongue-lashings.

By the time she'd slanted her head to the right, he'd managed to remove her coat and she had one hand on his beard, her fingertips pushing into his hair.

He pulled away and she followed, stretching closer to him like a sunflower to the sun.

"Congratulations," he whispered against her lips.

Blinking up at him, she had to recalibrate her thoughts and remind her knees how to hold her up.

"You mean..."

His lips parted into a slow smile. "You got it, Dimples. Reese loved you."

At the pronouncement of the *L* word, Rachel felt her heart stutter in her chest. Granted, Tag had been talking about his brother when he said it, but inside, she felt a definite lurching sort of *want*.

"Bobbie is emailing you the details. You have to meet with HR and give them your exact start date."

"Thank you." She threw her arms around Tag's neck and squeezed. He hugged her close.

"This was all you." His hands moved along her back, strong and sure, but gentle.

"About that."

"Don't worry about it, Dimples."

"I owe you an explanation."

"You don't owe me anything." Those hands kept soothing and she relaxed into him.

"I say I do," she said softly, stroking his chest and tipping her chin. "Name your price, Tarzan." She put a kiss on his mouth and his arms tightened further, tongues dancing as they kissed again. •

Time was lost.

"What'd you come up with?" she asked when he allowed her to catch her breath. His eyes were heated, his fingers digging into her hips.

"You. On your knees."

A smile curled her lips.

"Not like you think." He shook his head slowly. "I'm talking about you, ass in the air, me behind you. You don't think I put those mirrored closet doors in my bedroom for no good reason do you?"

A blush stole her cheeks and radiated to the roots of her hair as he kissed her neck, each sip of his lips on her skin tantalizing. Imagining him behind her, strong hands on her hips as he drove deep was…gosh. So sexy she couldn't think.

"Does now work for you?" she breathed.

"Before dinner?" He pulled back to cup her jaw, his eyes on hers.

"I'm only hungry for you." She backed away and lifted her dress over her head, dropping it on the ground next to her coat; then she shimmied out of her panties, careful to untangle them from her boots. Last to go was her bra, and his hungry gaze stayed glued to her breasts.

The moment she was naked, he splayed one hand over the center of her back and kissed her neck. From there he moved to her collarbone, sending shivers of pleasure over her. When his tongue slicked over one nipple, she moaned in the back of her throat.

He broke out of his casual lean on his desk to lift her into his arms, carrying her to his bedroom, where he tossed her down on the piled bedding. Digging the heels of her boots into the plush comforter, she maneuvered to the center of the bed. She turned her head to take in the mirror he'd mentioned earlier. Her hair was rumpled in the pattern of Tag's fingertips, her cheeks pink from Tag's rasping kisses, and with her spiky boots, nipples pointing, knees up and slightly open, she had to admit...

"I look sexy."

"You do." Tag hauled his shirt over his head, stripping his upper half before starting on his belt and pants. Soon he was as naked as she was and climbing over her, his head turned to the side to look at them in the mirrored doors across from the bed. His hair tickling her breast, he lowered his lips and kissed her shoulder, then kissed his way up her neck and flicked his tongue over her earlobe.

She tore her eyes from the sensual scene unfolding before her to look at him. "You made me feel sexy again."

He sucked in a breath that expanded his chest, eyes narrowing, mouth tipping into a prideful expression.

"The first time I touched you, you had to convince me, but just now? I stripped completely bare and you didn't have to say a word."

It'd finally happened. She was a confident, sexual being. She wasn't afraid of sex, or of her performance. The woman looking back at her from the mirror with the blue eyes at half-mast knew she deserved the man sliding his hand down her stomach to the space between her legs.

Simply amazing.

"You've always been sexy," Tag murmured. "Glad you finally see what I've always noticed."

A few lingering strokes with his fingers and Rachel stopped having her epiphany and closed her eyes. The next words Tag spoke came after she did, clutching around his fingers as her orgasm sent goose bumps to the surface of her skin. He put his lips to her ear, and the gravel in his voice sent a shudder down her spine.

"On. Your. Knees."

She wasted no time obeying, moving to her knees and watching as he positioned himself behind her. In the mirror she watched him roll on the condom, felt his hands move sensually over her bottom, and then along her spine and into her hair. He took a handful of her blond locks and bent over her, bracing himself on the bed with one hand as his cock slid expertly against her swollen center.

He tugged her hair, but lightly, and she caught a flash of the bold smile on her face in the mirror. Then her eyes were on the man behind her.

"Want it wild?" he asked, his voice a low growl.

"I want you inside me."

Another tug on her hair and he plunged deep. A sharp cry left her lips. He filled her, hot and thick.

"Now what do you want?" He slid out and then in again, his pace torturously slow. Her hair was still wound around his fingers, his hold steady more than forceful.

Amazing. How much more bold could she be?

"I want you to fuck me." She whispered her demand.

His shoulders lifted as he pulled in a deep breath. She'd never said those words in her life. Now that she'd tried them out, she was surprised to find she meant them. The animal in her responded to the animal in Tag, and she wanted to explore this with him. Every dirty little inch of it.

He released her hair, sweeping it over one shoulder and flattening his palm on her back. He traced a line to her bottom, which he then molded with his palms.

"Grab hold of those blankets, Dimples."

She watched him, in his element with calm control. Had he been holding back, waiting for her to come around this whole time? She clutched the blankets, anchoring herself to the bed, trusting him fully. When he slid out and back in again, she uttered a helpless moan. He bracketed her hips with his hands, drew back and thrust so hard the backs of her thighs slapped the front of his.

"Oh!"

"Oh, what?" he grunted as he drove into her again.

"Tag," she breathed, no, *panted*. She was soaked and so ready, the next plunge went deep and struck her right where she needed. She exclaimed his name again and again as he rode her hard from behind.

"There?"

"There," she affirmed, her entire body warming. Buzzing. Coiling in anticipation.

Fixed on that spot, he worked her into a frenzy, until she'd lost the ability to hold her head up and broke a fingernail while clutching the blanket. The bite of pain was nothing to the epic release that unfurled like silk.

Her soft cries met his potent growl, one that reverberated through her entire body. She managed enough strength to raise her head and take in the beauty of Tag coming. His pleated brow, the way his lips drew back over his teeth. His muscles stiffening, abs clenching...

He folded over her, breath heavy and hot on her shoulder blade before he covered the spot with a damp kiss. He left her body, and Rachel's knees went out from under her. She dropped to her belly, aware of Tag climbing off the bed to dispose of the condom. Then he was back, hand pushing her hair off her face and lips pressing to the corner of her mouth. He lay next to her on the bed, sweat beading his brow. A small smile tickled his mouth as he elbowed her.

"Dimples. Look."

Sleepily, she raised her head to rest it on her chin. Their reflections looked back at them, both satisfied. Tag's golden brown hair was as messy as hers.

"Who knew it could get better?" she asked.

Tag's head turned toward her and she faced him.

"Better than with your ex?" A hint of jealousy streaked his expression. She'd never seen that look on him before. When had Tag ever worried about his performance?

"Better than the first time with *you*," she said, laughing when he smiled. "Tag Crane."

"Rachel Foster."

They didn't say anything more for a long while. He simply lay beside her, occasionally tracing a finger down her arm.

In that moment she realized she'd been fighting a useless battle. She couldn't stop herself from falling for Tag.

She was already there.

CHAPTER 23

Tag drove Rachel to the corporate headquarters, a few blocks from the Crane Hotel. Convenient, since she now worked close by, and given the way his neck was itching, possibly encroaching on his territory. He hadn't been overwhelmed by her presence when she lived in the damn building or when he'd taken her to Oahu, so what was with the freak-out now?

Because Reese brought up Mom's death like some sort of pop psychiatrist.

Added to Luc's assessment of "spun," Tag had been thinking way too much about the future lately. In general, he was a "live in the now" type of guy. He'd like to get back to that and stop turning over what came next.

It didn't matter what happened in the future with Rachel. She was a thread in the company fabric, and that was the way things would always be. He'd dated Fiona, and she still worked the front desk at Crane Tower, and he had no problem talking to or seeing her.

Rachel is nothing like Fiona.

Wasn't that the truth? He'd seen a lot more of Rachel than any woman in his past. He'd been the one in heavy pursuit of her. She was wildly different than any woman he'd dated before her.

"I'm so nervous," Rachel said, echoing his ridiculous and borderline panicky thoughts. She looked out the passenger window as Tag pulled up to the curb in front of the building. Crane HQ was a high-rise, not as tall as the Crane, but had the same clean lines, glass, and black-and-white style as their hotels. His father had been a stickler about branding. Wisely so.

"Don't be nervous," he told both of them. "You've got this. Want me to walk you in?"

"No." Her eyes widened. "I'll die."

He had to smile. He'd glossed over the fact she'd cut him out of the resume/interviewing process, and really, what was there to fight about? She'd been fierce about her independence with money, so it shouldn't have come as a surprise she didn't want his help with this, either. But it bugged him all the same. Because he'd wanted to help. Wanted to take the extra incentive with her while she'd fought him every step of the way.

She dropped a quick kiss on the center of his mouth, but he cupped the back of her head and let his lips linger. Kissing her always brought him back to center. Back to what they had. Back to what mattered.

"Have a nice day, dear," he murmured.

"Thanks again." She took one more kiss before stepping out of the car and shutting the door behind her.

That evening, Tag returned to his penthouse with takeout Thai food. Rachel put in her first full day, so he expected her home—he glanced at the clock on the stove—right about now.

On cue came a knock at his door.

"It's open, Dimples," he called, but walked for the door anyway. He was halfway across the room and ready to tell her to stop knocking when the door opened, revealing a red-faced, red-eyed Rachel.

"Hey, hey," he soothed as he rushed to her. He bent to take her in, swiping a few stray tears from her cheeks. He took her purse and another heavy bag filled with files and set them on his desk. "What's wrong? What happened?"

"Nothing." She gave a hearty sniff. "I'm...stressed."

"Stressed."

"I have to go to Andromeda tonight for a shift." She swiped her eyes and backed away from him. "Bree is sick and there's no one else."

"You just worked ten hours."

"I was on my way over when I got the call. I'll have to wear my suit to the bar. She gestured down at the gray skirt and blazer over a silky-looking pale pink shirt. "I don't have a change of clothes." She dug through her purse and came out with a tissue. "I won't get done at the bar until three in the morning, and Bree and Dean both have the plague. I don't want to catch what they have. Is it okay...if I stay here?" Her mouth turned down. "It's only for tonight. And maybe tomorrow if they're still puking."

"Babe." He hugged her to him and kissed the top of her head, his heart crushing that she'd worried about asking. "You can stay."

"Thanks," she said, her voice watery. "I have to get going."

"Grab a bite. You're no good without fuel tonight."

Her stomach rumbled. He heard it.

"I don't have time. I have to brush my teeth, pull my hair into a ponytail..."

He caught her arm as she beelined for the bathroom. "Sit down. Take ten minutes to eat. I'll drive you to work."

"Really?" So much hope bloomed in those blue eyes. Did she really think she couldn't count on him? *Well, you have been acting cagey, Bucko.*

"Yes. Sit." He doled out a portion each of basil chicken fried rice and shrimp pad Thai onto a plate for her. While she ate, he called the front desk. "Fi, how quickly can you get me a pair of comfortable women's sneakers?" He moved his mouth away from the phone to ask, "Size, Dimples?"

"Oh, uh, eight."

"Eight," he told Fiona. "Thanks." He ended the call. "Ten minutes."

"She's going to find me shoes in ten minutes?"

"Crane Tower's front desk has a million connections."

Rachel sent him a grateful smile. Even with damp eyelashes, she looked a hell of a lot more relaxed than she did when she opened his front door. He hated that she had to work like a dog this week. He hated to see her this exhausted. This spent.

"Give me your apartment key." He held out a palm.

"Why?" she said around a bite.

"Because I'm going to pack a bag for you and set you up here."

"I can pick up something after my shift," she said with a headshake.

"You mean at three in the morning, before you have to get up at six and go to work?"

She frowned.

"You know what? Call in tomorrow at HQ. This isn't your fault."

"Absolutely not." Her frown deepened. "I can't call in my second day."

Her dedication blew him away. He admired that as much as he admired every other part of her.

"You could skip the bar shift, you know. You are quitting." He knew her answer before she gave it.

"No. They're *packed*. They can't run a shift without a bartender. Already, Trudy and Miles have been waiting on tables and popping behind the bar to pour beers. It's too much for two servers to run the bar and the restaurant."

"All right, then. Get ready, Dimples. I'm going to change and we'll get out of here in a few."

"Change? For what?" she asked as he walked to his bedroom.

"For my shift at the Andromeda."

* * *

Rachel would have been buried if Tag hadn't pulled his hair back, pushed up the sleeves of his Henley, and stepped behind the bar to help her out. He was in charge of simple mixed drinks and draft beers. No food orders, no money handling. That was his idea, and given Rachel would have been doing it herself anyway, having him there as a workhorse was a godsend.

She'd cried on the cab ride to Tag's and nearly collapsed from fatigue in his living room, but since then she'd tapped into her second wind.

Tag had been wonderful. He'd swiped away her tears, fed her, bought her comfy shoes, and drove her here. *And* was working with her.

The billionaire bartender.

"What's so funny?" he asked, pouring a chardonnay for a group of girls clogging the entire corner of the bar.

"How many of those have they ordered?" Rachel murmured, swiping a customer's credit card.

"I'm keeping track in my head. Don't worry."

"I'm not worried about you undercharging. I'm worried they'll be falling-down drunk by the time they leave." She tipped her head discreetly. "Although, one of those girls is suspiciously sober. I think she's ordering so you'll turn around to pour and she can look at your ass."

"You think?" He beamed.

"Careful."

"In the business, we call this tip talk," he said, pulling his shoulders back and elevating the glass of wine. "Just you watch how many tips I earn you."

She watched. Between making drinks and taking orders, she watched Tag laugh and lean, flex, and at one point there was a little dancing. The girls were completely starry-eyed and they kept ordering. When it came time to settle the bill, one of them made a show of jotting her phone number on the receipt.

By the end of the night, the women piled into a taxi, courtesy of Tag, who'd called one for them. He locked up after he came back inside. "Did I tell you, or did I tell you?"

"I hate to break it to you, but the biggest number on those receipts was a phone number."

"One of them left a C-note, princess. Check your till."

Her mouth dropped open. "Seriously?"

He put his hands on his chest. "Tip talk master."

She laughed, but the expelled breath was the end of her fuel.

"We're half-assing cleanup. I'm dead." She dropped the bar towel on a nearby table she'd intended on bussing. Instead she collapsed into a chair, the idea of wiping down two dozen tabletops making her want to cry fresh tears.

"Samuel," Tag said. She turned to see his phone pressed to his ear. "I need a car to the Andromeda Club in five."

What on earth...?

"Yep. That's the one. Thanks." He dropped his phone in his pocket, came out with his keys. "Stay put, Dimples. I'll grab your coat." He twisted a key off the ring and put it in front of her.

"What are you doing?" She blinked, bleary-eyed and pretty sure exhaustion had zapped her brain.

"I'm going to clean the bar, lock up, and make sure your kitchen guys do their shit. You're going back to my place and you're going to get some sleep."

"Tag, no."

He leaned over her, one hand bracing the back of her chair, the other flattened on the table next to the key. "I run Guest and Restaurant Services for a massive hotel conglomerate. I can handle shutting down a bar. You're going to my house." He kissed her, warm and delicious, then straightened. "Then you're going to put on one of my T-shirts and climb into bed."

Going to bed in one of Tag's worn cotton tees sounded like heaven after the day she'd had. He grabbed the bar towel and started wiping down tables, sending her a wink while she just...sat there, alternating between watching his ass and trying not to fall asleep.

The car came, and Tag buckled her in, kissed her again, and sent her on her way. Everything else was a blur, but she did manage a quick shower before pulling on one of Tag's T-shirts as instructed.

She was asleep as soon as her head hit the pillow.

* * *

"Coffee."

The intoxicating scent curled under Rachel's nose and she opened her eyes. Tag was leaning over her, dressed in sweats and a tee, his hair falling to one side. He lowered to the bed as she pushed up on one elbow and accepted the mug.

Any one of the women last night would have gone home with him if he'd shown an ounce of interest, yet Rachel was the one in his bed. The thought triggered a sleep-deprived smile.

"Sure you don't want to call in?" he asked, his lips tipping.

"What time is it?" the frog in her throat asked.

"Ten till six."

She groaned.

"Can you make it?"

"I can make it." She sipped her coffee and eyed him over the rim of the mug. "Thank you. For last night."

"You don't have to thank me."

"I couldn't have done it without you." She'd needed him. And when she allowed herself to lean on him, he didn't collapse like a house of cards. He'd ended up being as strong and capable as he appeared.

Even though she was tired, she made it through coffee and getting dressed—Tag hadn't had a chance to pick up her clothes from Bree's since he'd worked with her, but he'd arranged for someone to deliver a wardrobe for her. Rachel had found several white shiny bags on his couch filled with clothing and accessories, and her favorite perfume and makeup brand. She would have argued it was too much, but she was too busy being grateful.

The hours went fast except the ones between two and four o'clock—those dragged. Rachel finally finished her workday promptly at five. She called Bree to check on her. The worst of her friend's flu was over, and she had tonight off, so there was no need for Rachel to bartend again. Her relief was short-lived when Bree walloped her with news she hadn't prepared for.

"We're moving out this weekend, Rach. I'm so sorry to do this to you, but we were told the house was available sooner than we thought, and a friend of ours offered to take over our lease here, meaning we won't be penalized for leaving early. I figured since you were with Tag and you had a place to stay—"

"No penalty from me either," Rachel had said before Bree apologetically informed her further.

Rachel had spent her lunch and ten-minute break arranging for a storage facility and calling the apartment she'd wanted to put the deposit down on. More bad news: the unit she wanted to hold wouldn't be ready for two weeks.

Working for Crane HQ gave her a discount on hotel

rooms, but as she soon found out, even with a discount, the price of a two-week stay was much heftier than she would've liked.

She checked a few discounted hotels, and for fun, the Van Heusen, which belonged to Reese Crane's fiancée. She hadn't pulled the trigger on that yet, figuring she could talk to Tag tonight.

Over pizza they'd picked up on their way home, she and Tag camped out on the couch, swigged beer from bottles, and talked about their day. Her worries tumbled like shoes in the dryer, banging around in her head, unable to be ignored. Instead of sharing them, she took another drink of her beer and looked out the window at the sky, fading from purple-pink to yellow as the sun set behind the cityscape.

"What is it?" Tag asked.

"What is what?"

"You were chattering and now you're clamming up."

"No, I'm not." Yes, she was. Because her thoughts had turned deep and murky and bordered on terrifying.

"Dimples."

That one-word nickname bled the truth from her. She sighed and decided to tell him what was going on. From the beginning...then she'd see how far she got.

"My apartment won't be ready for two weeks. I put a hold on it over the phone today," she said.

"That's great," he said cautiously.

"Bree and Dean need me out by this weekend." She sagged on the couch. "I was going to stay at the Crane, but my first paycheck is another week out." Money problems. She hated sharing money problems with Mr. No Money Problems.

Predictably, he offered to fix it with a snap of his fingers. "I can comp one for you, Dimples."

"I don't want special treatment on the hotel room, Tag."

"It's not a big deal."

"It is to me." He was a big deal. This was a big deal. *They* were a big deal. But she couldn't seem to get any of those words out. Each time she thought of telling him how she felt, she clammed up, afraid to scare him off.

But he didn't scare off last night.

"So stay here," Tag said with a shrug.

She blinked at him. Had she really heard that?

His blue eyes held steady.

"I couldn't ask you to let me stay here for two weeks."

"You didn't." He leaned forward and kissed her. "I offered. Pretty much had to since you refuse to use me for my money."

His easy smile went a long way to easing her frayed nerves. She shook her head, still in awe of how he kept surprising her. "Thank you."

"Use me for my body, instead," he said, kissing her ear. The ear kiss turned to a neck kiss. By the time he'd palmed her breast and she'd turned her lips to his, he was lying on the couch and she was on top of him.

She pulled her lips away and tucked her hair behind her ear. "We always end up right here."

Large hands encircled her rib cage, warm and comforting. Tag was both of those things, proving to her with his actions she could count on him. Maybe it was time to stop being so afraid of scaring him off. He didn't appear scared. Not even a little.

"I like you right here," he said, his low tone trickling through her.

"I...like it too." *Chicken*. What an enormous chicken she was. So close to blurting "I love you," but she couldn't do it. Because she had no idea what he'd say. She bit down on her lip, her thoughts pinging from topic to topic.

"Now what are you thinking about?" he asked a minute later, smoothing those hands along her sides again.

"The wedding."

Was it her or had he stopped breathing for a second?

* * *

He had the sensation of standing on a ledge, about to topple off backwards. Everything Rachel hadn't said was reflected in her soft, blue-eyed stare. He'd been leaning into this—leaning into her. And suddenly, he wasn't confident he knew what he was doing.

He didn't need to label what was going on. They could just be them. Their relationship included overnights, sex, and food. Not...He swallowed, feeling nauseous. *Weddings*.

When he'd offered to let her stay here, he hadn't thought about it for more than two seconds. She was at his penthouse often, and she needed help, and as per her usual, she wasn't going to let him take care of it with money.

Inviting her to stay seemed like a good idea until she mentioned—

"My cousin's wedding is next weekend."

"Oh." He expelled a deep breath. *That* wedding.

"Tag?"

"Yeah." *Keep breathing. Be normal. Don't freak.*

"You're sure it's okay if I stay here?"

"I'm sure." Even as the words left his mouth, he didn't feel sure.

Admittedly, him comping a room for her was ridiculous. She was with him whenever she wasn't working. Her staying here was no big deal. He had tons of space.

He nodded to himself. Six thousand square feet should be enough space to share with one person. That niggling buzz that had started in the back of his mind when she said the *W* word was frustrating, but it would go away.

He hoped.

"It will only be two weeks," she said. "I can store my things in the meantime."

And now she was trying to be careful with him. He sat up and moved her so she was sitting next to him.

"I can take care of that for you." The moment he offered, she opened her mouth to argue. He didn't let her. "Those are my terms. I'm not fighting with you about this. You won't let me take care of a room at the Crane for you, then you have to let me help you move. You don't have time with two jobs, and Dean and Bree will be too busy moving themselves out to help you. Who else is going to do it?"

She closed her mouth and shook her head gently before admitting, "You make a good point."

He was tired of backing her into a corner before she let him do nice things for her. This entire situation was born out of dire need on her part rather than her letting him treat her the way she deserved.

It was like she only trusted him so far; then she cut him off. Maybe that was what was bothering him.

Jittery, he stood, closed the pizza box, and swiped his empty bottle off the table, unsure what exactly about this conversation was bothering him. Was it her mention of the one ceremony he'd always avoided? Or was it simply that she didn't let him in when he wanted to help?

"Another beer?" he offered, opening the fridge door.

"I'd better not. I'm still wiped from last night."

He stared long and hard at the bottles lined up on a shelf in the fridge, before shutting the door without extracting a beer for himself. Then he paced around the kitchen, restless. Rachel yawned, slumping down in the corner of the couch.

Their paces couldn't match less.

"I'm going to go to the gym for an hour or so. You good?" He could run off this frenetic energy and then maybe the fog in his brain would clear and he could get some sleep.

"I'm good." She peered over the back of the couch. "Thank you again."

"You're welcome." He hoisted the trash bag out of the plastic bin and tied it off. "I'll take this out, too."

She nodded. He nodded.

She hadn't been uncomfortable around him since the first time he asked her to touch him. He wanted to ask if she was sure this worked for *her*, but didn't want her to think he'd had second thoughts.

He watched her for a prolonged moment and then nodded again. "Be back in an hour, Dimples."

"Tag?" she asked when he was at the front door.

"Yeah?" He turned to see her gripping the arm of the sofa, her chin resting on her hand.

"Do you need me to make up the guest bed?"

He scowled. *What the hell?*

He shifted, the plastic bag in his hand crinkling.

"Sorry. I'm being weird," she said before he could argue. "Your bed. Of course."

At the very least.

"Okay, see you."

"Yeah, see you."

He collected his gym bag and took the trash with him when he went, calling goodbye over his shoulder. In the entryway, he paused long enough to look back at the door, trying to decide if he'd helped or hurt their situation.

He and Rachel were good in bed, good at dinner, good at hanging out. But living together? Even temporarily...

What had he done?

CHAPTER 24

"Good morning, Mr. Crane," Bobbie greeted Tag as the elevator deposited him in front of her desk.

"Reese in there?" he asked, forgoing his normal banter.

"What, no 'schnookums'?"

Bobbie's ultracasual reaction made him blink in surprise. "Sorry, off my game today."

In so many ways.

"I should say so." She didn't push him further, simply slipped back into her formal routine. "He returned from lunch ten minutes ago."

"Good."

Bobbie hit the intercom to announce him, but Tag mashed the button on her desk to open the office doors before she could. Reese, standing at his desk with a palm full of pink WHILE YOU WERE OUT notes, paused flipping through them. Behind Tag, the office doors whooshed shut.

"I need the number of your therapist."

"Nice of you to call as usual," Reese said, droll. "I don't have a therapist."

"She's at my apartment."

Reese's brow crinkled. "Who?"

"Rachel Foster." Tag walked to his usual seat, couldn't sit, so he paced to the window. He turned and pointed at Reese. "This is your fault."

His brother's frown intensified.

"You were the one spewing that shit about how Mom's death made the Crane boys scared of girls." He waggled his fingers in front of him, realizing he probably looked and sounded crazed. "So what did I do? I leaned in to it. I let it happen. I told myself I wasn't scared of anything, and now she lives with me." He crammed his hands into his jeans pockets. "Kind of."

Reese abandoned the notes and came out from behind his desk to stand in front of Tag. "I'm missing something."

"Her roommate booted her out of her apartment because they're leaving and transferring the lease. She was homeless. What was I supposed to do?"

"Be a good boyfriend and let her stay with you," Reese answered with a shrug.

At the word *boyfriend*, Tag's stomach flipped. He'd once told Rachel he wasn't boyfriend material, and no matter what he was "leaning in to," that hadn't changed.

"Maybe you do need a therapist. You're pale. Sit down."

Tag shook his head and bypassed the chair, pushing his fingers into his hair. "This isn't normal. Cranes are not normal. We're fucked up."

"You're normal." Reese was his usual calm, stoic self,

which was what Tag needed right now. "This is a big step and a first for you. Look at me. I holed up in a hotel suite like Howard Hughes last year."

Tag dropped his arms. "You need therapy, too."

"Probably." One side of Reese's mouth lifted. He gestured to the chair by his desk.

Tag dropped into it, one foot bobbing from too much coffee.

"How long has she been there?"

"Four days." Tag scratched his cheek. "She has no idea I'm in full-on panic mode."

"You're not in panic mode. You're fine."

Tag took a deep breath. He wasn't fine. Every passing day, he felt more trapped. Or... not trapped. Stuck. He was freaked. And this morning, he thought he'd figured out why.

"Remember when we were kids and Mom would be up packing our lunches, a cup of coffee by her elbow?" Tag asked. "Dad would come down, kiss her on the cheek, and pour himself a mug."

Reese frowned, his answer a simple, "I remember."

Tag swallowed down a bout of nausea and forced himself to continue. "Rachel was making a sandwich for her lunch this morning, a mug of coffee sitting next to her elbow. Sun was streaming over her blond hair. Then she looked up... and smiled at me. My heart just... stopped."

And time along with it. The surreal moment played out in slow motion, and Tag caught a glimpse of a future that scared him.

"I can't do this, bro." Tag's desperate laugh was dry and devoid of humor. "And I have no idea why."

Reese lowered onto his desk, perched on the edge

while looking down at Tag, concern evident on his features. Tag said nothing, just waited. There was nothing to say. He was a mental basket case who was freaking out because things were *good*. Now he was wondering if he'd missed the window to end things before they turned bad. He had no idea where the self-sabotaging thoughts had come from, so he had come here.

"You should leave," Reese said.

Tag flinched. "Leave?"

"Yes." Reese stood and smoothed his tie. "You have cabin fever. Get out of there."

"What, like move?" Tag asked with a laugh. Because seriously, what was his brother talking about?

"Hawaii," Reese said, deadly serious. "Blue ocean, bluer skies, sand, and surf."

Tag leaned back in the chair and narrowed his eyes. "What's going on?"

"I found some land in Maui. Perfect for a new build. I didn't want to ask you to go since you were busy with the bar projects, but now...Maybe you should go instead of me."

"I can't go to Maui." But man, did the idea of breathing clean ocean air appeal. He could leave his penthouse since it had inexplicably turned stifling.

"You can. You should. Before you do something stupid." Reese crossed his arms over his chest. "Like barricade yourself in a hotel suite and ask your wife for a divorce."

Tag remembered when Reese had gone through that. It was a rough patch both he and Merina had miraculously made it through together.

"You're never home this much, Tag. Normally, every two or three days you're gone."

He hadn't considered that, but damn, Reese was right. Tag typically traveled so much, he kept an overnight bag packed and ready. He'd been on one trip over the last several months, and it wasn't a trip he'd taken alone.

"Tell me about Maui," Tag said with a nod. A business trip might be just what his fictional therapist ordered.

"It's a perfect slice of land," Reese said with a smile that reflected his pride in finding it. "I wanted to go with an updated design for this one. Like we did in Miami."

"Miami." Tag practically salivated. Crane Miami with its ultra-svelte style and splashy lobby. The entire building lit up hot pink and electric blue at night. He rubbed his hands together, possibility blooming before him. What if Reese was right and what Tag needed was a project to sink his teeth into? A getaway to clear his head?

"Well?"

Breathe. Tag felt like he could breathe for the first time in days.

"I'm on it." He'd overseen grand openings for restaurants and bars for Crane Hotels, but he'd never been a part of choosing the plot of land one would sit on. He couldn't pass up the opportunity.

"Good. I'll email you the details and have Bobbie set an appointment with the Realtor," Reese said, then paused. "Tell me something. You're the pro at letting girls down. Refusing Rachel should be well within your skill set. Why didn't you?"

"I hate seeing her sad." The lost look on her face. Her fear that she couldn't tell him about her problems. She was so worried over him providing things for her. Didn't she see he could? That he wanted to?

But that wasn't the only reason.

"I care about her," Tag admitted.

Reese watched him for a moment. "I know."

His brother understood what he was going through. Being understood after feeling like he was losing his marbles was such a relief, Tag blew out a sigh, slightly embarrassed about coming in here and having a meltdown in front of a guy who had a tight grip on his faculties.

"Thanks, Doc." Tag pushed out of the chair. His brother had suggested he go to Maui for a good reason. Tag needed to go to Maui not only for himself but also for Rachel. For *them*. Before he went mental. "Guess I'm off to Maui."

"Send me a postcard," Reese said from his desk, flipping through the stack of pink notes again.

Tag turned for the door, feeling better and, oddly enough, worse. Part of him felt like he was running, but if he expected to figure out what had him knotted up, Hawaii could hold the answers.

In front of Bobbie's desk, Tag stopped and sent her a grin. "Darling, can you book me a flight to Maui?"

"Sure thing, sugarplum," Bobbie said with the smile he'd been trying to tease from her for years. "When are you leaving?"

* * *

"I already miss you so much!" Bree cried. Not literally, but her face scrunched up like she might cry at any moment.

"You are a broken record," Rachel teased. "I'll miss

you, too. At least we'll work my last shift here together."

"I guess." With an exaggerated pout, Bree continued, "You have a fancy job, and a fancy life, and soon you'll be married and living in Tuscany."

"I don't even like Tuscany."

"Love makes you do crazy things."

"I never said I was in love," Rachel said with an uncomfortable laugh.

Bree propped a hand on her hip. "I'm not blind, Rach."

"Miss, can I get a Monte Cristo sandwich to go?" a customer, waving a twenty, said at the worst possible time. Bree handled the transaction quickly and delivered an on-the-house Coke with a smile. Then she was back to Rachel.

"Besides, I can't be in love with him," Rachel said. "I don't think he's in love with me."

Bree clucked her tongue like Rachel was being petty. "Why would you say that?"

"Because he flew to Hawaii yesterday morning." He was excited about the trip—almost too excited. Seeing him jazzed about leaving stung.

Bree screwed her eyes up to the ceiling. "So?"

"*So?* He's been acting downright twitchy since he offered his penthouse as my home away from home, and then yesterday he was bouncing off the walls because he was going to Hawaii."

"Well, it *is* Hawaii. And you shouldn't be surprised. His job requires traveling."

"I *know* he travels. Traveling is not the issue." Rachel huffed, knowing she sounded petty and grouchy. "I'm excited to hear from him already. Like, I'm already *waiting* for him to call."

"That's because you love him." Bree beamed, fluttering her lashes.

Thank God Rachel hadn't told Tag that. He'd have booked a trip to the moon instead of Maui.

"He has been gone less than a day, and I miss him so much my chest hurts. I can't help but remember how much I depended on Shaun and how he ended up leaving. Tag hasn't given me any indication we'll stay together for the long haul."

"Do you want to stay with him for the long haul?"

Rachel pressed her lips together. She didn't know. Yes. No. Maybe. She needed a Magic 8 Ball.

"But he hasn't asked you to leave," Bree said.

"No, he's been intensely polite about my being there," Rachel said flatly. Her newfound situation smacked of what Lucas's wife, Gena, had told Rachel in that restaurant bathroom. Tag had a lot of girl *space* friends. Because he never wanted to hurt them, so he let them down as easily as possible. "Shaun slowly cut me loose, too, Bree. Months and months passed by before things imploded. I can't let that happen again."

Remembering the slow fade and painful breakup was enough to make Rachel break out in hives. Was she on the brink of another breakup like it?

"Rach." Bree's eyes filled with concern. "It makes sense for you to be nervous about where things are heading. Love is big and scary. You're both probably adjusting. I've seen you with him, and I've seen the way he looks at you. He looks like a man in love to me. Maybe he hasn't admitted it yet. To himself or to you."

Rachel considered the possibility. How long until he admitted it? Until she did? They could lose another season dancing around each other and never making any progress. She couldn't take that. Not again.

"Once he calls you'll feel better," Bree said. "I've said this before, but it bears repeating. Tag is not Shaun. He's not plotting your corporate demise."

Another customer sat at the bar, and Bree moved to greet him.

Rachel pulled her phone out of her pocket to check the time, calculating the flight to Honolulu, how long it'd take to land and arrive at the Crane Makai hotel...

Bree was right. Tag was nothing like Shaun. He bested her ex in every way. But she couldn't escape the idea that her loving Tag was a one-way street, and she knew exactly where that street ended—with her, alone, picking up the pieces on a life she hadn't ordered.

She needed to find out what was going on in Tag's head.

* * *

Tag called the next afternoon at one her time. She was typing an email and stopped midsentence when her cell phone showed his name. She slipped away from her desk and she stepped into the hallway by the elevators for privacy.

"Hi." She heard the breathlessness of her greeting.

"Hey, Dimples."

His rumbling, soothing voice made her miss him that much more. And it'd been one day. She was so screwed.

"I hear surf and sand." She pictured the beach. The blazing sun. Surfing. Part of her wilted when she wondered if she'd ever see Hawaii with Tag again.

"You can't hear sand." He chuckled, the sound easing her nerves.

"You know what I mean."

"I do. I wanted to call and check in. Have everything you need?"

"I'm not wanting for anything." She paused as a co-worker walked past her with a full cup of coffee. After he was gone, she decided to be brave and added, "Except for you."

"I like that." His tone dipped into a low, sexy tenor. "So. I have good news."

"The bar design is working?" Pride laced through her. She'd worked hard with him to make the Oahu bar project as seamless as possible.

"I think so, but that's not the news. I'm standing on a patch of ground where there will someday be a new Crane Hotel."

"Did you buy the land?" He'd mentioned he was going there to look at it.

"Not yet, but the Realtor is on his way, and I'm going to tell him yes. I already called Reese. It's perfect. I can envision the direction the hotel will face, where the bars will go—maybe your designs."

He sounded happy. Happy, and like he was a million miles away. From Chicago, from her heart.

"That's great," she forced out, feeling that gap widen further. She was ready to leap with him, but was he ready to leap with her? There was no way to tell for sure, and the timing was off...unless...She'd felt so distant from him lately. Like they hadn't been on the same page. She'd turned over and over the idea of him joining her at her cousin's wedding this weekend. Maybe he'd reconsider?

"I had a proposition for you, actually," she said before she lost her nerve.

"Let's hear it."

She swallowed and cleared her throat, willing herself to ask. No. She wouldn't ask. She'd tell him what she wanted. *Be bold.* After all they'd been through together, she should be able to speak her mind instead of tiptoe around him.

"When you get back," she said, "I'd like to take you to my cousin's wedding in Ohio." She held her breath after she asked, feeling like she was at the edge of a very steep cliff.

Tag didn't do weddings. Gena had told her that. Heck, *Tag* had told her that. She told herself she wasn't testing him, but in a way this felt like a test. An easy way to determine how "in" he was with her would be him either accepting or dodging that commitment.

"The...wedding?" His voice was cautious, lost beneath the wind blowing over the speaker of the phone.

"It's Saturday," she pushed. This was important to her. If they were going to be together, he couldn't shy away from a simple request. They would attend weddings and other family gatherings in the future if what they had grew into more. She wanted it to be more. "I know you won't be back home until Friday, but we can leave Saturday morning. It's only a six-hour drive."

More wind. Then silence.

"Tag?"

"I can't. I'm sorry." Gone was the light happiness in his voice, replaced by rigidity.

The answer hit her like a slap. He was saying no to so

much more than attending a ceremony with her. He was saying no to *them*.

"I'll have a lot of work to catch up on when I'm back. Especially if I pull the trigger on this deal. Oh, hey, the Realtor is here. I'll call later. And, Dimples, don't forget, the moving company is scheduled to be at your apartment this afternoon. Make sure they get everything they're supposed to into storage for you, okay?"

"Sure," she mumbled, feeling her heart crush like an aluminum can.

"Hey, why don't you take my Aston Martin to Ohio? Unless you prefer flying. I can book you a flight tonight if you text me the particulars."

"A flight?"

"Whatever you like, Dimples. I'm happy to help. Gotta go."

He hung up and despite his generosity and the sweet way he said her nickname, she still had the horrific urge to cry. She leaned against the wall and stared down at the floor, her mind muddy.

She wasn't going to drive Tag's two-hundred-thousand-dollar car to Derby, Ohio. And she wasn't taking a private jet, either. Her invitation to the wedding was about forging a real connection with Tag—about him overcoming his fear. She'd tackled all of hers, and at times, it hadn't been easy. Yet, he wasn't willing to leap that same hurdle for her.

Unacceptable.

She couldn't be the only one moving forward in this relationship. She couldn't be the only one wanting more, or they'd stay in this endless loop forever...or until one of them left.

She'd fallen in love with him. And while Tag was willing to provide moving trucks and fancy cars and private jets, he seemed incapable of giving her the one part of him she wanted most.

His heart.

CHAPTER 25

When Tag arrived at his penthouse, he was ready to drop. The overnight flight had been rough, and thanks to the cabin shaking like a Mexican jumping bean, he hadn't slept a wink.

Despite the motion sickness, he'd stayed awake and worked. Thanks to a long night of sleep deprivation, his brain was fuzzy and his head was throbbing, and all he wanted to do was fall into bed and sleep for days. He had to grab at least a few hours, or he'd be jet-lagged forever.

Despite the rough flight home and the hectic schedule while he was there, he was glad he made the trip. There had been a narrow window to buy fast and close quickly, and another party had been interested in the land. He and Reese had arranged to have their lawyer fly over to facilitate the agreement. And like that, the Crane Maui hotel had a foundation. Now it was done and Tag had never been so grateful to be at his own penthouse.

There was an added benefit to his trip: the relentless feeling of plummeting headfirst into Terror Town had dissipated. Whatever he'd been upset about while sharing his place with Rachel—whatever bizarre fear had rattled him—was gone. He'd missed Rachel so much, he could hardly stand it. He'd called and texted her a few times, but the long-distance contact hadn't been enough. He couldn't wait to wrap his arms around her, smell the sweet scent of her hair.

He stuck the key in the lock and let himself in, dragging his suitcase behind him. Rachel was standing in his living room, a sight for his incredibly sore eyes.

Like the first time he saw her outside his apartment building, he felt the hit low in his gut. At the time he'd been transfixed by her blond hair and full, glossed lips, and wondering what secrets this exquisite creature held. Now he knew. He'd had her blond hair wound around his fist, and he'd kissed those lips more times than he could count. He'd learned she preferred to sleep on her side facing the windows and that she always left her towel on the bathroom floor. She took her coffee black, her breakfast to-go, and always, always slept in pajamas. Even when he begged her not to.

A smile crested his mouth. God. He'd missed her.

"Hey. I thought you'd be at work." He wrapped an arm around her and held her close. His chest filled. "Mmm. You smell good." He kissed her hair, then moved to kiss her mouth, but she turned her face and pulled away from him.

Her eyes were shuttered, her mouth unsmiling.

What the hell?

She moved to a suitcase by the door—this one hers,

which stood next to another large bag. She hooked her purse onto her shoulder and tilted her head. "You're early. I thought you'd be home later today."

Her tone was flat. Her eyes were flat. In his head, a warning siren blared.

"I left right after the closing." His eyes tracked back to her luggage. "Dimples, what's going on?"

"I'm going to Ohio today," she said. Formally.

The wedding. Thank Christ. He'd thought for a second she was moving out. His brain was more sluggish than he'd thought. He was borderline panicked, and all she was doing was going on the trip she'd told him about.

"Right. Have a nice time. Are you taking my car?" He rubbed his eyes and yawned, feeling every minute of sleep he'd lost.

"I'm not taking your car, Tag." Her tone was still flat, her forehead creased.

Whoo-ooop! Whoo-ooop! The siren in his head screeched.

Okay. It wasn't just the jet lag. Something was definitely wrong.

"I'm going to need you to lay out what's going on," he said. "I don't like this."

"I didn't plan on doing this now, but maybe I should..." Her blue eyes held his, devoid of the heat and desire he'd grown accustomed to seeing there. In their place was acceptance. Pragmatism. "Things had to end sometime, right?"

End? His heart hammered double time. He released the death grip on his suitcase handle and came to stand in front of her.

"Hang on." He pushed the front door closed and put

his hand flat on the wood. He couldn't comprehend what she'd told him. It was like his mind was lined with fur. "I've had a long, sleepless night. An exhausting flight. Let's—"

"I had fun, Tag." Her smile was polite. "I don't want you to think I have any regrets, because I don't."

My God, she's seriously doing this.

"I can't thank you enough for all you've done," she continued. "You really helped me through a bad patch."

"Dimples, hang on." He pinched the bridge of his nose, his head pounding as hard as his heart. His head swirling, dizzy.

"I feel like it's best to end things now before it gets harder to walk away."

He opened his eyes to find her eyes swimming in sadness. He wasn't sad. His chest was as empty as if his heart had been scooped out.

"Who said anything about walking away?" he managed. Barely.

"You did," she said quietly. "In a million subtle ways. The way you left for Hawaii after I'd stayed with you for a few days. The way you have kept me as close as possible in bed, but as far as possible elsewhere. I'm not angry, Tag. I'm not. And this is a good thing for you. You're off the hook. For the wedding. For the future. It's better for both of us if we don't drag this out."

His synapses were running at a slog, but one thought snapped into place. "This is about me not going to a wedding?"

"It's okay. You are who you are, but I need to be who I am."

She might not be angry, but he sure as hell was. Pissed,

he stepped forward and looked down at her. "And *who are you*, Dimples?"

She met his gaze and said, "A woman who is capable of doing things without your help."

She didn't want his help any longer? After he'd closed the bar for her when she was ready to drop? After he gave her a place to stay, had offered his home and car and plane to give her whatever she needed? After taking the time to crack open the woman underneath the scared one she presented to the world?

"You mean now that you've taken everything you needed from me, you're good to go?" His nostrils flared, anger surging through him. Voice raised, he continued. "You found your sexual self and your ability to take no shit from your ex, and you secured the job of your dreams in a building with my goddamn name on it, and now you're *capable*?" he all but shouted.

Rachel blanched, her cheeks dulling. He'd surprised her, but what had she expected? For him to say "no problem" when she dumped him on his ass? She'd gutted him. He could barely process the pain lying in wait to flay him later.

"Glad I could foot the bill and help you through your life transition, Dimples," he said. Because right now, he was feeling pretty fucking used.

"That's not fair."

"No shit." He pulled the door open for her, his heart lurching and his nose stinging. "Have a nice life."

She looked like she might cry the tears he was viciously staving off, but then her phone chimed. One look at the screen and her face was once again placid. "That's my cab."

"Better catch it." That last word came out quiet. He

didn't move toward her an inch. She didn't come to him either, simply lifted her chin and collected her bags.

"Bye, Tag."

Then she was out the door.

And out of his life.

* * *

"She dumped you?" Lucas dodged a plastic toy, avoiding suffering a concussion by a very narrow margin. "Not now, sweets," he said to his daughter. "Daddy needs his brains right now."

Tag had driven to Lucas's after Rachel left. Tag had let her go, closing his front door and staring at it, his heart aching, his entire body buzzing and dull from lack of sleep. In his compromised state, he was afraid if he chased after her, he might drop to his knees and beg her not to leave.

He wasn't about to do that. He had some pride.

After pacing his penthouse like a caged tiger for the next twenty minutes, he'd conceded there was no way he could sleep, so he'd grabbed his keys and called Lucas on the way.

"She used me," Tag said now. He blinked, his vision grainy, brain set on stupid.

Lucas chuckled.

"What's funny?"

"You look more confused than angry. Like someone put Shakespeare in front of you and asked you to point out examples of iambic pentameter."

Tag felt his mouth screw to the side.

"Proving my point."

"I'm past angry. I was angry an hour ago when I opened the door for her to leave my house." But *angry* wasn't necessarily the right word. Hurt. Pissed. Confused. Yeah, confusion was his reigning emotion at the present.

Lucas handed the baby off to Gena, whose laser-like eyes fried into Tag like he was a rotisserie chicken. "Once the baby is down for her nap, I'll deal with you."

Tag watched her go, then refocused on his friend. "What'd I do?"

"It's what you didn't do." Lucas held up a finger to make his point.

Spreading his hands, Tag said, "Which was?"

"You could've gone to the wedding with Rachel."

"I have to work. She knows I have to work." That made sense, right? He couldn't be sure, since each thought sloshed in his brain like a tossing ship.

"Uh-huh. Also, you're allergic to weddings."

"I've been to plenty of weddings." Tag pushed his hair off his face and twisted it into a bun at the back of his neck. Why the hell was everyone's focus on weddings all of a sudden?

"Never with a date," Lucas said, crossing one leg at the ankle and resting a hand on his jeans. "We didn't take dates to weddings, because they'd get diamond-eyed when they stepped up to catch the bouquet toss."

"Diamond-eyed," Tag repeated. Another stupid term for another stupid thing he and Luc used to do together. "What the fuck is wrong with us?" Or, more aptly, since Lucas was happily married, what was wrong with *Tag*?

"The world may never know." Luc pushed off the couch. "You want some coffee?"

"Yeah." Tag wasn't any closer to arriving at an epiphany, but maybe coffee would help.

They bellied up to the bar—which was actually the kitchen counter. Lucas pressed a button on his fancy coffeemaker that ground the beans and started the pot brewing. By the time he had poured them each a cup, Gena swept into the kitchen, her daughter no longer in her arms.

"They're both down," she said, keeping her voice low. Then she pointed at Tag and handed him his own ass.

"You're a fucking moron." She smiled sweetly at Lucas. "Babe, pour me one?"

Lucas angled a glance at Tag, handed Gena a mug, and filled one for himself.

"Tag teamed," Tag muttered. "In this case literally." His joke had no hang time. It settled into the air like pungent gas. Gena even wrinkled her nose.

"Who was the last girl who dumped you?" she asked, eyebrows raised.

Tag blinked at Gena before shrugging. "I don't know." His mind flipped through his past dates like pages in a book. Slowly, given he was running at half-speed today. "I don't remember."

"Rachel," Lucas answered with a snap of his fingers.

"Bingo." Gena held up a hand and Lucas high-fived her.

Tag sent his buddy a glare meant to be a silent reprimand. Whose side was Luc on?

"She's right. No one's ever dumped you," Luc said, sipping his coffee. "It's your thing."

"It's not my *thing*," Tag argued.

"No," Gena interjected. "Your *thing* is breaking up with them before they break up with you. Letting them down easy so no one gets their feelings hurt. How many girls have you left in tears?"

"None." Tag knew the answer instantly. He didn't like tears. Didn't like sadness in general. He never wanted to leave a girl feeling less than good about the time they'd spent together.

"Rachel learned a lot from you, seeing as how she let you down the same way. I don't see you sobbing," Gena said.

"No, Rachel was very clear about what I meant to her. She thanked me for all the monetary goods and services I've awarded her and then left whole." His stomach soured and he pushed his coffee mug away. That wasn't true. She hadn't been whole. Tag hadn't missed the pain etched on her face as she stepped out the door.

But she'd torn him to bits, so he'd felt justified letting her leave hurt.

"I gave her everything she'd let me," he said. "Hawaii. Dates. Sex. She moved in. I kept trying to offer more, and she kept telling me no." He lifted a hand in frustration. He'd have done more. He'd have given her the damn moon. "I have to work one weekend, and she's done with me."

He drank the coffee anyway. Stomach be damned, he needed caffeine.

"Wow, how could she leave you after you gave her the contents of your wallet?" Gena asked dryly. Lucas stepped away from Tag to avoid getting hit in the cross fire.

"What the hell is that supposed to mean?" Tag's anger had peaked. He couldn't take any more women falsely accusing him today.

"What comes hard for you, Tag?"

"This conversation isn't exactly easy," he snapped, standing to flatten his palms on the counter.

"Money doesn't come hard for you," she said.

"You know what"—Tag held up his hands in surrender—"I'm not doing this. Luc, later man."

Gena, proving that Tag's size didn't intimidate her, moved to him and poked him square in the chest. "You bought her things. You took her to Hawaii. You had sex with her."

"Oh, and you think she didn't enjoy any of that?" Tag said in his defense, his heart twisting as memories of each moment they had together chugged through his brain like a railcar. The coffee on the beach at Oahu when Rachel sat between his legs, her head resting on his chest. The way she'd determinedly pushed up on her surfboard and then howled as she tumbled into the ocean. The shower where she turned him on and reclaimed her power at the same time.

"Those things come easy for you." Gena interrupted his thoughts, poking him again. "You're *good* at lavishing attention on women. You're *good* at flying to Hawaii in the company plane. I'm assuming by your reputation that you have the sex thing down."

"Damn straight," he couldn't keep from agreeing.

"Going to a wedding is *hard*," Gena said. "Telling her how you feel is hard."

Given the way the room swam, Tag was beginning to think Gena might have a point. The idea of telling Rachel his feelings—confronting his fears—was terrifying.

"Putting yourself on the line, telling her you're not going anywhere, is *hard*. She wants the hard thing from you."

Lucas snorted.

"Shut up," Gena told her husband.

"Sweets, you can only make so many 'hard' references before it starts sounding funny."

"This is your problem," she snapped. Luc's smile erased. Before Tag could become smug, she turned back to him. "You're little boys. Grow up. Rachel never wanted your money or your gifts, Tag." Her voice softened, she stopped poking him, and she patted his chest with the flat of her hand. "She wants your heart."

Like that, the clouds cleared from his head.

Rachel left not because she'd become whole and found herself after using him. She'd left because he hadn't given her a reason to stay. He hadn't stepped up when she'd needed reassuring the most.

He thought of Reese's words about their mother. How afraid of commitment Lunette Crane's sons were. Because they feared being left by another woman they loved. Tag had avoided commitment his entire life, breaking off relationships but maintaining his "good guy" status. Then he avoided commitment with Rachel, and she was the one who left him.

Tag had opened the door for her to walk out, but in truth, he'd opened it a long time ago. Lucas saw what was coming a mile away, and when he'd confronted Tag with it, Tag had been too chickenshit to admit the truth. To Lucas, to himself.

To Rachel.

"I love her," Tag muttered with a sad headshake. Reality came on like sobriety. With an ache after the numbness wore off.

Gena's hand left his chest. "Does she know that?"

Tag and Lucas exchanged glances.

She didn't. Or she never would have gone. If Tag knew one thing about Rachel, it was that she was cautious, until she wasn't. And when she wasn't, she threw herself in, body and soul. She'd thrown herself into him over and over. She'd flown to Hawaii with a virtual stranger, trusted him with her body when she tested the boundaries of her sexuality. She'd been the one trying not to take advantage of him by accepting his money or his help.

She'd been ready to step into him further, but now he could see the way she'd lingered on the edges, waiting for him to come around. And what did he do? He took a huge step away from her when she was the most fragile.

He flew to Hawaii instead of telling her how he felt.

Him not going with her to this wedding—especially after he'd been weird about her staying with him—had her believing he didn't care about her. And after she'd dated a guy who didn't give a shit about anyone but himself, was it any wonder she'd pulled the plug?

It's better for both of us if we don't drag this out.

She'd been protecting herself. And he'd missed the opportunity to tell her she didn't have to.

Tag blinked at Lucas, who wore a smirk.

"Have something to say?" Tag asked.

"Yup," Luc answered. "Do you have a tux to fit those circus-sized shoulders, or is the wedding casual?"

CHAPTER 26

Rachel sat on the rocker on her mother's back porch wearing a wrap sundress. The reception was in full swing in the backyard, her cousin having been married today in a disgustingly perfect ceremony.

Outdoor weddings in Ohio were tricky, but this spring day, the blooms were lush, the wind light, and the sun unstoppable. It was too early in the season for mosquitoes. Night had fallen, nothing but the occasional moth bumping into the porch light overhead.

"Hey, hon," her mother called, strappy sandals in hand as she navigated the walkway to her own house. The tent hovered in the background, separate bathroom trailer and all. No one had a reason to come to her parents' house unless they were sleeping here tonight. Rachel fell into that category.

"I'm moving in," she grumbled.

Her mother laughed as she sat next to her daughter

on the wide bench seat. "No. You're not. You belong in Chicago. You remember when you were here, bartending and working hard to fund school. Even those few months you spent in Florida were wrong for you. Chicago is your dream."

Chicago *was* her dream. When she'd worked at the marketing firm with Shaun and moved in with him, she'd been as duped as her dear mother into believing the city would give her everything she wanted. Instead, she'd ended up following one doomed relationship right into the next.

When she'd arrived at her mom's house yesterday afternoon, her dried tears had reemerged instantly. Then the dam burst and Rachel told her mom everything. About the breakup with Tag. About how she should have known better than to fall in love with a rebound. How she'd chosen Chicago's biggest playboy, so really it was her fault and not his. How she'd taken a page from his book and tried an I'm-okay-you're-okay breakup, only to find he was not okay and she was definitely not okay.

"I do miss you, though," Rachel told her mom.

"I miss you, too." Keri Foster smiled and pushed a few stray strands of hair away from Rachel's eye. "Couples fight, honey."

"Tag and I aren't a couple." She said it quickly, but the hurt didn't dissipate—it intensified. They'd felt like a couple to her. "It's for the best. We were a wrong fit from the start. He's not the man for me."

Lie, lie, lie. *Just keep lying to yourself and everyone around you, Rach.*

"He was so mad." A tear trickled from her eye and she swiped it away, angry she wasn't better at hiding her feelings.

"So fix it when you get home," her mom said, her rose-colored glasses everlasting. "It's fixable. You'll see."

"Keri." Her father strode into the yard toward the house. "Rach. Cake is being cut."

Her mom stood. "Come on, you look like you could use a slice of cake."

"A slice—I could use the whole cake."

Her mother laughed as Rachel stood. Keri wrapped her arms around her daughter and rubbed her shoulder. They walked to the tent, and Rachel made a point to pull herself together. This was supposed to be a happy occasion. Not one where she sulked and wallowed in regret over leaving the man she loved.

She'd never taken a moment to tell him that. Maybe she wasn't as bold as she'd thought. Or maybe she was foolish to think that Tag could change. Maybe he never would. Maybe he'd be single forever.

Hell, maybe *she'd* be single forever.

The cake was cut, bites fed, photos taken. It was sweet, she supposed. Some less cynical part of her could appreciate her cousin's happiness, anyway.

Rachel's parents had skipped the cake in favor of dancing. They looked good together. Her father's receding hairline and her mother's smile lines bespoke of the years that had passed. Of the life they'd shared together. A pang of longing shot through Rachel so fiercely that fresh tears stung the backs of her eyes. She wanted a life shared, she realized. A future with someone else was the real reward.

As if in answer to a prayer, a waiter delivered a glass of champagne to her. She put her hand on the stem and started to tell him his timing was impeccable when the overhead lights caught the edge of a diamond cuff link.

Wait.

She'd never seen a waiter wearing diamond cuff links. Wearing cuff links at all, she thought as she stared at one broad, tanned hand.

"Will there be anything else?" A deep, delicious voice washed over her. Goose bumps raised on her arms as she turned her eyes up to find Tag standing over her. He wore a tuxedo, which was ridiculously formal for the borderline casual summer wedding, but he didn't look ridiculous. Long hair flowing over his shoulders, bow tie perfectly tied, jacket and pressed shirt...He looked like the man who'd stolen her heart without her permission. Even now it throbbed painfully as if in response to being this close to its missing piece.

"What are you doing here?" Her eyes followed as he lowered into a plastic rental chair.

"I came here for you." His sideways smile went a long way to making her feel better. "You told me that on Oahu. Remember?"

Before she could reply, the DJ interrupted the music with an announcement.

"Ladies and gentlemen, we have a last-minute toast for the bride and groom from..." The DJ slid on his glasses and read from a card in his hand. "Taggart Crane?"

"I'll be right back, Dimples." Tag winked, stood, and then crossed the tent. Rachel watched him go, thinking of the first time she'd seen him on that city sidewalk outside of Crane Tower. And then again at Oliver's front door. He looked the same, tall, massive, too much hair, trimmed beard—but now he was so familiar that all of her ached to be closer to him. The attraction was foreign when she'd first felt it, but now she couldn't picture herself without him. He just seemed to belong wherever he was. Wherever *she* was. Here, at this wedding and wearing that tux, he belonged.

Because he belonged with her.

He took the microphone as feedback screeched from the speakers.

After a quick adjustment, the DJ gave Tag the thumbs-up.

"Good evening." Tag cleared his throat, adjusting his collar like he was nervous. "Been a while since my last public speaking gig," he said with an uncomfortable laugh, his voice notably subdued.

He was nervous. Rachel noted the way his hand shook when he swiped his fingers along his brow. Evidently, there were *two* things Tag Crane couldn't do well. Play pool and speak publicly.

"First of all, congratulations on your wedding." Tag waved at the bride and groom, who were across the room at the head table, wearing curious smiles. "I promise I won't be long. I already asked the photographer not to document this for your album."

The crowd laughed.

"The truth is, I didn't come here for you guys." Tag's voice dipped and his eyes found hers across the room. "I came here for Rachel Foster."

Gasps surrounded her as every pair of eyes migrate to her. She put her hand to her warm face and waited for him to say more.

"Ask my brothers and they'll confirm I'm not one to focus on the past or the future, which is why they put me in charge of throwing parties at Crane Hotels instead of assisting with new builds." He licked his lips before he continued with a slightly off-topic segue. "Parties are important. Parties like this one. Right? Weddings are a big deal because celebrating the present matters. I've always believed that. Living in the present is where it's at. Then I met Rachel—Dimples," he corrected with a flooring smile. "And while I never planned for our future, whenever I was with her, I knew I didn't want our present to end."

Her heart climbed into her throat and made her next breath a struggle.

"Isn't that what the future is?" Tag stepped off the stage and walked toward her as he talked. "The present continually unwrapping itself for years to come? When I was on Maui for work," he said, addressing the crowd with more confidence than before, "I stood on a piece of land where my company will build our next hotel. I could see it." He refocused on her. "Even though it wasn't there yet, I knew what it should look like."

When he reached her, he lowered to a squat, the microphone to his mouth, the only sign he was nervous evident in one shaking hand.

"I see us like that, Dimples," he spoke right to her, his voice even, his gaze unwavering. "We're not a bare patch of land, but we're not finished yet either. I can see more."

"You can?" she couldn't help asking, her voice watery from unshed tears.

"Yeah. I can." He drew in a quick breath. "I let you leave without telling you how much I love you. How much you've changed me. I didn't even know I was broken until I met you. Thanks a lot for that," he tacked on wryly.

The crowd chuckled again, eating him up. Tag had

never lacked charm. Never lacked honesty. There was so much sincerity in his words, but what was killing her was the way they matched the love swimming in his eyes.

She could see it. And she could feel it.

"I love you, too," she whispered.

He grinned then, the biggest smile she'd ever seen him wear. It parted his beard and showed off his teeth. He snatched her off the chair and lifted her off the ground, hugging her close as he kissed the breath right out of her.

Arms locked around his neck, his hair tickling her cheeks, she kissed him back. To the sound of whistles and applause, Tag let her slide down his long body until her heels once again touched the ground.

The DJ relieved him of the microphone and restarted the music. Couples resumed their dancing, and the tent filled with the low hum of chatter once again.

Tag swiped one palm down his jacket, then over his forehead. "That was terrifying, and you're looking at a guy who once jumped off a cliff face."

"Why'd you do it?" she asked, beaming up at him.

"It was my first time in Hawaii and one of the locals dared me to—"

She stretched on her toes and pulled his face down to hers, smothering his words with another kiss. By the time her lips left his, he'd wrapped both palms around her waist and rested his forehead on hers.

Eyes open, he murmured, "Because I love you and I want to spend the rest of my life with you. I wasn't sure if you'd forgive me if I called, so I thought if I showed up, you'd have to listen."

"Smooth," she said with a smile.

"Yeah, well. Work with your strengths."

"Get ready, single ladies," the DJ announced over the music. "Next up, we're doing the bouquet toss!"

"Oh no. Not that." Tag quirked one eyebrow and without warning, lifted Rachel into his arms.

She squealed and held on for dear life as he tromped out of the tent, his hold on her tight.

"What are you doing?" she asked through her laughter.

"Old habits die hard. I'll explain later." He tightened his hold on her and lowered his lips to hers. "Besides, I thought you'd be into this whole me-Tarzan, you-Jane thing."

She ran a finger over his soft beard, her heart full. She was right where she belonged—in his arms and in his heart. "Can I brush your hair later?"

He laughed before turning her on with another lengthy kiss. When he pulled away, it was only a scant inch so he could say, "Love you, Dimples."

To which she replied, "I love you, too, Taggart."

Ever since he returned from war missing a leg, Eli Crane just wants to be left alone. So why does his family keep interfering in his life, sending personal assistants to baby him? But when beautiful, undeniably sexy Isabella Sawyer appears at his front door, maybe a little company isn't so bad...

Isa can't deny the red-hot attraction she feels for this gorgeous and infuriating man. But she has a secret, one that could change everything. Will the sparks between them ignite or flame out?

A preview of
The Bastard Billionaire follows.

CHAPTER 1

The flames in the fireplace were nearly extinguished, the curtains on the high windows of Elijah Crane's office drawn. Rain pattered on the glass, providing a soothing backdrop for his work. He pecked at his keyboard, mind on the email, when a mousy, quiet voice lifted in the darkness.

"Mister...Crane?"

The only other light was the desk lamp and the slice of natural light that made its way past the doorless entry to his office. His newest temporary assistant stood in that light, her shadow a long wedge.

"Reese Crane called," she said as she walked into his office. "Your brother."

Like he needed that reiteration?

"I know who Reese Crane is, Melanie."

"He asked me to..." Her small voice grew smaller until it vanished altogether. The reason being because Eli had just taken a deep, rumbling breath and pushed himself up from the desk.

Slowly.

Let it never be said intimidation wasn't an art form.

He kept his eyes on the woman now standing at the other side of his desk. She was young, probably in her early twenties, and from what he'd gleaned in the last eight or so hours since she'd started this position, weak. He'd bet he could run this one off in record time. Not that he was keeping track, but maybe he should. He was getting good at it.

He blew out that same breath, keeping his lip curled, his expression hard. He let the breath end on a growl.

"What did I tell you this morning?" he asked, his voice lethal.

The temporary personal assistant currently putting a massive cramp in his style blinked big, doe-like eyes at him. "Not to interrupt you, but, Mr. Crane—"

"Not. To. Interrupt. Me." He made a show of pulling his shoulders straight and hobbling around the table. Her gaze trickled down to the prosthesis at the end of his right leg as he affected a limp. One he didn't have. One he'd trained himself *not* to have.

For some reason, the help found him more intimidating when he reminded them he was an amputee. He'd used it to his advantage on more than one occasion. "Do I look like I need to be bothered with trivial questions, Melanie?"

"N-no, sir, but it's about Crane Hotels, and I was hired to—"

"You answer to me," he told her point-blank. "I don't care if it's a memo from the pope. I asked not to be interrupted. I expect not to be interrupted."

"But the board meeting..." Melanie trailed off, her eyes blinking faster as if staving off tears.

Tough shit, sweetheart.

The sooner word reached his brothers that the ninth—or was Melanie the tenth?—PA to set foot in Eli's warehouse left in tears, the better. He didn't want to be bothered with Crane business. The thickheaded men in his family didn't listen when he'd clearly and concisely said no to a pencil-pushing position at the Crane home base, so he'd resorted to showing, not telling.

"Mr. Reese Crane said all you need to do is read and give your opinion. I can reiterate on the conference call for you," she squeaked.

He elevated his chin and stared her down. She didn't hold his gaze, her eyes jerking left then right and very purposefully avoiding dipping to his missing limb for a second time. Sucking in a deep breath, he blew out one word.

"Fine."

"Fine?" Melanie's eyebrows lifted, her expression infusing with hope. She was a sweet thing...Who was about to get a lesson in hard knocks.

"*Fine.* I'll give you my opinion." He lashed a hand around her wrist, snatched the folder from her hand, and tossed it into the fireplace. They were mostly embers now, but a single flame crawled over the edge of the folder, where it fizzled, then smoked instead of igniting.

Well. That was unimpressive.

"You-you're..." Melanie's fists were balled at her sides, her eyes filling yet again.

"Spit it out. I don't have all day."

"You're a monster," she said, then turned and ran—

yes, *ran*—from his office, through his living room, and to the warehouse elevator. He stepped out from behind his office wall to watch the entire scene, arms folded over his chest. There were only a few doors and walls in his place, so not much hampered the sight of another victory won by Eli "Monster" Crane.

He walked back behind the wall of his office and stomped on the smoking file folder at his feet. Once he was sure he wouldn't burn down his house, he chucked it into the wastebasket on the side of his desk.

"Sorry, Reese," he said to thin air. "You'll have to manage without me."

They'd managed without him for the years he was stationed overseas, so he didn't see why they couldn't put one foot in front of the next now. God knew being away for years hadn't improved Eli's ability to weigh in on financials.

His cell phone buzzed with a text—not from one of his brothers, but from a contact he'd made earlier this week. He felt a real smile on his face as he lifted the phone and walked smoothly from his desk to the kitchen.

Yep, still in business, it read.

He tapped a reply. *Let's talk more next week. Give me a choice of dates.*

Then he pocketed his phone and opened a beer, feeling a charge shoot down his arms. *This* was what he was supposed to be doing. Real work. Work that would change the worlds of men and women who'd made sacrifices. For their country, for their families. Men and women who'd returned home with less than they'd left with and were expected to drop back into the flow of things seamlessly.

Whenever Eli thought of the opening for chief operations officer of the gargantuan Crane Hotels, he felt two things. One, he had no time to trifle with meetings and operations of a hotel chain that had been humming along for decades without him. Two, his oldest brother had COO on lock. There was nothing Reese couldn't do, and the last thing Eli needed was to be in a position of power when he did not give a shit about it.

Eli's answer was a solid, resounding no. And if Reese and Tag—and hell, even his retired father—continued to push him about COO? No problem. Eli had become adept at running off PAs. In fact, he'd become more inventive about the ways he could get them to quit.

He covered his smile with the tip of the beer bottle and drank down half the contents.

Next, he'd move to a creepy mansion atop a hill so the villagers could murmur about the beastly man no one dared bother lest they suffer his wrath. He let out a dry chuff.

Sounded like heaven.

* * *

The phone was ringing off the hook today, which normally would be a good sign. But the caller on hold sent Isabella Sawyer's stomach on a one-way trip to her toes.

"Isa?" her assistant asked from her desk. "Do you want me to take a message?"

"No, Chloe, I'll take it." She didn't want to take it, but she'd take it. She shut her office door and in the minimizing crack watched as her best friend's face morphed into concern. Isa gave Chloe a thumbs-up she didn't quite feel.

Isa lifted the handset of her desk phone. "Bobbie, hello," she said to Reese Crane's secretary.

"Hold for Mr. Crane," Bobbie said in her usual curt manner.

She'd had similar conversations with Reese several times already. Ten of them to be exact. Isabella was pretty sure this was the "you're fired" call she'd been expecting three personal assistants ago. But that was okay, because she had prepared a response.

"Isa. Here we are again," came Reese's smooth voice. She'd met him once in passing, at an event she'd attended on behalf of her personal assistant company, Sable Concierge. Reese Crane was tall, intimidating, handsome, and professional. And married.

Not that he was Isa's type. Business guys in suits for clients, yes. Business guys in suits for dating potential, no thanks. She'd been there, done that, and picked up the dry cleaning.

"Mr. Crane, I'm sorry we aren't speaking under better circumstances."

"So am I. You promised me you'd found the ideal PA for Eli this time around."

Melanie hadn't exactly been second string, but Isa had already sent her top choices. Elijah Crane had chased off every last one of them. They were down to her assistant Chloe or a new hire named Joseph. No way would he last thirty seconds.

Isa refused to pull her other PAs off current assignments to cater to Elijah Crane. If she lost the Crane business, she'd need her current clients or they'd all starve.

"Solve my problem." Reese's commanding tone brooked no argument, nor should it. Isa was at his beck and call for one simple reason: his seal of approval would boost her budding business or, if she continued to fail at finding a suitable assistant for his brother, could tank it. She wanted a foot in the door with the elite in Chicago, and Reese held the key.

"I have a solution," she said. "A PA who has over three years' experience at my company, a decade prior to that working as right-hand woman at Sawyer Personal Finance, and I guarantee your brother absolutely will not succeed in scaring her away."

"And who is this maven?" he asked, but the lilt of his voice suggested he already knew.

"Me."

A quiet grunt that could have been a laugh came through the phone. "I take it you're not much of a wilter."

"No. I'm tenacious and stubborn."

"An exact match for Eli."

"Once I convince him to get more involved in Crane Hotels, I'm sure I can place one of our many qualified assistants in my stead. I do have a company to run."

She cleared her throat, her mother's scolding voice in the back of her mind. *Be polite, Isabella. No man likes a woman who disrespects him.*

"My foray as his assistant will be brief," she continued. "But there's no need for him to know I'm top brass. I'll act as if I'm number eleven and give him a run for his money."

"Eleven," Reese repeated, and Isa could have kicked herself for reminding him how many assistants they'd run through already.

"I apologize for the lack of follow-through you've seen so far. I appreciate you giving Sable Concierge another chance. My company is one I want you to lean on any time you're in need of help."

"Your company came highly recommended, Ms. Sawyer," Reese said, his voice softening some. Isabella knew why. Reese's voice did that whenever the topic of his wife came up.

"Thank Merina for me again," Isa told him.

"I will. Your success is imminent, I presume."

"You can bank on it." She said her goodbyes and hung up the phone, pulling in a steady breath. One more shot. She had one more shot to pull this off. No, Reese hadn't said it, but he hadn't needed to. She'd fire her if she were him. Wife-recommended or no.

Last fall, Isa randomly scored a position for one of her assistants at the Van Heusen hotel with Merina Crane. Merina had suggested Isa's company for Elijah's transition from the military to Crane corporate. In comparison to what Merina's brother-in-law had been through already, placing a PA should've been easy. Eli had already been through the physical hoops to regain his mobility using a prosthetic leg, and his warehouse home was equipped to accommodate his working at home.

The assistant's job was to help him field conference calls, answer and forward emails, and tend to the light load of work Reese had handed down to Eli to oversee.

Eli had done none of it.

Isa had sent in seasoned help each time, and a startling number of her employees left either in tears or so angry Isa nearly lost them altogether. Elijah, regardless of the team's sensitivity training and the day they'd all spent with a rehabilitation expert for amputees, was not an easy guy to feel sorry for.

He was "mean," according to one of her employees, "miserable" according to another, and to poor Melanie, who unfortunately had turned in her notice after her first and only day at Eli's, had referred to him as a "monster" on her way out the door.

Isa wasn't having it. If Eli sought misery, he could ruin his own life, not her company's future. She'd expected Melanie to last two days. She lasted half that. Isa believed in always being prepared, so she'd been training Chloe to run the office in case of just this circumstance. Isa could run Sable Concierge after hours, answering emails and returning phone calls during lunch or early in the morning.

As owner and operator, Isa was willing to do what it took to shove her business to the next level. If she had to work two jobs, so be it.

Elijah Crane hadn't given her much of a choice.

* * *

Eli sat at the kitchen table and watched the hubbub in front of him, chin resting in his hand, scowl on his face. His sister-in-law, Merina, was bustling around, setting the table. She paused in front of him.

"You look like your brother when you do that." She hoisted an eyebrow and dropped it.

"The one you married or Tarzan?"

"I heard that," Tag said, loping into the room with three bags from Chow Main, the best Chinese food joint in town. Eli's mouth watered at the sight of the generic paper-inside-a-plastic bag. On it, a yellow smiley face, and beneath that red lettering that proclaimed HAVE A NICE DAY!

Tag's girlfriend, Rachel, followed him, a bottle of wine in each hand.

"Hey, Rach," Merina greeted, setting the last place. She accepted one of the bottles and spun the label around. "Ohh, good choice."

"It's a customer favorite. Or was, when I bartended."

Reese filtered in next, wearing his suit from work. Merina loosened his tie, standing on her toes to press a lengthy kiss to his lips.

"Sexy man," she murmured.

"Vixen," Reese commented, his hand on her ass.

Patience shot, Eli gestured at the dishes on the table and bellowed, "Can someone please explain why we can't eat Chow Main out of the containers like normal human beings instead of dealing with this bullshit?"

He crossed his arms over his chest and glared at his family, all of whom had their eyes glued on him. Merina clucked her tongue. Reese looked mildly irritated. Rachel bit her bottom lip and stepped closer to Tag, who opened his mouth and let out a hearty laugh.

At that laugh, the tone of the room shifted back to light and fluffy, and the chattering continued as Rachel and Tag unloaded the food onto the table.

It seemed the only person Eli was capable of scaring off were assistants. His family was entirely immune to him.

"We're here," came a call from across the warehouse. Eli looked over to see his father, Alex, and his assistant, Rhona, file in together, her hand in his. It'd been recently discovered that Alex and Rhona were partnering in more than business, and since Eli's old man was retired and had been for some time, Eli guessed that Alex and Rhona were partnering more often than not on a personal level.

"Hey, Eli." Rhona pulled a patterned scarf from her neck—it was only September, so he had no idea why the scarf—and smiled brightly at him.

He lifted a hand and gave a brief wave. Rhona merged into the fray, cooing over the wine as Merina apologized about not knowing she was coming and pulled an extra set of dishes from the cabinet. A low sigh worked its way through Eli's chest as he watched.

Happy. Every last goddamn one of them.

"Beer, bro?" Tag asked, collapsing next to him into a chair. His brother's hair was down in golden-brown waves, his beard full like Eli's, but neatly trimmed, *not* like Eli's.

Eli accepted the bottle. "What, no frosted glass? Shouldn't we have coasters?" He gestured to the set table, in the center of which rested a bowl of oranges his last assistant brought over. She'd probably been instructed by Reese to monitor his vitamin C intake.

"It's been half a year, E," Tag said, leaning back in the chair and sucking down some of his own beer. "You're going to have to get used to us being in your face. We missed you." That last bit accompanied an elbow jab, and Eli, though he grunted on the outside, knew they'd missed him. *He'd* missed them. Just because his brothers' (and hell, now his father's) happiness was soul-sucking didn't mean he didn't love them. He just wished they'd be adorably coupled off somewhere far, far away from Eli's sanctuary.

"I can go out into public you know," he grumbled, setting the bottle down next to his plate. "You guys don't have to come in here and serve me."

"Oh, but we do, Lord Crane." Merina smiled as she leaned over and handed him a glass. "We know you don't want to deal with the public right now. Trust me, I spent enough time with the media breathing down my neck. I don't blame you."

Eli liked Merina. She was tough. She was bold and clearly had enough forearm strength to pull the stick out of Reese's ass. At least partway. Eli had never seen his oldest brother this . . . joyous. And now that Reese was living a utopic existence with his dreams coming true, he wanted Eli on board to tiptoe in the tulips alongside him.

No, Reese wasn't through pressuring Eli into coming back on at Crane Hotels full-time, but he had lightened up some. As evidenced when he returned to the dining room sans tie and jacket. Unlike Tag, Reese was always suited. Tag was the opposite, typically in cargo pants and a skintight Henley to show off the biceps he pumped into ridiculous sizes.

Eli was as comfortable in a suit as out of one. He could don fatigues, jeans and tee, or Armani and feel like himself. The clothes, in his case, did not make the man. Even his body didn't make the man, though Eli had worked his ass off to maintain his. The better shape he was in, the better he felt about the leg.

"The media doesn't give a shit about me," Eli said. Just the way he liked it.

"They will when we name you COO," Reese piped up.

Eli sent him a death glare. Reese didn't flinch. Eli's sleeve of tattoos and surly attitude didn't intimidate his oldest brother. Reese knew him when he sleepwalked to the neighbor's house, so he wasn't about to be intimidated by a grumpy ex-Marine.

"We found you a new PA," Reese said.

"No."

"She starts next week," he continued as if Eli hadn't spoken.

"Well done, Reese." Alex took his seat. He leaned an elbow on the table and smiled through a snow-white goatee at Eli, looking very "Most Interesting Man in the World" in that position.

"You're wasting your time. I've told you repeatedly, I'm not interested in Chief Pencil Pusher, but if you insist, Clip…"

Tag barked another laugh, proud to hear his nickname for Reese (Clip, short for Paper Clip) used by someone other than himself.

"You're the most like me, Eli," Alex said, starting up a familiar speech. Because Eli had heard it about a dozen times over the last five months, his vision had already begun blurring at the edges. "Reese has my business savvy. He was made for COO." On that Eli couldn't disagree. Reese bled Crane Hotel's black and white. "Tag is my free spirit, winning hearts."

"He won mine," Rachel said, sliding onto Tag's lap instead of her own chair. Eli looked past lowered eyebrows to see her nuzzle Tag, who smiled like a lovesick fool. Must be nice.

"But you, Elijah," his father continued. "You have my sense of duty. You have a lion's heart. That same sense is what propelled me into the service." Alex pushed up a sleeve, revealing a faded tattoo reading *semper fi*. Eli turned his arm to show off his matching tattoo. They did have that in common. "But now your duty lies elsewhere, son."

Here it came. *Don't say it. Don't say it.*

"It's time to be the man Crane Hotels needs you to be."

Next to Eli, Tag snorted. Reese even cracked a smile.

Eli referred to this as Dad's "Batman" speech. It always ended with that same ode.

"I'm busy, Dad," Eli said.

"We'll see."

"Okay, food!" Merina gestured to the spread. Typically, Tag ate three entrees on his own, but Merina preferred to have a bite of everything on the table. If Eli wasn't fast, she'd dig into his without asking. "Ohh, Eli. Your shrimp pad Thai looks amazing."

He made a shooing motion. "You have to give me an extra crab rangoon if you steal my food."

She slid a glance at Reese. "Did he used to be nicer?"

"No," Reese deadpanned.

So it went every other Friday since Eli had returned after leaving part of himself in Afghanistan. Yes, his leg, but also two friends. While he was away, a lot had happened to him, and as much had happened to his brothers. Reese was married, Tag, practically married, and Dad...whatever was going on there.

Eli understood that they thought he'd slip into the slot saved for him at Crane Hotels now that he'd retired from the military, but for him, it wasn't that simple. He didn't fit anywhere. A large part of him wondered if that was simply because he felt incomplete, and not for the reason anyone thought. He cared about different things now. He wanted different things now. He glanced around the table at his family.

Reese dished out some of his Mongolian beef onto Merina's plate while she stole a sip of his wine. Rachel slid off Tag's lap with a smile and Tag lifted her hand to kiss it. Rhona unwrapped a pair of chopsticks and handed them to Alex.

Eli didn't want what they had. None of it. His reasoning was simple.

He refused to want something he couldn't have. Life had spoken. He was listening.

He didn't need another relationship to be whole.

He didn't need anyone.

Fall in Love with Forever Romance

MISTLETOE COTTAGE
By Debbie Mason

The first book in a brand-new contemporary series from *USA Today* bestselling author Debbie Mason! 'Tis the season for love in Harmony Harbor, but it's the last place Sophie DiRossi wants to be. After fleeing many years ago, Sophie is forced to return to the town that harbors a million secrets. Firefighter Liam Gallagher still has some serious feelings for Sophie—and seeing her again sparks a desire so fierce it takes his breath away. Hoping for a little holiday magic, Liam sets out to show Sophie that they deserve a second chance at love.

Fall in Love with Forever Romance

ONLY YOU
By Denise Grover Swank

The first book in a spin-off from Denise Grover Swank's *New York Times* bestselling Wedding Pact series! Ex-marine Kevin Vandemeer craves normalcy. Instead, he has a broken-down old house in need of a match and some gasoline, a meddling family, and the uncanny ability to attract the world's craziest women. At least that last one he can fix: He and his buddies have made a pact to swear off women, and that includes his sweetly sexy new neighbor...

THE BILLIONAIRE NEXT DOOR
By Jessica Lemmon

Rachel Foster is surviving on odd jobs when billionaire Tag Crane hires her and whisks her away to Hawaii to help save his business. As things start to get steamy, Rachel falls for Tag. Will he feel the same, or will she just get played? Fans of Jill Shalvis and Erin Nicholas will love the next book in the Billionaire Bad Boys series!

Fall in Love with Forever Romance

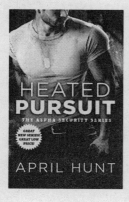

HEATED PURSUIT
By April Hunt

The first book in a sexy new romantic suspense series from debut author April Hunt, perfect for fans of Julie Ann Walker, Maya Banks, and Lora Leigh. After Penny Kline walks into his covert ops mission, Alpha Security operative Rafe Ortega realizes that the best way to bring down a Honduran drug lord and rescue her kidnapped niece is for them to work together. But the only thing more dangerous than going undercover in the madman's lair is the passion that explodes between them...

SOMEBODY LIKE YOU
By Lynette Austin

Giving her bodyguards and the paparazzi the slip, heiress Annelise Montjoy comes to Maverick Junction on a mission to help her ailing grandfather. But keeping her identity hidden in the small Texas town is harder than she expected—especially around a tempting cowboy like Cash Hardeman...

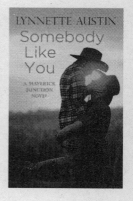

READ MORE FROM
JESSICA LEMMON

THE LOST BOYS SERIES
BOOK 1

MEET THE ULTIMATE BAD BOY...
AND A LOVE THAT CROSSES
ALL BOUNDARIES

LOVESWEPT